THE SEAMSTRESS

Sisters of Woodside Mysteries
Book 4

A Regency Romance

by Mary Kingswood

Published by Sutors Publishing

Copyright © 2019 Mary Kingswood

ISBN: 978-1-912167-21-0 (paperback)

Cover design by: Shayne Rutherford of Darkmoon Graphics

Author's note:

this book is written using historic British terminology, so *saloon* instead of *salon*, *chaperon* instead of *chaperone* and so on. I follow Jane Austen's example and refer to a group of sisters as the Miss Wintertons.

About the book: A traditional Regency romance, drawing room rather than bedroom.

Miss Fanny Winterton has only one wish in her romantic heart — to surrender to overwhelming love. She will accept nothing less than to be struck by the thunderbolt of everlasting passion. Real life isn't quite so obliging, however, so while she waits for the fires of love to ignite, she is content to ply her needle as a lowly seamstress for her noble patroness.

The Honourable Ferdinand Makenham has no wish at all to marry, until one glimpse of Fanny's sweet expression convinces him that he has found the love of his life. Now all he has to do is to persuade her to accept him, but is he romantic enough to win her affection? As he sets about his courtship, he and Fanny are drawn into the mysterious death of a young woman and life gets complicated.

Book 4 of the 5-book Sisters of Woodside Mysteries series, each a complete story with a HEA, but read all of them to find out all the secrets of the Winterton family!

About the series: When Mr Edmund Winterton of Woodside dies, his daughters find themselves penniless and homeless. What can they do? Unless they wish to live on charity, they will have to find genteel employment for themselves. This book is set in England during the Regency period of the early nineteenth century. Book 0 takes place 5 years before books 1-4, and book 5 ten years later.

Book 0: The Betrothed (Rosamund) (a short novel, free to mailing list subscribers)

Book 1: The Governess (Annabelle)

Book 2: The Chaperon (Lucy)

Book 3: The Companion (Margaret)

Book 4: The Seamstress (Fanny)

Book 5: Woodside

Want to be the first to hear about new releases? Sign up for my mailing list at: http://marykingswood.co.uk

Table of Contents

The Winterton family

Hi-res versions of all family trees available at:
http://marykingswood.co.uk

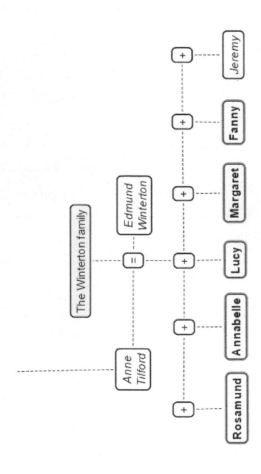

The Dalton family

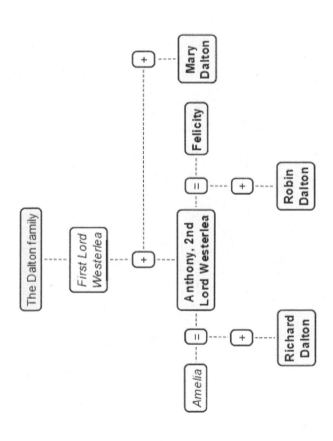

The Dalton family

First Lord Westerlea

+

Mary Dalton

Felicity

= + Robin Dalton

Anthony, 2nd Lord Westerlea

= + Richard Dalton

Amelia

The Makenham family

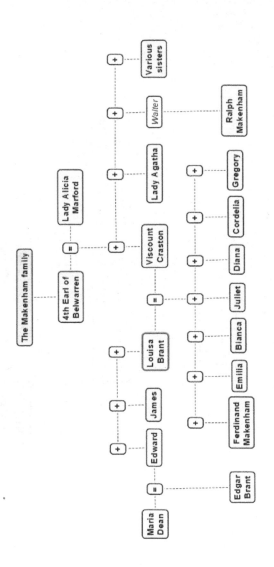

1: A New Home (January)

The Honourable Ferdinand Alphonse Makenham, son of Viscount Craston and grandson of the Earl of Belwarren, was embarrassed. This was not a situation which occurred with frequency, for Ferdy was as socially adept as he was well brought up. He could move with ease in every setting where a gentleman might find himself, and acquit himself well in every one. There was no circumstance which discomfited him, no place where he might not happily pass, no crisis which he could not address with aplomb and grace.

Except for one, and that was his grandfather's house on Christmas Day.

It was the tradition within the family that everyone who was capable of travel converged on Abbeymount at the tail end of the year, there to celebrate every birth and betrothal and marriage in the last twelvemonth, and mourn every death. The house was vast, with entire wings which stood empty for eleven months of the year, but in December every bed was filled and the house was stuffed to the rafters with Makenham and their cousins the Brants and Marfords and Deans and Carmichaels and Missenthorpes. And Christmas Day brought the dark moment of Ferdy's year, the great feast of Christmas and the reason for his discomfort.

For Ferdy had had the misfortune to be born on Christmas Day twenty-five years ago. That was excuse enough for his every childhood foible, his most unfortunate mishaps and his most excruciating failures to be brought out for inspection, laughed over and passed on to the next generation. One day, far in the future, when he was grey and stooped and had finally stepped into his grandfather's shoes as the Earl of Belwarren, his relations would still be chortling over the occasion at the age of two years when he had been violently sick over the Dowager Duchess of Camberley, or when, on his first attempt to mount his pony unassisted, he had contrived to seat himself facing the tail. Would he ever be allowed to forget the time he had teased the peacocks on the south lawn, and one of them had chased him all the way down to the icehouse, where he had hidden, terrified, for three hours? And then there was the incident with the Bishop, which even now made Ferdy hot with embarrassment to recall. How he wished that his relations would quietly forget his childhood misdemeanours and treat him as the responsible adult he now was. Or, failing that, that he had been born on any other day of the year.

But there was no escaping it. The aunts sighed over him every year on this day, remembering his auspicious arrival, his father's first child, for coming so soon on the heels of his Uncle Walter's untimely demise that it had seemed like the hand of Providence. As one heir departed, another had arrived, with the whole family gathered to celebrate it. And celebrate it they had, every year thereafter, and if Ferdy had grown somewhat reconciled to the attention, the mortification never diminished.

After the feast was the especial humiliation of his grandfather's speech, which always involved some kind of present. It was never a horse or a curricle or something of the like kind that Ferdy might actually use, or at least exchange for a better version, more to his taste. No, it was always some outlandish piece of jewellery, such as no man had worn anytime these last fifty years, or a book, perhaps, and what need had Ferdy for a book? He already had a Bible, a psalter and a copy of Debrett's Peerage, and he could not see what purpose any additional book might serve. He had left all that nonsense behind when he had waved farewell to his last tutor.

But this time his grandfather surprised him.

"My good people," he bellowed, the better to be heard by the one hundred and twenty persons gathered at his exceedingly large dining table, "we are here today to celebrate two births — that of our Lord Jesus, and that of my grandson and heir, Ferdinand. The former took place this morning in church, and the latter here and now. Let us all drink to Ferdinand's health and wish him a joyous and pleasurable year to come."

That much was entirely as usual. Everyone raised their glasses, and drank, and settled down to hear what present Ferdy was to have this year. But then the earl veered away from the usual speech.

"This year is a very special one for Ferdinand, as it was for Craston and as it was also for me. For today Ferdinand reaches the age of five and twenty, and this is the year he will marry, just as his father did at that age, and just as I did also at the same age. It is the way of the Makenhams, to marry at twenty-five, and I have no doubt that Ferdinand will do what is expected of him. To this end, therefore, the present I bestow on him is a very particular one. Today I present my grandson with the key to his house, number Twenty-Five Harlington Terrace, Sagborough, the place where he will bring his bride. Congratulations, Ferdinand."

And so saying, he placed an ornate key, decorated for the occasion with ribbons, on Ferdy's plate. There was a murmuring of approval, and some applause, and someone slapped Ferdy painfully on the back. Ferdy stared at the key before him as if it might jump up and bite him on the nose. To the world it might appear to be only a key, but to him it represented the bars of a cage.

When the ladies had withdrawn, with many a knowing glance at Ferdy, the gentlemen moved around the table and clustered in groupings of their choosing, the grandfathers at one end around the earl, the fathers in the middle and at the further end, the young men gathered around Ferdy in varying degrees of sympathy.

"Lord, Ferdy, you must have guessed how it would be," his cousin Ralph said, reaching a well-manicured hand for the port decanter. "Five and twenty is when the heir marries, and five and twenty you are."

"Oh yes, but... the house!" Ferdy said. "Never expected the house. Bride first, *then* the house, that is the proper way of things."

"Not for the Makenhams," said Edgar, another cousin. Ferdy had a great many cousins, but these two were his particular friends. "Have their own proper way of doing things, the Makenhams."

"Confound it, though," Ferdy said gloomily. "Married! Me! It hardly bears thinking about. I mean, a woman about the place, always."

The others murmured in sympathy.

"Pretty bad," Edgar said. "Horrifying."

"Oh, not *that* bad," Ralph said, with a wink and a grin. "A house of your own, Ferdy, and no need to leave it for a man's pleasures. It could be worse."

"Still horrifying," Edgar said firmly, and Ferdy could not but agree with him.

When the men started to drift away, the earl came and slapped Ferdy on the back. "Come into the book room with me, m'boy, and have a brandy, eh? You too, Craston."

Making a face of mock alarm to his friends, Ferdy followed his father and grandfather out of the Long Gallery, where they dined when the house was full, and then along twisting corridors to the book room. Despite the face-pulling, he was not afraid of his progenitors. His school friends had told dire tales of beatings and worse, of parents who constantly berated them for the smallest misdemeanour, or forced them to follow a particular career against their inclinations. Ferdy had never encountered such difficulties. His parents and grandparents had uniformly applauded his successes, and treated his mishaps lightly, as humorous escapades that might befall anyone. They had never quibbled at his expenditure, or denied him horses or clothes, or looked sternly at him and told him how disappointed they were in him. He got along with them remarkably well, in fact.

But now they wanted him to marry, and Ferdy was not sure he could oblige them.

The earl's book room was tucked away in a secluded part of the house. Unlike the rest of Abbeymount, this part was not built on a grandiose scale, and the book room would not have looked out of place as the housekeeper's room. The furnishings were elderly and worn, the carpet threadbare and the curtains moth-eaten. The shelves held a mismatched assortment of ornaments, including a wooden horse Ferdy had laboriously carved at the age of ten as a present for his grandfather.

The earl turned genially to Ferdy as they entered the room. "There now, we rubbed through that tolerably well, eh, m'boy? Only one mention of the Bishop, eh? 'Pon my soul, you colour up as easy as a girl, sometimes. Craston, do the honours, will you, while Ferdinand and I get comfortable."

Ferdy's father poured the brandy while the earl took the wing chair on one side of the fire, and gestured Ferdy to its partner on the other side, for Ferdy was the guest of honour today. Viscount Craston, having handed round glasses, brought forward a smaller chair.

"Well now, you look as nervous as a kitten, boy," the earl said. "It is not so bad being married, y'know. Not so bad at all, eh, Craston?"

The viscount shook his head. "No, indeed. Best thing I ever did, getting married. You will love it, Ferdy. So comfortable, having a lady to arrange all those delicate little touches that make the place a proper home. Meals always on time, the house run just as it should be, and a nursery filling up, you see. What could be pleasanter?"

Almost anything, in Ferdy's opinion. Instead, he said plaintively, "But who am I to marry?"

"Why, whomsoever you please," the earl said in surprise. "What, did you think we were about to foist some fubsy spinster on you in an arranged marriage? You must think us positively medieval, m'boy." The two men chuckled.

"No one is going to force you into anything you dislike," the viscount said, smiling. "Once you turn your mind to it, however, you will start to view every eligible female in a new light."

"Turn my mind to it?" Ferdy said, dazed. "How do I do that?"

"That part is already accomplished," the earl said smugly. "We have sown the seeds of the idea in your brain, y'know, and you have your house now, all ready and waiting. You will see the ladies differently now."

"You can look around you when you go up to London in April," the viscount said. "You will soon find someone you like, and with your address you will have no trouble fixing your interest."

"Aye, he is very personable, I grant you," the earl said. "He dresses too plain, though. A man needs a bit of colour about him, and a decent quantity of lace. I say nothing about powder and wigs, for good riddance to all that, but I do like to see a bit of lace about the cuffs, if a gentleman is to distinguish himself from his land agent or banker."

Ferdy smiled, and said nothing, perfectly assured that his attire was both fashionable and elegant, in the restrained manner of the London saloons. Here in Yorkshire, the more flamboyant styles could often still be seen, although his grandfather, for all his yearning for lace, restricted his desire for colour to a brocade waistcoat.

"Ah, that is the fashion, these days," the viscount said. "Dark colours everywhere, and only the neckcloth showing any liveliness at all. It is all that fellow Brummell's fault. But Ferdy's style is much admired, and is quite copied by the young bloods, so I am told. Nobody would ever take him for a banker."

Ferdy bowed modestly at this compliment.

The earl grunted. "Well, I have no doubt he can take his pick of the ladies. Once they understand him to be looking to be riveted, they will be all about in a trice, and he may look as high as he pleases. A title in the future, and an excellent fortune — I shall increase your allowance immediately, m'boy. How does fifteen hundred a year suit you? You will need a good income to maintain that house in the proper manner, and do some entertaining, you know. Get Agatha to help you with that. She knows how best to do these things, but do not worry if it gets expensive. If you find you need more, just say so. And when you marry, you will need a great deal more and you will not find me ungenerous, not at all."

"You are too kind, Grandfather," Ferdy said. "But how will I choose a wife? What must I look for? What sort of dowry?"

"Ha!" His grandfather took a long swallow of brandy. "That would be very tawdry, to choose a wife for the purse she brings with her. No, m'boy, you may have a free hand to find a woman who pleases you, but you must be very sure that she is the right one for you. It is a lonely business being an earl, and you must have a woman by your side who makes you happy, above all else."

"Happy. I see," Ferdy murmured, wondering how an earl who had just left a dinner for one hundred and twenty relations could describe himself as lonely.

"You must be in love with your wife, of course," his father said.

"In love... But... but how will I know? How can I tell when I am in love?"

His father and grandfather both chuckled. "You will know," his grandfather said. "Twenty-four hours after I took possession of the house at Twenty-Five Harlington Terrace, I was just emerging from the snuff shop in Sagborough, and almost bumped slap into my Alicia, and I knew at once."

"It was the same with me," the viscount said. "I had barely been in the house a week when I went out, only to the post office, as it happened, and a lady's carriage had become entangled with a pig wagon, and I stopped to render assistance, and there was my dear Louisa."

Ferdy smiled and nodded, having heard the tales before, usually with more embellishments.

"So I will just know..."

His father and grandfather smiled benevolently at him, nodding, but Ferdy was no nearer understanding just how he was to find a wife, or even whether he wanted one.

~~~~~

Fanny was sure she must be the most fortunate creature alive. When poor Papa had died leaving his four unmarried daughters penniless, it had seemed like the end of the world, yet now they were all safely employed in pleasant occupations. Annabelle was to be a governess, and no one could deny her aptitude for books and learning. Lucy, the most sociable of them, was to act as chaperon to two young ladies making their come-out and what could be more romantic? And shy Margaret was to live secluded with two elderly aunts, which would suit her retiring nature admirably.

As for Fanny herself, she was to be of service to Lady Harriet Hay's project helping women who had fallen into difficulties to return to respectability. She was not entirely sure what those difficulties might be or why it rendered them less than respectable, but she was sure that any assistance was to be commended. Lady Harriet had once called them *'my fallen women'*, but when Fanny had asked what they had fallen from, Lady Harriet had looked at her thoughtfully for a moment, and then said, "Let us call them *unfortunate*, Fanny. They are unfortunate women, and it is best not to enquire into their histories."

So it was that Fanny found herself travelling north with Lady Harriet in the greatest imaginable comfort, the carriage as snug as snug could be, every inn perfectly accommodating and every attention paid to them. They travelled with Lady Harriet's sister-in-law, Miss Marina Hay, and Miss Marianne Trivers, whose journey would reunite her with her uncle and aunt, who had made her their heiress. A second coach conveyed the bulk of the luggage, as well as the lady's maids of Lady Harriet and Miss Trivers.

Fanny had no lady's maid. At home at Woodside, she had shared Janet with her three sisters, but mostly they had laced each other's stays and tended each other's hair. Now there was no one to help her with her curling papers, or advise on which gown to wear. Her sisters were scattered about the country, and Janet was gone with Lucy, and Fanny must learn to do her own hair. It was fortunate, then, that she had nimble fingers and a way with a ribbon or a few beads or a strip of lace, to make something out of nothing. It was why she had been engaged by Lady Harriet, after all, for her skills with a needle.

"Are you not terrified, Miss Winterton?" Miss Trivers said one evening, as they waited in the private parlour for Lady Harriet and Miss Hay to join them. "Leaving everything you know behind you, and journeying all alone to foreign parts — I should be terrified. Indeed, I *am* terrified, even though I already know my uncle and aunt."

"Oh, I am a little *nervous*, naturally," Fanny said. "Lady Harriet has been so kind to me and I should not like to disappoint her. But there is nothing to terrify one. I am not alone, after all, and Yorkshire is not exactly foreign parts."

"But very wild," Miss Trivers said. "Still, we are both of us alone, in a way, for we have both left sisters behind us, and neither of us has any friends in Yorkshire. Not of our own age, I mean. Even Miss Hay is quite old."

"She is eight and twenty," Fanny said, trying not to laugh, for her eldest sister was seven and twenty, and not in the least old.

"Exactly! Quite old, and Lady Harriet is positively elderly. She must be well over thirty. Will *you* be my friend, Miss Winterton?"

"Of course I will!" Fanny said at once. "As far as my duties permit, of course. How kind of you to ask me. I should be very honoured, Miss Trivers."

"Oh, but you must call me Marianne."

"And you must call me Fanny."

And so it was that Fanny arrived in the small town of Sagborough in the northern county of Yorkshire already in possession of a friend. She thought herself very blessed.

~~~~~

For one reason or another, it was near the end of January before Ferdy took possession of his house. After the celebrations of Christmas at Abbeymount, he spent a week with his parents at Lennister Hall, and then there was an old school friend to be cheered up, recovering from an unfortunate bout of measles, and so the month drifted away. But eventually, he made his way to the unprepossessing market town of Sagborough. It was already showing signs of advancement, in the numerous mills and manufactories lining the canal at the eastern end of town, and the road from York was edged with many new buildings to house the mill workers and managers and engineers such industries required. Further on, the brand-new hospital was still being built, and not far away was a new school.

But the centre of the town boasted a number of fine edifices from the medieval period onwards, and on a quiet side street lay the splendid frontage of Harlington Terrace. Ferdy had never seen the house before, for it had been rented out for years, but as his carriage drew up outside number Twenty-Five, he had to confess himself rather impressed. The house, like all those in the street, was double fronted with a porticoed entrance and at least five stories, not counting the basement and attics. And all of this was his! Naturally, it was not comparable to the vast splendour of Abbeymount, or even the more modest scale of Lennister Hall, but still, it far outclassed his modest rooms in the town house in London.

As his travelling carriage drew up outside, the front door opened and out streamed a line of servants. His grandfather had said airily that the servants were in place, but Ferdy had hardly expected a butler and no fewer than three footmen for a bachelor household. His carriage door was opened by one footman, another let down the steps, and a third offered his arm, a service which Ferdy declined. He descended to the street, gazing up in some awe at the property which was now his.

Voices nearby caused him to turn his head. At the house next door, another carriage was drawn up, and three ladies were alighting, amidst the usual bustle of such occasions. His new neighbours, he supposed. His practised eye weighed them up instantly. One older woman, married, he thought, with clear London style about her. A spinster, with practical garb, who might be a companion, perhaps. And a third, younger than the others, in mourning, her clothes cleverly created but rather plain. The two older women ascended the steps to the front door without looking his way. The younger one hesitated, looking up at the house before her much as Ferdy had looked at his own, with surprise and perhaps a little awe.

And then she turned her head and looked at him, with a delicate little smile playing about her lips.

That smile! Ferdy stood stock still on the pavement, mesmerised by her smile. He had never in his life seen a lady, old or young, married or spinster, rich or poor, with a smile of such enchantment. Her whole expression was filled with sweetness.

She turned and followed her companions up the steps and into the house. The door closed behind her, the carriage rolled away and the street was empty of all but Ferdy's own carriage and servants.

19

But Ferdy knew. Confound it, his father and grandfather had been absolutely right after all. He had no idea of her name or connections or situation, but he knew. He had met the lady who would be his wife.

2: *Ferdy Goes To Church*

"He is still standing there," Miss Hay said, twitching the curtain aside and peering down into the street. "Ah, now his butler is coaxing him inside. Well, well, well, but he is a curiosity, I think."

"Do you always have this effect on gentlemen, Fanny?" Lady Harriet said in amused tones. "For if so, I must tell you that it will become very tedious to have the street littered with pole-axed young men turned to statues."

"Oh, *no*, indeed not," Fanny said earnestly. "Although Mr Hawes was so kind as to say that he was struck dumb when he first saw me, but I think that was just a poetic way of speaking. And Thomas Claremont followed me around at my first ball without saying a word, but then he had never before seen me in a ball gown and with my hair up. But just standing frozen in place like that — I should be mortified if it were a common occurrence. Now if it were Miss Trivers, I could understand it, for she is twenty times more beautiful than I am, but we had already left her at her uncle's house."

Miss Hay laughed. "Oh, Fanny, no! She is twenty times more beautiful than *I* am, there is no question about that, for my features have never been better than serviceable, but you have a very delicate sort of prettiness that is not just in the common way."

Fanny could not answer this, for naturally she could not comment on her own appearance, but nor could she disagree with the first part of the comparison. Miss Hay had the sort of washed-out, sandy complexion that was quite out of fashion, and perhaps would always be so.

The housekeeper came into the room just then with tea and toast and fruit for the ladies, who fell on the modest repast with enthusiasm, having had nothing to eat since breakfast.

"Mrs Bell, who is the gentleman going into number Twenty-Five?" Lady Harriet said through a mouthful of buttered toast. "He must be staying, for he brought a quantity of luggage. Is he a nephew of Mr Welbury?"

"Mr Welbury moved out before Christmas, milady. Given notice to quit a year ago, he was. The house is taken by a Mr Makenham now. He was expected today, so perhaps that was him you saw."

"Oh, one of the Makenhams! But that does not help, for there are hundreds of them scattered about. A dreadfully respectable family. I know one or two of the girls. Oh... I wonder if it might be Ferdy? Was he excessively well-dressed, Fanny? I did not notice."

"He seemed very stylish, to me," Fanny said. "He reminded me of Mr Dalton, my brother-in-law. He is fearsomely fashionable, but in a restrained sort of way."

"Well, we shall find out soon enough," Lady Harriet said comfortably, and laughed. "I imagine he will be keen to make our acquaintance, and I confess to some interest in him, too. I shall tell Dr Hay to call upon our new neighbour as soon as may be. Good heavens, is that the time? We must think about dressing for dinner. Come along, Fanny, I will show you to your room."

The house had formal rooms on two floors, with family bedrooms on the floor above. Fanny's room was on the floor above that, with a lower ceiling but the same size as Miss Hay's room, Lady Harriet assured her. It was almost twice as large as her room at Woodside, which she had shared with Margaret. Apart from the bed and the usual furnishings, the room boasted two huge wardrobes, into one of which a maid was assigning Fanny's clothes as she drew them from the travelling box. Lady Harriet opened the other, to reveal shelf after shelf piled high with gowns and pelisses and bonnets and shawls.

"These are all for you," Lady Harriet said. "The fruits of my little project, for you to show off. The girls make up gowns to a basic pattern, then the ladies who buy them alter them to fit and add little decorative touches to make them their own, you see. You are skilled with a needle, so your first task will be to alter these to your own ideas, and then you will wear them as you go about here and there, and everyone will see what may be achieved."

"I cannot wear these, Lady Harriet. There are ball gowns here, and nothing suitable for deep mourning."

"Oh — true enough. I had forgotten. Well, there is black stuff at the shop. Get the girls to help you with them, and then you can prettify them. You will not be in mourning forever, and I shall want you at all the public assemblies. Heavens, did you think you were to be hidden away behind the shop, plying your needle until your eyes fail? Not in the least! I want someone young enough to show off the gowns for the unmarried ladies. Miss Monkton, the proprietrix of the shop, is well enough but... rather matronly. Your presence will establish our reputation wonderfully, although, I confess, Fanny, I had not expected you to be so attractive. I thought, with four sisters all unmarried, that you would all be frights, and I could depend on you settling here and being a great help to me for years. But now that I have seen you, and the effect you have had on a certain young gentleman, I suspect you will be married within the year."

"Oh, *no*, Lady Harriet, I am sure I shall not be," Fanny cried distressfully. "For I have no dowry at all — I am quite penniless and in paid employment, and not at all a suitable person for any respectable gentleman to marry. Perhaps if I am very fortunate, I may in time marry an apothecary or some such."

"Well, our smitten young man next door is no apothecary," Lady Harriet said with a smile.

"Smitten young men do not always offer for one," Fanny said sadly. "All young men have to marry *prudently*, or so Rosamund says, and since Papa disgraced himself by losing all his money, we cannot expect to find good husbands. Rosamund spends every spring in London, so she knows about these things."

"She does not know everything, however," Lady Harriet said crisply. "If I were to let my sister-in-law have the dressing of you — Connie is the Marchioness of Carrbridge, you know, and frightfully stylish — and take you to town in the spring, I guarantee she would find you gentlemen enough who would not care tuppence about your lack of fortune, or what your papa may have done. She could probably get you a title, too, if you were so minded."

"Oh, *no!*" Fanny cried. "As if I cared about titles! I shall never marry unless I am very much in love with my husband, and he with me. There must be love, or marriage would be insupportable."

"Ah, Fanny, what a romantic you are. When you have seen a little more of the world, I hope you will appreciate that a husband and wife may be perfectly at ease together without being head over heels in love. Respect and friendship and consideration for the comfort of the other is all that is necessary. And money enough to live upon helps, too."

"Oh, how sad," was all Fanny said, wondering if Lady Harriet and Dr Hay enjoyed a marriage based only on respect and friendship. The whole journey north, Lady Harriet had not mentioned her husband, and Fanny had not liked to enquire about him, but this conversation inspired in her a great wish to see him and judge for herself.

The reality was something of a disappointment. Dr Hay was in appearance a male version of his sister, tall and thin, with the same sandy hair and pale eyebrows that gave Miss Hay's face such a faded appearance. They both looked so fragile that the least puff of wind would bowl them clean over. And of Dr Hay's attachment to his wife, Fanny could not detect any sign of romantic love at all. He addressed her as Lady Harriet, and was unfailingly polite to her in the most gentlemanly manner, enquiring with the greatest attention of her stay in the south, of the friends she had visited and of her journey north. But he addressed Fanny in the same courteous manner and his sister likewise, so there was nothing to be deduced from that. Fanny concluded that such a marriage was beyond her understanding.

The final member of the household was Mrs Hay, the widowed mother of Dr Hay and Miss Hay, who was so deaf that every word had to be repeated and shouted, and even then she missed two words out of three. But she smiled benignly on all of them, and enjoyed every item of food that was put her way, and afterwards played cribbage with ferocious determination. Fanny liked her at once, and wished she were her mother, too.

Then she went to bed in her spacious room, and gave sincere thanks to God for the good fortune which had brought her from tragedy to this welcoming family in the north.

~~~~~

Ferdy had discovered his neighbours' names almost at once, although the name of the young lady took some work by the servants to be revealed. It was fortunate, however, that the neighbouring kitchens abutted each other, with a low wall beyond, where the kitchen maids and footmen were accustomed to loiter when the weather permitted, while waiting to be summoned to their duties. So it was that before Ferdy went to bed that first evening, he knew that the lady with the enchantingly sweet expression was Miss Winterton from Brinshire, who was there to work for Lady Harriet Hay's little project to provide sewing work for disadvantaged women.

He was immediately alarmed. " Disadvantaged? You mean—? She is not herself—?"

"No, no, sir," said the impassive butler, who was retailing the snippets of gossip to the drawing room from the yard below. "She is to assist with the shop, I believe. She is a lady, sir, respectable but impoverished."

"A lady. Yes, of course. She could not be otherwise," Ferdy said distractedly. He was sitting in solitary state with the port decanter, as information was relayed to him bit by bit. "Miss Winterton. Of Brinshire."

Ferdy waited at home for three days, to be quite sure not to miss Dr Hay's visit of introduction. He was not without callers. A Mr Malpas was his first visitor, a portly gentleman, who confessed immediately that he knew himself not to be Ferdy's social equal, but, in his position as Mayor of Sagborough, wished to welcome him to their humble town, hoped he would attend the fortnightly assemblies at the King's Head, advised him that the best shops were along York Road and Mill Road, and cautioned against certain establishments hard by the canal, which were known to be disreputable.

His second visitor was Mr Plumstead, the clergyman at St Peter's, the parish church.

"Matins at eight, Eucharist at ten and Evensong at six, if you have not had your fill of the Almighty by then," he said cheerfully. "Shall I have a pew set aside for you, sir? Mr Welbury's pew would be suitable for a gentleman such as yourself, sir. Mr Welbury was the gentleman who had this house before yourself, sir."

"What happened to Mr Welbury?" Ferdy said cautiously. "I have tossed him out of his house, seemingly, and I should not like to toss him out of his pew as well."

"Bless you for the thought, sir," said Mr Plumstead, chuckling, "but he's gone to his daughter in Leeds. Glad to go, too, if you ask me, for all he grumbled about it, but he grumbled about the stairs here even more."

"Ah, an elderly gentleman."

"Indeed, not at all like yourself, sir. There's many a young lady's heart will be gladdened to know of a fashionable young gentleman such as yourself moving to our humble town. What brings you here, sir, if I may make so bold as to ask?"

"Family tradition," Ferdy said, not paying much attention, for he was wondering if one particular young lady's heart would be gladdened by his arrival. "The Eucharist — that would be the usual service for the families here, I imagine? My neighbours, for instance, the Hays — they would attend that service, would they?"

"Oh yes, sir. All the Quality such as yourself is at the Eucharist, sir, so you will meet them all there. All those from this part of town, that is."

"That sounds perfect for me, then," Ferdy said happily. "And I am sure that Mr Welbury's pew will suit me admirably."

After that, there was a steady stream of town worthies eager to make his acquaintance. Sagborough boasted a couple of baronets and one or two gentlemen who liked to winter in town and enjoy their estates during more clement seasons, but these lofty individuals remained unseen. Instead, most of his callers were what his cousin Ralph called the fringe people — attorneys and retired army men, younger sons living on the edges of good society, cutting a dash in a cheap, unfashionable town and always hoping for an invitation to stay with grander relations from time to time.

Ferdy found them uniformly friendly and welcoming, seeming delighted to make his acquaintance. Some even remembered his parents living at number Twenty-Five many years before, and talked affectionately of the then Mr Henry Makenham and his lovely wife, and what a lively couple they were, with a ready wit and up to every rig, and how the joke with the piglets was still talked about. Ferdy smiled and nodded, and tried to reconcile the impish pair so described with his rather staid parents.

By the end of his third day in residence, he had acquired a troop of new acquaintances, two invitations to dinner, three to evening or card parties and one to a ball. He accepted them all unhesitatingly, for only by going about and getting to know everyone would he be sure to bump into Miss Winterton again. But then, eventually, Dr Hay came.

He was an unprepossessing man in appearance, tall and thin, as if stretched, with reddish hair and a weaselly sort of face. However, Ferdy had long since learnt not to judge a man by his physical appearance, which was not his fault. His clothing was a far better guide to a man's character and aspirations than the colour of his hair. Dr Hay dressed soberly but well, without excess or aspiration to fashion, and looked every inch the provincial gentleman of means. He talked sensibly, too, speaking at length of his work at the new hospital. Ferdy had already discovered that this enterprise, funded by the Marquess of Carrbridge, was in fact the Hay Hospital, and Dr Hay was chief director of all that went on there. One wing was already finished and in use, a second was nearing completion, and there was a plan for a third, and a row of alms-houses, too.

Dr Hay talked also about his wife, the sister to the Marquess of Carrbridge, and his own sister, who was herself very learned in medical matters, it seemed, and he even mentioned his mother, who lived with them. Ferdy was far too polite to ask directly, but eventually, just at the point where Ferdy had almost given up hope, he mentioned Miss Winterton.

"We have a guest staying with us just now. I believe you noticed her the other day, for you arrived at much the same time."

"The young lady in mourning? One must always be sympathetic towards one so young wearing black gloves," Ferdy said.

"Indeed," Dr Hay said gravely. "Miss Frances Winterton, or Fanny, as she is known."

Fanny! What an enchanting name...

"Her father died recently, leaving his daughters indigent, so she is to work for Lady Harriet. She is a talented seamstress, I understand."

"A seamstress," Ferdy repeated, remembering the cleverly contrived pelisse and bonnet, plain but beautifully made. Talented indeed, if she had made those herself.

"You must come for dinner one evening," Dr Hay was saying, as he rose to leave, but Ferdy barely heard him, and made his responses automatically. Fanny! Her name was Fanny...

He went the very next day to return Dr Hay's call, but he was out, so Ferdy could only leave his card. Still, he was not disheartened, for the next day was Sunday, and he would see her then. She must be at church, surely.

He was early for the service, walking briskly up Harlington Terrace and across the main road to the imposing church of St Peter's. The sexton showed him to his pew, a well-favoured spot a few rows from the front. From there, he had an excellent view of the Hay family as they arrived to take their places — Dr Hay, leading an elderly woman on his arm, then his wife and sister, and at the back, a neat figure in black, was Miss Winterton. Fanny! They sat several rows in front of Ferdy, so his view was of the back of Fanny's head, giving him ample opportunity to observe that she sat almost motionless for the entire time, with no shuffling or looking about. When the service ended, and the party left the church, she walked with dainty steps at the back of the group, her head demurely lowered, so that he saw nothing but a small expanse of one cheek.

He was not deterred. He made his way outside without haste, spotted the tall figure of Dr Hay at once, talking to another man, and the small, black figure standing nearby. He set off determinedly—

"Mr Makenham, sir! Mr Makenham!" The clergyman, puffing his way through the crowds, his clerical robes flying, one arm waving. "Oh, Mr Makenham, one moment of your time, sir."

Ferdy tried not to sigh audibly. "Mr Plumstead, your servant, sir. Most interesting sermon. Very thought provoking."

"Ah, yes, but never mind that," the vicar wheezed, out of breath after his dash across the churchyard. "I have just discovered, sir, that you are the scion of Lord Belwarren. That you are, in point of fact, his heir. Mrs Malpas has just informed me of it, which I had not at all realised when I assigned you to poor Mr Welbury's pew, sir. I do trust you will overlook my little mistake, but you may be sure that a better pew will be found for you before next Sunday. Pray forgive me, sir."

"Nothing to forgive," Ferdy said at once. "No, no — I assure you. Think nothing of it. Very happy with Mr Welbury's pew. Never had a finer pew. Perfectly admirable pew. Good day to you, sir." Out of the corner of his eye, he saw the Hay party moving slowly away towards their waiting carriage.

Mr Plumstead flapped his hands about in distress. "No, indeed, sir! Pray allow me the very great liberty of disagreeing with you! You are no mere gentleman, but the grandson of an earl. You are an Honourable, sir! You must have an appropriate pew for your rank."

The Hay party were ascending into their carriage, and Ferdy regretfully turned his full attention on the little clergyman. "Does God care more for Honourables than mere gentlemen, Mr Plumstead?"

The vicar's eyes twinkled merrily. "Not in the least, sir, but the good people of Sagborough do. They would have you in your rightful place, or know the reason why. And besides, what if some of your noble relations were to visit you here in our humble town, and be forced to sit in the middle of the church, with the baker only two pews behind! No, sir, it will not do."

"I take your point, Mr Plumstead," Ferdy said gravely.

"Our two baronets have the highest rank, and therefore the most forward pews, and then Sir Lawrence, and then Lady Harriet Hay, but then you yourself would be above her in precedence, I imagine, so—"

"Oh, must it be done by formal precedence?" Ferdy said, amused. "But that is more difficult, for you see my father is a viscount, and the eldest son of a viscount ranks quite high, only just below a baron, and above both the younger son of an earl and the eldest son of a baron. Baronets are much further down the list. But I think you will find that Lady Harriet Hay has the highest rank of all, for she is the daughter of a marquess, you know."

Mr Plumstead's mouth flapped open, then closed again. "Oh dear. It is more complicated than I had supposed. I had better look it up."

Ferdy laughed. "For myself, I had far rather stay where I am than offend anyone by asking them to move to a lower pew. I do not come to church to display my rank, Mr Plumstead."

Mr Plumstead bowed with great respect, Ferdy bowed in his turn, and, since almost everyone else had now departed from the churchyard, he walked home in some disappointment. But even if he had not yet spoken to the intriguing Miss Winterton, he had at least seen her again, and knew that he would have the pleasure of seeing her every Sunday thereafter. And if that were to be their only meeting place, he must hope she was not prone to chills or fevers or fainting fits or other ailments that might keep her away.

Fanny! Sweet, smiling Fanny. And healthy Fanny, he must hope.

3: Miss Kelly's Finest Gowns (February)

Fanny breakfasted with the family the next morning, although Lady Harriet informed her that this would not be a regular occurrence.

"The shop opens at seven, but Miss Monkton and her mother manage the early callers, who usually only want a ribbon or a pair of gloves. But you must be there by nine, to assist with those looking for a complete gown, or wanting advice. A great many ladies come in to ask our advice and then go away without buying anything." She sighed. "I do not know how we are supposed to turn a profit when a customer steals all our ideas and then runs off to her usual seamstress. However, let us not repine. These things always take time, do they not? You will stay until three or four or whenever the shop becomes quiet. Most of our customers dine early, so they are seldom out after three. It is not a long walk but you must always be accompanied by a maid or footman. William or Withers will take you there each morning, and Miss Monkton will assign someone to accompany you home. Ah, Bridget, come in. Fanny is nearly ready to go. Fanny, this is Bridget Kelly, who is in charge of my little project."

"Oh, I thought you were in charge, Lady Harriet," Fanny said in surprise.

"Her ladyship's our patroness," Bridget said, with a quick laugh. "But she's too grand for shop work. It's trade, isn't it? So she foots the bills, and we do the work."

Lady Harriet said primly, "I am not too grand, I hope, but I can be more use to you by taking a more distant interest, and lending an air of respectability to the project. Go and fetch your bonnet, Fanny. Bridget will take you to the shop today, and show you everything. Off you go now, and be sure to be back before five, because Dr Hay likes his dinner on the dot of six."

"Yes, Lady Harriet. Thank you." Fanny scrambled down from the table, abandoning her half-eaten toast and almost a full cup of coffee, and dipped a curtsy before leaving the room.

"May I come upstairs while you put your bonnet on?" Bridget said, heading for the staircase even before Fanny had had a chance to reply. She sat on the bed, looking round the room with great interest. "Lucky you! This is a fine room. Ooh, may I look at your clothes? Professional interest, you might say."

"Of course," Fanny said with a gurgle of laughter. It was impossible to dislike Bridget, for all her forwardness. She was not a handsome woman, plain-faced and with a nose too large for her face, but her expression was lively and the mop of blonde curls protruding from her very dashing bonnet softened any harshness in her features. She was somewhat above thirty, Fanny guessed, and unmarried, although wearing clothes that any fashionable wife would have been happy to own.

"So much black!" Bridget said, as Fanny tied her bonnet ribbons. "Your father, isn't it? How long will you be in mourning? Because it might cast a damper on the customers."

"I had not thought of that," Fanny said. "Oh dear me! But there is a back room, is not there? Where the sewing is done... I can hide in there, and help with the stitchery, just at first."

"Oh, but her ladyship wants you in the shop with the customers," Bridget said dubiously. "Well, we'll just have to see. Are you ready? Goodness, that's a very fetching bonnet! How pretty you are in it. Did you make it yourself? You'll be a great asset to us, that's certain. Come on, then. No, not that way," she said with a laugh, as Fanny headed for the stairs. "This way. It's the back stairs for you now, my girl."

"Oh yes. Yes, of course." Fanny crept after her, very subdued.

They clattered down the uncarpeted back stairs and out through the tradesmen's door beside the kitchen, across the yard and past the coach house and stable into a lane. This brought them out onto the York road, where they crossed over, passed a few shops and then turned down another street, with *'Mill Road'* carved onto a stone high on the side of the first house. More shops, and then one with a sign reading *'Miss Kelly's Finest Gowns For The Discerning Lady'*.

"Here we are," Bridget said cheerfully, pushing open the door, so that the bell above it jangled clangorously.

Inside, the room was so dark that Fanny had to pause while her eyes adjusted. Gradually the room came into focus, a long, thin room the full width of the double-fronted shop. To one side of the door, a counter was backed by the myriad small drawers found in any haberdasher's shop. On the other side, a smaller counter fronted large drawers and open shelves, where heaps of materials lay. There was a strong smell of tobacco.

A large lady of middle years materialised out of the gloom at the back of the shop. "My dears! Come in, come in, come in! There now, you must be Fanny Winterton. Let me look at you, my dear. Oh, so pretty! But oh deary me, you are in mourning of course. You poor dear creature, how miserable you must be. But never fear, we shall cheer you up." And she wrapped Fanny in her ample, poplin-clad arms, wreathing her in the overpowering scent of lavender water.

When she could get a word in edgeways, Bridget said, "This is Miss Monkton, Miss Winterton. Oh, and here is Mrs Monkton, her mother. This is Miss Winterton, Mrs Monkton."

Mrs Monkton was almost as large as her daughter, and just as enthusiastic in her embraces, despite her advanced years. Fanny feared she would be squashed to death if she received just one more such hug. Fortunately the doorbell clanged again and a customer came in, so the Monkton ladies were diverted. Bridget whisked Fanny through a door and into a room filled with light.

For the second time, she had to wait until her eyes adjusted, but the noise of girlish squeals gave away her location long before she could see it — this must be the sewing room. Again, she was hugged, although more decorously and when she could see again, she found herself surrounded by smiling faces.

"Oh, the bonnet!" someone cried. "Please, please, please can I have a closer look?"

"Ooh, look at these sleeves," someone else said.

"Such tiny buttons! What is underneath the pelisse? May we see?"

Laughing, Fanny surrendered her bonnet, gloves and pelisse, which were carried off triumphantly to the long worktable to be examined. They would have liked to strip off her gown, too, but Bridget protested.

"Let her be, you lot! Good grief, she's only just got here. Miss Winterton, this is Ruby and that's Martha... Edith... Joan... Susan... Hannah..."

Fanny nodded to each one, but her head was spinning with all the names of these poor unfortunate women. Although they did not look terribly unfortunate to her, for they were respectably dressed in plain round gowns, all in drab or dark colours, and none of them showed signs of illness or deformity. Some of them were very pretty, too. They all wore matron's caps, so she supposed they were unfortunate in being widowed young.

Now that she could see, she understood why the room was so dazzling, for large roof windows let in a great deal of light. It was not a sunny day, but nevertheless the room was bright enough to work at delicate stitchery without candles. The room was dominated by a long worktable, strewn with half sewn gowns, with shelves full of lengths of material and drawers for needles and thread lining the walls.

After a few minutes, Bridget shooed the seamstresses back to work and led Fanny through another door. Beyond was a long kitchen where a single cook worked.

"This is Rose," Bridget said. "Rose, this is Miss Winterton."

"Well now, you're very welcome, miss," Rose said. "Let me just get this pie into the oven, and then we'll have a sit down and a bite to eat. Did you get your breakfast this morning, miss?"

"A little," Fanny said.

"Then a little more wouldn't go amiss, would it? There now, that's the pie away. Bridget, pour some ale for us and I'll see what there is to eat."

Within a few minutes, the three ladies were established at one end of the kitchen table with slices of cake and pastries and bread and a cold pigeon pie. There was only ale to drink, so Fanny sipped it delicately, not wishing to offend, but disappointed that there was no tea.

"Now, Miss Winterton," Bridget said. "You've seen everything, so what do you think?"

Fanny swallowed her mouthful of cake and took a sip of ale to give herself time to think, but even so, she could not work out what answer was wanted. In the end, she could only say, "About what, precisely, Miss Kelly?"

"Why, about the shop, of course. You're a lady so give me your honest opinion — if you came here as a customer, would you buy anything here?"

"I would not," Fanny said at once, "for I have no idea what is being sold. There is nothing to indicate the goods for sale apart from the sign over the door."

"Now isn't that just what Lady Gilbert said when she was here?" Rose said. "You need to put something in the windows, she said."

"But how can we?" Bridget said. "Our gowns are just roughly tacked together, mostly, so the customer can finish it off to suit herself. And if we put the other things in the window — gloves or ribbons or whatever — we upset Miss Walters or Mrs Turnbull or Miss Crisp. Lady Harriet doesn't want us setting up in opposition to the established milliners and haberdashers."

"What is the one thing you sell that nobody else has?" Fanny said.

"Why, our half-finished gowns, of course."

"But where are they?" Fanny said.

"On the shelves... wait, let me fetch one." Bridget jumped up and dashed out of the room, returning moments later with one of the bundles of material that Fanny had seen before. But when Bridget shook it out, she could see that it was a gown inside out and loosely tacked together.

"If I were a customer," Fanny said slowly, "I should like to see what I were buying, but I should also like to see the finished gown."

"But the ladies finish them off themselves," Bridget said. "They add their own trimmings."

"Then show them what they might do with such a gown," Fanny said. "Or perhaps two different versions, one plain and one more elaborate." Bridget opened her mouth, then snapped it shut again thoughtfully. "And the shop is too dark," Fanny went on.

"We can't afford a great many lamps," Bridget said.

"Then paint the walls white, and the ceiling, too, for it is a horrid shade of greyish-brown."

"This used to be a snuff-seller's shop," Bridget said, amused. "It still smells to high heaven, doesn't it?"

"Bowls of flower petals here and there," Fanny said. "Fresh flowers in summer. And rugs on the floor, soft draperies across the door, more comfortable chairs than those hard wooden things."

"Our customers are not gentry," Bridget said. "They don't expect comfort. They walk here in the rain and drip all over the floor and leave puddles on the chairs."

"Wooden chairs in wet weather, then, but you want them to be comfortable, because that way they will buy more," Fanny said. "They may not be gentry, but everyone wants to be treated as if they were. When my sisters and I go—" She stopped, as grief burned through her momentarily. She took a deep breath, then continued with only the slightest wobble in her voice, "When we used to visit the mantua maker, it was like calling on a friend. She gave us tea and buns, or lemonade, and we sat on the sort of sofas that one might see in a drawing room. She had a private room for her favoured customers, and one of her assistants would show the materials while Madame discussed the latest fashions and pointed out ideas from the journals. Do you have journals?"

"A few, in the sewing room. And we have a private room," Bridget said. "These are interesting ideas."

"And glass-fronted cabinets," Fanny added. "Show them gloves and bandeaux and necklaces and fans, so they will say: look, this necklace would be perfect with this gown. That is how they do it in town, my oldest sister, Rosamund, says. One goes in for a length of ribbon, and comes out with a new fan and evening gloves and three pairs of stockings."

They left Rose to her kitchen chores, and walked slowly around the shop again, while Bridget mulled over Fanny's ideas. Then several customers arrived, and everyone jumped to attend to them, Fanny included, and so began her life as a shop girl.

~~~~~

'Dear Fanny I have arrived safely Margaret'

~~~~~

FEBRUARY

Ferdy set about the task of making Miss Winterton's acquaintance with determination. He accepted every invitation offered him, he was assiduous in repaying calls and he walked about the streets at likely times when a young lady might be abroad. Despite all his efforts, he was disappointed. After the third indifferent dinner and the second dull card party, he began to suspect that Miss Winterton had not yet been introduced to Sagborough society. Nor was she present at the first assembly he attended, although since she was in mourning, perhaps that was not a surprise. He saw nothing of Dr Hay, either, and although he had left his card at number Twenty-Six three times, the gentleman had not called again, and Ferdy supposed that the acquaintance must now be given up.

Church was his one hope, but on his second visit to St Peter's, the vicar again sank all his plans with another long conversation about pews, wherein he agonised at excessive length about the proper protocol for assigning them. Ferdy cared nothing for pews, was perfectly happy with the one he had and had not the least desire to change, but for the second Sunday in succession he was obliged to feign interest while, in the distance, Miss Winterton walked away from him. It was most frustrating.

However, he was too well-bred to display any sign of his disappointment. He bowed civilly to Mr Plumstead, and when the dreary hours of Sunday were over, he began another week of morning calls, and evenings filled with dancing and conversation or cards, playing whist or speculation with equal willingness, and all of it carried out with a ready smile and expressions of pleasure. And if he found little to interest him in Sagborough society, he soon found himself a person of the utmost interest to the local population. It had not taken them long to discover, as Mr Plumstead had, that he was not just any Mr Makenham, but *the* Mr Makenham, heir to the earldom of Belwarren, and therefore a person of the greatest consequence in the town, and especially to the unmarried young ladies.

Ferdy was used to that, of course. He had been a future earl from the moment of his birth, and a catch on the marriage mart from his first steps into society at the age of sixteen. He had early learnt to deal with ambitious young ladies and their even more ambitious mamas. He knew perfectly well how to avoid unwanted entanglements and depress pretensions, but it was always done with courtesy and a smile, so that no one ever felt slighted. Previously, he had kept his distance from habit, having no thought of marriage in his mind. Now, he kept his distance because he had glimpsed his future wife, and no one else would do.

Even if he had so far failed to encounter Miss Winterton again in person, he occasionally had the pleasure of hearing her spoken of, and learning tiny snippets of information about her. One evening he dined with Mr Adam Trivers and his wife. They had a niece, Miss Marianne Trivers, who was both pretty and well-dowered, but to his relief no vulgar attempts were made to push her into Ferdy's way. He did his duty, however, by sitting next to her at dinner.

"Have you lived in Sagborough long, Miss Trivers?" Ferdy said politely.

"Only two weeks or so. My older sister married recently, and Mr Porter very kindly offered a home to Mama, too, so my Uncle and Aunt Trivers asked me to live with them here."

"And how do you like Sagborough?"

"Very well, although it is very small. Bristol was a very busy, bustling place, and Sagborough is much quieter. I am not quite accustomed yet. But it is very pleasant here, I am sure," she added hastily. "I shall like it well enough in the summer, when we can get out onto the moors. So romantic, moorland."

Ferdy was not much enamoured of moors, having grown up surrounded by them, so instead he said, "Bristol is a great distance away, I believe, and travelling in January, too — you must have had a difficult journey, Miss Trivers."

"Not in the least," she said, with a shy smile. "I was very fortunate, for my aunt is acquainted with Lady Harriet Hay, who also lives here, and she was so very kind as to allow me to travel in her carriage, together with Miss Hay and Miss Winterton, and even with four of us, we were not in the least squashed. It was the most comfortable journey imaginable."

Ferdy was immediately alert. "Lady Harriet has a generous spirit towards those less fortunately circumstanced than she," he said carefully, hoping this might trigger more talk of Miss Winterton. But he was to be disappointed.

"I am sure she has," Miss Trivers said. "I should love to interest Lady Harriet in Celia Drabble, who would be such a success if only she had a sponsor to help her into society. Do you not think Celia is the loveliest creature imaginable?"

Ferdy had met Miss Drabble several times, for her widowed mother was sister to Sir William Harbottle, one of the town's two baronets, and was therefore invited everywhere. He glanced down the dining table, to where Miss Drabble sat listening to the mayor prosing at some length. There was not the least doubt that she was a great beauty, but he already knew that she had not a penny piece for dowry, since several kindly souls had already warned him away from her on account of it. Celia, it seemed, was to depend upon her looks to make her fortune. And perhaps she would do so, with but a little expenditure, but she wore the saddest gowns Ferdy had ever seen, drably unfashionable and clearly let out around the bodice.

So he said merely, "Miss Drabble is indeed very beautiful."

"You spend the season in London, Mr Makenham. Do you not think Celia would turn heads even there? Surely there can be few so lovely anywhere. She would make a great match, would she not, if she were to go there?"

"Perhaps," he said cautiously.

"Oh." She looked crestfallen. "You do not think she would be a great success if she went there?"

"There is more to a successful season than a beautiful face," he said gently. "Nor does a man marry solely for such surface considerations."

"Oh, but Celia has many accomplishments — she paints and sings and is very well-read. I cannot do half so much."

"Accomplishments are not enough either. There are also considerations of rank, of wealth, of connections. All these things a gentleman will weigh when choosing a bride."

"Oh. She has none of those," Miss Trivers said in a small voice. "So perhaps her beauty will not help her to make a splendid match."

Ferdy made some non-committal noises, but his thoughts were entirely taken up by another young lady who had no rank or wealth or connections, but who might nevertheless make a splendid match, if only he could meet her again and get to know her.

4: An Old Friend

Ferdy was disconsolate. In his two weeks at Sagborough, he felt he had made no progress at all in his pursuit of Miss Winterton, and was not at all sure how best to proceed. Subtlety had got him nowhere, so perhaps it was time to enquire more directly about Lady Harriet's project. Yet every feeling revolted at the prospect. But then he had a piece of luck. He was mooching along the main street, idly looking in shop windows and examining every woman dressed in black with a keen eye, when he heard himself accosted.

"Ferdy? Ferdy Makenham, as I live and breathe!"

He turned, and then smiled in recognition. "Gil Marford! Upon my soul, what are you doing here?"

"Why, I live here now. But you here? You look as out of place as lupins in December, in all your London finery."

"One must not let one's standards slip just because one happens to be in the far north," Ferdy said complacently, knowing that he had correctly adjusted his dress for his current residence. Not everyone, however, noticed subtleties such as a coat that was two years old and a simplified neckcloth arrangement. "And I live here too, I would have you know."

He smiled genially at his friend. Lord Gilbert Marford was as different from Ferdy as it was possible to be. He was the ne-er-do-well youngest brother of the Marquess of Carrbridge, with a reputation for wildness of every kind. Ferdy thoroughly disapproved of him, but, being of similar age and moving in the same circles, they had been thrown together somewhat in their early years. Now he was glad of a friendly and familiar face.

Marford smiled back. "Really? Oh, famous! Why Sagborough, of all places?"

"Family tradition," Ferdy said. "My father lived in the house at one time, and my grandfather before him, so I must take my turn. I am neighbour to your sister, Marford."

"Hatty and that dry stick of a husband of hers?" Marford said. "That was a queer business. Never thought she would marry at all, and she had no need to — had a house and a good independence. Ah, but there is no knowing when matrimony will strike a person down. Look at me, for instance."

"Heard about that," Ferdy said sympathetically. "Well — heard a lot of rumour about it. Not half of it true, I expect."

"Oh, I expect it was all true enough. It was a rum business, but it turned out well in the end." He grinned mischievously, and Ferdy was conscious of a pang of envy. He had never wanted to be like Gil Marford in character, but oh, to have even a tenth of his good looks and charm and way with the ladies. He had only to turn his blue eyes on them and they flocked around him with adoration written on their faces, whereas Ferdy's flocks had greater admiration for his future title and fortune than his person. "I say," Marford went on, "why not come and take your pot luck with us this evening? Lady Gil will be delighted to see you."

"No pot luck," Ferdy said firmly. "That always goes badly. The husband says cheerfully that his wife will be very happy, and she, poor lady, is forced to smile and pretend that half a dozen plain dishes and a single remove is as good as two full courses, and claim she does not mind a bit and do come again any time. And then they hiss at each other over the card table, and she cries and he sulks, and the poor guest goes home wishing he had stayed in his own house.

No, no pot luck, if you please, but have your wife invite me in the regular way and I shall be delighted to dine with you."

Marford laughed and agreed to it, they exchanged cards and Ferdy went home in a much more mellow frame of mind.

~~~~~

'My dear Fanny, How charming you make it sound, and such fun, to be spending all day in a dress shop. Lady H's unfortunates sound like a lively set of young women, but perhaps you should not mingle with them quite so much, Fanny dear, for they may talk about subjects not fit for your ears. And so nothing more has been seen of the young gentleman who was so taken with you? Ten to one he was struck with indigestion at that moment, and it was nothing to do with you at all, but even if it was not, his singular failure to make himself known to you suggests that it was an aberration, so you should not get your hopes up, dearest. Have you made any other acquaintances in Sagborough? You do not mention any evening engagements, and I do not like to think of you sitting at home night after night, all alone. Do try to get out a little if you can. Your fond sister, Rosamund.'

~~~~~

Fanny rather liked being a lowly seamstress. When the shop was quiet, she worked in the sewing room with Lady Harriet's unfortunate women and that was very homely, not terribly unlike sitting in the morning room at Woodside with her sisters. These women were constantly chattering, too, just like Lucy, and Bridget was often there to scold them gently into busyness, just like Annabelle, and there were one or two who said nothing and bent their heads to their work, just like Margaret. It softened the emptiness inside Fanny a little.

But in truth these women were nothing like her own sisters. Their accents were harsh, and there were one or two she could barely understand. And then most of their talk was about their children, which was interesting but not a subject to which Fanny could contribute. They talked about men, too, and that was more familiar, for although the men they liked were farm workers or footmen or blacksmiths, they still liked to talk about roguish eyes and strong muscles and the likelihood that a certain one might be wanting a wife. But it was sad listening, for they often ended with the words, "But he'd never want to marry someone like me." And that was a sentiment Fanny could sympathise with, for she was in much the same position herself. Whoever would want to marry Fanny Winterton, brought up as a lady, but a lady no longer?

The shop had been transformed, on Fanny's advice. A painter had come in each evening after the shop closed to repaint the walls and ceiling in a pale colour. Each window now boasted three mannequins, one showing the roughly tacked gown, and the others two variants of the finished garment, one plainer and one more elaborate. There were fashion journals scattered about on low tables beside soft chairs grouped in a circle, and ladies were beginning to come in to sit and read the journals and chat. Before they left, they often bought a new brooch or fichu or silk flower from one of the new display cabinets scattered around. But they seldom bought a gown.

One day, when Fanny was engaged in dusting the display of fans, two ladies entered the shop, one older and one but a little younger than Fanny. The younger one had perhaps the most beautiful face Fanny had ever seen, more beautiful even than Rosamund. And yet, her clothes were dull and a little shabby, made more for durability than fashion.

The older woman's eyes fell instantly on Fanny. "Mourning gowns!" she declared in a booming voice. "Do you supply mourning gowns? For that would be such a comfort for those newly bereaved, to come here and buy a gown or two, almost ready to wear and no need to worry about dyeing and whatnot."

Fanny curtsied respectfully low, as she had been taught to do for customers. "I do not believe we do, at present, ma'am," she said. "But it is an excellent notion. I shall suggest it to Miss Kelly when next she visits."

The older woman raised a quizzing glass to her eye. "Hmm. I do not know you, miss."

"I am Fanny Winterton, if you please, ma'am." Fanny dipped another curtsy.

"That gown of yours — was it made by the girls here?"

"Indeed it was made here, but by my hands, ma'am."

"Those sleeves — very pretty. Very neat. I like the way they sit. Celia, come and look at these sleeves. Do you think you could make 'em?"

Celia fingered Fanny's sleeves delicately, and then shook her head. "It is a very complicated design, Mama. All these little tucks..."

"I should be very happy to help," Fanny said. "Perhaps I might demonstrate how it is done? All of our prepared gowns come with enough fabric for a sleeve of this type."

"I cannot afford to buy another gown just yet," Celia said sorrowfully.

"Oh, of course," Fanny said hastily. "One must eke out one's allowance. It is so tiresome when one sees the most charming material, yet it is quite out of reach, but one must be prudent."

Celia smiled a little at this. "Mama says we must have food on the table before we think of clothes."

"And coals for the fire," her mother said, with a rueful grimace. "Luckily it has been a mild winter, so I might be a whole chaldron to the good, come Lady Day. Ah, Jane, there you are." She bustled away to talk to Miss Monkton.

Fanny felt desperately sorry for Celia, who was as beautiful as a princess, yet would never find her prince in such drab clothes. Such a waste, for it was still possible to look stylish at very little expense. On impulse, Fanny said, "Would you let me examine your gown? For it might be possible to make some small changes to the sleeves without the expense of a new gown."

Willingly, Celia removed her pelisse, and Fanny fingered the fabric. "I could do something with this, if you wish it. Or a different gown, if you have another one you would like dressed up a little."

"Oh... you are so kind, but I do not think we could afford even that."

Fanny reached out a hand to her. "Oh, pray do not worry about such matters! I shall be perfectly happy to do this for you as a favour, for with your looks you deserve to have quite the most ravishing wardrobe. Well, perhaps to do the thing properly would take quite a lot of money, but a very little effort with the needle will make all the difference, you will see."

"Fanny?" Miss Monkton's sharp tones cut across this impassioned speech. "I trust you are not planning to provide services at no cost to our customers? I am as fond of Celia as anyone, for she is the daughter of my dearest friend, but we cannot simply give away our efforts to anyone."

Fanny went hot with embarrassment, but she did not hesitate. "I beg your pardon, but I sew in the evenings for my own pleasure. I may do so for this lady, may I not?"

Celia's mother cast shrewd eyes on Fanny. "Just think, Jane, if Celia could make more of an impression on society than my widow's mite can achieve for her, and it were to be known that this shop were responsible... imagine how it would enhance your reputation."

"Well..." Miss Monkton looked from one to the other. "Perhaps just this once."

Celia's face lit up, and her mother smiled too. But after they had gone, Miss Monkton said to Fanny, "That was generous, child, but you must not make a habit of it. Lady Harriet would not like it to see shopkeeper's daughters dressed up like ladies. One must have the distinction of rank preserved, or where would we be? Much as I would love to see Celia Drabble well-dressed, it is not for us to interfere. If her mother has no money for decent clothes, and no skill to make them, then Celia must trim her expectations accordingly."

"But she is so beautiful!" Fanny cried. "She should marry a duke, who would not care about her lack of dowry."

Miss Monkton laughed. "Aye, and perhaps he would not. But he might care a great deal about her indigent family. None of the Drabbles have two pennies to rub together, and not exactly quality, if you take my meaning. Barbara herself is a lady through and through — well, she is a Harbottle, after all — but the rest of them scrabble by as best they can. I would love to see Celia make a great match, but her husband will have to be both wealthy and tolerant, poor man."

"Poor Celia," Fanny said sorrowfully.

~~~~~

Aunt Agatha arrived in a whirlwind of camphor-scented worsted to rescue Ferdy from his bachelor existence. Lady Agatha Makenham was not quite fifty, one of those women who exist in every family — an awkward debutante and reluctant participant in the marriage mart, who had finally come into her own around the age of thirty, donning a spinster's cap with relief, and devoting the rest of her life to supporting her numerous married relatives. Every Makenham knew perfectly well that if there should be an outbreak of measles, a broken arm or a difficult baby, Aunt Agatha must be sent for at once, and all would be well. She had an inexhaustible supply of remedies for illness, of games to alleviate boredom and of scurrilous gossip to cheer harassed parents.

Now she was come to bring a female element to Twenty-Five Harlington Terrace, and play hostess at Ferdy's exclusive dinner parties. There was no point in having a house of his own if he did not entertain a little, and if he were to oblige his father and grandfather in marrying soon, he would need to be able to entertain ladies as well as gentlemen.

Aunt Agatha bustled in at two in the afternoon. By four, she had rescheduled all the meals, supervised the rearrangement of the furniture in the drawing room and morning room, instructed the butler to polish the silver to a receipt of her own devising and sent word to the coal merchant to present himself at eight o'clock sharp the following day to explain the poor quality of his goods. From Ferdy she demanded a list of all the principal ladies of the town, and all his social engagements.

"So you are dining out this evening?" she said, her sharp eyes scanning the paper he had provided. "Lord and Lady Gilbert Marford?"

"Yes, but I will cry off, of course, now that you are come, Auntie."

"Nonsense. Where is that footman, the one with the yellow hair? What is his name?"

"Hill, Auntie."

"Hill. Good. Scratch a note to Lady Gilbert that I have arrived and that you will be bringing me with you this evening, and Hill will run round with it. Where do the Marfords live?"

"Harkwell Road."

"Well, this is a small town and it is not far, I daresay. The fellow has long legs, he can lope round there in five minutes. Come along, come along, Ferdy. Do not stand about gawking in that foolish way. Write the note."

"Yes, Auntie."

Ferdy tried not to smile as he wrote his note, a little more politely phrased than Aunt Agatha's peremptory instruction. He would have given up the dinner engagement, naturally, for one could not desert a guest on her first evening, but it was the very last thing he had wanted to do. Lord Gilbert Marford was brother to Lady Harriet Hay, and surely she would be invited to a dinner at her own brother's house? And if Lady Harriet were invited, then very likely her house guest would also be invited. And even if she were not, meeting Lady Harriet socially would give him an excuse to pay another morning call at number Twenty-Six, and not be confined to

Dr Hay's rather gloomy masculine domain. He needed every opportunity he could muster to enter the Hays' society, for how else was he to get to know the elusive Miss Winterton?

Well, if all else failed, there was always Aunt Agatha. She had once rather famously managed to get herself invited to dinner at the Royal Pavilion at Brighton, a feat never achieved by any other Makenham, so inveigling her way to a meeting with Miss Fanny Winterton would not tax her in the slightest. Not that Ferdy had any intention of telling her about the lady, but somehow Aunt Agatha always wormed her way to the heart of the matter. No secret could be kept from her for long.

One way or another, he was determined to meet the lady with the sweetest expression in the world, and every day brought him a little closer to achieving his objective.

5: Dinner With The Marfords

Ferdy allowed a little extra time for dressing that evening. He was fastidious in his habits, following the precepts of the great Mr Brummel in wearing clothes that were perfectly cut, tasteful rather than extravagant, and being always immaculately groomed. He bathed first, therefore, and then shaved for the second time that day.

His drawers and a shirt of fine lawn went on first, then he sat for some time while his valet tended to his hair, making a few delicate snips here and there before his expert fingers created the windswept style Ferdy favoured. His hair was the bane of his existence, for it curled rather more than he would like, and made certain styles all but impossible for him.

The silk stockings and knee breeches went on next, followed by the most difficult part of the operation — tying the neckcloth. His under-valet held a dozen cloths of tonight's chosen size and shape, starched to exactly the right degree, while Ferdy attempted the desired style. Tonight was a lucky one, for he was satisfied with only his fourth effort. The valets smiled, pleased. Ferdy was pleased, too. No one else would know or care that he had created a perfect Mathematical, nor how long it had taken to achieve, but he would know, and that inner knowledge warmed his heart.

The rest was easier. A waistcoat of burgundy figured silk picked out with delicate grey embroidery, a single fob hanging at the waist, a coat of black superfine, polished shoes, hat, gloves and cane. His valets stood side by side, smiling, as Ferdy admired the effect in his dressing glass.

"You look splendid, sir, if I may say so," the senior valet said.

Ferdy turned to him in surprise. The man was rather stiff, as a rule, and rarely commented on Ferdy's appearance. "I look like a gentleman, Wrackham," he said.

"Exactly, sir."

Ferdy laughed. "I look well enough. Thank you both. I do not expect to be late tonight."

"I shall wait up for you myself, sir," Wrackham said, with his usual rigid bow.

Ferdy made no comment on this, for usually it was Wright, the under-valet, who peeled him out of his clothes at the end of the evening, but it was a matter for the two of them to decide.

With a nod to the two, he made his way down the stairs to begin the evening, giving no further thought to his appearance, and turned his mind to the pleasures of good food, good wine and good company at Lord and Lady Gilbert's.

Lady Gilbert turned out to be a quiet, unassuming person, not at all high in the instep. She was not in the least the sort of society prize who would normally draw the attention of the son of a marquess, especially one with Gilbert Marford's reputation as a ladies' man. However, Ferdy knew that they had had rather an unconventional meeting, and they seemed a contented pair. As for the guests, he had assumed it would be another motley collection of town worthies, but instead he found himself mingling with some of Sagborough's principal residents.

Sir William Harbottle and his good lady were a well-matched pair, both tall and long-limbed, with sharp eyes that ranged over Ferdy and sized him up knowingly.

"So you are Belwarren's heir, eh?" Sir William said, his keen eyes lingering on Ferdy's carefully contrived neckcloth. "And how shall you like being an earl, boy?"

"Not at all," Ferdy said promptly, "since it will mean the demise of both my father and grandfather. Prefer them alive, to be honest."

Sir William uttered a bark that might have been amusement. "True enough, true enough. I hope you will be more punctilious about attending the House than Belwarren has been. I have *The Times* sent to me so that I can follow everything that happens in the both Houses, but Belwarren's name has not been mentioned since he was introduced."

"The Makenham tradition is to leave politicking to those clever enough to understand it," Ferdy said.

"Hmm. He has Whig tendencies, I hear, so it may be all for the best."

As Ferdy had hoped, the Hays were invited, although sadly this did not include Miss Winterton. However, Lady Harriet and Miss Hay were of almost as much interest to him. He knew Lady Harriet slightly already, for the noble families could scarcely avoid some acquaintanceship. Although they must have nodded to each other a hundred times at balls and routs, somehow their paths had never particularly crossed before.

"Well, Mr Makenham, we meet properly at last," was all she said, laughing at him, and he had a mortifying suspicion that she was remembering him standing transfixed on the pavement outside his own house. She was placed at the opposite end of the dinner table from him, but he heard her rattling away to her brother and Sir William. Ferdy was glad he was not sitting next to such a chatterbox.

Miss Hay was a pale copy of her brother, and like him also in aptitude, for she discussed medical matters quite freely at the dinner table, and when the subject turned to politics, she offered her opinion on that subject, too, debating spiritedly with both Dr Hay and Sir William.

The talk was a little above Ferdy's head, but he employed the time gainfully by chatting comfortably to Lady Gilbert about the shops of Sagborough, especially those of interest to ladies seeking to improve their wardrobe. By this subtle means he was able to discover at least three possible places where Miss Winterton might be found, without once asking a direct question. Several times during the evening her name was mentioned by one or other of the guests, but although Ferdy started whenever he heard it, he heroically said nothing, letting the conversation drift on. Soon enough he would be properly introduced to the mysterious Miss Fanny Winterton, but he was not impatient, and he was determined not to reveal his intentions too soon. On the whole, he was quite pleased with his inscrutability, and relieved that Lady Harriet said nothing about his embarrassing transfixion.

His complacency was short lived, however. When the carriage had taken them home again, Aunt Agatha marched Ferdy into the drawing room, where a fire and candles still burned, and a tray of brandy and sweetmeats had been left out on her instructions.

"Now then, young man, you had better tell me all about Miss Fanny Winterton."

"M-Miss Fanny Winterton?" Ferdy said, aiming for insouciance, but realising almost at once that Aunt Agatha would see straight through him.

"Ha! Come along, Ferdy. Out with it."

He heaved a rueful sigh. "How do you always know?" he said, smiling affectionately at her. "No use trying to bamboozle you."

"You forget that I have known you since the day you were born. When you are feigning disinterest, the tips of your ears go bright red."

"Do they really?" Ferdy said, instantly diverted, jumping up to examine his ears in one of the mirrors.

"Of course, and after the incident with the bishop—"

"Yes, yes, but that is old history," Ferdy said testily.

She laughed. "Then come and sit down, drink up your brandy like a good boy and tell me about this Miss Winterton. All I have gathered is that she is staying with the Hays, that she is in mourning, and that she is helping Lady Harriet with some scheme or other. Hatty Marford always has some project on the go. One of those busy females who is never at home, always dashing about here and there. Last I heard it was orphan girls. These fallen women are a new start."

"Miss Winterton is a lady of mystery," Ferdy said gloomily, plunking himself down on an overstuffed chair, and wincing. "Upon my soul, this furniture is uncomfortable. It is not even stylish. One does not mind being uncomfortable if one knows oneself to be at the forefront of fashion but— Yes, yes, stop scowling at me, Auntie, I am getting to Miss Winterton, but there is little to tell. I have seen her once on the day I arrived, and twice at church, but never to speak to, and we have not even been introduced."

"Ah. So this is not a growing attachment on your part, and you are just another foolish young man taken in by the sight of a pretty face. I had expected better of you, Ferdy. You have been on the town for years, so I should have thought you immune to such trivialities."

"A pretty face is hardly a triviality," Ferdy said with feeling. "If one must look at it every day for forty years and more, one would prefer it to be worth looking at. But that is not it, not at all. She is not a diamond of the first water, I will grant you. Not bracket-faced, you understand, but she would be nothing in town. But there is such a sweetness in her expression, such innocence — I have not the words to describe her. One would need a poet to do justice to her, I fear."

"Hmm." Aunt Agatha looked at him assessingly. "Well, it is not hopeless. Once you *have* met the chit, you may well find she has a dreadful accent or has no proper thinking, or possibly no thinking at all. So many of these girls nowadays dress up prettily and can play a tolerable tune on the pianoforte but are incapable of holding a conversation. They think of nothing but gowns and balls and beaux, and one fears for the welfare of their children with such brainless mothers."

"She is not brainless," Ferdy said with a smile. "No one wearing so elegant a pelisse could be brainless."

Aunt Agatha laughed out loud at that. "Really, Ferdy! She has a clever mantua maker, that is all."

"She is a seamstress, and therefore makes her own garments, and I have never seen a pelisse with quite that style of shoulder puff. And in velvet, too! Not an easy task. And at church, she wore a different one, in merino wool with some exquisite stitching detail. She cannot be at all brainless with such an eye for style."

She shook her head, but she smiled, too. "Ah, Ferdy, you judge everyone by the clothes they wear."

"Of course. The naked form is no more than nature unadorned — all one may say is that it is tall or short, rounded or slender, the limbs increased, perhaps, by a man's occupation or habits, or shrunken and withered with age. But the garments he dons speak of his place in the world, his rank, his wealth, his good taste, his education, his ambition, his morality. Clothes are the carapace of civilisation. A man's clothes say what he is, and what he would like to be, and what he would like the world to think he is, even if he is not. When one sees a man fully dressed, be his garments the finest tailoring in the world or the simplest homespun, one sees what he truly is. One of my tutors told me all that. He was a prosy bore on the subject of the Black Death or cyphering, but he was absolutely right about clothes."

Draining her brandy glass and setting it down on a side table, she reached for a marzipan sweet. "That is a bit subtle for me. I either like the way a person dresses or I do not. What did you make of Lady Gilbert's attire?"

"A simple gown, well made from good quality material, and not over embellished. A self-effacing style of dress, that does not want to be the centre of attention yet tries not to embarrass her husband's rank. I think she made it herself, although she has not Miss Winterton's skill. Lady Gilbert is not yet comfortable in her position in society, for all her pleasing manners."

"You can read all that from one gown? She is an odd sort of wife for a marquess's son, I grant you. Did you hear the accent?"

"She is a Kentish physician's daughter, although she did not put herself forward during the medical discussion."

"Unlike Miss Hay. How do you read *her* gown? Did it speak to you of her brazen lack of feminine humility?"

"There you see a lady who simply does not care what the world thinks of her appearance. It is not just the gown, Auntie, it is everything — hair, jewellery, gloves, shoes, stockings. One notices when there is a hole in a stocking, as with Miss Hay, and I swear that her hair had barely been brushed. Such presentation is deplorably lax. Lady Harriet is equally unconcerned, although in a different way. She probably orders new gowns twice a year from the same *modiste*, and then wears them repeatedly until her maid quietly burns them. Her outfit tonight was five years old at least, and more appropriate for Carlton House than a quiet dinner in Sagborough. It is an affront to decency to make so little effort. Most people would disdain to wear anything so ill-thought-out, but then she is a marquess's daughter and cares nothing for the opinion of lesser mortals."

"At least she is not one of those dreadfully affected people who look down their noses at everyone," Aunt Agatha said. "Well, if we are to get to know your Miss Winterton, it must be through Lady Harriet, so I shall call on her tomorrow. I believe my age and prior acquaintance with the family will allow me to make the first call, despite her greater rank. And I must visit Lady Gilbert, of course, to thank her for our very pleasant evening. Shall you send flowers, Ferdy?"

"Of course, and a little note."

"Ah yes, you are so good at these delicate little touches. There now, you need not sit up with me any longer. I shall just have a touch more brandy, and make a list of tasks to begin tomorrow, but you may go off to your club or your gaming den or drinking party, or whatever you young men like to get up to after respectable folk have gone to bed."

Ferdy laughed. "You are mistaking Sagborough for London, Auntie. Everyone here is in bed by midnight, respectable or otherwise."

"How dreadfully dull," she said with a knowing smile. "Shoo, now. Leave an old lady in peace."

"Old lady, indeed!" he said affectionately.

He kissed her cheek, and went dutifully upstairs to Wrackham's ministrations and then bed, although it must be confessed that sleep did not come to him as easily as usual. His thoughts were very much in the house next door, wondering which room was Miss Winterton's and whether she was at that very moment lying awake too.

~~~~~

'Dearest Fanny, You sound very happy in your wintry northern fastness, but then I know how you make the best of everything. Are you truly contented in Sagborough? It sounds an interesting little town, and there is something in what you say of it being much cosier than a great city, and yet so much bigger and more convenient than Frickham. And a circulating library! How glorious to have such a facility, and directly opposite your little shop, too, so you need only cross the road to find some wonderful new tome to while away the quiet hours. I do hope you have some quiet hours, dearest, and are not working every waking moment. Do not do too much fine work by candlelight, for it is ruinous to the eyes. I hope the weather improves soon, for spring cannot be far away now. Your loving sister, Annabelle.'

~~~~~

Fanny sat alone in the drawing room, rereading all the letters from her sisters. It reassured her to feel that tiny contact with them. As she read, she heard their voices in her head, and saw their animated faces smiling and laughing, teasing each other, and it made her feel a little less lonely. Old Mrs Hay had snored for a while after dinner, then woken up to eat a bite of supper before retiring to bed. Fanny stayed on, however, her sewing cast aside, rather curious to know how the evening had gone. She had not realised before that one of Lady Harriet's brothers lived in Sagborough. Lady Harriet had six brothers, seemingly, and Fanny had not quite got them straight. The eldest was Lord Carrbridge, of course, a marquess and therefore unimaginably grand, but the others all got muddled up in Fanny's mind, and Lady Harriet chattered away so fast that it was impossible to disentangle one thread before she had moved on to some other topic entirely.

Close to midnight, when Fanny was just beginning to think of giving up and going to bed, the sounds of a carriage drew her to the window. Peeking from behind the curtain, she watched it pull up outside number Twenty-Five. The footmen jumped down from the back of the carriage to open the door and let down the steps, and light streamed out from the front door in welcome. A lady descended from the carriage first, a rather stout middle-aged lady, who waved away the attentions of the footmen and strode up the steps into the house.

Then a man descended, a man so exquisitely dressed that even from her perch some distance above him, Fanny recognised the quality of his coat, the shapeliness of his hat and the gold finish on the head of his cane, glimmering in the lamplight. Even the polish on his shoes reflected the light, and as for his neckcloth — it positively glowed, it was so white. And so beautifully arranged! She had never seen anything like it.

Descended to the pavement, he paused and looked up at number Twenty-Six as if searching. With a squeak of alarm, Fanny slipped out of sight behind the curtain. By the time she had plucked up the courage to peer out again, he had gone, and the carriage was setting off for the coach house.

But she knew him. She had not seen him since that moment when they had both alighted from their carriages at the same moment, and their eyes had met, but she could not mistake him. No one else looked quite so stylish, and there was an air about him that was not arrogance, but rather an assurance that he was a man perfectly fitted to his setting and to the occasion. He was a man of fashion — no, that was not quite right. He was a man of impeccable taste and she felt, as she had felt from that first moment, that she would like to know more of him, and discover whether he was the pattern card of sartorial elegance he appeared to be, or whether he was just a dandy.

She did not even know his name.

6: *The Seamstress*

Lady Harriet's carriage brought the Hays home not long afterwards, and they drifted into the drawing room, Lady Harriet talking at a rapid pace, as always.

"— and it is very tiresome, but I shall have to get the lawyers involved to sort out the mess. I shall write to London tomorrow and tell them— Oh, Fanny, did you wait up for us?"

Fanny bobbed a curtsy. "May I fetch you anything? And did you have a lovely evening?"

"You want to hear about your love-struck young man, I daresay," Lady Harriet said, laughing loudly. "Ah, Bell, some tea, as soon as may be, but nothing to eat. Well, Fanny, he was there, and it *is* Ferdy Makenham, as I should have guessed, from all the capes on his great-coat that day we all arrived here. Such a fribble! I am sure no one else spends quite so many hours in front of the looking-glass."

Miss Hay tittered, but Dr Hay said quietly, "I thought him rather well-dressed, if you ask me, without undue ostentation. Some of these London fellows are too dazzling for words."

Lady Harriet cast her fan onto one chair and her gloves onto another, and flopped onto a sofa near the fire. "No, I assure you he is a fribble, and almost as bad as Gil, although his shirt points were lower, I grant you. Do you not agree, Marina?"

"Certainly," Miss Hay said. "I cannot like a man who spends longer than I do getting dressed. It is a foolish kind of vanity. So long as a man looks respectably the gentleman, I ask nothing more of him. And he said nothing of interest, nothing at all. He had no desire to talk about politics or the hospital or any serious matter. He was telling Sir William how he tied his neckcloth, if you please! As if anyone cared for that! Did he speak more after the ladies had withdrawn, Perry?"

Dr Hay considered the question carefully. "I cannot say that he did. Harbottle and I had the best of the conversation, assisted by Lord Gilbert. Makenham was only animated when the topic turned to horses or shooting or some such. I daresay a young man such as he is not greatly interested in the French trouble."

"Well, he should be!" Miss Hay said hotly. "If something is not done about this Bonaparte fellow, and soon, who knows where it will end? Lord Gilbert said that his uncle had word that..."

Fanny crept towards the door. When Miss Hay began to talk about the French it made her head ache. She dropped into another curtsy, Lady Harriet waved a languid hand and she was able to escape to the solitude of her own room. She undressed, carefully folding each garment and placing it neatly on its shelf, put on her thickest nightgown and slipped between the cold sheets, shivering, for the maid with the warming pan had long since been and gone. Her last waking thought was that it must be very pleasant to meet a young man who talked about how to tie a neckcloth and not about the trouble with France.

And now she had his name. Mr Ferdinand Makenham.

~~~~~

'Dearest Fanny, How exciting it must be to live right in the town, so that everything you want is but a short walk away and the pavements are swept and clean. There is so much mud about at the moment after all the rain we have had! There is no going anywhere, by carriage or on foot. But at least we have had no snow recently which

is the greatest blessing. Is it hard work, being in a shop and sewing all day? When one enters a shop as a buyer, the occasion is filled with excitement, for one gets to explore all those wonderful little drawers of buttons and feel the softness of the ribbons and perhaps one buys something or perhaps not, but for the person in the shop, smiling at every customer and bringing out all her goods and not even making a few pennies sometimes, it must be very hard. I do not think I could smile all day, hour after hour, being pleasant to everyone who comes in just in case this is someone who will actually buy something. But you are so good-natured, Fanny, that perhaps you do not even see the hardship. You do not complain in your letters, but that is just like you, dearest, always to see the best in everyone. Be sure to wrap up warmly when you go out, for even if there is no snow, the wind can be biting and you must not take a chill or fall into a fever, not without your sisters there to look after you. Your affectionate sister, Lucy.'

~~~~~

Fanny soon discovered that the other seamstresses lived a short distance away from Sagborough, in a property of Lady Harriet's called Westbury House. It was some five miles by road, but under two miles if one walked along the canal. In the winter, it was too dark to go that way after the shop had shut for the day, so two or three of the women stayed for the week with the Monkton ladies above the shop, returning to Westbury House after church on Sunday, when another group would stay. Others came each morning with the sun and returned home before dusk had made the tow path too treacherous.

It was from this latter group that Fanny began to make friends, for she, too, was sent home before sunset, and the women accompanied her along Mill Road, across York Road, and then into the lane that ran behind Harlington Terrace. When she turned into the gate beside the coach house for number Twenty-Six, the others continued down the lane to the far end of Harlington Terrace, across another road and so to the canal.

Fanny liked being part of their big, noisy group. It was almost like having her sisters around her again, although, if she closed her eyes, she would never make such a comparison. Their accents reminded her of the harsh cawing of crows, and several of them wore wooden clogs that clonked on the cobbles as they walked. But Fanny liked their cosy chatter, and the affectionate way they spoke of their children and worried about them when they had the slightest sniffle. None of them wore wedding rings or ever mentioned husbands, and Fanny had begun to have some inkling of the nature of these unfortunate fallen women and what it was that they might have fallen from. But naturally she could not ask about such matters.

One morning, Fanny was busy in the sewing room when Miss Monkton came in carrying a large package wrapped in brown paper and string.

"Ah, Fanny, I have a task for you. You are to go to Mrs Malpas on York Road with these three gowns, and fit Miss Malpas with the two gowns her mama bought last week."

"Me?" Fanny said, wide-eyed.

"It must be you, Fanny," Miss Monkton said firmly. "You're the only person presentable enough to send into the best parts of town who can also place a stitch. Take your work basket, for you will need to do a fair bit of sewing. I daresay they have made a hash of putting those gowns together, but do the best you can, you know. If we can turn out the mayor's daughter creditably, it will enhance our reputation enormously."

"Take more than a few stitches to do that, I reckon," Edith said.

"Now, now, let's not be unkind," Miss Monkton said. "Miss Malpas may not be blessed with great beauty, but she's a very good-natured girl, by all I've heard. Besides, Mrs Malpas wishes to buy a dozen gowns from us, so we will be very civil about the whole family. You may get your coat and go at once, Fanny."

"Yes, Miss Monkton." But when she had her pelisse and bonnet on, she said timidly, "If you please, Miss Monkton, I am not sure of the way. In which direction must I turn on York Road?"

"Bless you, child, Martha will go with you to show you the way. She will carry everything, you know, and hold pins and so forth while you do the fitting, but do not let her speak to Miss Malpas." She went on half to herself, "Yes, it must be Martha, for she is no use here, except for sweeping the floor and holding things. She is no seamstress! She was a housemaid before, you know."

"Before?" Fanny said. "Before she came here, you mean?"

Miss Monkton threw her an odd glance. "Aye. Came from Norfolk or Essex — somewhere down that way. Ah, there you are, Martha. Are your shoes respectable? Do watch where you walk when you cross the street, for you do not wish to be dragging mud or worse over Mrs Malpas's fine carpets. There, now. Off you go, and no dilly-dallying."

As soon as they stepped outside the door, a bitter wind caught them and tossed the ribbons on Fanny's bonnet about her face.

"Oof! Nippy out here," Martha said cheerfully. "Best walk fast to keep warm." So saying, she set off at a rapid pace that had Fanny half running to keep up.

The mayor's house was one of the best houses on the main road through Sagborough, considerably larger and newer than those on Harlington Terrace. Fanny was half way up the steps to the front door when Martha hissed at her.

"Wait! You might be able to go that way, but I have to go down, not up." She pointed to the narrow steps down to the area.

"Oh. Of course." Rather subdued, Fanny followed her down to the servants' door, where a harassed scullery maid with soapy hands opened the door and looked at them enquiringly. Fanny said, "We are here to attend Mrs Malpas and Miss Malpas for a fitting."

"You from the dress shop, then? Come inside. Wait 'ere." She waved them in, shut the door and disappeared down a long, narrow corridor, leaving a wet trail of drips to mark her passage.

The two women stood in silence. The narrow space behind the lower door was as black as a coal-cellar, the only light coming from narrow windows over the door. Dark paint added to Fanny's feeling of having fallen into a pit. Yet it was only the servants' quarters, she reminded herself. Woodside's nether regions were no different. But there she had been a daughter of the house, treated with deference, not left in the dark to wait on a summons from above.

When her eyes adjusted to the gloom, Fanny looked about her with interest. Further down the corridor, a female voice and the metallic clang of pans suggested the cook and kitchen maid were hard at work. Down another corridor lined with doors, two male voices, perhaps footmen. A bell clanged somewhere nearby, and the scullery maid reappeared, still dripping, and dashed past them to see which bell it was. "Drawing room!" she yelled, before retreating once more to her dish washing.

A door opened and a butler emerged in a rush, pulling on his coat. He stopped when he saw Fanny and Martha.

"Ah, from Miss Kelly's establishment, I take it. You are late. Follow me."

He took the stairs at some speed, causing a housemaid with mop and bucket to flatten herself against the wall as he passed. Fanny followed more slowly, taking the steep steps more cautiously. "Come along now!" the butler said impatiently, ushering them through a door into the hall, where he almost collided with the housekeeper.

"Mr Wilson, you are wanted in the drawing room, I fancy," she said tersely.

"Thank you, Mrs Hargreaves, I am on my way. I shall just direct these persons—"

"The shop girls? I shall take care of them, Mr Wilson. No need for you to trouble yourself. If you would be so good as to inform the mistress that they are here, I will convey them to Miss Emmeline's room myself. By the *back* stairs." With the merest raising of one eyebrow, she managed to put the flustered butler in his place. Turning without haste to Fanny and Martha, she looked them up and down, before her gaze came to rest on Fanny. But she said only, "This way."

She led them out of the hall and down the full length of the house, then through a door to the uncarpeted back stairs. Fanny followed meekly, uncertain whether it was worse to be called a shop girl or a person. She tried not to be humiliated, for she would have to accustom herself to such slights.

Miss Emmeline's room was an odd mixture of battered, elderly furniture and the most exquisitely luxurious carpets Fanny had ever seen. Even Westerlea Park had nothing so fine, and here was a bedroom fitted out with the richness of a palace, but only on the floor. It was odd.

The lady's maid was already there, an elderly woman, grey haired and frail, gently laying out gowns on the bed.

"The girls from the mantua maker, Miss Tripp," the housekeeper said.

"Ah, at last. Thank you, Mrs Hargreaves, very kind of you. Has Madam been informed?"

"Mr Wilson is apprising the mistress at this moment. Do you require any further assistance on this occasion, Miss Tripp? I can send Maria up to you if you wish. We don't want you over-exerting yourself again."

"How kind of you but I believe I can manage, Mrs Hargreaves."

"Very well, Miss Tripp. I shall—"

The end of the sentence was lost as the door flew open and two smiling faces, giggling together, burst into the room.

"Fanny! I so hoped it would be you!" And Fanny found herself wrapped in a silken hug.

"Marianne! I mean Miss Trivers — how lovely to—"

"None of that '*Miss Trivers*' nonsense," Marianne cried. "We are friends, remember? So you must call me Marianne, always."

"Oh no! It would not be proper at all, not now," Fanny cried. "You are a lady and I am... a shop girl. A *person*."

"You are still my friend," Marianne said stoutly. "But it is the most infamous thing, for my aunt will not let me visit you at all, and so Emmy had this clever idea... oh, this is Emmy, Fanny, and you are going to rig her out in the first style so that she may snare her admirer and be a countess one day."

Fanny turned for the first time to Miss Emmeline Malpas, and her heart sank. Her large frame and bulky hands might, perhaps, be disguised, and the straight, sandy hair would yield to curling papers, but the pasty complexion and prominent teeth were greater difficulties. There was no escaping the fact that Emmy Malpas was a very plain girl indeed.

But Fanny would never be so hard-hearted as to make the slightest adverse comment. "What a lovely figure you have, Miss Malpas."

"That's just what I've been telling her," Miss Tripp said, beaming. "All the gentlemen like a lady who *carries* herself well, shoulders back and best foot forward."

Marianne and Emmy giggled behind their hands.

"Now, Miss Emmy, slip out of that gown and into this one, so that the seamstress can see if anything needs to be done. I must just have a word with Mrs Hargreaves."

She bustled out of the room, and the muted sounds of hissed voices filtered through the closed door. Fanny took off her bonnet and pelisse, and began to unbutton Emmy's gown, while Martha unpacked the parcel, and Marianne sat on the bed, beaming happily at Fanny.

"I am so happy to see you, Fanny, you cannot imagine. I so missed our chats, and it was abominably lonely just at first. It is so shabby of Aunt Eve and Uncle Adam to stop me from seeing you, but they are dreadfully stuffy and expect me to make a very good match, so they do not think I should be intimate with a seamstress."

"That is perfectly proper," Fanny said, sliding the gown off Emmy's broad shoulders. "I am not a fit person for you to associate with."

"Oh, pooh! That is all nonsense! Luckily, I met Emmy at my very first assembly here. We bumped into each other at the door, and there we are! We have become the best of friends, have we not, Emmy?"

"Oh yes," Emmy said, in a soft voice, so quietly that Fanny could barely hear her.

"But you were not at the assembly, Fanny dear. Does Lady Harriet not allow you to attend?"

"I am still in mourning," Fanny said, lifting the new gown over Emmy's head. "I cannot possibly think about dancing, not when Papa... not so soon."

"Oh no, of course not. But you will come later, I hope? Everyone goes to the assemblies here, even Emmy's milliner was there, and one or two farmers were pointed out to me, perfectly respectable-looking persons. One would never know to look at them. So you see, you need not scruple to come along too."

"I shall take Lady Harriet's advice on the matter," Fanny said firmly, as she smoothed out Emmy's skirts, and stood back to look the gown over with a critical eye.

"You must come!" Marianne said robustly. "I shall tell Lady Harriet so the next time I see her. The assemblies are such fun, and

Emmy has a beau already, and such a distinguished one — the heir to an earl, would you believe!"

"He is not my beau," Emmy said in her quiet way, but blushing all the same. "He stood up with me first because of Papa, I expect, but Papa became very excited about it, and gave Mama a hundred pounds to buy me some new gowns and furbelows."

"And *I* told her about your shop, Fanny," Marianne said, "and how she might buy twice as many gowns for the money if she but does a little sewing herself. Was that not clever of me?"

"Oh yes!" Fanny said. "Martha, some pins, if you please. Yes, hold the pin cushion up for me to reach. What is he like, this... this gentleman who is *not* a beau? Is he very handsome?"

The two girls considered this carefully. "He is not exactly *handsome,*" Marianne said eventually, "but very refined and aristocratic in his appearance. He dresses rather plain, I thought, but his manners! Oh, my dear Fanny, his manners are exquisite. Very London, Aunt Eve said. Very polished. *Such* a perfect gentleman!"

Martha grunted, and the others all turned to look at her, startled. "Beg pardon," she muttered, very red. "Pin caught me."

"Is there blood?" Fanny cried. "Do you need a handkerchief to bind it?"

But Martha shook her head, so Fanny turned back to the gown she was pinning. The others lost interest in Martha very quickly.

"Uncle Adam said he was a coxcomb, but I saw nothing outrageous in his attire," Marianne said.

"Oh, no! Very well turned out, I thought," Emmy said. "And *such* an excellent dancer. So elegant. I am very clumsy, as a rule, but he made me feel almost graceful. And when I almost went wrong, he guided me the right way so smoothly that even Papa did not notice. But when he took me back to Mama after the dance and I apologised for almost treading on his foot, and said I was not very familiar with the steps as yet, he was so kind as to say that he would not have guessed it."

Marianne chuckled. "There, you see! We shall have you married in no time."

"Oh, *no*, Marianne, no!" Emmy said, blushing violently. "He was only being polite to me. He did not distinguish me in any way."

"Apart from dancing with you before all the other young ladies," Marianne said, laughing. "You will look very fine together, I assure you. Fanny will make you some wonderful gowns, and then you will be a splendid pair altogether. Mr and Mrs Ferdinand Makenham."

Fanny concentrated on the task of pinning the gown, and said nothing.

7: The Housemaid's Tale

Fanny spent several hours trying to impart some semblance of elegance to the two gowns Miss Malpas had inexpertly stitched together. This involved much unpicking and reworking, but with some new frills and ribbons and a little delicate embroidery, she managed to cover up the worst errors and imbue the gowns with a little style. With a promise to return on the morrow to assist with the new gowns, she and Martha wearily packed up their things and made their way down the back stairs to the servants' quarters and thus out to the street.

When they emerged it was already beginning to grow dark, and a sleety wind nipped at their faces and crept through their winter-thick garments to chill them to the bone.

"At least we have not far to go," Fanny said cheerfully. "And the wind is at our back. That is a mercy, at least."

But a mere five minutes of trudging through the winter gloaming, with the sleet rapidly turning to snow, reduced them to stoical silence. The lamplighters were already out, but the brave pools of light still left a quantity of unlit gloom along the street. Martha's steps slowed and then stopped altogether.

"I hate winter," she muttered.

Fanny was peculiarly sensitive to the sentiments of others, however well concealed, and she was aware now of some distress in

Martha. What it was that had upset her she could not say, but something had, and ever since she had pricked her finger she had been silent, her face closed up. She had done whatever Fanny had asked, but sometimes she had not responded at first to questions or requests, seeming sunk in her own thoughts. Now she stood, head down, lost in misery. Fanny knew it would not do to take her back to the shop and the busy sewing room, with its noise and laughter and constant teasing. What Martha needed was somewhere quiet, and a sympathetic listener, if she should wish to talk.

"There is no point in going all the way back to the shop only to turn round and set out again in half an hour," Fanny said slowly. "There is an inn on the corner there. Shall we get some coffee to warm us? We can watch for the others coming up Mill Road from there."

"I can't afford no coffee," Martha said sullenly. "I've no money at all till next quarter."

"I have coins," Fanny said. "We can get warm, and have a comfortable coze, and perhaps, if you wish it, you can tell me what it is that is troubling you."

Martha looked sideways at her, but then nodded curtly and strode away to the inn. The tap room was not as warm as Fanny might have wished, for the door constantly opened as patrons came and went, but it was free of wind and sleet and the penetrating cold of a February afternoon. They ordered coffee, and then found a quiet corner by a window where they could watch for the other women from the shop heading home.

The coffee was not very good, but it was warm and that was all Fanny asked of it at that moment. For a while they sat in silence, sipping their coffee, and savouring the respite.

"Do you want to talk about it?" Fanny said as the silence lengthened. "Of course, if you do not, I shall *quite* understand, for sometimes a matter is too affecting, too *dreadful*, to be shared, but

Mama always used to say that a trouble shared is a trouble halved, so if you wish to—"

Martha's face lit up with a wide smile as abruptly as the sun emerging after a rain shower. "My ma used to say the same thing! How funny! Not that *my* trouble can be halved," she added in an undertone. "It is just... those young ladies see only one side of these rich gentlemen. This Mr Makenham — I know nothing of him in particular, but they're all alike. To *your* kind, they're all smiles and perfect manners, but to *our* kind... No, let's not speak of it. You shouldn't know anything about such things."

"You mean, I suppose, the... the *difficulties* in which you find yourselves. Lady Harriet calls you *unfortunate*, and although I do not understand exactly what that means, I am not stupid, Martha. I do have an inkling, for you all have a child and... and no husband. And that is a great tragedy, to fall so deep in love that—"

Martha gave a great crack of laughter. "Love? Aye, there's some that fell in love, right enough, and hoped the blighter would marry them, but most of us..." She sipped her coffee, eyeing Fanny warily. "Most of us were wronged, Miss Winterton, without any thought of love. In service, usually, or working at an inn or such like. I was a housemaid at... well, never mind the name. I'd like to forget it, I can tell you. A grand house near Grantham, in Lincolnshire. Doing well there, too, so I was, and would likely have been head housemaid in a few years. But there was a gathering there in the summer of three years ago. Lots of young ladies and their mamas, and lots of young men, too. Great dinners and outings and dancing and all sorts of entertainments. They put on a play one afternoon, and another day there was archery, with all the young gentlemen showing off to the ladies. Well, you've moved in that world, you know what it's like. They like their fun, don't they? And it's not always archery they want, not the men. They come in the night and take what they want and go away again." Her face darkened. "They think they have the *right*," she said, with a spurt of anger. "They think we're just there for their pleasure."

"That is indeed very bad," Fanny said, not entirely understanding but thinking that taking things in the night sounded very wrong.

"Aye, so it is, very bad, but—" Again she stopped. "Look, you really shouldn't know about this sort of thing. You're a lady, you shouldn't know nothing about what men and women do."

"But I am not a lady any longer," Fanny said sorrowfully. "That part of my life is over, and now you — all of you from Westbury House — are my friends, and I do think I *ought* to know about you, do you not agree?"

"Hmpf," Martha said, taking a deep breath. "Maybe. He was handsome, I'll give him that, the one who wronged me. Handsome and smiling and... and *strong*. Nothing I could do about it. Before he went, he put a sovereign on the bed, as if that made it right. I asked him for his name, in case... in case... well, the worst happened, and he laughed at me. *Laughed!* It were just a game to him, just a bit of fun. But then he told me. Edgar Brant, his name was. *'Where will I find you?'* I asked him. He laughed again. *'In Yorkshire,'* he said. Then he went, and he left the next day, and I never said nothing, hoping... you know, that it would be all right. But it wasn't of course. He'd left me with a babe, and I was turned off and that was that."

"But it was not your fault!" Fanny cried, horrified. "Oh! I have just remembered when the farrier's boy married the apothecary's daughter, and Mrs Sheridan said it was not *her* fault. I have never realised what she meant by it until now, but I always wondered why everyone was so upset, because usually a wedding is a happy occasion."

"Aye, well, at least she got a husband out of it, which is more than I did," Martha said sourly. "I got my lovely boy — that was the only good thing to come out of it, as far as I was concerned. The darlingest babe you ever saw, and such a lovely smile, and I never blamed *him*, even though he has his father's eyes and reminds me of him every time I look at the poor mite. I came looking for the blackguard, of course. What else could I do? My ma was dead, and my pa was away at sea, and my sisters were in service too, and couldn't help. It was for *him* to make things right. So I walked all the way from Grantham to York in the middle of winter, and there I would have died, too, except that I took shelter in the church on Ousegate. The verger found me and took me to the rector, and his wife looked after me and helped me birth my lovely babe and then told Bridget Kelly about me."

"So now you are safe," Fanny said. "No one can hurt you now."

"Pah!" Martha spat. "*Safe!* Oh aye, safe enough, but I'd had a *life,* I'd had a place and prospects, and I was *respectable*. He took all that away from me. A sovereign — that's all my life was worth to him, may his evil heart burn for ever. And they're all the same, these men. They take what they want and then they just... walk away. I don't suppose he's thought about me since he left that house, but me? I've thought about *him* every waking minute of every day. His face is burned into my mind, and one day I'll find him again and—" With frightening rapidity, the violent anger dissipated. "Lord, I'm scaring you, aren't I? You've gone as white as a sheet!"

"It... it is so shocking," Fanny whispered, but the most shocking part was the violence in Martha, her face contorted with rage. Fanny shuddered to imagine a meeting between Martha and this man whose face burned into her mind.

"Aye, but— Oh, look, there's the others now. Come on, let's go."

This conversation affected Fanny so powerfully that as soon as she reached number Twenty-Six, she went straight to her room and wept and wept. At such times, the longing for her sisters almost overwhelmed her. Rosamund, of course, would simply have told her to pull herself together, in that bracing way she had, but Annabelle would have held her hands and spoken soothingly, Margaret would have hugged her tight and Lucy would have marched up and down, voluble and angry on Martha's behalf. And in a little while, Fanny would have felt better.

Instead, Mrs Hay's maid, Draper, had come to do her hair and found her weeping and still in her morning dress. Draper had quite rightly ticked her off soundly, for one must be considerate of the servants, Mama had always said, for their lives are hard. But even though Fanny had apologised profusely and scrambled into a fresh gown as quick as may be, Draper still grumbled and there was nothing more lowering to the spirits than a lady's maid berating one. Then, not surprisingly, Fanny had been late for dinner and put everyone out, and she could not help sniffling a little over the soup.

Lady Harriet waited until the footmen had withdrawn before saying, "Really, Fanny, whatever is the matter with you today? What has happened to put you so out of frame? Did you have a problem with Emmy Malpas?"

"Oh no, my lady, no, although I had to remake both gowns, and I am to go back tomorrow to help with the new ones. No, it was Martha, my lady. The talk of the ladies' gentleman admirers upset her and when I asked what the matter was, she told me... she... she told me... what had happened to her," she ended in a whisper.

"What a foolish girl she is!" Lady Harriet said, with some force. "Really, I have no patience with her! I gave Bridget strict instructions that her girls were not to talk about their pasts with you, and that, after all, is why we let you live here with us, instead of over the shop, to try to shelter you from such things. They all tell sad stories, Fanny, but you must not make too much of it. As often as not they brought their downfall upon themselves by laxity in their morals."

"Oh no, for Martha said—"

"No, no, I beg you, do not repeat her words. I am sure it is a tragic story — they all tell tragic stories — but one never knows quite where the truth lies. Now, do not look so shocked, child."

"She is an innocent, as the Good Lord intended all young ladies to be," Dr Hay said in his ponderous way. He set down his spoon and steepled his fingers. "Miss Winterton, remember that people like Martha have not had the benefit of an education, as we have, and their minds have never been attuned to rational thought. Like children, they cannot discern right from wrong, and when they fall into error, then, as children do, they attempt to conceal the truth. It is not a lie, exactly, but rather a smudging of the truth, to justify their wickedness in their own eyes."

"Oh," Fanny said, pondering this new vision of the world where truth could be smudged, and wondering how it was possible for anyone to go to church week in and week out, and yet be unaware of right and wrong.

"Some of them are born liars," Miss Hay said calmly. "I do not know this Martha, but I have met women in the disreputable areas who will look one straight in the eye and tell the most outrageous fibs."

"I cannot like it when you go to these back streets, Marina," Lady Harriet said.

"No, indeed! You are very brave, Miss Hay," Fanny said. "I should be terrified to go to such places."

"I insist she takes a footman with her, and no purse to tempt the little pickpockets," Lady Harriet said. "It is all I can do, however, for she insists on going there."

Miss Hay smiled, her face softening. "How could I not? Such people cannot afford to come to the hospital, and even the cost of an apothecary is beyond their means, but I have a little medical knowledge that Peregrine has shared with me. I can do some good for these people, and they are grateful, I assure you. But many of them have no scruples at all about begging or stealing or lying, if it will benefit them. I have learnt not to trust anything they say, Fanny, so save your sympathy for those who deserve it."

"Oh," Fanny said, rather faintly, for how could there be a creature alive in the world who did not deserve sympathy? It was inconceivable. She did not like to disagree openly with any of the

Hays, for they were wiser and more worldly than she was, and were her benefactors, moreover, but sometimes their opinions shocked her.

"Quite so," Lady Harriet said briskly. "It is not sympathy they need, but a helping hand to lift them up when they fall from grace. That is what we all do, in our different ways, from Christian charity. But I confess that I had not fully considered the consequences of your involvement, Fanny. Your innocence must not be corrupted by these women, but what I am to do with Martha now I cannot guess. She has not been a success as a seamstress, that much is certain, and her bitterness makes her a poor influence on the other women."

"Does she have enough work to occupy her?" Dr Hay said. "Idleness is fatal in such cases."

"That is true," Miss Hay said. "It may also be that she would respond better to a more conventional setting. Can we find her a place in service?"

"Excellent idea!" Lady Harriet said. "She was a housemaid once, so she had better come here to start with. Patty has not come on as I had hoped, so she can go, and Martha may take her place."

"Oh no! Poor Patty!" Fanny said. "I did not intend... oh dear."

"You are far too kind-hearted," Lady Harriet said gently. "She is uncomfortable in such a large household. I will find her another place, have no fear. And please let us have no more weeping for any of these women, for it is rather distressing, Fanny. If one weeps for every sadness in the world, one would never leave off. Shall we have the soup removed now?"

For the rest of the evening, Fanny did her very best not to weep, for she did not want to distress anyone. Still, she was sadly low in spirits, contributed nothing to the conversation and went early to her bed. There she lay, her head spinning with fragments of Martha's words and then Dr Hay's, trying to reconcile the story told with all the passion of a wronged woman, with the physician's view of a child concealing her misdeeds.

And then she considered all the young men she knew, and wondered if they, too, crept through night-darkened houses taking what they wanted. Boys she had grown up with, like the Claremont brothers. Rosamund's husband, the very polite Mr Robin Dalton. Her former admirer, Mr Roland Hawes. And the well-dressed young gentleman next door, Mr Ferdinand Makenham. And how would one ever know?

She shivered, and curled up beneath the covers with her eyes closed, resolutely reciting the Pater Noster under her breath and awaiting sleep.

~~~~~

"Ferdy, have you taken out a subscription at the circulating library yet?" Aunt Agatha said.

Ferdy was hiding away in his book room, reading the Court Circular in the latest newspaper to reach Sagborough from London, already several days out of date.

"Circulating library?" He waved his hands towards the depressingly large number of well-filled book cases. "Why should I have the slightest inclination to do so?"

"Because it is on Mill Road, and directly opposite *Miss Kelly's Finest Gowns.*"

"Miss Kelly's—? Who is Miss Kelly? I do not know a Miss Kelly."

"Miss Kelly is the person who manages the shop where Miss Winterton may be found."

"Ah." Ferdy got the point. Folding the newspaper neatly, he said, "Auntie, I feel a sudden yearning for a novel to read. A *new* novel, one not already supplied in this hideous room."

"Do you not like your book room, Ferdy?" Aunt Agatha said, laughing. "You will never be short of reading material. I cannot imagine how your father and grandfather accumulated so many books, because they were no more bookish than you are."

"This place reminds me of school," he said gloomily. "Something to be read every lesson, and two pages of translation from the Latin every afternoon! Can you imagine how hideous? And those Romans were a dreadful warlike people, always off conquering and annihilating and decimating populations. You cannot conceive the amount of blood in a Latin text. Perhaps I will have the books boxed up and the bookcases taken away, and—" He had a sudden vision of Miss Winterton walking into the room. *'Where are all your books?'* she might say, and naturally a man should have books in a book room. Besides, she might be bookish herself. This was an uncomfortable thought, and reminded him that he still knew almost nothing about her. "But not yet," he finished lamely.

"Shall we walk down to Mill Road before it gets too dark? There is snow coming, so Poole says, but if we leave now, we shall not have to rush."

"Leave now?" Ferdy said, in scandalised tones. "But it will take me at least half an hour to change for a walk."

"You look well enough to me," Aunt Agatha said. "No one will notice."

"No one will notice!" Ferdy was almost apoplectic with disbelief. "Impossible, Auntie. Quite impossible. We shall go tomorrow."

"We might be snowed in tomorrow," she said, laughing at him.

They were not snowed in, but the rain was unremitting, so there was no going out in it. However, the following day was Sunday, and another tantalising glimpse of Miss Winterton. Even the rain held off, so the congregation emerged from church into wintry sunshine. To Ferdy's amusement, Aunt Agatha set herself the task of distracting Mr Plumstead and assuring him that she was perfectly delighted with her pew, and could imagine no finer pew in the whole of Christendom.

Ferdy moved smartly out of the clergyman's range, fixed the Hay party in view, and began to work his way towards them. He was not so crass as to approach them directly. His social skills had been honed in the saloons and ballrooms of London, and so he moved smoothly through the crowds gathered outside the church, exchanging a word with one here and another there, allowing them to think he had no other object in view but to engage them in conversation, while all the time pursuing an end of his own. He smiled, he bowed, he made polite enquiries and he moved on until he came, as if by chance, face to face with Dr Hay. To one side of him, deep in conversation with the Harbottles, were the Hay ladies. Behind him, her eyes demurely lowered, stood Miss Winterton.

Ferdy made some comments about the weather to the physician, and enquired politely whether his hospital were full to overflowing with winter chills and fevers, to which Dr Hay responded with equal civility. But Ferdy's eyes kept straying to the small, black-clad figure waiting quietly.

Exactly as he had hoped, Dr Hay, seeing the direction of his gaze, said, "You do not know our young guest, I believe?"

"I have not yet had that pleasure."

He turned to her and said, "Miss Winterton, would you allow me to introduce to you our neighbour on Harlington Terrace?"

"Oh, oh, of course! Delighted!"

And there it was again, that sweet smile that had so enchanted him, and had haunted his dreams, and many a waking moment too, framed in the most charming bonnet that contrived to be starkly plain and yet undeniably fashionable, at one and the same time.

"This is Mr Ferdinand Makenham, Miss Winterton, grandson to Lord Belwarren of Abbeymount. Mr Makenham, may I present to you Miss Winterton of Woodside, in the county of Brinshire."

"How do you do, Miss Winterton," Ferdy breathed, then executed his very best bow.

She curtsied demurely, then smiled even more widely. "I am so happy to make your acquaintance at last," she said. "For we arrived on the same day, both strangers to Sagborough, and I have wondered very often how you were and whether you had grown accustomed to the town. Do you like it here?"

She gazed up at him in the most artless manner, her eyes lambent, and Ferdy, fluent, sophisticated Ferdy, who had talked without hesitation to three princes, seven dukes and any number of lesser nobles, who moved with equal facility amongst the *haut ton* and market town squires, who was never without the perfect rejoinder in any conversation, found himself utterly lost for words.

8: Meetings

Fortunately for Ferdy, Aunt Agatha escaped the voluble clergyman at that moment and appeared at his elbow. "Ah, there you are Ferdy. Good day, Dr Hay. Oh, but is this another neighbour?"

"Um... yes, indeed. Auntie, allow me to introduce to you Miss Winterton of Brinshire. My father's sister, Miss Winterton. The Lady Agatha Makenham."

After the usual exchange of civilities, Aunt Agatha drew Dr Hay aside with a question about the hospital, and Ferdy was left smiling down at Miss Winterton. Or rather, she was smiling up at him, and he could not prevent himself from smiling back. How idiotic he must look! And still he could find no words. He knew he was staring, but was powerless to stop himself.

How pretty she was, now that he saw her at close quarters. Not beautiful in the classical style so admired in London, but her countenance must be pleasing to the most fastidious observer. Her skin was smooth and clear, her dark hair neatly drawn away from her face and her eyes — ah, her eyes held such depth, a man might drown in her glance. And the sweetest little mouth, so soft and... and...

"How charming that your aunt has come to stay with you," she said. "Is Lady Agatha to make a long visit?"

He almost said, *'Until I marry,'* but stopped himself in time. "A while, yes. I cannot... cannot entertain without a lady as hostess."

"Oh, do you plan to entertain a great deal? That will make you very popular," she said, making him laugh.

"I do hope so," he said, and then she laughed, too.

Lord, how sweetly she laughed, one hand raised to hide her mouth, but her eyes twinkling up at him. She was just the right height for a lady, he decided, for if he were to hold her in his arms, her head would rest so comfortably on his shoulder.

"Ferdy? *Ferdy!*" His aunt tapped him on the arm. "The Hays are leaving now."

And with another shy smile and a little curtsy, Miss Winterton turned and walked after the Hays with dainty steps. Ferdy watched her, mesmerised. As the footman handed her into the Hay carriage, she turned and looked back at him, giving him a last glimpse of her lovely face, and Ferdy felt that life could furnish no greater bliss than to be privileged to see such a face.

"Ferdy! Are you listening to me?"

"Auntie?" he said vaguely, his gaze fixed on the carriage door closing, and the horses starting into motion as the footman jumped up behind.

"Shall we go home?" Aunt Agatha said. "It is too cold to stand about here, do you not think?"

"Hmm?"

"Home, Ferdy! Goodness, you are in a bad state. Let us go home and get warm."

"Home. Yes, home, and at once, for I have letters to write. I must write to Lennister and Abbeymount and tell them that I have found her."

"Found whom?"

"My future wife, of course."

Ferdy was out and about at the unprecedented hour of eleven the following morning, hustling Aunt Agatha to Mill Road and the circulating library to take out a subscription, despite his horror at the uncountable numbers of books he saw there. Then he dragged her home again and sat her down at the old-fashioned writing desk in the morning room to send out invitations to dinner.

"Really, Ferdy, I shall need to talk to Poole and Eduarde first. There is no point inviting twenty people to dine if there is only plate for a dozen, or if there is no fish to be had."

"There are chairs and spoons and dishes enough for twenty-four, I have already checked with Poole, and the cellar is well stocked, so you may be easy on that head. And since my grandfather has seen fit to inflict a highly expensive French chef on my bachelor household, Eduarde can earn his keep and turn two pigeons and four pig's trotters into an exquisite meal."

She smiled and shook her head, but settled down to compile a list of all those who had entertained Ferdy and were now owed hospitality in return. "This is all for Miss Winterton, of course," she said, as she added the Hays to the list.

"Of course," Ferdy said. "How else am I to get to know her better?"

But this happy scheme turned to dust only two days later. Lady Harriet's elegantly scripted reply informed them that she and her husband and Miss Hay would be delighted to dine with Ferdy and his aunt, but Mrs Hay and Miss Winterton were unable to accept their kind invitation.

Ferdy was sadly cast down by this setback, but naturally his guests could not be allowed to suspect his disappointment. He had never before had occasion to play host, but he knew perfectly how it should be done. The invitees enjoyed an elegant repast with excellent wines, the conversation was lively and not too erudite, the young ladies provided some gentle music and there were three card tables set up besides. The whole was followed by a light supper, and everyone expressed pleasure in the company. It was not until Wright had readied Ferdy for bed and left him alone that wistful thoughts of Miss Winterton's little face intruded into his musings and left him empty and a trifle sad.

Even so, he was not disheartened. Each day he made his way to Mr Rackham's circulating library, there to linger near the window, his gaze fixed on Miss Kelly's shop across the street. Sometimes, if his visit were late in the afternoon, he was rewarded by a glimpse of his object, as Miss Winterton set off for home, but since she was invariably surrounded by a cluster of other women, her companions in drab working clothes and with brash accents audible even through the glass, he hesitated to approach her. It was enough, however, to have seen her, for in no other way might he encounter her, apart from church. He could not pay her morning calls, and she was never seen in society.

But one day he was lucky. A footman he recognised from number Twenty-Six came down the street and entered the shop, and five minutes later Miss Winterton emerged alone, with only the footman in attendance, walking three paces behind her.

He seized his opportunity. Abandoning the book he had been pretending to examine, he dashed out into the street. "Miss Winterton! Miss Winterton!" She stopped, turned, looked up at him enquiringly, and he almost lost the power of speech. With the greatest effort, he said, "I... erm, wondered if we might be... erm, going the same way? Perhaps I may escort you?"

"Oh, Mr Makenham, I am so pleased to see you! I wished to tell you myself how sorry I was that I could not accept your very kind invitation to dinner."

"I was sorry, too," he said, his throat oddly tight.

"It was not that I did not wish to, but I do not go into company just yet," she said. "It is not two months since Papa died, and I could not participate in any amusements."

"Your feelings do you the greatest credit," he said, then, finding it easier to talk now that he had begun, he went on, "When do you feel it would be proper for you to venture into society again?"

"I do not know. I cannot tell. I have sought my sisters' advice, but they all offer different opinions, and Lucy is already attending balls, although not to dance, naturally. She is acting as chaperon to two girls just out, so she is forced to do so, although I do not think she has many qualms on the subject," she ended sorrowfully.

"One must decide such matters according to one's own sensibilities," Ferdy said gravely. "Your sister, perhaps, is a person who does not feel as deeply as you do, Miss Winterton. Only you may decide what is appropriate for you, although it must be said that society at large tends more to your sister's view of mourning."

"Oh. You think, then, that I am wrong to stay in seclusion?"

"Right or wrong is for you to judge and no other, Miss Winterton, but only the highest sticklers would censure you for dining amongst friends occasionally, even in full mourning."

"Oh. Do you think so?" There was note of surprise in her voice. "I should very much like to do so," she said in her guileless way. "It is a trifle dull staying at home night after night, and sometimes with only old Mrs Hay for company, but I should not like to leave her all alone. That would not be right, would it, Mr Makenham?"

"I do not know Mrs Hay very well," Ferdy said gently, "but I suspect that she is quite accustomed to spending an occasional evening alone." He hesitated, but she had asked for his opinion, so he went on, "There is also your own wellbeing to consider, Miss Winterton. To remain cloistered from society when you are used to all your sisters about you must be very lowering to the spirits. It might do you good to go into company occasionally — just now and then, you know."

"Just now and then — oh yes, I can see that that might be beneficial. One does become a little melancholy when one has no one to talk to, it is true. If it were just now and then... perhaps I will ask Lady Harriet's opinion on the matter."

As they turned into Harlington Terrace, he said, "Will you come in and see Aunt Agatha, Miss Winterton?"

"Oh, how much I should love to, but I may not. I am sent for to help Miss Hay with her packing, and make some alterations to her gowns."

"Her packing? Is Miss Hay going away?"

"Oh yes, Lady Harriet and Miss Hay are going to Drummoor for a few days — the Marquess of Carrbridge's seat."

"They are leaving you here alone, Miss Winterton?"

"Oh no, sir, no, not at all! Mrs Hay stays behind, for she goes nowhere now, and Dr Hay will be here in the evenings. Oh look, you have a visitor!"

It was true enough, for a hired post-chaise was drawn up outside number Twenty-Five, and several figures could be seen moving about on the pavement, and in and out of the house. As they drew near, one figure in particular was familiar to Ferdy, a man whose many-caped greatcoat pronounced him a man of decided fashion.

"Edgar? Great heavens, what are you doing here?"

"I came to see — oh!" He turned, startling as he realised that Ferdy was not alone. "Oh, I beg your pardon, Ferdy. I was not aware... do not let me disturb your perambulations, for I would not for the world separate you from the company of your charming companion. Do, pray, ignore me altogether, I shall not mind a bit in such a cause."

"Really, Edgar!" Ferdy said, laughing. "Miss Winterton, would it be presumptuous of me to present my cousin to you?"

"Oh, your cousin! Oh, indeed, I should be delighted!"

"This is Mr Edgar Brant. Edgar, this is Miss Winterton of Brinshire."

Edgar executed a flourishing bow, but Miss Winterton froze. "Mr Brant? You are Mr Edgar Brant?"

"I am, madam. Are we acquainted? I am perfectly sure I should have remembered, if so."

"Oh no, not at all, but... oh, I beg your pardon, sir, I am very pleased to meet any relation of Mr Makenham's. And now, sir, you will excuse me, I trust, for Miss Hay will be waiting."

Ferdy bowed, she curtsied and then she scuttled away to number Twenty-Six, the footman in stoical pursuit.

"So that is the lady?" Edgar said, watching her disappear into the house next door. "Pretty, but... not such as would turn your experienced head, I'd have thought, old boy."

"She is everything that is enchanting," Ferdy said firmly, ushering his friend up the steps into number Twenty-Five. "So what brings you to Sagborough, Edgar?"

"Why, you do, Ferdy," he said in surprised tones. "Or rather, Miss Winterton. You wrote to your mama, and she wrote to mine, and now the females of the family are all a-twitter, in hourly anticipation of an announcement, so I came to see for myself. Ah, Lady Agatha, how do you do? But I need not ask — I see you are in fine fettle, as always. You look younger every time I see you, I swear it."

"And I see you are as audacious a flatterer as always, Edgar. How delightful to see you! Were we expecting this visit? Perhaps Ferdy forgot to mention it."

"Thought I'd surprise you, dear lady. But if you have no room..."

"Nonsense! Always room for *you*, but good gracious, Edgar, is that coat the latest thing in town? How glad I am to be female and not have to wear anything quite so... dramatic."

Edgar took this in good part, for he was a man who set great store by wearing the most fashionable styles, and would have been mortified for his attire to attract no comment.

They enjoyed a convivial evening. Edgar brought them up to date on the latest family news, for his parents lived but seven miles from Abbeymount and the two families met very frequently. In return, Ferdy told his friend of his modest progress with Miss Winterton, and his ventures into Sagborough society.

"So you go to these subscription balls, do you?" Edgar said with a visible shudder, as they drank tea after dinner. "Market town assemblies are the very devil, Ferdy. No, really, very bad *ton*. No fashion, no breeding, no manners — dreadful, and you find out afterwards that the prettiest girl is a farmer's daughter or some such. And if Miss W don't go, what is the point?"

"I enjoy the dancing," Ferdy said simply. "Almack's is all very well, but one likes to get a bit more lively sometimes. It is great fun, and I shall drag you to the next one, whether you will it or no. You will be all the rage, I promise you. If you think Sagborough is a place of no fashion, then it behoves you to set the standard."

Edgar raised an eyebrow, but preened a little, too. "Well, that is a good point. Why, I daresay they imagine *you* to be the height of fashion, Ferdy."

"Oh indeed. You must disabuse the population of such misguided opinions, for I assure you, I am much admired at present. I am believed to be quite a *nonpareil*."

"Well, if *that* is what the locals think, we should fetch Ralph here, for his style would cast both of us into the shade."

"Me, perhaps, but not you, Edgar," Ferdy murmured. "Definitely not you."

"Do you truly think—? Oh, you're bamming me, Ferdy, you dratted fellow."

Ferdy laughed, and Edgar was too good-natured to take offence. His response was interrupted, however, as Poole sidled in and bowed to Ferdy.

"Lady Harriet Hay to speak with you, sir."

"With me?" Ferdy said, astonished. "Lady Harriet? At this hour?"

"Oh dear!" Aunt Agatha said. "I do hope nothing untoward has occurred. Do show her in at once, Poole."

But before the butler could move, Lady Harriet swept into the room, her gaze raking over the three occupants and settling on Ferdy, her eyes flashing with anger.

"Lady Harriet, what a pleasant surprise," Aunt Agatha said, with a polite smile, as the butler quietly withdrew.

"Lady Agatha," she said curtly. "Mr Makenham."

"Do you know my cousin?" Ferdy said calmly. "Mr Edgar Brant of Cressington Manor. Lady Harriet Hay, Edgar. Our neighbour."

"Mr Brant," she said, not bothering with even the hint of a bow. "Mr Makenham, whatever are you thinking, to be lurking about the streets, and following Miss Winterton home? I will not have it, do you hear?"

"Will you sit down, Lady Harriet?" Ferdy said. "Some tea? A glass of claret, perhaps?"

She ignored these civil overtures. "I will not have it, Mr Makenham. You must leave her alone."

Edgar sidled towards the door. "I think, Ferdy—"

"No, do stay, Edgar. If Lady Harriet does not scruple to speak her mind before you, neither need I. But it would be more comfortable for all of us if you would take a seat, Lady Harriet."

She looked at the two men, unable to sit until she did so, and with a huff, planted herself on the very edge of a chair.

"Let us speak frankly," Ferdy said, flicking the tails of his coat as he sat, and crossing his legs neatly at the ankles. "When a gentleman wishes to become better acquainted with a lady, there are certain courses open to him. He might pay the lady a morning visit. He might invite her to join a pleasure party of his devising. He might hope to meet her in society, through mutual friends. None of these avenues are available to me with respect to Miss Winterton. Therefore what alternative do I have, but to lurk about the streets, as you so trenchantly phrased it, and offer to escort her home when the opportunity presents itself? She was not unwilling to be so escorted, you know."

"I am sure she was not, because she is as innocent as a child, and knows no better."

"There is not the least impropriety in a gentleman escorting a lady to her door, especially with a footman following behind."

"It is not that!" Lady Harriet cried. "But she is not a lady, Mr Makenham."

"She is a gentleman's daughter," he said at once, with some heat.

"So she is, but her position now is precarious. There are those who would see her as nought but a seamstress, a lowly employee who plies her needle for money. I hope her status as my guest protects her to some degree, but whatever she once was, she is not a lady any longer."

"But if she were to marry a gentleman, she would become so again!" Ferdy cried. "And in time, a countess."

Lady Harriet's mouth made an astonished circle. "Oh, *marriage!*" she said, with a long exhalation.

"Yes, marriage, of course. What else? Good gracious, did you think—? No, no, I assure you my intentions are entirely honourable. Great heavens, Lady Harriet, what an opinion of me you must have."

Lady Harriet laughed suddenly. "I hardly know you well enough to have formed an opinion of your character, Mr Makenham, but when a young man shows a marked partiality for a young woman who has neither father nor brother to protect her, has no dowry and is living in greatly reduced circumstances outside good society... forgive me, but it is a natural mistake to make. And so after one glance on the doorstep and a few words exchanged after church, you have decided to marry her, have you?" She laughed again. "I wish you joy, Mr Makenham, but such hasty matches rarely bring true contentment."

"Really, Lady Harriet, you must think me a perfect mutton-head to marry on such flimsy grounds, but I should certainly like to become better acquainted with Miss Winterton, and you could help me, if you chose."

She smiled then. "What, encourage my very best seamstress to leave me? That would be a great loss to me. Fortunately for you, Mr Makenham, I wish only the best for Fanny, and such a match would be wondrous great for her. Indeed, she could hardly do better, but have you thought whether your grandfather might not quite like his heir to marry so low?"

"I shall solicit his opinion on the matter, certainly, and that of my father and mother also, but ultimately the decision is mine to take. And Miss Winterton's, of course."

"Then I will not hinder you," Lady Harriet said. "I shall be away for a few days, but when I return perhaps we shall have a small dinner for friends and neighbours, and I shall encourage Fanny to relieve her mourning a little. After that, it will be up to you to secure your bride if you can, Mr Makenham."

She laughed again, as if certain his suit would not prosper, but Ferdy suppressed his annoyance at her high-handed attitude and rose to bow politely.

At last he felt he was making progress.

9: A Confrontation (March)

MARCH

~~~~~

'My dearest Fanny, What a vivid imagination you have, in seeing romantical entanglements everywhere. Just because I admire a man's shapely legs does not mean I am in imminent danger of falling in love with him. Besides, Mr Audley is the most dreadful flirt, and one cannot believe a word he says. I want nothing to do with him. But what about you? Do tell me more about this mysterious neighbour of yours who is the grandson of an earl, and although one would never take such a thing into account, it might just happen that you will fall in love with him and there is no doubt that it would be the most comfortable thing in the world not to have to worry about money ever again. Not that one falls in love in that convenient way, and I know that you would never, ever marry a man unless you were quite <u>violently</u> in love with him, Fanny dear, but only think how pleasant it would be to fall violently in love with a man who will be an earl one day, so do tell me everything about him. Is he handsome? You said he was well-dressed, but that does not tell me much, except that he has a half-decent valet and tailor. Is he one of those horridly fashionable types, with shirt-points so high and starched he looks up at the sky the whole time? Such puffed-up gentlemen make me laugh, although naturally I do not mean that I should laugh at <u>your</u> gentleman, if he should happen to be a puffed-up type, no no no, I

did not intend to say— Oh dear, I am getting in a muddle, but I am sure you know just what I mean, sister dear. But if you do not wish to talk about your mysterious neighbour, at least tell me more of the women you work with, who sound very lively company. And are you happy, Fanny? Do answer me truly, for when I cannot see your face I cannot tell when you are just being brave. Your loving sister, Lucy.'

~~~~~

Fanny was distressed. For all that the Hays had told her not to extend too much sympathy for undeserving people like Martha, still she could not but feel acutely for the poor woman. Whatever the cause of her problems, and whether she had brought about her own loss of respectability, the truth was that she had brought forth a child outside the sacred bonds of marriage, and had thereby lost everything she held dear. Fanny could not quite imagine herself in Martha's place, but there were certain aspects of her case that were all too real to her. She too had lost her entire family, her place in society and her respectability. Even though she lived under Lady Harriet's roof, and was therefore sheltered from the worst of society's scorn, she worked side by side with her ladyship's poor unfortunates and was well aware of the averted eyes when they walked together through the town. Martha and her friends might look like ordinary hard-working women, but the burghers and matrons of Sagborough knew who and what they were.

And now, here was Mr Edgar Brant, the cause of all Martha's difficulties, living in the very next house. He was a close friend of Mr Makenham, too, who seemed such a pleasant and gentlemanly person, and yet might be just as wicked as his friend.

What ought she to do? Fanny went over and over it in her mind. Should she tell Martha? Patty had found another place, although as a chamber maid, not such congenial employment, but she seemed pleased about it, and Martha had already moved into the attics of number Twenty-Six, returning to Westbury House to see her little boy only on Sundays. The servants were very unobtrusive, but Martha was now and again to be seen with her ash bucket and brushes, tending the fires, or running up or down stairs with her feather duster. She smiled and told Fanny that she was contented enough with her lot — *'I like being a housemaid, miss, my boy is well looked after at Westbury House and I can still see him every Sunday, so it suits me well'* -- so perhaps she would be better knowing nothing of her seducer's residence next door, for it could do no good.

Even while Fanny dithered over the question, she feared that the servants might resolve it without her aid.

"Is there much... *mingling* between number Twenty-Five and... and the neighbours' servants?" she had asked Draper one evening, as the lady's maid was dressing her hair.

"Ha! I'll say there is." The junior servants, she was told, exchanged what Draper described as *'idle tittle-tattle'* over the low wall separating number Twenty-Five from number Twenty-Six, and the footmen, grooms and coachmen from several establishments in Harlington Terrace liked to spend an occasional convivial evening at the Bridge Inn by the canal, enjoying a tankard or two of the landlord's finest ale and regaling each other with stories about their employers.

"Worse than the maids for gossip, the men are," Draper had said with a disparaging sniff.

So Fanny knew it was only a matter of time before the name of Mr Edgar Brant reached Martha's ears, but still she could not quite bring herself to be the one to convey this dreadful news, so she pushed the thought aside.

Fanny returned from the shop one afternoon escorted by the most amiable Mr Makenham, who by happy coincidence had again chanced to be in Rackham's Library just as she emerged and had gallantly offered her the support of his arm. Such a kindly young man, although a little shy. When he had deposited her at her own door and made his farewell bow, Fanny had settled down to enjoy a cup of tea with Mrs Hay. As that lady was not a great conversationalist, Fanny was left to her own thoughts.

They were rather agreeable thoughts, for Mr Makenham was a personable young man with excellent manners, not to mention that he was heir to a title and a substantial fortune, and so Fanny was engaged in running through the names of Sagborough's young ladies for a match for him. She had a strong partiality for Miss Trivers, of course, who was her friend, but Marianne seemed happy to relinquish the field to her friend, Miss Malpas, although it had to be confessed that her looks were against her.

But then there was Miss Drabble. She was so beautiful that Fanny was convinced she was destined to marry well, and here was the perfect match — a radiantly lovely young lady and a young man of great charm must inevitably be well-suited. Fanny had been permitted to make up only one gown from the shop for Celia, but then she had had rather an ingenious idea. Lady Harriet had filled Fanny's shelves with an array of delightful gowns, none of which she could wear while she was still in mourning. She had asked Lady Harriet, therefore, if she might adapt them to fit Celia's rather larger frame, and thus improve her wardrobe. And to her infinite delight, Lady Harriet had merely laughed and said that she had no objection, so long as Celia told enquirers that her gown came from Miss Kelly's shop, when asked. The improvement in her appearance was so great that Fanny could not imagine she would see another Christmas unwed, and perhaps it would be Mr Makenham who carried off the prize.

Fanny set no store by his seeming fascination with her, for she was entirely ineligible to marry a man of rank. To be sure, he looked at her with a degree of admiration, that she could not deny, but his attentions were no more than the commonplace courtesies any gentleman would offer to a young lady. Even if he should be so foolish as to disregard her lowly status and lack of dowry, she had given him not the smallest encouragement.

She could hardly have done so, for she was not in love with him, and this, Fanny felt, was an absolute prerequisite for marital bliss. It was inconceivable to contemplate marrying without the most violent and unwavering affection, on both sides. She had been so shocked when Rosamund had decided to marry Mr Robin Dalton that, even now, she could barely speak about it. Rosamund had been betrothed first to the elder brother, Mr Richard Dalton, and although she had laughed and denied any feelings of love, they had known each other for ever, so there must have been a very deep affection. But when he had fallen from his horse and died just days before the wedding, Rosamund had calmly married his younger brother, a man she had known for no more than a few weeks. Such behaviour was incomprehensible to romantic Fanny. When she married, she would be head over heels in love, and even if she was not entirely sure how this desirable state might manifest itself, she would know it when the time came.

With Mr Makenham, therefore, she was confident that any regard he might have felt for her on first making her acquaintance was of the slightest kind, and, without encouragement, would die away most speedily. She did not go into society, so they could not meet often, and he would soon turn his attentions to those young ladies who were available to him. Such as Miss Drabble, she hoped. How she wished she could attend the assemblies so that she could see for herself whether he favoured one lady over another! Yes, she was sure he must be drawn to Miss Drabble, for not only was she as beautiful as the day, she was well-read and spoke four languages and could paint and draw and sing and no doubt had a great many other accomplishments, too. No, it could not be many months before Mr Makenham would—

These happy thoughts were disturbed by a commotion in the hallway one floor below.

"Whatever can that be?" she cried, forgetting that only Mrs Hay was in the drawing room with her.

"Eh?" the old lady said. "What is it, Fanny?"

"People shouting, ma'am. *Shouting! In the hall.* I shall just go downstairs to see... *SHOUTING! DOWNSTAIRS, MA'AM!*"

"Ring the bell for Poole," Mrs Hay said. "No need to shout for a servant."

"Pray excuse me," Fanny said. *"EXCUSE ME! I MUST JUST GO..."*

"As you please. Has the gong sounded?"

"Not yet, ma'am. *NOT YET.*"

So saying, she dashed out of the room and hastened down the stairs. The housekeeper, footman and both lady's maids were collectively haranguing a figure in a brown woollen gown who was calmly tying the strings of a bonnet in the hall. Then, with a swirl of her cloak, she made for the door.

"Martha? Martha, what is the matter?" Fanny cried as she descended the last few stairs in a breathless rush. "Why are you going out of the front door? What has happened?"

"*He* is next door," she hissed. "Mr Edgar Brant. He has been living just a few feet away all this time, and he will answer to me for his crimes."

The housekeeper shook her head vehemently. "You can't go accusing gentlemen, you silly girl. Take your bonnet off and come to my room. We'll have a glass of something — the mistress won't mind this once — and you can tell me all about it."

"No," Martha said, pushing forwards again. "No, no, *no*. Don't try to stop me, Mrs Bell. I'm going to see him and have it out once and for all, and I am leaving by the front door because I'm going to talk to him as a wronged woman and not as a servant. I want him to know what's happened to me, what he's reduced me to."

"Martha, no!" Fanny cried.

But by this time, Martha had dragged open the front door and stood poised on the top step. A gust of icy wind blew in, with a hint of sleet in the air.

"Martha, don't do this!" the housekeeper cried. "You'll be turned off and then what will become of you? You mustn't!"

"I don't care! What does it matter now anyway? My life is ruined, and it's all *his* fault. He'll pay for this. He *ought* to pay."

And so saying, she marched out into the freezing air, the sky dark with snow, and set off down the steps.

Mrs Bell threw up her hands in dismay. "Will you look at the foolish child! William, run after her."

"No, let me go," Fanny said. "At least I know Mr Makenham, I can explain it to him, and perhaps it will help... somehow."

"Wait — you need a cloak!"

"It is only the house next door, no distance at all." And so saying she plunged out of the house and down the steps. The wind tore at her skirts and whipped her hair about her face. Impatiently she brushed it away, but it blew back instantly and she gave it up. It was but a few steps down to the street, then she ran along the pavement after Martha, already stamping up the steps of number Twenty-Five. Fanny started up the steps just as the door was opened by a very grand butler.

His face closed up when he saw Martha. "Through the area," he said, pointing firmly to the basement steps.

Martha looked disconcerted for a moment, but then she recovered. "I have business with Mr Edgar Brant," she said, lifting her chin defiantly.

The butler looked her up and down as if she were something the stable cat had dragged in. "I very much doubt that."

Martha opened her mouth to argue, but Fanny put a hand on her shoulder.

"Is Mr Makenham at home?" she said to the butler, with her pleasantest smile. "Would you be so good as to tell him that Miss Winterton wishes to speak with him on a matter of some urgency."

"I shall enquire, madam. If the young person..." He looked disdainfully at Martha. "...would care to—"

"She is with me," Fanny said firmly.

The butler hesitated, looking from one to the other. He knew his duty, and under no circumstances could he admit Martha through the front door, in her humble servant's clothes. But Fanny's appearance was not much better, with neither coat nor bonnet nor gloves, and her hair disordered by the wind, and she was not a person he had previously admitted to the house.

"Oh, this is ridiculous," Martha said, and marched straight past the astonished butler.

"Oh dear! Oh, Martha, no!" Fanny cried, following her into the hall.

Two footmen emerged from the servants' stairs, and a third from some inner room, and from the merest flick of the butler's head understood the problem and seized hold of Martha. She yelled her displeasure, the butler remonstrated with her and Fanny could only wring her hands and cry, "Oh no! Oh, pray do not hurt her! If we could but speak to Mr Makenham! Oh dear!"

A door opened and there was Mr Makenham himself, unruffled, perfectly calm. "Poole? What is going on? Oh — Miss Winterton! I beg your pardon, I did not realise... Peters, Hill, unhand that young lady at once. Poole, what on earth are you thinking, to leave Miss Winterton standing in the hall with the door wide open on a day like this. She must be frozen. Come into the book room at once, Miss Winterton, and your friend, too. Poole, desire Lady Agatha to step down here, if you please."

The butler bowed, his face impassive. One of the footmen rushed to close the door, and the others became statues, immobile and blank-faced. With a bow, Mr Makenham ushered Fanny and Martha into his book room and firmly closed the door on the servants. The room was dark, the curtains already drawn against the wintry afternoon outside, and only a few wall sconces threw pools of light onto a reading chair, a desk, a small table.

"Do come and sit by the fire, Miss Winterton. Good gracious, the matter must be urgent to bring you out of doors in such weather without even a cloak. Let me put some more coals on the fire. Ah, there now, much better! Do take this chair, and your friend may sit just here. Will you take some refreshment?"

"Oh no, thank you! You are very kind, sir, but we shall not detain you for long. I must — I do! — beg your forgiveness for intruding in this irregular way." She sat on the edge of the chair he indicated. The argument with the servants had rattled her, and now that it was come to the point, she rather wished herself a hundred miles away. Still, his composure brought her reassurance. At least he was not angry with her!

"You are always welcome here, Miss Winterton, formally or otherwise," he said, smiling at her. "I am sure you have a very good reason for your visit."

As he gazed into her upturned face, there was a glow in his eyes that there was no mistaking, and Fanny could not help blushing at the intensity she read there.

He pulled up another chair to sit beside her, and said quietly, "Now, Miss Winterton, in what way may I be of service to you?"

He was as calm as if she were paying a commonplace morning call. Still his eyes were fixed on hers, and it was as if no one else were in the room. She was vaguely aware of Martha, still standing near the door, thrown off-balance by this gentle reception, but Fanny's attention was all on Mr Makenham, and for a moment she was silent. She had followed Martha in a moment of impulsive haste, and had had no time to consider how to manage the business. Indeed, she had supposed that Martha would say what needed to be said, and that her own role was no more than as a supporter, to help get past the suspicions of the servants. But Martha was silent, and the duty of explaining their precipitate arrival fell to Fanny.

"This is Martha Smith, Mr Makenham. She is one of Lady Harriet's... um, protégés, and... and..."

"I want to talk to Edgar Brant," Martha said loudly.

There was a cough from a dark corner, and a face emerged from the gloom. "I am Edgar Brant." The tone was puzzled, and rather hesitant.

Even without the many-caped greatcoat, Mr Brant was an impressive figure, not in size but in the exuberance of his dress. Where Mr Makenham was all elegant restraint, Mr Brant tended to excess. His shirt points were high and well-starched, his coat was padded at the shoulders, his buttons large and his waistcoat a garish masterpiece of the tailor's art. Unfortunately, the effect of all these extravagances gathered into one person was rather overpowering.

Martha gasped, and started towards him, then stopped. "No... no, you ain't him. You're Edgar Brant? Of Yorkshire?"

"I am."

"Oh. Then... then he lied to me, the twisty, deceitful *Devil!*"

She plopped down onto the nearest chair and burst into noisy sobs.

"Oh, I say," Mr Brant murmured. "No need to cry, madam, I'm sure. Not as bad as all that, surely. But... not sure I understand, actually. Who has lied?"

Mr Makenham looked enquiringly at Fanny. How awkward it was! She blushed but answered with tolerable calmness, "The gentleman who... who *wronged* Martha told her his name was Edgar Brant."

"Ah." Mr Makenham nodded understandingly.

"Not me!" Mr Brant said indignantly. "I would never—! Quite inconceivable! No, no, some mistake, I fear. It must have been some other fellow. Gave my name, the bounder. Or... or I suppose it could have been a distant relation. Edgar is a common family name, so... could be a cousin, perhaps. But not me. Definitely not me."

"I believe Miss Smith has accepted that point," Mr Makenham said, moving towards Martha's chair. "Edgar, some brandy for the lady, if you please. Now, Miss Smith, take my handkerchief and dry your eyes. There, now, that is better. Thank you, Edgar. Here, Miss Smith, take this and have a little sip."

He knelt in front of Martha, holding the brandy glass out to her, but she gave a quick shake of her head. Although she was mopping her eyes frantically, there was no diminution in the flow of tears. Her shoulders shook as she sobbed convulsively.

"Now, Miss Smith, do try a little," Mr Makenham said in the gentlest tones imaginable. "It will do you a great deal of good, I am persuaded. There now, well done. A little more? Excellent. You will feel the warmth inside, and you will be calmer directly, and then perhaps you may be able to tell us what your purpose was in seeking out this man. Did you feel a great affection for him, perhaps?"

She laughed through her tears, then, but there was a hysterical edge to it. "I wanted him to *suffer*, the way he made me suffer," she said, her voice harsh after Mr Makenham's soft tones.

"And how did you plan to do that? If he is a gentleman who abused you and yet abandoned you to your fate, then I do not suppose him to have any proper feelings, Miss Smith. If his own conscience did not bring him to do what is right by you, I cannot think he would be brought to remorse by any words of yours."

"Not *words*," she spat. "I want to *hurt* him like he hurt me." She reached into a pocket, and, to Fanny's utter shock and horror, drew forth a long, thin blade. "I want him to *pay* for what he did. You men, you just take whatever you want and walk away, and you shouldn't be allowed to get away with it, injuring honest folk like that. I was all right before he came by, I had a good place, I had prospects and he took *everything* away from me, *everything*, and I want him to pay the price for that!"

10: An Assembly

"You are quite right," Mr Makenham said to Martha, his voice so quiet Fanny could barely hear his words. "That is abominable, and any man who mistreats a woman in that way is wicked indeed. But this is not the answer."

Gently he detached the knife from her grasp, laying it carefully on a table, and she offered no resistance. Her sobs had ceased as her anger had risen, but the tears still tracked silently down her face, unheeded now.

The door opened, and Lady Agatha bustled into the room, with a maid in attendance.

"Ah, Aunt Agatha," Mr Makenham said, still kneeling on the floor, yet perfectly composed, as if it were the most normal thing in the world. "Miss Smith is... upset. Perhaps...?"

"Of course. Come along, dear. Belinda will take you downstairs and you can tell her all about it. I am sure we can find some cakes and— What do you like to drink, dear? There now, dry your tears, everything will be perfectly all right, you will see."

With such gentle burbling, Lady Agatha encouraged Martha to rise from her chair and suffer herself to be led away, although she snatched up the knife as she left, pushing it back into her pocket. With a sigh, Mr Makenham rose to his feet and turned at once to Fanny.

"Miss Winterton, this is a most unfortunate affair. How distressing for you! May I offer you something? Some brandy, perhaps?"

"Oh no! Thank you, but not brandy, although I am a little— Perhaps some Madeira? If you have it?"

"What an excellent idea. I shall take some too, I believe. Edgar?"

Again it was Mr Brant who poured and fetched and then melted away into the shadows, and Mr Makenham who proffered the glass of wine, and sat opposite Fanny sipping from his own glass. His fingers were slender, she noticed. Such graceful hands he had! She had a longing to see him dance, for she knew his arms would be positioned just so, and the hands placed with all due elegance. He would be a fine dancer, she was sure.

"Are you warm enough, Miss Winterton? Shall I send for more coals?"

"Oh no, I am perfectly warm, thank you. And thank you so much for treating Martha so kindly. She… she was very upset, and when she produced that knife—!"

"I doubt she would have used it, however," Mr Makenham said. "She must have felt so desperate, and… helpless. One feels so inadequate when all one can offer is sympathy."

"Oh yes," Fanny said. "And one cannot help but sympathise with anyone in such a position. At least, *I* cannot, although Miss Hay said one should save one's sympathy for those who deserve it."

"And who are we to determine who might deserve our sympathy and who might not?" Mr Makenham said at once. "Every creature on earth deserves our sympathy and aid, in my view, from the criminal on the gallows upwards."

"Oh yes!" Fanny cried. "Yes, indeed. I am entirely of your opinion, Mr Makenham. Poor Martha!"

"Yes, poor Martha," he said gravely.

~~~~~

Ferdy's thoughts after this incident drifted rapidly away from the unfortunate Martha and settled on the much more attractive personage of Miss Winterton. Fanny, that was her name. He thought about Fanny as he dressed for dinner, he thought about her in the drawing room before the meal, and he thought about her during dinner, too, and it was not until Aunt Agatha withdrew and he was left alone with Edgar that he was forced to set aside these agreeable thoughts and exert himself. Even then, he found that Fanny intruded into the conversation, to the point that even Edgar noticed.

"Have to say, Ferdy, that you are as besotted a man as I've ever seen," Edgar said, helping himself to port. "Got you properly dazzled, she has. Be leg-shackled before you know it. Take my advice — head for Lennister or Abbeymount immediately or it will be too late."

"But I *want* to be leg-shackled, Edgar," Ferdy protested. "Do you disapprove?"

"Of marriage in general? Not at all. It is a perfectly sound plan for other people, but not for you, Ferdy. You and me and Ralph — the Terrible Triumvirate, you know? Stick together no matter what, and that means no interfering wives. You know how it will be, she will smile oh-so-prettily and say *'But why are you leaving me all alone and going off to wherever-it-is?'* in a wheedling voice, and you will be overcome with remorse that she has only twenty servants, six children, three sisters, four aunts and a couple of cousins to bear her company, and you will never be able to go anywhere without her ever again."

"But I have not the least wish to go anywhere without her," Ferdy said, smiling beatifically. "I cannot think of anything I should like better than always having Fanny with me."

"Oh, it is *'Fanny'* now, is it?" Edgar said gloomily. "It is a settled thing, then. There is no saving you, my friend. Doomed, that's what you are."

But Ferdy only laughed.

When they returned to the drawing room, Aunt Agatha said cheerfully, "So, when is the next assembly to be? For I give you fair warning, I am minded to go with you."

"Truly?" Ferdy said. "You want to see how badly the locals dance? They are very enthusiastic, I grant you, but gracefulness is an alien concept to them."

"But you go, and you are dragging Edgar with you, and I should like to go too."

"Why?" Ferdy said, narrowing his eyes suspiciously. "What are you up to now, Auntie?"

She had the good grace to look conscious. "I am not *up to* anything, exactly, but it is the very best way to obtain all the latest gossip, and I should like to know more about your Miss Winterton. And also this business of the house."

"House? What house is that?"

"The one where all these fallen women live — West-something."

"Westbury House?"

"That is it," she said, pleased. "There is some legal dispute about it and I am curious to know more about that. Besides, if Edgar is to go to the assembly with you, why should we not make a proper family expedition of it?"

So it was that, only a few days later, the master of ceremonies banged his staff, and announced to the interested townspeople assembled at the large upper room at the King's Head the names of the Lady Agatha Makenham, Mr Ferdinand Makenham and Mr Edgar Brant. All three of them caused a stir amongst the good people of Sagborough. Ferdy was already identified as the heir to a title and a substantial fortune, and therefore of the utmost interest to the unmarried young ladies. Lady Agatha, as a titled lady, brought consequence to a town which boasted few scions of the nobility. A number of matrons at once determined to make her acquaintance, the better to sprinkle their conversations with lesser personages with those magical words, *'As Lady Agatha said to me…'.* And as Ferdy had predicted, Edgar attracted attention for other reasons entirely. As soon as he walked in and stood, as if posed, in the doorway, all eyes turned his way. Mr Edgar Brant in full evening dress was a wonder to behold, and the people of Sagborough accorded him the proper degree of awed respect, and if one or two tittered behind their fans, he studiedly ignored such ignorance.

Ferdy walked around the room with Aunt Agatha on his arm with the object of introducing her here and there. He need not have worried. The first person they encountered greeted his aunt like an old friend, on the basis of a half hour meeting at Lady Gilbert's house, and ten minutes of conversation in the apothecary's shop while waiting to be attended to. She was carried off triumphantly to sit beside Lady Harbottle and Lady Gilbert on the seats at the head of the room reserved for noble ladies and their particular friends.

Ferdy was free to look about him for a partner for the next dance. His practised eye ran over those few young ladies still sitting on the seats lining the sides of the room, too poor or plain or boring to interest anyone else. His eye ran on, stopped, returned. Was that Miss Drabble in a very fetching gown with the most fashionable style of sleeve? Someone had been expending some trouble on her dress, and money, too, for that was surely the work of an expensive *modiste*. It was too splendid a gown to sit unnoticed in a corner, when it would display to much greater advantage in the dance.

He made his way slowly towards her, edging past the dancers, exchanging a word here and there with acquaintances, of which he had a great many already, despite his recent arrival. Miss Drabble was sitting beside her mother, her gaze fixed on the couples weaving about in the dance, and one foot kicked out repeatedly, lifting the hem of her gown, as if she could not bear to be still.

Mrs Drabble, more occupied in watching the non-dancers, saw Ferdy first, and nudged her daughter to awareness. He watched her face change to surprise, and then, touchingly, hope, before she blushed a little and lowered her gaze.

Ferdy made his greetings, enquired politely whether Miss Drabble might be engaged for the next two, and if not, might he have the honour? And having secured her hand and made her blush even more, he sat down to talk composedly to Mrs Drabble until it was time to lead her daughter onto the floor.

"And who is your fine friend?" Mrs Drabble said.

Ferdy did not need to see where she pointed with her fan to know who she meant. Edgar was parading slowly around the perimeter of the room to be admired. "My cousin, Mr Edgar Brant," he said.

"What a splendid young man," she said. "Sagborough is not at all accustomed to such magnificence. We are most honoured. Do tell me, Mr Makenham, is that style of dress in vogue in London? I am not very familiar with the fashions, I confess."

"I assure you, such attire is regarded as the height of fashion... in certain circles," he said.

"In certain circles. I see. It seems to me that fashion is often incompatible with comfort. His head looks most awkwardly positioned, held so high that he must have the greatest difficulty in seeing anything below his nose. I confess, Mr Makenham, I prefer the way you dress, although you also look very fashionable to my rustic eyes."

Ferdy responded gravely, "I too am regarded as the height of fashion in certain circles. Certain *other* circles. If you could see another of my cousins, Mr Ralph Makenham, you would observe yet a third style of fashion. There are many fashions in London."

She smiled, and he saw that she understood him perfectly well.

The dance ended, and Ferdy led Miss Drabble onto the floor to begin the next set. This gave him a further opportunity to observe her gown, which swirled elegantly around her legs as she moved. He was impressed, but it would not do to say so. He knew better than to pay any girl a compliment on her appearance, unless he wished her to believe he intended to offer for her. So he talked of nothing very much, and she replied with perfect composure, without the least nervousness. She danced well, too, and he could not but feel she was wasted on the wallflowers' benches.

Ferdy's next partner was Miss Marianne Trivers, and here he knew to be even more circumspect. Whereas Celia Drabble was an exceptionally beautiful girl, she had no dowry and no likelihood of marrying someone with Ferdy's prospects, so there were no expectations there. Marianne Trivers was another matter altogether, for she was both pretty and an heiress, exactly the sort of girl who might have ambitions to be a countess one day, so he took particular care not to arouse false hope in her.

She was indeed ambitious, but not for herself. "Do you not think Celia is looking well tonight, Mr Makenham?"

"I have never seen her looking better," he said, with perfect truthfulness.

"You move in London society, so you must know all about the latest styles. Is Celia's gown made according to the current modes? It seems very lovely to me, if a little... plain."

Ferdy looked at Miss Trivers' gown, with its overskirt heavily encrusted with spangles, and frills and bows on the bodice, and could see at once why she considered Miss Drabble's gown to be plain. "Miss Drabble's gown is indeed very fashionable, Miss Trivers," he said. "The intricacy of the sleeves, the shape of the back of the bodice and the way the skirt drapes just so, all of these details were to be seen in London last season, or at the earliest, the one before. But a young lady does not dress only by fashion. She must also take into account her rank and position in society, her fortune, her age and her disposition."

"Her disposition?" Miss Trivers said, smiling at him. "How does a lady's disposition manifest itself in her gown?"

"Why, a lady of retiring manner will choose to wear clothes that do not draw attention to her. If she is more outgoing, then her mode of dress will be likewise flamboyant. And if she likes to dance, her gown will swirl about her as she moves, just as Miss Drabble's does."

"Oh. I had not considered that aspect of the matter."

"Miss Drabble's gown may look plain," Ferdy said, "but it is perfectly suited to a young lady of gentle birth making her debut in society, who loves to dance."

"And the colour exactly matches her eyes," Miss Trivers said, with a deep sigh. "That is why Fanny chose it. It was her gown, you see, but she altered it to fit Celia for she said it would suit her perfectly, and so it does. Fanny has so much romantic sensibility in such matters."

Ferdy's heart squeezed momentarily. "Fanny?" he said, his voice not quite steady. But how like her to make over one of her own gowns for a friend. Dear, generous Fanny!

"Fanny Winterton. You must know her, she is your neighbour."

"Ah, yes, Miss Winterton." He breathed carefully to keep his voice level. "I do not know her well, for she does not go into society."

"No, and it is the most infamous thing! I know she is in mourning, but one need not stay secluded entirely, do you not agree, Mr Makenham?"

"I... it depends upon the lady's inclinations, naturally."

"True, but I do so wish I could find some way to meet Fanny. We became such friends on the journey north, but now I never see her, and if she were to attend these assemblies, why, we could meet without the least censure. She need not dance at all, but it would be so comfortable to sit and chat, for she is the most charming company and enters into all one's feelings. There would be no impropriety in her coming here, would there? Mrs Young is here tonight and she is still in full black for her husband. I cannot see the least impropriety in it."

Ferdy had every sympathy with her viewpoint, wishing very much to see Fanny himself, but he could not offer advice on such a subject, so he responded merely that it was very sad if one could not meet one's friends on such an occasion. He was left to reflect on Fanny's good nature, in generously giving her own gowns to Celia Drabble.

~~~~~

Lady Harriet and Miss Hay returned, and a date for the dinner was set. There would be twenty at table, Fanny discovered, and there was a certain excitement amongst the servants, for it was a rare event for Lady Harriet to hold a formal dinner. She occasionally entertained members of her own family, and she returned hospitality, but only one or two couples at a time. However, this was the first time the dining table would be extended to its maximum reach.

Fanny had only two full evening gowns in mourning colours to choose from, and one was in depressing bombazine, which made her feel too much like a widow. It reminded her of Lucy's gowns after poor Walter had died. So she chose her black velvet, and felt she was close enough to half-mourning to wear her pearl necklace and add some cream ribbons to her hair.

Draper came early to finish dressing her, so Fanny was the first down to the drawing room and had a few minutes to compose her thoughts before the Hay family arrived, and then the guests began to trickle in, the least important first — a doctor friend of Dr Hay's, and the Plumsteads — then the two baronets and their ladies, followed by some of Lady Harriet's relations. Last, but by no means the least in Fanny's eyes, the party from number Twenty-Five was announced.

Until she saw Mr Makenham in full evening dress, Fanny had not truly appreciated the glory of his sartorial elegance. Or perhaps it was the contrast with his two relations. Lady Agatha was an imposing figure in purple satin, complete with befeathered turban and diamond necklace. Mr Brant dazzled the company with a bright green coat, embroidered orange waistcoat and a whole line of fobs at his waist. Beside them, Mr Makenham was a model of restraint in plain shoes buffed to a high gloss, immaculate silk stockings and knee breeches, a silver waistcoat adorned with but a single fob, and a neat dark blue coat that fitted him perfectly. Above it all was a snowy neckcloth arranged with mathematical precision, pinned with a small diamond, and hair that was fashionably disordered. Fanny let out a soft "Oh!" of appreciation as he walked across the room behind his aunt to greet Lady Harriet. Even his bow was elegant, and perfectly judged for the occasion.

"He is a very fine young man, is he not?" whispered Mrs Plumstead, who shared the sofa with Fanny.

"Oh yes!" she breathed.

"I'll wager he's the talk of London town."

"He must be, yes."

"I would never have thought of marrying green and orange together, but it certainly attracts attention. Goodness me! I can scarcely take my eyes off him."

Fanny realised belatedly that the clergyman's wife was speaking of Mr Brant. What on earth to say of such attire? "He is certainly very colourful," she said, ruthlessly suppressing the words that sprang first to her mind, such as *'garish'* and *'hideous'*. "Mr Makenham is dressed very fine, too," she added.

Mrs Plumstead turned surprised eyes on her. "You regard such plainness with favour, do you? For myself, if a man has a position in society, he should dress accordingly, with a bit of a flourish. He should set himself to be noticed, and not be mistaken for a well-to-do vicar who has not even bothered to brush his hair. The distinction of rank, my dear."

Fanny thought that Mr Makenham looked nothing like a vicar of any sort, and far from not brushing his hair, she guessed that his valet had laboured for some time to achieve the windswept effect.

She knew from her brother-in-law, Mr Robin Dalton, how many hours were required to perfect just such an understated look. But even Mr Dalton would look a shade over-dressed beside Mr Makenham.

She sighed with pleasure.

11: *Dinner At Number Twenty-Six*

Fanny and Mrs Plumstead were obliged to leave off this conversation as the two gentlemen in question made their way towards them, exchanging a greeting before moving on and finally settling further down the room, Mr Brant beside Dr Hay's friend, Dr Wellbeloved, and Mr Makenham beside old Mrs Hay. Not long afterwards, William announced dinner and the guests began to rise from their seats and move towards the door. Fanny, being the lowest ranked in the room, held back. She was used to a degree of formality in the process, with the highest-ranking gentleman escorting the highest-ranking lady. At Carrington Hall, Lady Elizabeth Drake was something of a stickler, and always organised the pairings herself, and ordered the seating at dinner, too. Here, there was no such tidiness, and most of the group left in a more or less random gaggle. Mr Brant gave his arm to Mrs Hay, and Lord Montague and Lord Gilbert escorted their wives, but the rest went through anyhow.

"Miss Winterton? May I have the honour of escorting you to dinner?"

"Oh, thank you so much, Mr Makenham," she said, with a smile of pleasure. "I am so glad someone knows the correct form. Oh dear! I did not mean... it was not my intention to criticise, for so many members of the nobility must know each other well, I daresay. They need not stand on ceremony with their own kind."

"They need not," he said, as they began their descent of the stairs, "but for myself, I like to see the thing done properly, two by two and all arrayed in rank. It makes for a more rational entrance to the dining room, I feel. More rational, but not always so enjoyable. Had we processed by rank, I should have been escorting Lady Montague Marford and you would have been on the arm of one of our two physicians."

"How clever you are to work it out so quickly!" she said, blushing a little at the subtle compliment. "I am hopeless with such matters, for I had not guessed your rank to be so high. Do honourables rank above baronets?"

"It depends on the honourable's father," he said gravely. "My father is a viscount, so that sets me above the baronets, but well below the sons of a marquess."

"Oh. How complicated it is," she said. It was a relief, in many ways, to be a mere seamstress and not have to worry about such things.

In the dining room, most of the ladies were already seated, but Mr Makenham led Fanny to a spare seat and then sat down beside her. She was glad of it, for one never knew who one might be sitting next to in such company, and Mr Makenham was a familiar and friendly face. Her other dinner companion was more daunting, being one of Lady Harriet's brothers, Lord Montague Marford. Whatever was she to say to a brother of the Marquess of Carrbridge? For a while, as they all drank their soup, little was said by anyone. But eventually the soup was removed, and as the joints were being carved, Lord Montague turned politely to Fanny.

"It is always distressing to see a young lady in the black of deep mourning," he began. "It is your father whom you mourn, I understand, Miss Winterton?"

"Oh yes, my lord. Papa died at the turn of the year after a very short illness, although he had not been quite himself for some years, so it was not unexpected."

"But still a shock, no doubt," he said. He had a very gentle voice, and his face was filled with sympathy. "And you have been forced from your home, too, and separated from your family. But how bravely you have undertaken the long journey from Brinshire, under the most trying of circumstances."

"Oh, but I have been excessively fortunate, my lord! I have been so lucky as to be taken up by Lady Harriet, who has treated me quite as one of the family, so it is a pleasure to help her with her charitable project. And the work is most congenial, so I have not the least reason to repine. I am very comfortably situated, I assure you. Do you live in Sagborough too, my lord?"

"No, I live in a small village called Kirby Grosswick, where my parish is." A clergyman. She had not guessed that. "We are staying with Gil and Lady Gil until after the Easter ball next week, or at least Lady Monty is. I shall go home for the services and return to Sagborough in time for the ball. The whole family descends on Sagborough twice a year, for the Easter and harvest balls. Do you know Lord and Lady Carrbridge?" She shook her head. "You will like them. Lady Carrbridge is from Brinshire, too, so you will be able to have a comfortable chat about old friends and familiar places."

Fanny could not imagine having a comfortable chat to a marchioness about anything, but she smiled and nodded. Mr Makenham drew her attention after this, by helping her to portions of various dishes, and Lord Montague turned to Mrs Plumstead on his other side.

Once she had eaten a little, she set down her knife and fork and said, "I must tell you, Mr Makenham, that you were quite right in what you said to me the other day."

"Was I?" he said, his mouth quirking into a little smile. "In what way was I right?"

"You told me it would do me good to go into company, and it is true, for I have been looking forward to this evening for days, and I am enjoying myself excessively."

His face broke into a wider smile that lit his whole face and gave such a sparkle to his eyes that her breath caught in her throat. She had seen him smile many times, for he was a very sociable man and smiled a great deal, but those smiles, she now realised, were merely his pleasantly polite expressions. This was a different smile altogether, warm and infused with happiness. Yes, her words made him happy.

When he answered, however, his voice was calm. "I am very glad to hear it, Miss Winterton. Might I presume to entertain you at my own table the next time I send out my cards?"

"Oh, indeed, I should like that very much! Thank you, sir!"

"And perhaps I may see you at the Easter ball?"

"Oh — do you think—? But I need not dance, need I? And it would be so enjoyable, even to sit and watch the dancing. It would not be improper, would it?"

"Not at all, in my view, Miss Winterton, and it would give your friends an opportunity to meet you again. Miss Trivers told me at the last assembly how much she misses your company."

"Oh, how kind of her. How very kind. I miss her, too, but of course it is not an acquaintance she can pursue, now. Did you dance with her? She is so pretty, is not she? And did you dance with Miss Drabble, too? She is so, so beautiful! I do not think I have ever seen anyone so beautiful in my life. Rosamund is said to be a beauty — my eldest sister, you know — but I do think Miss Drabble outshines her. I am sure all the gentlemen must be violently in love with her, and she is so accomplished, too! I wish I had a tenth of her looks. Do you not think her loveliest creature, Mr Makenham?"

"She is indeed a very handsome young lady," he said, "but... but it usually takes more than beauty to entice a man to fall violently in love. There is also temperament and good humour and... well, one must feel comfortable with a lady. One must feel as if she is the only woman in the world."

His eyes gazed into hers with such fiery intensity that she had to look away, turning quickly back to her plate. Fortunately, he was very well-bred, for he calmly changed the subject, asking her about Woodside, and they talked for the rest of the meal in the most companionable way about houses. She told him all about her own home, and the grand houses she knew in Brinshire, like Westerlea Park, Lord Westerlea's seat, and Carrington Hall, where Lady Elizabeth Drake lived. In his turn, he told her about his father's cosy house, Lennister Hall, and his grandfather's rambling principal seat, Abbeymount, the deficiencies of which he described in vivid terms.

"It sounds delightful," Fanny said wistfully.

"You consider smoking chimneys and rattling shutters delightful, Miss Winterton?" he said, smiling. "And the food is always cold before it reaches the dining room."

"That might be amended," she said. "Burners in the pantry would keep the food hot. But how romantic to live in a house with so much history, where every room has so many memories."

"I suppose it *is* romantic," he said. "I had never thought of it that way. I love Abbeymount in the summer, when the whole vast estate is there to be ridden across or walked over, and the air is balmy. I like it less well in the winter, when the wind howls round and the snow traps everyone indoors and the house seems far too small. Perhaps it is always so when families are gathered together like that. Everyone becomes a trifle short-tempered. Or perhaps it is just that my grandfather loves to fill the place at Christmas, and all the elderly aunts and uncles forget that one is five and twenty, and treat one like a schoolboy."

"You are so lucky to have enough relatives to fill Abbeymount," Fanny said wistfully.

At this point they were interrupted by Lady Greenfoot's booming voice from across the table. "Mr Makenham! Do tell us, if you please, when you will be going to London? I have a package that you might take to my sister, if you would be so obliging. You will not leave before the Easter ball, I trust?"

"No, indeed, Lady Greenfoot. In fact, I shall not be leaving at all, for I have no plans to be in London this spring."

"You will miss the season? How singular! I thought all you fashionable young men like to strut about in town. But Lord Belwarren will be going south soon, I am sure? I knew him well when I was a girl, and perhaps for an old friend he might—"

"He is already in London, my lady. He has been there since January."

"What, so soon? London is very thin of company before Easter, and I cannot imagine what he finds to do there so early in the year."

Mr Brant, who sat beside her, murmured something inaudible, but she shook her head, and said loudly enough for half the table to hear, "Government business? What government business? I cannot imagine what that might be. Lord Belwarren has no position in government."

Lord Gilbert, on Lady Greenfoot's other side, offered his services in getting her package to London, and then pressed her to try one of the lobster patties, and since her ladyship was more interested in food than the Earl of Belwarren, the subject was dropped, and the conversation became more general.

~~~~~

Ferdy could not recall a happier evening. When he, Edgar and Aunt Agatha gathered in their own drawing room for a brandy later that evening, he could not suppress a huge grin, even though he supposed he looked completely idiotic.

"So, what do you think of her now?" he said eagerly.

His aunt looked at him quizzically. "Does it matter what I think?"

"I value your opinion, naturally," Ferdy said, offended. "You can judge her impartially, as I cannot. Besides, you will share your opinion with Mama and Papa, so I hope you *do* like her. Your recommendation would carry a great deal of weight."

"Oh, so you are not going to marry in the face of family opposition, then?"

"Well, of course not! If you dislike her, then you would have good reason for that. *Do* you dislike her?"

She laughed. "Not in the slightest. There is nothing about her to dislike. She is not encroaching, which is the most important thing. I cannot abide persons who *insinuate* themselves, and suck up to anyone of rank. She is neat and well-mannered, neither too forward nor too shy, and she is no blue-stocking, that much is certain. You would not be comfortable with an opinionated woman. That Miss Hay! Upon my word, I never saw the like! Your Miss Winterton is far more the thing."

"Edgar?" Ferdy said hopefully.

"Oh, no use asking me," Edgar said, pulling a face. "They are all alike to me, these girls. But she seems a taking little thing, as girls go."

"She is!" Ferdy said happily. "Very taking. So you will tell Mama all of this, Auntie?"

"You may tell her yourself. She will be here tomorrow."

"Here? Tomorrow? Mama?" Ferdy said blankly.

"Just so. You did not suppose she would allow her eldest son to choose a bride without having a good look at the lady first, did you? Really, Ferdy, you ought to know Louisa better than that. And she will be here for this ball that the locals are so excited about."

"Excellent! Can we squeeze in a dinner before then, do you suppose?"

"I guessed you would want to do so, and everything is in hand, nephew."

"Auntie, you are a treasure," Ferdy said, giving her his deepest bow.

She laughed, but she looked pleased, all the same.

Ferdy walked about on air after such a successful evening, his thoughts entirely taken up with Miss Winterton. Fanny. His courtship had at last made a beginning, and had not been ineffective, he felt. She had been perfectly open and friendly with him, without the least hint of reserve or disdain, and he was optimistic of a positive outcome in due course. But there was time enough, and he would not rush at the fence and risk a premature fall. He had already told his parents that he would not be in town that spring, the better to pursue his suit, and perhaps by the summer he could approach Fanny directly and put it to the test.

He was so energised that he could barely sleep, and was up with the dawn and out of the house even before breakfast. The streets of Sagborough were already a-bustle, as men of business finalised their affairs before Easter, and housewives prepared for the feast on Easter Sunday. Ferdy walked briskly down one side of the York Road and had begun the return journey on the other side when he became distracted by the window of a jeweller's shop. There was a seed pearl necklace with a sapphire pendant that would suit Fanny admirably. He was considering whether to enquire further within, when there was a delicate cough nearby and he became aware that he was being addressed by an unknown man of distinguished appearance.

"My dear sir, I must apologise in the most abject manner for intruding upon your cogitations." The stranger removed a very stylish beaver hat and swept it into a low bow. "I do trust that when you hear my plight you will overlook my impertinence in addressing one wholly unknown to me, for I am but a stranger in your fair town, and you look like the very man to assist me."

Ferdy made a small bow of acknowledgement. The voice was cultured and although his clothes bespoke a man of greater income than taste, he was not so outlandishly attired that Ferdy was offended to be seen with him. Ever polite, he responded, "Naturally I will be pleased to offer you whatever aid may be within my power."

"You are too good, sir. Too kind altogether. But I knew at once that you were the very man to answer my question, for — if you will permit me to say so, sir — yours is quite the finest neckcloth arrangement I have yet seen since I left my home last Friday."

Ferdy bowed again, not immune to the value of the compliment, even from a man whose own neckcloth showed a sad lack of proper starching.

"The problem I have encountered, sir," the man continued, "is that my valet has most unfortunately neglected to pack sufficient neckcloths for my needs, and matters are becoming desperate. Might I make so bold as to enquire the source of your own neckcloths?"

"Ah. These came from a place on Oxford Street, London," Ferdy said.

"I might have guessed as much," the stranger said. "The quality of the linen is such that I should have realised at once. Then is there nowhere in this town where I might obtain material of a similar quality?"

"As to that, I have not lived here long enough to need to buy such goods," Ferdy said. "However, there is a linen drapery in the next street which looks respectable enough. Allow me to accompany you there."

"You are all goodness, sir. Might I know to whom I am indebted for this assistance?"

"Ferdinand Makenham. My card."

"Thank you, thank you. How kind. And mine, also. Roland Hawes of Kellingborough in Staffordshire."

"Staffordshire? That is... not in these parts. You are a long way from home, Mr Hawes. What brings you to Sagborough?"

"I am here to find an old acquaintance who moved here a few months ago. As soon as I have remedied the deficiencies of my wardrobe, I shall begin my search, but one likes to look one's best."

"Oh, certainly, certainly," Ferdy said with some feeling. "One should always present one's best face to the world. But perhaps your friend would be the proper person to advise on your purchases."

"No, no," Hawes said, with a satisfied smirk. "A lady would know nothing of such matters."

"Ah, a *lady*," Ferdy said. "How romantic! And you have no other acquaintance in Sagborough?"

"None, sir. Not a soul."

"Then you must come to dinner," Ferdy said firmly. "I am entertaining a few guests on Thursday, and you will be most welcome. If you find your lady friend, then she will be welcome too. Where are you staying?"

"At the Carrbridge Arms."

"Excellent choice. I shall have my aunt send you an invitation."

Having reached the linen draper's shop and agreed that the quality was good even if the prices were shockingly high, the two parted on the best of terms. Ferdy went home for breakfast in a very contented frame of mind, both flattered by admiration of his carefully contrived neckcloth and pleased to assist, albeit in a very small way, in the progress of a romance.

12: Dinner At Number Twenty-Five (April)

Ferdy was on the doorstep of number Twenty-Five later that afternoon as an antiquated travelling carriage drew to a halt. The butler and two footmen descended to the pavement with measured steps, but Ferdy bounded down, and flung open the carriage door.

"Mama!" he cried. "Here you are at last! Welcome to Harlington Terrace. Or welcome *back*, I should say."

"Ferdy, dear boy! Were you watching for us? How thoughtful you are." She took the arm he offered to aid her descent, and looked up at the house, just as Ferdy had done two months earlier. "Ah, dear number Twenty-Five. Such happy memories."

Lady Craston was a softly rounded woman, whose shape was not flattered by the columnar outline of modern gowns. Her portrait over the stairs at Lennister Hall, in the vast hat and full skirts of fifteen years ago, captured her at her motherly best. Now she clasped her eldest son to her pillowy bosom.

"How are you, dear?" she said. "Ah, looking well, I see. Good, very good. What a pleasure it is to see you again."

"And you, Mama. Oh — and Cordelia, too. And Emilia. How kind of you all to bring your feminine charms to lighten my bachelor life."

Lady Craston laughed merrily. "Ferdy, if anyone else said such a thing, I would think it the most outrageous flummery, but you truly mean it, I believe."

"Of course I do," he said, surprised. "I am delighted to see you, however unexpected. All of you. I only hope we have enough rooms."

"The girls will share, of course, but Agatha has it all in hand."

"Naturally she does," Ferdy murmured. "Whatever would we do without Aunt Agatha? Do come inside out of this cold wind and have some tea while the luggage is unloaded."

They drifted up the steps, Lady Craston leaning on Ferdy's arm, although she was perfectly fit and had no need of the support. The two girls bounced up the steps arm in arm, twittering excitedly. Ferdy smiled to see them. Cordelia was his youngest sister, just seventeen, and about to enjoy her first season in London. Emilia was the eldest, and at four and twenty was close to permanent spinsterhood. All the Makenham girls were handsome and well-dowered, so there was no obstacle to marriage, but so far Emilia had not been tempted.

Ferdy introduced the servants to the new arrivals and ordered tea in the drawing room, but it was not an easy task to get the three ladies up the stairs, for they wanted to examine every room on the ground floor first. If two of them were got to the foot of the stairs, the third was sure to have vanished into the dining room or Ferdy's book room or the card room. Even when they were all gathered in the hall again, they exclaimed over the furniture.

"What an ugly mirror," Cordelia said, pulling a face as she adjusted her curls after removing her bonnet. "I do not know how you can bear to look in it, Ferdy."

"I never do, I assure you. Emilia, do not disappear again, I beg you."

"Never? Not even a last peek before you go out?"

"Why would I need to? Wrackham would tell me if there were anything amiss with my appearance."

"Come along now, girls," Lady Craston said. "Let us have some tea. Ah, Agatha, dear, there you are!"

Finally, the ladies ascended the stairs and settled in the drawing room with tea and macaroons.

"Well now, this is very pleasant," Lady Craston said. "You are very obliging, Ferdy, not to make a fuss about us descending on you like this, when Agatha clearly neglected to tell you anything about it."

Ferdy laughed. "You wrong her, Mama. She told me all about your arrival, although not until midnight last night. I admit that the inclusion of Emilia and Cordelia in the party is a delightful surprise."

"Well, I hope it *is* delightful, because I should like them to stay all summer, if it is not terribly inconvenient for you."

"All summer? But what about Cordelia's season? It is all arranged, is it not?"

Lady Craston sighed, and set down her teacup. "It is, or rather, it was, but she has developed a distinct *tendre* for a chap in York, some distant relation of the Marfords. When you wrote to say that you would be staying here for the summer, it seemed ideal. Cordelia can stay with you, with Emilia to bear her company, and this fellow can stay with his cousin who lives here. That way they can get to know each other a bit better and see if they would suit. No point spending a fortune on a season for the girl if she has already set her heart on someone. And if it falls through, there is always next year. Although it does seem quite a settled thing. He is very keen, this Whittleton fellow. Jules or Julian or some such."

"Julius Whittleton," Cordelia put in, with a hint of a blush.

"Julius, yes. Very personable and sings like an angel. Beautiful voice. I do like a man who can put so much feeling into a song. There cannot be much wrong with anyone who can perform heart-rending duets in Italian."

Cordelia laughed. "He is shockingly unsuitable, Mama. You really should be forbidding the banns instead of encouraging us. He manages a gaming house, Ferdy, can you imagine?"

"Good heavens! Truly? A gaming house?"

"It is a perfectly *respectable* gaming house," she said, eyes brimming with laughter. "Very exclusive. It is owned by Lord Humphrey Marford, and is quite the finest such establishment in the North of England, according to Julius, although to my mind a gaming house is a gaming house, whoever owns it. Lord Humphrey can get away with such an association, for no one would dare to disoblige a marquess by cutting his brother, but Julius is too insignificant to merit such protection. He is quite an outcast to good society."

"But however did you meet him?" Ferdy said.

"I was in York for some gown fittings and I bumped into him in the street. Sent the poor man flying and broke his umbrella into the bargain. He walked me back to the hotel, found out who I was and lurked about the place until he bumped into me again. Mama got tired of finding him always underfoot, so she invited him to dinner. He arranged for us to go and stay with Lord and Lady Humphrey for a while, but now that everyone is haring off to London, we need a way to meet regularly. You do not mind, do you, Ferdy?" she added anxiously.

"Of course not," he said. "Happy to play matchmaker, although — well, no matter."

"No, tell me all, Ferdy," Cordelia said. "If you know something to his disadvantage, I would sooner know of it now than find out when I am three steps from the altar. Does he keep mistresses and so forth?"

"I never heard so. Not that you should know anything about such matters, at your age," he said disapprovingly. "Honestly, young ladies are outrageously forward these days. I know nothing bad of this Julius himself, but all the Whittletons are very much the poor relations to the Marfords. Hangers-on, most of them, if not outright fortune hunters, so I hope you will assure yourself that his admiration is for your person and not your dowry."

"You need not worry about that, Ferdy," Lady Craston said. "He told me as much himself, and that he has tried his luck with one or two heiresses in the past. Very open about it, but he is not a poor relation any longer. He takes a share of the profits from Lord Humphrey's gaming house, and has made a very pretty fortune from it. He is well able to keep a wife, I assure you."

"And will be even more so if he has Cordelia's dowry in his hand," Ferdy said seriously. "Truly, Mama, be cautious."

"Good heavens, Ferdy, how medieval you are getting!" Cordelia said huffily. "If Mama and Papa approve of him, I shall not regard *your* opinion, you may be sure."

"But I shall," Lady Craston said with a frown. "Ferdy has excellent judgement, and he will be keeping a close eye on this Julius fellow over the summer."

"Well, that is the outside of enough!" Cordelia cried. "Is Ferdy to say who I marry now?"

"Not at all," Ferdy said imperturbably. "Just keeping a brotherly eye on my sister, that is all. On *both* my sisters. What about you, Emilia? Sagborough is a trifle short of eligible bachelors, but I am sure we can find someone for you. I believe the vicar has an unmarried uncle somewhere about the place, and you will not object to his rheumatism, I am sure. He is very sprightly for his age."

She laughed at his teasing. "Oh, you are too kind, but there is no need to worry about me, Ferdy. There must be a spinster in every generation to take care of everyone. I intend to be the next Aunt Agatha."

The present Aunt Agatha laughed heartily at this ambition.

"Well, this is all very pleasant," Lady Craston said. "Agatha, I will take a little more tea, and Ferdy can tell me all about his Miss Winterton."

"Oh, do!" cried Cordelia. "How very unlike you, Ferdy, to fall violently in love. She must be excessively beautiful to draw your notice, when you have had every diamond in town at your feet for years. You are quite the most eligible bachelor around, now that Ramsey is leg-shackled."

Ferdy demurred modestly at this, but went on, "She is not excessively beautiful, no, but she is no antidote, you may be sure, and she is such a gentle, sweet-natured little thing. You will like her, I am sure, Mama."

"I daresay I shall, for Agatha has given me a very promising report of her, and if she is all that you say, then you will not hear any objection from me, and your father will follow my lead. He always does."

"But a seamstress, Mama," Emilia said quietly. "It is all very well for Cordelia to marry her gaming house fellow if she pleases, for a fifth daughter need not consult any wishes but her own, but Ferdy is the heir. I have nothing against the lady, you understand, nothing at all, but he could do a great deal better."

"There is no better wife for a man, whether he be high or low, than the one in his heart," Lady Craston said firmly. "I should like Ferdy to marry, if only to cut Ralph out of the line of succession, for he is far too rackety for my liking, but as to whom he should choose, I leave to him to determine. A man knows what kind of wife would suit him best, Emmy dear. All I ask, Ferdy, is that you do not rush into anything, for too much haste can be fatal. Get to know her properly first, then you may decide."

"That is my plan, Mama," Ferdy said, but despite the calmness of his voice, his heart was singing inside. His mother would not hinder him! He had hoped it would be so, but her abrupt arrival had raised a doubt in his mind. Perhaps she had come to put a stop to it? But no, just as he had guessed, his romantic mother would not stand in the way of his happiness with the woman he loved.

~~~~~

Twenty-Five Harlington Terrace was now filled with girlish chatter all day, and began to feel over-full. Edgar, never at his best in female company, acquired a hounded look and Ferdy took him out of the house as often as possible.

Just when Edgar was beginning to talk about decamping altogether, at which Ferdy denounced him as cowardly in the extreme to leave him alone with four females, the masculine side of the household received an unexpected fillip in the person of their cousin, Ralph Makenham. Ralph was the handsome one of the three cousins, the one with the sparkling blue eyes and roguish grin that set feminine hearts a-flutter, the one who flirted and teased and stole kisses when he could. There were worse rumours about him, too, but Ferdy gave no credence to them.

He had always envied Ralph just a little, though. Ralph was one of those men who did everything well. He rode superbly, drove to an inch, was a bruising boxer and an expert swordsman, shot well and danced with a litheness that made him even more popular than Ferdy at a ball. And all of these accomplishments were reflected in a broad-chested, muscular figure that looked effortlessly graceful whatever he did. Where Ferdy laboured with his valets to achieve his unostentatious style, Ralph seemed to throw clothes onto his back in a casual manner and yet still looked every inch the debonair man of fashion.

His presence was welcome, nevertheless, and with the house now satisfactorily full, Ferdy now began to turn his attention to the Easter celebrations, of which the first event was his own dinner, where he would have the inestimable pleasure of entertaining Miss Winterton in his own home.

~~~~~

APRIL

Not even their greatest friends would describe the Makenham family as clever. Good-humoured, people said of them, or even more ominously, respectable, but not clever. A great-uncle of Ferdy's who had had a distressing tendency to talk about planetary orbits and quote lengthy passages in Ancient Greek had been speedily shipped out to India, where he had fallen into a fever and died within weeks of his arrival. The family was very sad, naturally, but felt it was probably for the best.

Ferdy had received a great deal of education, as befitted a future earl, but as his mama had not wished him to go far away to school, and he himself had had no inclination for university, his learning had been a hodgepodge of methods and subjects, at the whim of his teachers, his parents and Ferdy himself. There had been a governess in his early years, then a tutor, then two years at a school in York, followed by a succession of tutors, both general and specialised, supplemented by occasional lessons from his sisters' governesses, the chaplain and whichever relations took it upon themselves to improve his knowledge.

He was not, therefore, uneducated, but there were noticeable gaps in his learning. Geography was one such area. He could recite to a nicety the names of all the posting inns between York and London, the distances between them, and which were honest and which could provide enough hot water for a bath. But as to towns, rivers and counties, he was a trifle hazy. Given a map of England, he could only reliably point out London, York, Brighton and Bath. On the counties, he knew none beyond the Ridings of Yorkshire. Had he been asked about Miss Winterton's home county of Brinshire, for instance, he would have said only that it was somewhere to the south of York, but not as far south as London. Of Mr Hawes' home in Staffordshire, he knew just as little. If he had taken the trouble to look up Hawes' estate of Kellingborough on the map, he would have been astonished to find that it was not even ten miles away from Miss Winterton's home of Woodside.

And if Ferdy had done all that, he would not have been quite so shocked to discover that the lady Mr Hawes sought was none other than Fanny Winterton.

The evening had started so well, too. Ferdy had had the inestimable pleasure of introducing Miss Winterton to his mama, and seeing them chatting together in the drawing room in the easiest manner possible. His mother had a comfortable way with everyone, and Miss Winterton, despite her youth, was not overawed by rank, and so they got along famously. It was only when other guests arrived and were introduced to Lady Craston, and Miss Winterton very correctly rose to make room for them, that Ferdy was able to draw her away to the far corner of the room and talk to her himself. So it happened that he was sitting beside Miss Winterton when the drawing room door opened.

"Mr Roland Hawes," Poole intoned. Ferdy heard the name, and rose to his feet smoothly to greet his guest.

Miss Winterton heard it too, and gave a little squeak.

Ferdy looked at her in surprise. Her face, normally wreathed in smiles, was ashen, her mouth an 'O' of shock. But there was no time to wonder at it. Good manners asserted themselves, and he made his way across the room to receive Mr Hawes, and introduce him around the room. He made it a slow progress, starting at the furthest extremity of the room, to give Miss Winterton time to compose herself. But eventually the moment could not be avoided.

"Miss Winterton, may I present to you Mr Roland Hawes of Kellingborough in Staffordshire. This is Miss Frances Winterton, sir, who is another of my neighbours."

Hawes started violently at the first sight of her, and for a moment seemed speechless. But he quickly recovered his wits, made her a florid bow and said smoothly, "Miss Winterton, this is the most delightful surprise! And yet not such a surprise, I fancy, to discover you here, amongst the finest of Sagborough society, as your manifold charms entitle you to be. I need not enquire as to your health, for your countenance is as fair as I ever saw it, and your eyes dazzle with their brilliance."

Ferdy would have been mortified to inflict such grandiloquent utterings on any lady, and expected Fanny to give Hawes a rapid put-down. Instead, she blushed prettily and said, "Oh, you are too kind, Mr Hawes! Such flattery! But you have always had such a way with words — so *poetic*. Do sit down beside me, and tell me how you are, and all you have done since we last met. At the Claremonts' ball in November, was it not? Are you making a long stay in Sagborough?"

Ferdy drifted away from them, not wanting to hear such happy chatter directed at any man other than himself. Hawes was handsome enough, he supposed, in a commonplace sort of way, but now that he looked more carefully at his evening dress, he saw that the breeches were rumpled, the coat ill-fitting and the neckcloth sadly uneven. He could not see what Fanny, so precisely dressed herself, could see in such a man, especially one with such fawning manners. Yet it was clear that she liked and even admired him, and that her admiration was returned. She was, in fact, the very person he had come north to find, and Ferdy had facilitated their reunion, to his own great loss.

He was empty inside, with such a pain in his heart as he had never experienced before. The woman he loved had eyes only for another, and one so little worthy of her. He could not look at the two of them, for whenever he ventured a glance, Fanny was leaning towards Hawes with flushed cheeks and shining eyes, her lips slightly apart, and Hawes was smirking in a smug, self-satisfied way that was beyond all bearing.

Good breeding was all that got Ferdy through the evening. He smiled, he talked composedly to his dinner companions, he moved around the drawing room later ensuring that all his guests were suitably entertained, arranging card tables for those so inclined, and gathering the rest into friendly groups, and no one to look at him would guess that his heart was torn into tiny shreds.

That night, after Wright had left him, he lay in bed curled into a miserable ball, and wished he had never bumped into Mr Roland Hawes.

13: *The Easter Ball*

Fanny could not sleep that night. Mr Hawes in Sagborough! It was beyond anything! Yet why was he there at all? He had not mentioned any business which had brought him north, nor friends that he might be visiting — in fact, he was staying at an inn. So what had brought him to Sagborough, of all places? Her heart whispered that perhaps he had come for her, but she could not quite believe it. He had had enough opportunity to offer for her, had he wished to make her his wife. For two years he had buzzed around her like a persistent bumble bee, never quite leaving her alone but never quite getting to the point, either. Even when Papa had died, and she had been faced with leaving her home and taking up a menial occupation to survive, he had not offered. One letter of condolence, beautifully worded, but no visit and no offer of marriage.

Yet now, three months after Papa's death, here he was again and just as attentive as ever, just as fulsome in his compliments. But something had changed. Not in Mr Hawes, for he appeared to her to be exactly the same as always, but perhaps Fanny herself had changed. In Brinshire, Mr Hawes had seemed like a sophisticated man of the world, handsome, elegant and well-spoken. Compared with the other young men Fanny knew, like the Claremont brothers, the Bowens or the Sheridans, he was of a different class altogether, a little older, more gentlemanly and dazzling to Fanny's younger self. But now she had another point of comparison, and alongside Mr

Makenham's impeccable person, with his gentle mode of speech and his perfect manners, Mr Hawes seemed to shine a little less.

Was she in love with Roland Hawes? She was not at all sure that she was. When she had first known him, she had found his attentions flattering. His flowery compliments had made her feel like a princess, and she had walked about with a joyful spring in her step. Despite this, her heart did not hammer in her breast when she saw him, nor was she unaware of anything else when he was beside her. Most telling of all, she had scarcely thought of him since her arrival in Sagborough. Apart from which considerations, she could not quite forgive him for not offering for her long ago, when she would have accepted him without a second thought. There was something odd about a man who paid court to a woman for more than two years, off and on, and yet still failed to propose. If he were to propose now, Fanny was by no means certain that she would accept him. He remained the most appealing gentleman of her acquaintance, but she was unconvinced that her happiness lay in such a quarter.

Such thoughts seemed remote from her everyday life. At night, she was Miss Winterton of Woodside, dining with the most notable residents of the town, and wondering about a possible suitor, as if nothing at all had changed. But during the day, she could not deceive herself. She was a hired shop girl, no different from the apothecary's niece she saw helping her uncle in the shop, or the girl who swept the floor in the haberdashery. Fanny worked in a shop, just as they did, plying her needle with Lady Harriet's unfortunates, discussing with customers how to make up the partially-prepared gowns the shop sold, and advising on the latest fashions. She may have been paid a quarterly salary rather than a weekly wage, but she did not deceive herself as to her reduced circumstances.

Truth to tell, she rather enjoyed the work, which happily kept her too busy to repine upon her situation or to miss her sisters. She had quickly found herself in demand as a source of guidance regarding colours and styles. Many a patron had been deterred from purchasing something unflattering by Fanny's gentle words.

"Oh, do you like that?" she would say to a very young lady, as she held a vividly toned length of material against herself and looked at Fanny for approval. "Such a strong colour, do you not think? Now with your delicate complexion, you could wear something much more subtle that would not detract from your looks. This pale pink would cast such a lovely glow upon your cheeks, do you not agree?"

Or to a matron, she would say, "Oh yes, the white muslin is very pretty indeed, but this jade one would *so* enhance your lovely eyes."

And sometimes she would even suggest ways of dressing the hair, or which necklace to wear. In such quiet ways were the less well-to-do ladies of Sagborough gently led into a degree of elegance.

For herself, Fanny still wore black, but she had begun to think about the next stage of her mourning. In January, she had thought that a full year of mourning for poor dear Papa would hardly be enough, but now that she had begun to go out a little, her opinion had altered. All her sisters had now moved on to half-mourning and perhaps, with the Easter ball not far away, she should do the same. Besides, it would soon be spring, despite the unseasonably cold weather, and lighter colours would be pleasant for warmer days.

So she made up a small collection of gowns in grey and lavender, and added white to some of her black gowns, and began to count the days until the ball. Her first ball for months! And even though she would not dance, she could not suppress a shiver of anticipation whenever she thought about it. However, she was the only member of the household looking forward to the occasion.

Lady Harriet protested volubly at the command of her brother the marquess that all the family attend, for she was not fond of large social occasions, she declared. "Give me a good dinner, with good company and lively conversation, and some cards or a little music afterwards, and I am content. I have surely done my duty at enough fashionable squeezes over the years to be let off a public ball in Sagborough." Then, with a sigh, she added, "Still, the family has an obligation to create a spectacle for the amusement of the local people once or twice a year, so it must be endured, I suppose. Just as long as I need not dance. I have never been a good dancer, and must surely be past the age of such humiliation now." But she laughed as she spoke, so Fanny suspected that she was not as cross about it as she sounded.

Two of the marquess's brothers and their wives descended on the house for several days, so that the usual calm of the household was disrupted by booted feet rushing up and down the stairs, and loud male voices. Lord Humphrey was particularly hard on Fanny's nerves, for he was a large man with a flamboyant taste in waistcoats, and every room he entered instantly seemed too small. Lord Reginald and the two ladies were less trying, but even so, Fanny was glad to be out of the house during the day.

On the day of the ball, the shop was closed and so Fanny kept to her room, to be out of the way as much as possible. Then there was a great to-do about baths and dressing and an early dinner, which made Dr Hay very fretful. He and his sister did not feel themselves bound by the marquess's whims, so they were to stay at home, but Lady Harriet, still grumbling steadily, had put on one of her elaborate London gowns for the event.

The ball was not a subscription event, like the assemblies, but was open to all comers. The assembly room above the King's Head was too small for such a gathering, and therefore the coach barn behind the Carrbridge Arms was cleared of all its vehicles, bales of straw and broken items of furniture awaiting the carpenter, and converted into a tolerable ballroom. Fanny was pleasantly surprised when she walked into it and saw flowers and carpets and draperies and a proper wooden floor for the dancing. Braziers burned here and there to take the chill off the air, and there was a dais at one end for the orchestra, and another at the other end with seats for the gentry, with many servants attending. Tables running the full length of one side held an array of punch bowls, jellies, hams, pies and sweetmeats.

Lady Harriet's brothers and their wives had gone ahead in their own carriage, and Lady Harriet had fussed and dithered so much that she and Fanny were late in getting away. Consequently, the dancing was well underway when they arrived, but they found seats on the dais and ordered some punch. A footman snapped his fingers and a maid appeared bearing a tray of glasses.

"Martha!" Fanny cried, in pleased recognition. "I had no idea you were to be here. Are you working, and not dancing?"

"Earning a bit of extra money, and a whole day off tomorrow," Martha said. "I'll be finished when you lot all go home, and that's when things get serious here."

"Serious?"

"The serious drinking," Martha said with a smile. "It gets pretty rowdy. Some of the young gentlemen stay, but it's not fit for ladies."

Drink in hand, Fanny settled down to watch the dancing. She saw Mr Makenham at once, for no one else was quite so elegantly attired, and she was not surprised to see that he was a graceful dancer, too. Mr Brant was also easy to spot by his colourful attire. He stood with his cousin, Mr Ralph Makenham, watching the dancing, but not taking part. Marianne Trivers was partnered by a rabbit-faced young man with an ill-fitting coat, who kept moving in the wrong direction. Celia Drabble was dancing with a man who looked large enough to be a blacksmith, who was gazing at her with so much adoration in his eyes that he barely remembered to move at all, and she had to keep nudging him. Of Mr Hawes there was no sign.

The set ended, the dancers dispersed and Fanny found herself surrounded by rustling silk, waving fans and feminine chatter as the wives of all Lady Harriet's brothers descended on them. Lady Harriet was wrapped in embraces, and then the ladies turned their attention on Fanny.

"Oh, my dear, you must be poor Miss Winterton. How do you do? I am Lady Carrbridge," said a person in an exquisite gown of figured silk, the spider-gauze over-gown edged with such delicately worked silver flowers that Fanny was breathless with admiration. Fortunately, she was not required to speak, for Lady Carrbridge rattled on at a great pace. "But what a charming gown! Did you work the bodice yourself? How cleverly you have interwoven the grey, white and black. I must remember that for the next time one of the great-uncles meets his demise, for one does like to have a little something to lift a mourning gown above the commonplace. Oh, I beg your pardon, my dear, do you know everybody? Let me see... oh, here is someone you will not know. This is Mrs Merton, my cousin and our land agent's wife. I have no idea where the men have got to..."

"The punch bowl, I expect," one of the ladies said, and they all laughed and joked about their husbands, twittering like a flock of exotic birds in their turbans and jewelled combs and waving feathers. Fanny watched in silent bemusement. So this was what a marchioness and her family looked like!

Lord Carrbridge, when he appeared with his brothers around him, was a most distinguished-looking man, who chaffed his sister with a twinkle in his eye.

"Hatty, what are you doing sitting about in this dull way? Why do you not dance? Let me find you a congenial partner. There is a blacksmith without a partner near the door, and a fine-looking farmer over there who—"

She burst out laughing. "Merciful heavens, Carrbridge, spare me the dancing, I beg of you! I have obeyed your summons to attend, but that is where I draw the line. I shall walk about and talk to your blacksmith and farmer, if you wish, but no dancing, if you please!"

And so saying, she jumped to her feet and strode away.

Lord Carrbridge raised an eyebrow. "She used to *like* to dance," he said plaintively. "Is she all right, do you suppose?"

"Maybe she is increasing," Lord Montague said in his soft voice. "That often makes a lady less energetic than usual."

"Unlikely," Lady Carrbridge said crisply. "Well, even if Harriet does not wish to dance, I do. Come along ladies, the music is starting up again. Shall we find ourselves a handsome farmer apiece?"

Lord Carrbridge laughed as the ladies disappeared down the steps to the dancing area, and sat himself down beside Fanny, arms folded, legs stretched out, for all the world as if he were in his own drawing room. Even though he was a marquess and therefore a terrifyingly grand personage, he was still a friendly man who was happy to make conversation with a mere seamstress for half an hour. He pointed out various important people from the county, and one or two who were rather infamous. He was also a magistrate, so had had occasion to pass judgement on many of those now dancing vigorously below them.

"I once had Humphrey up before me," he said conversationally.

"Lord Humphrey?" Fanny squeaked, shocked. "That must have been a mistake, surely?"

"Oh no, not a bit of it. He had stolen some jewellery from one of the aunts — just as a game, you understand. I decided not to have him transported."

"Oh!" Fanny said, eyes wide, before realising that his eyes were twinkling. "Oh, you are teasing me! You would not really have done so, naturally?"

"Oh no. Quite fond of the fellow. Besides, there was no harm in it — just a prank. I fined him, and made him apologise and give a barrel of ale to the constables, but he had to spend a night in gaol before the hearing, so I think he was adequately punished for his impudence. Besides, not sure New Holland is quite ready for Humphrey. Ah, friends of yours, Miss Winterton?"

Mr Brant and Mr Ralph Makenham, who were not dancing, made their way onto the dais and claimed seats either side of Fanny, while Lord Carrbridge rose with a bow, and joined a noisy gaggle of his brothers just behind them. Fanny did not mind Mr Brant, who was very polite and gentlemanly despite his garish clothes, but she was not at all sure what to make of Mr Ralph Makenham. He was very handsome, to be sure, and his clothes fitted him well, showing off broad shoulders and muscular thighs. One felt he was more at home on the hunting field than the drawing room, however, and there was something overpoweringly masculine about him that unsettled Fanny.

"Devilish boring affair," Mr Brant said. "So many bucolic millers and wheelwrights."

"Some of their daughters are quite pretty," Mr Ralph Makenham said. "Hoy! Fellow! Bring us some punch."

"Punch!" Mr Brant said in disgusted tones.

"It will have to do, since there is nothing stronger to be had," Mr Ralph said. "You must be bored beyond belief, Miss Winterton, since you cannot even relieve the monotony by dancing."

"Oh, no, indeed I am not, sir. It is most enjoyable to watch everyone in their finery, and all having the most delightful time. No one can be miserable at a ball."

"Except Edgar," Mr Ralph said, laughing. "He is—"

A huge crash, mingled with the tinkle of broken glass, brought all conversation to a halt momentarily. A maid carrying a tray of punch glasses had tripped on the steps leading up to the dais.

"Oh! It is Martha! Poor Martha!" Fanny cried, half-rising from her seat. "I must go to her."

Mr Ralph grabbed her arm. "Sit!" he said peremptorily. "It is not for you to scamper about with the servants."

"But I am a servant myself," she said, stiffening at his touch. "I am not too proud to help a friend in trouble." He was still holding her arm. Startled at his brusqueness, she pulled out of his clasp.

"I beg your pardon," he said, but he sounded huffy. Then, in calmer tones, he went on, "It is not in your best interests to associate with the servant class, Miss Winterton. In your position, it would be prudent to look about you for a husband as soon as may be."

"Thank you for your advice, sir, but I have no wish for a husband. My present situation is perfectly satisfactory to me."

"Is it indeed? Then perhaps Mr Hawes has journeyed here in vain. Or it may be that you imagine a bigger prize is within your grasp, eh?"

"I cannot imagine what you mean, sir, but I beg you will say no more on the subject," she said stiffly.

He chuckled, but made her a small bow of assent, watching her with a lazy smile on his face, his eyes bright. He was a handsome man, there was no doubt about it, but there was something about his manner that set Fanny's back up. How dared he tell her what to do!

Eventually the punch arrived, and the gentlemen became a little less testy, entertaining Fanny with anecdotes of their numerous relations, and for a few minutes she felt less of an interloper and almost a part of their extensive family. How wonderful it would be to have so many cousins and aunts and uncles, and always have someone to talk to and go walking with, someone to share the excitements or disappointments of the day. Someone who would make her feel a little less alone, and prevent her from missing her sisters quite so much.

Another dance ended, and now Mr Ferdinand Makenham could be seen making his way through the throng towards the dais where Fanny sat. Even in the midst of the crowd he stood out. He was not of above average height, nor were his shoulders as wide as his cousin Ralph's were — in fact, he was rather slender for a man. Yet his perfectly-fitted plain dark coat and the immaculately starched whiteness of his neckcloth set him above all others, in Fanny's eyes. He was quite simply the most elegant man in the room, and she could not help but admire him.

"Your servant, Miss Winterton," he said, executing a courtly bow. "Ralph, why are you not dancing?"

"I stood up with the beauty, Ferdy. What more do you expect of me?"

"Miss Drabble? Indeed she is lovely, and very fetchingly attired, but there are any number of pretty young ladies you might try your charms on. The heiress, for example."

"Heiress?" Mr Ralph sat up straighter. "Where? Will you introduce me, Ferdy?"

"You already know her — Miss Marianne Trivers. Over there, talking to the military man. You had better make haste if you wish to secure her, for ladies love a man in regimentals."

With a quick farewell, he was gone, Mr Brant trailing in his wake, and Mr Ferdinand took a seat beside Fanny. "Should you like something to eat, Miss Winterton? I understand there is to be no proper supper hour, so one may eat a little of this, a little of that all evening." She agreed that she would indeed like some food, so he waved down a passing footman and gave orders for some platters to be brought to them. "There now, Ralph may do the pretty to Miss Trivers, and we may sit up here eating and drinking and making sport of the labouring dancers below us."

Fanny smiled at this sally, but said, "Is he so *very* poor?"

"Who, Ralph? He is not poor at all. He has a very cosy little estate in the East Riding, and a good competence to live upon. Why do you—? Oh, the heiress!" He laughed. "Ralph *would* like to marry an heiress, I believe. There is no man so rich that a fat dowry would not enhance his comfort, Miss Winterton."

"But to marry for such a reason!" she cried. "Marriage must be about love, Mr Makenham, for love is everything! How should a man care for a dowry, when he sees the blush upon his true love's cheek, or her eyes flashing with brilliance? *'What is the glory far above All else in human life? Love! Love! There is no form in which the fire Of love its traces has impressed not. Man lives far more in love's desire Than by life's breath, soon possessed not. If all that lives must love or lie, All shapes on earth, or sea, or sky, With one consent, to Heaven cry That the glory far above All else in life is— Love! O, Love!'* Is it not so, Mr Makenham?"

He stared at her, wide-eyed, and then leaned forward, speaking in a low voice. "Oh yes! Indeed it is so, Miss Winterton. You are quite right — love is everything. Never were words so true."

His gaze was so penetrating that her breath caught in her throat, and for an instant she felt dizzy and light-headed, as if she had drunk champagne too quickly. Briefly she wondered if she were about to fall insensible to the floor and make a spectacle of herself.

But then he moved apart a little and smiled his gentle smile, so full of sweetness, all the intensity washed out of him, and the moment passed. She breathed again. Whatever had happened there between them? But it was gone, and they could be comfortable again.

14: Watching The Dancing

Ferdy licked his lips, trying to still his frantically thumping heart, struggling desperately to bring himself back to calmness so that he might not alarm her further. Heavens above, he had for a moment quite forgotten that they were in full public view in the middle of a ball. Another second and he would have declared himself on the spot, and perhaps frightened her away for good. But he had seen something in her eyes — shock or fear, he could not be sure which was uppermost — and that had, most fortunately, brought him crashing back to earth. He must not rush his fences! Slowly, slowly, he must move slowly, no matter her impassioned speeches that *'All else in life is Love!'*. He had been so caught up in the moment that he had almost imagined that she was talking about *him*, that she loved *him*, but he had realised his error just in time.

He scrambled around in his disordered brain for some topic of conversation that would be less dangerous. He dared not mention Mr Hawes, not with the poetry of love still burning her lips and setting her lovely eyes on fire. He had no wish to know her feelings on the subject of Roland Hawes. Nor did he want her to search the crowd below the dais for that gentleman and notice him transfixed in the orbit of Celia Drabble, as he had been almost since his arrival, for such a sight could only give Fanny pain. What a clod pole that man was! He had only to reach out his hand to make Fanny his, or so it seemed to Ferdy, yet where was he? He should be here, beside the woman he had travelled so far to find. Whatever was he about? It was incomprehensible.

Yet what else could Ferdy talk about? He watched Ralph's lithe body heading across the room towards Miss Trivers, and felt, as always, that little prickle of envy. Oh, to be so athletic, so vigorous, so *manly*. What lady could possibly see Ferdy and his cousin in the same room and not be drawn to Ralph's magnetic masculinity? Ferdy was a gentleman to his core, but Ralph was a Corinthian, admired by men and women alike, whose stature did not depend on the degree of starch in his neckcloth. Even Edgar liked to trail about in his wake, and surely Fanny must find him even more magnetic.

The thought made Ferdy so dejected that he could barely speak. But speak he must, after that impassioned speech of love. He could not leave it hanging between them, rendering him speechless. It was essential to exert himself, and return the conversation to the commonplace again.

He cleared his throat. "The ladies have put up a splendid show this evening. How many of them derive their stylishness from your efforts, Miss Winterton?"

She dimpled so adorably that he almost lost the power of speech again. "Several. Celia Drabble, for one. Mrs Young. Mrs Wrackham. Oh, and Miss Malpas." She turned a mischievous grin on him. "Mr Malpas wanted to rig her out in prime style in the hope of attracting the eye of a very eligible gentleman, newly arrived in town."

"Did he indeed? And was the ruse successful?"

"Only you can answer that, Mr Makenham," she said, chuckling.

"Only I can—? Oh! Oh, I see. Good heavens. I do not think— Upon my soul, I never thought— Miss *Malpas?* Good heavens, no. Impossible."

"Naturally," she said serenely, and for a moment his treacherous heart skipped a beat. Was she about to acknowledge that his affections were already engaged? But she went on composedly, "You will marry someone of your own rank, of course. Everyone knows that is how it works."

Ferdy took a deep breath. Here was an opportunity he could not miss. "Rank is less important than... than finding someone who suits one. Someone who inspires one with the greatest respect and... and affection. Love."

"Oh yes, *of course* there must be love. But you must marry a lady who is used to your way of life, who can take her place beside you at court and manage that wonderful house you will inherit — Abbeymount? The mistress of Abbeymount! Only a woman born into the nobility can bring the necessary grace to such a role. It is only fitting. Oh look, Mr Ralph is a splendid dancer, is he not? He and Marianne make such a handsome couple, do you not think?"

Ferdy gave it up, and since he was soon joined by his mother, red-faced and puffing after her exertions on the dance floor, there was no further opportunity for conversation with Fanny.

"Merciful heavens, but I am getting too old for reels," Lady Craston said, collapsing into a seat beside Fanny. "Not that I am not enjoying myself enormously, but a little rest would set me up nicely for the next cotillion. Ferdy, would you be a good boy, and fetch me some punch? I am sure Miss Winterton would like some too. Goodness, it is hot in here. Gracious, is that Gil Marford in the set over there? Who is the lady with him?"

"That is Lady Gilbert, my lady."

"Upon my soul, Gil Marford dancing with his *own* wife! Whoever would have thought it? He has quite a reputation, you know — well, perhaps you don't, but it is so. Or *was,* in any event. Living a blameless life now, is he? That would be the first time ever. Ah, thank you, Ferdy. Are you going to dance again? If so, do not feel you have to hang about my skirts, you know."

"I wondered if Miss Winterton would care to stroll about a little, and watch the dancing from closer quarters. What do you say, Miss Winterton? Are you minded for a little exercise?"

"You are very kind, sir. Thank you! If Lady Craston has no objection—?"

"Heavens, no! Off you go, child. If you are passing the pies, there is a raised game pie which is rather good, or you might try the crab patties, if there are any left."

He offered his arm, and his heart somersaulted alarmingly as she rested her dainty hand on it and rose from her seat. With a neat curtsy to Lady Craston, she moved off beside him, and he had to work very hard not to grin inanely. How exquisite she was, everything about her so neat and precise — her gown, her little hand, her delicate steps, her demurely lowered lashes. And how fortunate he would be if he could persuade her to walk beside him through life, and not just around the perimeter of the Carrbridge Arms coach barn.

His pleasure lasted no more than ten steps, at which point the overdressed form of Lady Harriet bore down on them.

"There you are, Fanny. I have ordered the carriage. Let us collect our cloaks, for we are going home now."

"Of course, Lady Harriet."

"If Miss Winterton wishes to stay a little longer," Ferdy said hopefully, "she may go home with Mama. There will be room enough in our carriage for one extra."

"Oh no, I could not!" Fanny said at once, looking up at him in dismay. "Lady Harriet's convenience must be my first consideration. How kind of you to suggest such a thing, Mr Makenham, but I must go with Lady Harriet."

He bowed, she curtsied and within seconds she was gone, following Lady Harriet's imposing figure across the dais. As she disappeared through the door leading to the ladies' cloak room, she turned, saw him standing forlornly and gave him a little wave. All his disappointment melted away, and he smiled and waved back.

He flopped down in the empty chair beside his mother.

"You truly like her, I think," she said.

"I do! She is everything that is charming, and would suit me admirably, I am convinced of it! But... she said... she said that I should be looking for a wife from amongst my own rank. *You* do not think so, do you? Someone suitable? An earl's daughter or some such — Lady Something."

"Heaven preserve me from Lady Somethings. Starchy, top-lofty creatures, the lot of them, always insisting on protocol and precedence. We want none of that in *this* family. The Makenhams have survived four hundred years since the first barony without the least scandal or misadventure, always perfectly respectable, because we never got ambitious or political or clever, and we kept well clear of all the stuffy Lady Somethings. You marry someone who will make you comfortable, Ferdy. That is what your father did, after all. My papa was barely a gentleman, you know. Never even kept a decent carriage, only a gig, and had not a penny piece for a dowry. It was beyond my wildest hopes that Henry would look twice at me, so handsome and well-mannered as he is, and me nothing to look at, even in my prime. But here I am, and I made very sure he did not regret his choice. It has all worked out very well. So you may choose whomsoever you please, so long as she is a good-humoured girl with no fancy airs, thinking herself too grand for the likes of us. Mind you, she must not be so timid that she is terrified of the housekeeper, either. Your Fanny will do as well as any other. Although, it must be said, Ferdy, that you do not seem to have got very far with her. With your address, I was certain you would have fixed your interest with the girl by now."

"It is... awkward," he said. "She is at work all day, and has only recently begun to accept evening invitations. And now there is Roland Hawes."

"Yes, he was very attentive the other night. But do you know where he is tonight?"

"Dancing attendance on Celia Drabble," Ferdy said, with a lift of one shoulder. "I do not think Fanny noticed, however."

"She noticed," his mother said firmly. "A lady always notices, but she is too well-bred to show any dismay. It cannot be denied, Ferdy, that her behaviour is impeccable. As to Mr Hawes, either he will come to the point or he will not, and either she will accept him or she will not, and you cannot interfere with that. All you can do is to make very sure that she knows your intentions."

"And how do I do that?"

"Court her, dear boy. Send her flowers, write poetry in her honour, pay her those little attentions that signal a more than common interest."

"*Poetry?*" Ferdy said, in tones of the utmost revulsion. "Really, Mama! You must have windmills in your head if you imagine that I am going to compose verses for Fanny, or that they would be in any way tolerable if I did." He had a sudden suspicious thought. "Did Papa write poetry to you?"

She went rather pink. "Well, no, as it happens. But he did say that my eyes were the colour of the sea once, which is almost the same thing."

"What sort of sea? A summer's day blue sea? A cloudy day grey sea? That greeny colour like the painting on the stairs at Lennister? That is not poetic, it is silly, if you ask me. Besides, your eyes are brown, and the sea is *not* brown."

"Oh yes, but that just makes it *more* poetic. Have you heard anything from your father, by the way? Or your grandfather? They have been in London for positively *weeks*, and they tell me nothing."

"Only the usual, who they dined with and who was seen at the club and who has a— Well, you know, matters of male interest."

"Oh, mistresses, and so forth. Do not take me for a green girl, Ferdy. I do know about such things. I have always wondered, does your father—?"

"Not that I ever heard," Ferdy said hastily. "Would you want to know if he did?"

She thought about that for a moment. "Probably not. It pleases me to imagine that he has never looked at another woman since the day he met me, and he does nothing to suggest otherwise. When you are married to your Fanny, you must make sure to do the same. Tell her every day how much you adore her. A woman does like to be adored. Do you know, it is getting rather rowdy down amongst the dancers. Perhaps it is time we ladies left. Would you be a good boy and gather everyone up, if you can extricate Agatha from her set? I do not think she has sat down all evening. Where does she get her energy?"

"I shall order the carriage for you, but tell Smart he need not come back. It is a fine moonlit night, so Edgar, Ralph and I will walk home."

As it turned out, neither of Ferdy's cousins was amenable to this idea.

"Leave so early?" Ralph said. "The evening is just getting interesting."

"By interesting, I assume you mean drunk, noisy and building up nicely to a fight," Ferdy said. "Things will get messy before long. You had much better come with us."

Ralph only laughed at him. "Sounds like fun. I am not afraid of a mill, even if you two are. I enjoy a good set-to. Off you go, you hen-hearted pair."

Edgar hesitated. "Walk home? Can we not get a hackney?"

"None to be had in Sagborough," Ferdy said.

"But the streets will be crawling with footpads and cut-purses, Ferdy."

"It is no more than a five-minute walk," Ferdy protested. "There are two of us, and we both have canes with which to lay about any assailant. Really, Edgar, this is a most law-abiding town, with very little crime anywhere, except in the prices at the linen draper's, and *that* you will find in any town. Even if the place were to be awash with prospective footpads, they will all be in here tonight drinking the free ale, so we will be perfectly safe. However, you are welcome to stay with Ralph if you prefer a mill to a quiet walk home. I do not like the sight of blood myself, but—"

"No, no!" Edgar said faintly. "No blood, if you please. I have an abhorrence of violence. But still — high-handed of you, Ferdy, to dismiss the coachman like that. Should have asked."

"I beg your pardon, Edgar, but it is done now. Shall we go?"

Edgar made no further protest, but he spent the entire walk jumping at every shadow, and lashing out with his cane at any particularly menacing bush or stray tree branch. It was amusing, but Ferdy wished he had remembered just how jumpy Edgar was at night. He disliked causing his cousin such discomfort.

For himself, he rather liked the quiet streets, the rowdy barn left behind and just the occasional hoot of an owl or rustling behind a garden wall to disturb the night air. The coolness cleared his head and brought his thoughts into sharp focus. Not that his thoughts were particularly cheerful. His mother was right — he had made little progress with Fanny, and although he was tolerably certain that she liked him and enjoyed his company, he could see no sign of partiality in her. She treated him as a pleasant acquaintance, exactly as she treated everyone else.

No, not everyone else, for there was one man for whom she displayed more than friendliness. Mr Roland Hawes. Ferdy could not forget Fanny's face when she had first seen him, and the way she had leaned towards him so attentively, eyes wide and lips slightly parted. If she had ever looked at Ferdy that way, he would have ordered his wedding coat already.

Yet Hawes had neglected her shamefully at the ball, not even sitting with her or exchanging two words. He had arrived late and spent the rest of the evening never moving more than five paces from Celia Drabble's side. What was the matter with the man? He had travelled all this way to find Fanny, had fawned over her at Ferdy's house, hardly noticing anyone else in the company, yet now he ignored her. It was incomprehensible.

Still, it gave Ferdy an opportunity. If he could only dream up a way to draw Fanny's attention to himself, and convince her that his suit was serious... But he had not the least idea how to do it. Ralph, he knew, would have managed it in an instant, but how did he do that? Was it a natural gift, or was there a trick to it? Courtship was a mystery to Ferdy.

They reached Harlington Terrace without mishap, and Edgar headed straight to the drawing room.

"A nightcap, cousin?" Ferdy said gently.

"A large brandy to settle my nerves," Edgar said. "Stay and talk to me for a while, Ferdy, for heaven's sake! You know what Fellowes is like, so relentlessly cheerful, it is so lowering when all one wants to do is to be left in peace and not... not *jangled*."

Ferdy laughed. "Very well, but really, Edgar, you should not be browbeaten by your own valet."

"It is all very well for you, Wrackham is so starchy and too much on his dignity to gab away, and Wright takes his cue from him, but Fellowes feels it to be his mission in life to chivvy me out of the dismals. I know I should chastise him for it, but just imagine if he should give notice! He has such a way with my boots that I cannot bring myself to risk it. Oh, the horror of bringing another valet up to scratch! No, it is not to be thought of! Ah, thank you," he said, as Ferdy pushed a glass into his hand. "You are the best of good fellows, you know. Quite my favourite cousin."

"What, even above Ralph? You honour me indeed, Edgar," Ferdy said, executing an elegant bow. "Such a compliment rounds off the evening in splendid style. Good heavens, what do you suppose these pink things are?" he went on, lifting the lid from a dish of sweetmeats. "Some little treat for the ladies, I daresay. Aunt Agatha is such a treasure, to think of such matters."

"You see, that is what I like about you," Edgar said, flopping into an over-stuffed chair. "You are never out of humour, even when I get crotchety or Ralph growls at everyone or your house is invaded by a parcel of females. And the most astonishing thing is that you truly do not mind."

"Why should I mind my mother and sisters visiting me? I enjoy their company."

Edgar shook his head in disbelief. "Well, I do not, but I contrive to keep out of their way most of the time, so their presence does not distress me any more. How long do you suppose Ralph will be?"

"You know Ralph. He might be out all night. You had best not wait up for him," Ferdy said.

"But I could not sleep a wink. I should be lying in my bed listening to every passing footstep or distant cry, and imagining him being murdered for the sake of a few guineas."

Ferdy suppressed a sigh. "Then let us play piquet for a while. I might have a brandy myself, if we are staying up." He found cards, dragged a small table across to Edgar's chair, and then a chair for himself. "Here — you cut to decide the dealer."

They played for a little over an hour, and Ferdy was just wondering whether he would need to send for fresh candles when a slight noise was heard from below, and then the distinct click of the front door closing quietly.

"At last!" Edgar cried, jumping up and scattering cards. "Here he is!" He raced out onto the landing.

It was indeed Ralph, but not the immaculate, insouciant Ralph of earlier that evening. This Ralph had a face as black as thunder, and was drenched from head to toe.

When he saw them, he sighed. "So much for my hopes of returning undetected."

"Great heavens, whatever happened?" Edgar said. "Is it raining?"

"No, it is *not* raining, you imbecile," Ralph snarled. "I... got wet, that is all. Fell in the horse trough, if you *must* know. Things got a bit... physical, and several of the riffraff thought it would be amusing to put the nob in the water. But I know their faces! They will get their come-uppance. Dammit, I never imagined they would put one over on me. Glad you stayed up, are you? Now you can have a hearty laugh at my expense."

"Not laughing, dear boy," Edgar said. "Not amusing at all. Shocking thing to happen. You see, Ferdy? If I had stayed with Ralph as you suggested, that would have been my fate, too, and my lungs are so delicate."

Ralph laughed, but it was a harsh, brittle sound. "My lungs are not especially delicate, but it is damnably cold wearing wet clothes, I can tell you."

"Of course it is," Ferdy said. "Go upstairs at once and get stripped off, while I get someone to stoke up the kitchen fire and send up hot water."

"No, no, no! I want no fuss," Ralph said. "If the whole house knows of my misadventure, my humiliation will be complete. My man is discreet, and if you two can keep your mouths shut, no one else need know."

"Oh, of course, of course," Edgar said. "Not a word to a soul."

"You may depend upon our discretion," Ferdy said.

And with that, he doused the candles and they all went upstairs to their beds.

15: After The Ball

Fanny enjoyed the Easter ball quite as much as she had expected, given that she could not dance. She had had the most splendid view of the whole room from her perch on the dais, she had been surrounded by company all evening, and she had tried some of the food on offer, which was hearty, filling food but tasty. The punch had been rather too strong for her liking, so she had drunk only a few sips.

The shop, like many in the town, did not open the day after the Easter ball. Dr Hay and Miss Hay had gone out early to the hospital, and Lady Harriet had gone to visit her relations for the day, so Fanny had only old Mrs Hay for company. Fanny was very willing to make conversation with the old lady, but it was like walking uphill against a very stiff breeze.

"Are you warm enough, ma'am? WARM ENOUGH? Shall I BUILD UP THE FIRE? Is there a DRAFT FROM THE DOOR?"

"Who is at the door, dear?"

"No one. I was talking about THE FIRE."

"A buyer? Have they decided to sell, then?"

"No, ma'am, I meant—"

"It is so awkward. And now the lawyers have to sort it out. Would you ring the bell, dear? Tell William to put more coals on the fire. Such a dampness in the air today, but we will have snow before the week is out, mark my words."

"Snow? In April?" Fanny murmured, but she rang the bell, gave the orders and abandoned any further effort to communicate with Mrs Hay.

For a while she tried to write to Rosamund, but it was so awkward. She had written to tell her sisters that Mr Hawes had appeared in Sagborough, and she had told them about the Easter ball. Now they would be waiting to hear what had transpired, and although there was much that could be said, she could not mention Mr Hawes at all. What was there to say? That he had arrived late, and had not even sought her out? He had known that she would be there, he must have known where she would be, yet he had made not the slightest effort to find her. She had not expected him to sit out all the dances just because she herself could not yet dance, for that would be foolish, but she had expected some attention from him, if only the courtesy accorded to an acquaintance in a town where he was a stranger.

Of Miss Celia Drabble, she was determined to say nothing. It was perfectly natural that Mr Hawes should wish to dance, and perfectly natural also that he should be drawn to the most beautiful woman in the room. Fanny could not blame him for that, not in the least! But as to what it meant, she could not be certain and so it was better to say nothing at all. Having, therefore, nothing of great moment to impart to Rosamund, her pen stilled and eventually she laid it aside and took up her needlework instead. There was always solace to be found in perfectly placed stitches. Not that she was in need of solace, naturally, she reminded herself sharply. She was perfectly content, after all. What possible need could she have for solace?

When the doorbell rang, she was engrossed in a tricky section of the bodice, her needle flying, her mind fixed on the image of the finished gown, with Emmeline Malpas in it, drifting down a garden path in high summer beneath an arch of roses — cream roses, she hoped, for that would best set off this particular shade of pink. So when there was a knock at the door and William entered, she jumped in surprise.

"Are you at home, madam?" the footman said, proffering a salver to Mrs Hay.

"Oh," she said in a quavering voice as she read the cards. "Oh my. Do show them in, William."

The footman disappeared, and returned a few moments later. "Lady Craston, Lady Agatha Makenham, Miss Makenham, Miss Cordelia Makenham."

Suddenly the room was full of female voices, the swirl of velvet and worsted and bonnets with nodding feathers. Fanny jumped to her feet, sliding round the worktable to fix herself in an unobtrusive corner, out of the way. But after making their curtsies to Mrs Hay, the Miss Makenhams bore down on her and wrapped her in warm embraces, with the scent of jasmine and oleander, exactly as Rosamund wore, and Fanny's eyes filled with unaccustomed tears.

"So happy to see you..."

"... not a moment free last night..."

"... so sorry you could not dance, but..."

"... was it horrid, having to sit and watch everyone else enjoying the music?"

They stopped and looked at her, heads tipped to the side, waiting for her reply.

"Oh no, I was perfectly happy!" Fanny cried. "*Perfectly* happy. Never better entertained in my life."

Then she stumbled back onto a chair and broke into violent sobs.

They were so sympathetic. Pulling up chairs, they arranged themselves so that they all had their backs to the rest of the room, so as not to draw attention to Fanny, and then kept up a duet of murmured nothings, feeding her a supply of dry handkerchiefs, until she was a little more composed. Behind her, Fanny could hear Lady Craston and Lady Agatha conducting a shouted conversation with Mrs Hay, and having the same difficulties that she had had, and that made her laugh.

"There, that is better," Miss Makenham said. "You have a little more colour in your cheeks now, Miss Winterton. You poor, poor dear. Where is everyone? Why do they leave you here all alone with the old lady?"

"Oh, but that is *quite* all right, and I do not mind a bit, although it is a *little* difficult to talk to her, and I am not normally here anyway, except that just today the shop is closed. Lady Harriet has gone to call upon the marquess and marchioness, and Dr and Miss Hay have gone to the hospital, for she helps him with his work there sometimes. Miss Hay is very knowledgeable upon medical matters. Oh, I do beg your pardon. So foolish of me to become so tearful for no reason at all, except... except that you remind me of my sisters..." And that unleashed another flood of tears.

After a while, Lady Craston came over and chased her daughters away. "Go and help Agatha shout at Mrs Hay," she said cheerfully. "There now, dear, you look very peaky, and do not imagine you can pretend everything is going on swimmingly for it is painfully obvious that it is not. You should not be alone here with only an old lady for company, and I do not approve at all of you mixing with these women of Lady Harriet's. Are they in the shop with you?"

"Oh, no, no! They never go into the shop. Only Miss Monkton and Mrs Monkton, her mother, are in the shop. And Miss Kelly, sometimes. No, the... the *unfortunate* women are in the sewing room at the back."

"Ah! And you do not go in there, I hope?"

"Oh, yes, I do, quite often. When I am not needed in the shop, for Miss Monkton and Mrs Monkton manage most of the customers, but I am called in when there is a young lady, because I always wear the shop's gowns, you see, all made up, so that customers can see what is possible. But mostly I sit in the back room and sew, with the other seamstresses, and then we all walk home together. I beg your pardon, my lady, is that wrong of me? For Lady Harriet said—"

"Lady Harriet!" Lady Craston snapped. Fanny felt tears welling up again, but the viscountess went on in a softer tone, "No, no, I am not cross with you, child. Indeed, who could possibly be cross with you? Ferdy was quite right. No, you are doing just as you ought, and following Lady Harriet's instructions, I daresay. She has no younger sisters herself, so she does not appreciate— How old are you, child?"

"I am twenty, my lady."

"Twenty. Hmm. And as innocent as a babe newly born. Well, I shall speak to Lady Harriet and see if we cannot contrive some better arrangement."

"Oh, but I had much rather you did not!" Fanny cried in some alarm. "I *must* work, you see, otherwise I shall have to go to the poor house, or… or go and live with Rosamund as the poor relation that no one wants."

To her surprise, Lady Craston laughed. "I do not think it will come to *that*. You will have a husband before you are much older, that much is certain."

"Oh, no! No, no, no," Fanny cried in anguish. "I shall not marry just to escape being poor. That would be the most dreadful thing — so mercenary! I could not. And I do not know anyone suitable in my level of society, so you see, it is impossible, and I must do everything within my power to keep my employment."

Lady Craston gave her a strange look, and opened her mouth as if to speak, then closed it again, perhaps thinking better of it. Fanny was relieved. If only people would stop assuming that she would marry! She was sunk so low that no right-minded gentleman would want to marry her, and even if, by some miracle, a man might be found who was prepared to overlook such a disgraceful connection to his family, there was the question of love. She could never, ever marry without love.

Once again, the idea of marriage sent her thoughts skittering dangerously close to Mr Hawes. Well, she would not think about him! She was not in the least disappointed that he had so badly neglected her the previous evening... No, not *neglected*. She must not think that of him, for it implied some omission on his part, or some expectation on hers, and naturally there was nothing of the sort. He could not always pay her the sort of attention she had enjoyed at the dinner next door, when he had barely looked at another person all evening. Why, he had been quite— no, not ill-mannered towards the other guests, no, not at all. It was just the excitement of seeing a familiar face again, and now that they had caught up with all their news, he was no more to her than any other acquaintance, and she was *certainly* not disappointed... Not in the least disappointed... just a little puzzled, perhaps.

Lady Craston smiled, her head tipped to one side just as her daughters had done. Fanny had the feeling that some response was expected of her.

"I beg your pardon, my lady. I was... I was..."

The viscountess laughed, a deep, mellow rumble that Fanny found oddly comforting. Her ladyship was such a *maternal* figure. One felt quite easy with her, as if one had known her forever. As if she were one's own mother.

"You were wool-gathering, my dear. But no matter, it was nothing of consequence. Are you at home all day? Perhaps I shall send Ferdy round to amuse you. He is very good company, you know."

"Oh, yes, indeed he is! But pray do not if... I mean, he might have made other arrangements. He will not want to be sitting about watching me sew."

Lady Craston laughed again. "You are a sweet child, and I swear we shall have you married before the year is out, whether you anticipate it now or not. Good day to you, my dear."

~~~~~

Ferdy was very fond of his female relations, but four of them at breakfast was at least three too many. Aunt Agatha he could manage, because she talked only of what tasks she had planned for that day, and then swept away to do them as soon as she had finished eating. She usually left a list of tasks for him to accomplish too, but at least she gave him a little time to contemplate the day in silence.

There was no silence to be had with Emilia and Cordelia in the house. They talked unceasingly from the moment they woke until the moment they laid their heads on the same pillow at night, and neither of them had a sensible thought in their heads. At least, nothing that met Ferdy's idea of sensible thought. If they had discussed their gowns, or the most fashionable ways of dressing hair, or even the quality of various styles of umbrella, Ferdy might have felt that the breakfast hour was not entirely wasted. He might have been able to contribute to the conversation, and guide their minds into proper channels.

But no, all they could think of was books. Having dismissed the contents of his book room as *'stuffy old sermons and peculiar poetry'*, their first task on venturing onto the streets of Sagborough had been to take out subscriptions at the circulating library, and thither their feet directed them on an almost daily basis. And then they sat about reading aloud to each other, and discussing their reading constantly. It was incomprehensible to Ferdy, for what was there to say about books? Who needed more than the Bible, a prayer book, a peerage and perhaps, at a pinch, the collected works of Mr Shakespeare?

As soon as he could, therefore, he escaped the chatter and retreated to the sanctuary of his book room. Since Edgar and Ralph seldom rose before noon, he could be sure of some blessed quietness for a while. He had letters to write — there were always letters to write, for he had a great many relations who seemed to spend their lives quill in hand, and must all be replied to — but he was too restless for letter writing. He bethought himself of his mother's words, that a lady liked to have poetry written for her, and he knew there were poetry books on the shelves of his book room. Perhaps he could make use of all those books for once?

He pulled out a random selection, opened each of them at the shortest poem contained within, and sat down to study them. Now, study of any sort was not something that came naturally to Ferdy, but he persevered. Whenever he wavered and felt drawn to read the newspaper instead, he remembered Fanny's enchanting little face. Then he would smile and turn with renewed energy to the yellowed pages spread before him.

He worked for more than an hour, after which, feeling that he had grasped the essentials of the business, he drew forth a sheet of fresh paper, prepared a pen and settled down to write a poem. Immediately, he hit a problem. It was the custom to dedicate the poem to its intended recipient, but this was a puzzle. How to address his love? Not as *'Fanny'*, certainly. He did not yet have the right to use her Christian name. Yet *'Miss Frances Winterton'* seemed overly formal. And then, *'Miss Winterton'* was surely too abrupt a greeting.

In the end, he settled on the rather more discreet *'To a fair young lady of the poet's acquaintance'*, which sounded suitably romantic. He had no sooner written the words in his very best script before the dreadful thought occurred to him — was it too subtle? Would she even know that she was the subject of the poem? She might read it and suppose that it could not be about her, because her hair was dark, not fair. Would she understand that he meant that the whole of her was fair? It was a different word — or was it?

He threw down his pen in disgust. Poetry was far too difficult, and he had not yet written a single word of the poem itself.

Relief arrived in the person of Poole, bearing a card on a silver salver. "A Mr Roland Hawes to see you, sir. Are you at home?"

"Most definitely, Poole."

Ferdy jumped up from his seat at the desk and went out into the hall to greet his visitor and usher him into the book room. Madeira having been poured, pastries procured and the health of both parties established, Ferdy was about to progress to the weather, when Hawes gave a little cough, perhaps of embarrassment.

"I wonder, Mr Makenham, whether I might be so presumptuous as to ask your advice on a matter which has been concerning me rather, of late? Pray tell me at once if I am too impertinent, but I realised the instant I met you that you were a man of impeccable taste, and would fully understand every nuance of correct behaviour."

Ferdy was not impervious to such a glowing accolade. He inclined his head, and said, "Any advice I may be able to offer will be yours, Mr Hawes."

"You are most gracious, sir. How very generous of you! The problem... and here I anticipate your response, for I am certain you will tell me that such a matter is no concern of yours, but I have no father, no uncle, no brother to whom I might turn. I have no female relations, either, apart from one elderly aunt, but the female mind is too delicate, too sensitive to be brought to bear on weighty matters, I find. Apart from my dear mama, of course, but all *other* ladies are too easily distracted by surface considerations, are they not? For a proper, reasoned discussion of any matter, one must turn to a fellow gentleman."

"Oh, quite, quite," Ferdy said.

"And so it is that I make my humble request for counsel to your good self, sir, and trust that you will hear me out, I pray."

"By all means," Ferdy said, mellowing towards Hawes. Such reticence was a sign of proper feeling in a man, yet clearly he was in need of a friendly ear to hear his story. Ferdy had always been a good listener, and so he set down his Madeira glass, leaned back in his chair and prepared to listen.

"It is a matter of some delicacy," Hawes said. "It concerns a lady, one with whom you are acquainted."

For the first time, it crossed Ferdy's mind that he was placing himself in a position to receive confidences which he might not wish to hear. Yet he could not now easily draw back, and in moments, Hawes had realised his worst fears.

"In short, Mr Makenham, I wish to know whether you think I should marry Fanny Winterton."

16: *Morning Calls*

Ferdy froze. But he had no opportunity to collect his scattered wits to reply, for Hawes ploughed on, impervious.

"Not, you understand, that I expect you to say, *'Yes, you should marry Miss Winterton'* or *'No, you should give up the idea and look elsewhere'*, but you are a man of sophistication, Mr Makenham, who mingles with the greatest minds of our age, and must have a fair idea of the considerations which a man must undertake when approaching marriage. I reached the conclusion two years ago that I should marry, for my affairs are now in such good order that the estate may bear the extra expense of a wife. For a lady is an expense, is she not? It must be so, for a man must clothe her in sufficient style to enhance his position in society, and not skimp. And then there are children, and extra servants, and education to think of for the sons, and all of it a drain on one's purse. One must live within one's means, must one not?"

Ferdy had recovered himself sufficiently to murmur some agreement to this unexceptionable doctrine.

"So my primary concern," Hawes went on, "was to find a lady of means, one with a suitable dowry. Yet the very first lady to catch my eye was Miss Fanny Winterton. How large was her dowry? Who could say? Not her father, certainly. My tentative enquiries led me to suppose that there would be little to spare for any of the daughters, for the father was quite rolled up. All to pieces, so it was said. Yet Miss Winterton was so charming in her person, so appealing to my inexperienced eyes that I was drawn in, and it is not boastful of me, I flatter myself, to observe that I could well afford to take a wife with the most modest of dowries. My financial situation is such that it could be done without undue economy."

He paused here, presumably to be congratulated. "It is fortunate indeed where such is the case," Ferdy managed.

"Indeed. There are many far wealthier than I who could not say as much, but I have always been a careful manager of my money, just as my mama taught me. So that course was open to me, yet still I hesitated. Miss Winterton is quite delightful, of course — well, you are yourself acquainted with her, so you are familiar with her many attractions—"

"She is a most charming person," Ferdy said with some feeling.

"—so you will appreciate how torn I was. And was I, perhaps, misled by the constrained nature of society in Brinshire? In a wider society, Miss Fanny Winterton of Woodside might appear to less advantage. I took the audacious step of travelling to Hampshire, the better to make a judgement on my future."

"Indeed?" Ferdy said, becoming irritated by this disparagement of Fanny's manifold charms. Appear to less advantage, indeed! As if her star could shine less brightly even in the most exalted company. He disliked the man more with every minute that passed. But good manners kept his voice level. "And how did Hampshire answer?"

"Not at all," Hawes said in sorrowful tones. "The society there was even thinner than in Brinshire. If I had wanted an elderly widow, I could have had my choice of them, but as for the young females... no, it did not answer. I returned to Brinshire determined to make Miss Fanny mistress of Kellingborough. But the rumours about her father's position were flying, and then he died and set all to rest. Did I wish the name of Hawes to be associated with such mismanagement? I could not do it. My mother would never have approved such a union, and that must be my best guide, naturally."

"Naturally," Ferdy said tersely, tiring of this recital.

"However, once she was no longer before me, thoughts of Miss Winterton would keep intruding into my mind. Was she as attractive as memory made her? I resolved to seek her out, and indeed it was so. The sweetest young lady it had ever been my pleasure to meet."

"Indeed she is!" Ferdy cried.

"But then, a rare piece of good fortune. You introduced me to not one, but two jewels beyond price, Mr Makenham. Miss Drabble is the most beautiful creature I ever beheld, and then there is Miss Trivers, who is very pretty also, and an heiress to a substantial fortune. So you see my dilemma, sir. Which of the three would be the most suitable to be mistress of Kellingborough, a property of some substance, though I say so myself? Which of the three would best enhance my position in society? The beauty who would grace my dining table with her presence and give me magnificent children? Or the heiress who would secure my finances and do away with all worries of that nature? Or Fanny, who is well-bred and pliable, but has neither wealth nor great beauty? Do you see the difficulty? What is your advice? How may I choose between them?"

Ferdy had never been one to allow his temper to control him, and indeed little ever ruffled his serenity, but his wrath was great at these words. He dared not let his anger show, however, for it might have exactly the wrong effect. Oh, how tempting it was to steer Hawes away from Fanny! It would take but a few words, to suggest that perhaps Miss Trivers' dowry should be his object, or Miss Drabble's beauty. Hawes was sufficiently in thrall to Ferdy that perhaps it would do the trick.

But there was Fanny herself to consider. He could not forget her sweet face turned towards Hawes with such happiness in it. If she were truly in love with him, then it would be wrong of him, very wrong, to take any steps to turn Hawes away from her. And if, in the end, Hawes should make his offer, it would be from love, nothing but love, for he had made it very plain that nothing else drew him to her, and if so, he would cherish her as she ought to be cherished.

So even as he shrivelled a little inside at the thought of Fanny's happiness depending on this self-centred man, Ferdy composed himself and said with tolerable equanimity, "You honour me with your confidences, Hawes, but I regret that I cannot advise you."

"Oh," Hawes said, in surprise. "You disappoint me, sir. I had thought you a man of some perspicacity."

Ferdy could think of no better answer than the truth. "I cannot advise you because I am not a disinterested party."

"Not a—? Oh! Then you want one of them for yourself? I may as well go home at once then." He laughed, not seeming put out by this. "Why, the heir to a title and a fine fortune into the bargain — mine is nothing to it, nothing at all. None of the ladies will look at *me* if the Honourable Ferdinand Makenham is hanging out for a wife. Is that why you are here, then? To find yourself a wife? When you have all of London at your feet, I daresay? Hmpf. But there are some good fortunes to be picked up here in the north, and you need not look for a title, I suppose, so you scoop up an heiress. Miss Trivers, then, is the lady. I thank you for your frankness, sir, and it makes my dilemma a little less tricky. But you need not fear that I will interfere with your plans. Miss Trivers is yours."

Ferdy jumped to his feet, too angry now to mind his words. "Mr Hawes, you malign all three ladies if you suppose that any one of them would be mine for the taking, or yours, for that matter. Not every young lady is so dazzled by a man's prospects that she will marry him regardless of character or principle or affection. If you truly want my advice, then it is this — choose the lady you love the best, the one you want to spend the rest of your life with, and then see if she will have you. That is all."

"Love?" Hawes said, bewildered. "You would rest your whole future on so ephemeral a sentiment as love? Surely marriage is a matter of the utmost seriousness, to be undertaken only after the most careful consideration? It is a matter of prudence, or so my mama was wont to say. Prudence at all times and in all things, that was her maxim, and one which I follow to this day. It has stood me in good stead."

"Then your mama—" Ferdy began hotly, but at once stopped himself. It was the height of bad manners to criticise a man's mother, no matter the provocation. "Your mama sounds like a sensible lady. You should take her advice, not mine."

"Ah, if she were still on this earthly plane, I would do so," he said sorrowfully. "She left me alone in the world twelve years ago last November, and I feel her loss keenly, you may be sure. Poor Mama! Yes, she would tell me to be prudent, no doubt about it." He laughed, then, and the sound grated on Ferdy's nerves. "*You* may speak of love, if you like, Mr Makenham, for a future earl may marry without much regard for prudence, but most men are not so fortunate. Well, prudence would suggest Miss Trivers, but if you have already selected her... I mean, fallen in love with her—"

"Do not consider any words of mine when you make your choice," Ferdy said hastily. "If prudence suggests Miss Trivers... in fact, if you feel that your late lamented parent would approve Miss Trivers, then by all means pay your addresses to her. I would not for the world stand between you and your mama's choice of bride."

"Well now, that is very magnanimous of you," Hawes said, draining his Madeira and rising to his feet. "Not that I am sure that Mama *would* have approved of her, to be sure, being so close to trade as she is. Perhaps Miss Winterton—"

Ferdy could listen no more to Hawes' disordered maunderings. "You will forgive me, but I have... business matters to attend to," he said wildly, hoping Hawes would not notice the desk spread with poetry books.

"Of course, of course! So obliging of you to give me so much of your valuable time. With such condescension, such affability, you will be such an asset to the ranks of the nobility when your time comes,

Mr Makenham. I am proud to number you amongst my acquaintance. Never shall I forget your kindness to a stranger…"

Ferdy rang the bell, and to his infinite relief Poole appeared instantly. "Mr Hawes is leaving now, Poole."

"…on that day. I cannot sufficiently express my gratitude…"

"Good day to you, Hawes. Thank you for calling." He followed Hawes out into the hall, where one of the footmen impassively helped him on with his greatcoat and another handed him his hat and gloves, while the butler ushered him through the front door.

"…such good breeding! Never seen the like!" Hawes cried, peering round Poole's imposing bulk. "So kind! So very—" Poole gently closed the front door on him.

"If he ever calls again, I am *not* at home," Ferdy said, before storming back into the book room and slamming the door.

For several minutes, he paced about the room, fuming. Eventually, catching sight of his glowering countenance in an ill-placed mirror, he laughed at himself and picked up the latest London newspaper as a distraction. It was full of the early arrivals for the season, their balls and card parties and pleasure outings. It was the first time in years that he would not be numbered amongst the crowds thronging Almack's, and he was smitten with longing to be there, to dance properly again, to be part of the glittering London season. Then he remembered Fanny's dark eyes gazing at him, and her lovely smile, and ruthlessly he set the idea aside. Next year, he would go to London. Next year, he might be able to take his wife with him.

A sharp rat-a-tat-tat on the door was instantly followed by his mama's anxious face, still in her outdoor bonnet.

"Are you all right, dear? Poole said… I am certain he must be mistaken, but he said you had *slammed the door!* Can this be true?"

Ferdy gave a rueful smile. "I believe I did shut the door rather forcefully."

"Oh, Ferdy! Whatever has happened? I have never known you to get upset to the extent of... of *violence*, even against a door. You were always the most mild-mannered of my children. Never gave me the least concern, not like— Well, that is neither here nor there, and she is safely married now, and Rufus may have the taming of her. But *you!* Ferdy, this is not like you."

"It is not, but it is all over now. Will you take a little Madeira? There may be some ratafia about the house. Or tea? Tea would set you up perfectly."

"Brandy," she said crisply, flopping into a chair and untying the ribbons of her bonnet. "A large measure. Upon my soul, Ferdy, I was quite worried for a moment. Whatever happened?"

"I have had Mr Hawes here, that is what has happened." Even as he spoke, Ferdy felt his anger building again.

"Oh no!" his mother said distressfully. "He is not betrothed to Miss Winterton?"

"No, no! Nothing of the sort," he said, handing his mother her brandy. "He only came to talk, and I cannot tell you about it for it was all in confidence. But he said such things about her, Mama!"

"Oh. Disparaging things?"

"Yes! Not... not insulting, exactly, but he does not appreciate her as he should. He spoke of her — of all of them — as though he were wanting to buy a *horse*. Good breeding, magnificent children, that sort of thing. Oh pray forget I spoke! It was all said in the strictest confidence."

"All of them? He has other candidates?" she said thoughtfully. "Miss Drabble, perhaps. He seemed very attentive last night."

Ferdy opened his mouth to speak, and then closed it again.

"Yes, yes, I quite understand," Lady Craston said. "You cannot betray a confidence. Who else might he have met? Miss Malpas? Ah, no. Miss Trivers, then? I can see by your face that I am nearer the mark. Oh! He is not setting his sights on Emilia or Cordelia? Surely not!"

"He did not mention either of them, but I am sure that they will make their way onto his list, just as soon as he discovers the size of their dowries."

"Well, he is welcome to try," his mother said, with an easy laugh. "But if he has not yet spoken to Fanny, there is still time. You must fight for her, Ferdy!"

He heaved a great sigh, hurled himself into a chair, then sprang up and poured himself a brandy. "I am not much for fighting, Mama," he said forlornly. "Never have been. The sight of blood makes me feel sick, and as for men hitting each other — no, I could not."

She laughed again, and her comfortable presence reassured him. If she were not cast down by Hawes' behaviour, then Ferdy need not be either. Hawes was not the only man to respect his mama's opinion.

"Ferdy, no one expects you to call Hawes out or anything of that nature. You are far too sensible to fight a duel over Miss Winterton. Or for any reason, I am sure. No, all I mean is that you must not give way to despair. If this Hawes fellow is dithering, then you have a chance to snaffle the prize from under his nose."

"Fanny is not a prize to be snaffled, Mama," he said gently. "She has a mind of her own, and if her heart is set on Hawes, I would not stand in her way. Her happiness is more important than my own."

"Oh, Ferdy, what a kind soul you are! But this is not a moment to stand aside in gentlemanly fashion. Fanny is not betrothed, and there is all still to play for, and do not look at me in that speaking way, for heaven's sake! I know it is not a game and she is not a prize and so forth, but if you want her, then you must do something about it."

"I have been trying to write poetry, but I am not sure it will answer," he said gloomily.

Again his mother laughed. "Oh, forget poetry. You do not need poetry to make yourself attractive to the fair sex. You have so much address that all you need to do is to be your usual charming self. Why not go and see her now? She is alone with the old lady."

"She is at home? Now?"

"Certainly she is, for we have just been there. Off you go now and bear her company for a while. You may cheer her up, poor thing, for she was very low when we saw her, and you will be just what she needs to lift her spirits."

Ferdy needed no second bidding. With only the time taken to change his clothing from top to toe and add a greatcoat, hat, gloves and cane, he was ready to step outside his own front door, walk a few yards along the street and up the steps to number Twenty-Six. A bitter wind swirled around him, but he disregarded it, warmed inside by the prospect of seeing Fanny, his dear, sweet Fanny, in a very few minutes.

17: Sketches And Sleeves

Inside the door of number Twenty-Six, there was the business of cards and the footman ponderously climbing the stairs, then the welcome news that the ladies would receive him, after which he could hand over his outer garments and climb the stairs himself. He was announced, he entered the room and there she was.

Slate grey was her colour today, a simple round gown in some kind of jaconet or cambric, very plain but trimmed with twisted black ribbons about the bodice and sleeves which lifted it from the ranks of dullness to tasteful restraint. He could only admire her sense of fashion and decorum.

He made his bows to the ladies, and Fanny rose to curtsy to him. Then he turned to Mrs Hay and Fanny sat down at her worktable again and took up her sewing. Her chair was set at an angle to him, so even as he shouted his polite nothings at the old lady, he could enjoy watching Fanny's profile as she worked.

Ferdy managed five long minutes with Mrs Hay before he felt that duty had been done and he could escape to the worktable and draw up a chair beside Fanny. A pair of footmen appeared with trays of refreshments. He chose a glass of Madeira and a macaroon, but she refused everything.

"Will you not join me in a glass of something?" he said gently. "You work so hard that you should keep up your strength."

"Oh, how considerate you are, Mr Makenham, but be assured that I am not over-worked nor do I need to recruit my strength. I shall partake of a substantial dinner later, and we eat early here, so there is no danger of starvation. But how are you? Did the dancing wear you out last night?"

"Not at all. I did not stay long after you had left."

"I daresay such an evening is very tame to you, who must be used to the finest company. How delightful it must be to dance at Almack's, with the ladies in their London silks and jewels, and the gentlemen all dressed as fine as you were last night. How I should love to see *that*."

Her face was alight with enthusiasm, her eyes luminous and shimmering. *'The gentlemen dressed as fine as you were last night.'* For a moment, his breath caught in his throat and words failed him. He had hoped he was past that stage of helpless inarticulacy with her, but sometimes she took him by surprise. Wildly, he stumbled upon the first thing that caught his eye, the partly-finished gown spread out on the worktable.

"What are you working on? Is it for yourself?" It was a foolish remark, for it was a fine gold silk, not at all suited to her delicate complexion, even had she not been in mourning.

"No, it is for Miss Malpas. Is it not the perfect colour for her colouring? Her mama will insist on putting her in pink — I do not know why so many mamas think their daughters look well in pale pink, for very few of them truly do. This is much more the thing, and if I can dissuade her away from quite so many diamonds, she will look lovely."

"It is a beautiful silk," he said, running a little of it through his fingers appreciatively. "Lady Carrbridge wore something very like it last season, with a white sarsnet over-gown embroidered with tiny birds in gold thread and spangles — very striking."

"I do not think I can manage birds," Fanny said thoughtfully. "Margaret is the one who does all the delicate embroidery, and

Annabelle is clever at trimming bonnets, when one can prise her books from her hands."

"And the other two?" he said, thrilled by these disclosures.

"Lucy..." She laughed suddenly, and the room seemed filled with warmth. "Lucy talks too much ever to make anything. And Rosamund has never needed to. She can put on anything, and look well in it. Once, she needed a ball gown in a hurry, for there was something wrong with every one she had and no time to make anything new, so she found an old one of Mama's, quite five years out of date, and she looked lovely. Rosamund always looks lovely. There!" She spread the gown out on the table. "I have finished the bodice, all but the final fitting, but I cannot decide what to do with the sleeves. I was going to overlay the fabric, like so—" She gathered up a piece of fabric and twisted it about, but it sprang apart again. "You see, the silk will not lie well that way, so I shall have to think again."

"There was a very pretty type of sleeve I saw once or twice last season that might work," he said, pulling out his notebook and a pencil. With a few quick strokes of the pen, he drew a different kind of sleeve. "There! Do you see how it goes? It is a little fuller, but it might work."

"Oh yes! That would do very well." She pulled the fabric into a different arrangement. "Like so? Yes, I could manage that. Thank you, Mr Makenham! How knowledgeable you are. The fashion journals are hard to understand, sometimes, and there is no one at the shop who can offer suggestions, but you draw so clearly. I am so glad you called today."

Again he found himself breathless. "I... I am pleased to find you at home, Miss Winterton. You are not often here."

"Oh no, but the shop always closes the day after the ball, so I am here all morning, and I can still do my work, of course. I should not like to be idle, but it is very pleasant to have someone to talk to. It is such a kindness in you to call, and Lady Craston and Lady Agatha and the Miss Makenhams, too. Such a pleasure to see them, so kind as they are. Except that... except that your sisters... they reminded me a little of my own sisters, and... and I was a little tearful, but your mama was so, so kind to me."

Her eyes filled with tears even as she spoke, and Ferdy was overwhelmed with a desire to sweep her into his arms and hold her close to cry on his shoulder until she felt better. If only he could! One day, perhaps, he would have that right, but not today.

"You must miss them very much," he said softly. "And your home, where you lived for many years, I daresay."

"All my life," she whispered. "I was born at Woodside." One stray tear trailed forlornly down the softness of her cheek. "But I must not repine," she went on, straightening her back. "I am very lucky to have such good friends and congenial employment. There is nothing at all to cry about, and crying never made anything better. So Rosamund says."

"Missing one's home — one's family — is perfectly natural," he said quietly. "When I went away to school, I was appallingly lonely, just at first. I was only a weekly boarder, but even so, everything was strange and harsh and... and no one cared. I was just another miserable schoolboy. I managed almost two years before Mama decided that I was better off at home. There were tutors after that, but I have never forgotten the wretchedness of being away from home for the first time."

Her eyes were huge. "Oh, yes! It is very miserable, and even though one knows it must be so and it is all for the best, one cannot help but wish it had not been necessary."

"It does get easier, Miss Winterton. With every day that passes, the misery recedes a little and one's new surroundings become familiar and comfortable. This sense of loss will pass, in time."

"Oh but... two years, you said. And you were still unhappy, or you would not have gone home."

"Ah, no, I was happy enough at school by then, except for the bookwork. I have never had much aptitude for book learning. The words will not behave themselves, somehow, especially Latin words. No, there were... other reasons that necessitating my leaving." He flushed uncomfortably.

"I see. Pray forgive me, I did not mean to pry," she said. "Would you like a little more Madeira, Mr Makenham?"

His glass was empty. How had that happened? "If you will take some too, Miss Winterton."

She smiled, and his heart turned an alarming somersault. "Madeira in the morning is apt to make my head ache, but perhaps a macaroon..." She jumped up and carried his glass to the sideboard where the trays had been left, refilled his glass and returned with both the glass and a plate of macaroons. He sipped and she nibbled, her needle set aside for once, their chairs not two feet apart.

Ferdy had the most extraordinary sensation of lightness, as if he had been wandering through a great mansion of many rooms, all of them cold and empty and austere, but now he had found one filled with warmth and light and joy and bright colour. There was a rightness in his world such as he had never experienced before. Fanny was not just another pretty young woman moving through his life for a brief time, coming closer, then passing by and moving away again, like a partner in the dance. There was some indefinable connection that bound them together. Ferdy was not a fanciful man, and he was certainly not poetic, but he knew that he had crossed an invisible threshold and the moment needed acknowledgement.

He set down his glass and cleared his throat. "The second year at school, there were some boys there, ones I had not encountered before, or perhaps had never noticed. They took me in dislike, for some reason. At first it was just words. They taunted me, called me names, that sort of thing. Then it was pushing and shoving. My clothes were damaged, my shoes disappeared one day. It was a challenge, and if I had... asserted myself, fought back, I imagine I would have won their respect and they would have left me alone. But I am not that kind of person. It is an abomination to me, such behaviour. My parents taught me to be unfailingly polite, and the habit is hard to break. Eventually they got rougher, and when I went home one day, Nurse saw the bruises and told Mama and that was the end of it."

Her eyes were wide, the macaroon suspended halfway to her mouth, quite forgotten. "But that is dreadful! Such contemptible behaviour! Everyone is entitled to be free from such obnoxious people. Were they punished, those wicked boys?"

He smiled wanly at her outrage. "No. I simply left the school, and no one asked why. It is… not unusual in schools."

"Were you not afraid of them?"

"Of course! It was terrifying, but… there was not much to be done about it, except to endure. That is all any of us can do, when life is miserable."

She nodded, gazing at him in concern, the macaroon forgotten. "How brave you are! But why would anyone do such a thing?"

Impossible to answer that fully. He would probably never reveal the truth — how it had all started when Edgar had joined Ferdy at the school. Poor Edgar! He had been the early target, and the bullies had turned on Ferdy when he had remonstrated with them. And Ferdy had simply refused to fight, accepting whatever pummelling they chose to inflict. He had no older brother to protect him, and Ralph had already left to go to Harrow. Such an odd, helpless feeling to be so treated, and yet there was the satisfaction of not showing his tormentors the least sign of fear.

"Who can say?" he said with as much lightness as he could manage. "I had my revenge later when we met again in town. Two of them applied to join one of my clubs, and I saw to it that they were blackballed, and perhaps they did not receive as many invitations as they expected to the most prestigious occasions." He smiled a little.

"If one makes an enemy of the grandson of an earl, one must expect certain consequences. I have always been very good *ton*."

"Oh, yes, I am sure you are!" she cried in her artless way. "You always know just how to go on in every company, and in London you must be a person of the greatest consequence. How splendid it must be to mingle with all those elegant people, and you as fine as any of them. I had thought my brother-in-law, Mr Robin Dalton, the best dressed gentleman of my acquaintance, until I met you. You must know Mr Brummell, too. Does he dress as well as you do?"

Ferdy was absurdly pleased at this tribute, but he declaimed any superiority over Brummell. "Perhaps one day you will meet him and judge for yourself," he said gravely. "Many think he dresses too plain, his coats too dark and severe, but I admire his style greatly."

"Then I am sure I should too," she said with the utmost simplicity.

He inclined his head in acknowledgement, although he felt sure she truly meant it, and was not merely paying him an empty compliment. She was the most enchanting creature, and he was dizzy with love for her.

The clock struck the hour and she jumped up. "Oh no! It is five o'clock already. I must wake Mrs Hay and then go and dress for dinner, for Mrs Hay's maid very kindly attends me and I should not like to delay her."

"Upon my soul, is it so late?" Ferdy said, standing too. "You must be wishing me long gone. How rag-mannered of me to overstay my welcome. Pray forgive me."

She smiled so prettily that his heart, already unsteady, lurched even more. "Oh no! Nothing you do could possibly be *rag-mannered!* It has been such a pleasure to talk to you, Mr Makenham. I am so glad you came."

With a very few more words of farewell to the two ladies, Ferdy went downstairs and collected his hat, gloves, coat and cane from the footman, the man's face clouded with disapproval of a gentleman who stayed more than the prescribed half hour on a morning call. Ferdy beamed at him, bade him a cheery "Good day, my good fellow," and walked the few paces back to his own front door. A few flakes of snow drifted about his shoulders, but that just made him smile even more broadly. He cared nothing for snow, for Fanny thought him the best dressed man she knew! She valued his opinion! Nothing he did could possibly be rag-mannered! She even thought him brave! No one in his whole life had ever thought him brave before. Ferdy was euphoric.

~~~~~

The snow fell in earnest all evening and was still falling the next morning. Ferdy made discreet enquiries about his neighbours through the servants, and discovered that although Dr Hay had gone to the hospital as usual, all the ladies were at home. Accordingly, he felt drawn to pay another morning call at number Twenty-Six, to enquire if the ladies had need of his services to obtain urgent provisions, in view of the adverse weather.

Lady Harriet raised an imperious eyebrow. "Really, Mr Makenham, if we were starving to death, we might contrive to send the footman out to procure some stale bread or rat-bitten cheese rind."

He smiled, his good-humour unimpaired. "So you would, Lady Harriet, and indeed, it would inconvenience my valets greatly if I were to struggle through a foot of snow to obtain such delights for you. My boots would be quite ruined."

"The damp air might soften your neckcloth, too," she said, shaking her head at him.

"That would never do," Ferdy said with mock horror. "On second thoughts, you are quite right — it should not be attempted. My offer is withdrawn forthwith. I shall endeavour to be an agreeable guest by making polite conversation instead. Shall we talk about the weather?"

She laughed outright at that. "Pray do not, for it makes me cross, since it delays my departure for London. Snow in April — who ever heard of such a thing? Yorkshire is such an abominable place to live. At least this troublesome weather cannot be of long duration. We are too close to spring for any lengthy freeze. But you need not play the part of an agreeable guest with me. Go and talk to Fanny, Mr Makenham, or draw some more sleeves for her, for we have heard nothing since yesterday but of your kindness in helping her and your skill with a pencil."

Ferdy was very ready to do as he was bid, and having carefully arranged beforehand that the inhabitants of number Twenty-Five would call at set intervals during the morning, so that there was a constant coming and going, he contrived to sit unnoticed in quiet conversation with Fanny for more than an hour before good manners and Lady Harriet's pointed remarks drove him back to his own house.

The following day they were still snowed up, but his mother sent a note next door inviting the Hay ladies and Fanny to join the Makenham ladies to while away the hours. Edgar and Ralph soon had card tables going, but Fanny sat with her sewing and Ferdy was seldom far from her side. Never had he been happier, and especially so as no sign was seen of the dithering Mr Hawes.

Snow in April could not last for long, however. On the third day, the sun was out, the melt was underway and Fanny had to return to her duties at the shop. The streets had been cleared to some extent, but were still filthy with mud and slush, so the carriage was called to convey her to the shop and return her in the middle of the afternoon. Ferdy, his chair lodged near the window of his book room, observed her departure and return covertly from behind the curtain. It was too soon to pay another visit, and the next day was Sunday, but perhaps he could go on Monday, if she returned early again, or else he would resort to the circulating library once more. He could not bear to pass three days together without talking to her.

But late that afternoon, Ferdy was sitting, rather bored, in the morning room and just beginning to think about dressing for dinner and pondering which waistcoat to wear, when there was a loud knocking at the front door, followed almost at once by an agitated jangle of the bell. Poole's voice could be heard murmuring in the hall, and then another voice, high with distress... a very familiar voice.

Ferdy tore out of the morning room and down the stairs.

"Miss Winterton? Whatever is the matter?"

"Oh, Mr Makenham, I am so glad to see you! Please, please will you help me?"

"In any way that I can. Will you come upstairs? The ladies are all in the morning room."

"No, no, it is you that I need. Something dreadful has happened, I am sure, and I need your help. I am sure you will be able to help me. I know I can depend upon you, Mr Makenham."

"Of course you may, but tell me what has occurred."

"It is Martha!"

"Martha? Who is Martha? One of your friends?"

"Yes... well, no, not really. She is one of the housemaids, and she has vanished, completely vanished. She has not been seen since the night of the ball, and she could be lying injured somewhere and no one seems to *care,* but I must do something, and if you will not help me I shall look for her myself."

And then she burst into tears.

18: Searching (May)

Fanny allowed herself to be led upstairs and wrapped in Lady Craston's kindly arms. "*Do* come in, dear, and tell us what the problem is."

"But there is no time to be lost!" she wailed. "Martha could be lying injured somewhere. I must find her!"

A handkerchief was thrust into her hand. "Dry your tears, Miss Winterton," Mr Makenham said. "Take a deep breath to steady yourself... and another... and now tell us all about it, slowly and clearly. We must hear everything first, and then we will decide what is best to be done."

His calm voice was infinitely reassuring, as she had known it would be. Her first thought had been that Ferdy would know what to do, that he would help her, and she had not been wrong. So she perched awkwardly on the edge of a chair, taking deep breaths as instructed, which did indeed steady her. He always knew what was best! It was such a comfort to have him there. The others in the room — the ladies, Mr Brant and Mr Ralph Makenham — looked concerned, but it was Ferdy who knelt beside her chair stroking her hand, exuding calm encouragement. Another deep breath, and then she plunged into her story.

"Martha was helping at the ball at the Carrbridge Arms," she began. "Serving drinks and so on. A little extra money, she said, and a whole day off afterwards. She did not return to the house that night, but everyone assumed she had gone to Westbury House to see her little boy. Then the snow came and no one worried, for surely she had stayed there, safe and sound. But the shop reopened today and the women who came from Westbury House said that she had not been there. They assumed that she was here in Harlington Terrace. Everyone thought she was somewhere else, so no one looked for her until today. Miss Kelly has asked everywhere in Sagborough that Martha might have gone, but no one has seen her. The last time anyone saw her was at the ball, and I am sure some dreadful accident has befallen her. Will you help me to look for her?"

Mr Makenham nodded, but it was Mr Ralph who spoke. "This girl is in the Hay household, so it is for Dr Hay to search for her, is it not?"

"But he will not!" Fanny cried in distress. "He says that she is a grown woman and may go away if she pleases and he will do nothing, and Lady Harriet and Miss Hay agree with him, but she would not go away, I am sure of it, not without giving notice. She had a good place and she was glad of it, and she would not leave her son behind at Westbury House."

"What about her husband?" Miss Cordelia said, puzzled. "She must be married if she has a son."

"Widowed," Lady Craston said firmly, with a little shake of her head towards Fanny. She remembered then that a young lady like Miss Cordelia should know nothing of such matters. Fanny herself should know nothing of such matters, in fact, and it made her sad to think that she now moved amongst women who could not be openly spoken of in respectable circles. Perhaps that was why Dr Hay would not search for Martha, because she was a fallen woman and not worthy of such concern.

"It is very wrong of Dr Hay to make no effort to find Martha," Mr Makenham said, with a little frown. "She is in his care and he has a responsibility towards her. There must be a search for her, at least, and if he will not undertake it, I shall."

"Lord, Ferdy, ten to one Hay is right," Mr Ralph said. "There are all sorts of strangers in town for an event like the Easter ball, and the girl probably took the chance to move on. There were Romanies on the York road—"

"Martha would not go off with the Romanies!" Fanny cried hotly.

"—and any amount of odd types on the canal, and hanging around the streets. Maybe she met someone she knew, or decided to return to her former home."

"She would never abandon her child," Fanny said.

"But still, to imagine her lying injured!" Mr Ralph said scornfully. "You have too vivid an imagination, Miss Winterton. I am sure your friend is perfectly safe. There was a great deal of ale and punch consumed that night, and any number of people needing to sleep off an over-indulgence."

"Not for three days," Mr Makenham said sharply. "This is unhelpful, Ralph. Where is Poole? Ah, there you are. Tell Wrackham I want my oldest coat and boots right away, and have Hill and Crouch ready to accompany me in five minutes."

"Right away, sir?" Poole said, blanching. "Mr Wrackham will not like that, sir."

"Yes, right away, immediately, *this minute*," Mr Makenham said tersely, "and if Wrackham feels it beneath his dignity to follow my explicit orders he has my permission to find himself another post. This is an emergency, Poole."

"Very good, sir." But he looked unconvinced that Wrackham would understand the urgency.

"Now then, who is coming with me?" Mr Makenham said. "Ralph? Edgar?"

"My chest, Ferdy, my chest!" Mr Brant protested in faint tones.

Mr Ralph laughed. "Really, Ferdy, what is the haste? Report the matter to the constables in the morning, if you must, but it is madness to be scrambling about in knee-deep snow at the drop of a hat. Are you planning to miss dinner on account of this disappeared nobody?"

"Of course, if need be, and if you ever again suggest that any person, however lowly, is *nobody* then you are no friend of mine. Miss Winterton, do you go back to number Twenty-Six now and I will report my findings to you later this evening."

"Oh, but I will come with you! I know the ways Martha might have taken."

"Then you shall explain them to me before you go, but you will not, under any circumstances, take any part in the search for your friend. No, no arguments, if you please. I insist upon this."

"You are very good, sir, and I am so very sorry to be a trouble to you."

His serious expression lightened for a moment and his voice was softer as he answered, "Not the least trouble in the world, I assure you, if it will alleviate your worry somewhat. If your friend is anywhere to be found, then I shall find her, you may be sure."

With that Fanny had to be satisfied. *'If your friend is anywhere to be found...'* And what if she were not? Fanny shivered.

Later that evening, she was called out of the drawing room by William. "Mr Makenham is wishful to speak to you," he said, with an audible sniff. "Downstairs. Says he won't come up to the drawing room."

When she saw the state of him, Fanny was horrified. His boots and the hem of his greatcoat were a foot deep in mud, at least, and he was spattered from head to toe with more. But he bowed in correct form, as if he were every bit as immaculate as usual.

"Pray forgive my unkempt appearance, Miss Winterton, but I wished you to know at once that I have found no sign of Miss Smith, and it is too dark to continue this evening. Besides, I have the canal path to search next, and I should not care to miss my footing and fall in, not when the water must be quite freezing."

"Oh, dear! You are all goodness, Mr Makenham. I am so sorry! How uncomfortable you must be, when you are always so very particular about your appearance. I am dreadfully sorry."

"Gracious me, I do not regard a little dirt," he said, with a sudden smile of such sweetness that Fanny could not help smiling back. "I shall continue in the morning, as soon as there is light enough to see by."

"Oh, how *kind* you are," she said, resting one hand on the sodden sleeve of his coat.

"Do not come too close," he said in alarm, taking a step back. "My coat is of no account, but I should not like to stain such a beautiful gown. That colour suits you admirably, Miss Winterton."

She blushed then, seeing the admiration in his eyes, but said composedly, "Thank you, sir, but pray do not linger here talking to me. Go home and get out of those wet clothes as soon as may be. I only hope you may not catch a chill."

"I am never ill," he said, with another smile, but he bowed and made his farewells promptly, leaving no trace of his presence but a muddy mark on the hall rug, which William eyed disapprovingly.

~~~~~

For three days, as the snow was replaced by steady, bone-chilling rain and every path was mired to bog, Ferdy searched high and low for Martha. One morning he took Ralph with him, and another time it was Bridget Kelly. Lady Harriet, seeing that he was truly concerned, contributed her footman to the search. Ferdy enquired at every inn and tap-room in Sagborough and round about. He asked the gossipy ostlers at the post-houses, and he asked the taciturn bargemen, but no one had seen any sign of Martha. He told the whole to the constables, and dragged them along on his travels too. But in the end he was obliged to give it up.

"I am very sorry, Miss Winterton, but your friend has vanished without trace. I can do no more. The constables know all, so they will continue to make enquiries as they go about their business, but for myself I have exhausted all possibilities. I wish it could be otherwise, but regrettably I cannot give you any better news. All I can say with certainty is that, while I have not discovered any sign of Miss Smith, it is also true that I have uncovered no evidence that she has come to harm. That, I hope, brings you some comfort."

"Oh yes, and I thank you from the bottom of my heart for all that you have done. You have left no stone unturned, and it is not for want of trying that Martha could not be found."

"No, indeed," Lady Craston said, for they were sitting in the morning room of number Twenty-Five. "No one could have done more, Ferdy. But wherever the poor girl is, she is beyond reach. You must give it up now."

"But where could she have got to?" he said fretfully. "She must be somewhere."

"People do go missing, you know, dear," Lady Craston said. "It happens all the time."

"But how?"

Ralph said in a lazy drawl, "She could have had a drink or two after the ball, and climbed into a wagon to sleep it off. When she woke up, she found herself miles away, perhaps, and no means to get back to Sagborough."

"Yes, but—" Ferdy began, but Fanny laid a hand gently on his sleeve.

"Pray do not!" she said softly, and her luminous eyes almost unmanned him.

"Quite right, dear," Lady Craston said briskly. "You have done more than anyone could have expected of you, Ferdy, but to no avail. The girl is gone, and I daresay we shall hear no more about her. It is best to set it behind you now."

"Of course, Mama," he said, but privately he knew the mystery would continue to puzzle him. Whatever could have happened to Martha Smith?"

~~~~~

'Dear Fanny. Thank you for your letters. I am quite well. Aunt Letty is a little better. Aunt Pru is quite well. Yesterday I walked to church by myself. Aunt Letty's son is to visit. I hope you are well. Margaret.'

~~~~~

MAY

After the late snow, Yorkshire lurched directly into spring. Every tree burst into leaf and every garden into bloom, seemingly overnight. The roads cleared, and everyone of any importance packed and moved south, for the main London season was just beginning. Lady Harriet and Miss Hay were amongst the first to travel, although they were to visit friends before making for London. Lady Harriet had a seemingly inexhaustible supply of friends. Lady Craston, too, went off to London, taking Mr Brant and Mr Ralph with her, but Mr Ferdy remained, as did Lady Agatha and the Miss Makenhams.

There was a change to Fanny's routine at this time. Lady Craston had come one day and spent almost an hour closeted with Lady Harriet, after which Fanny was told she was not to mingle with Lady Harriet's unfortunate women again. She would go each morning to the shop, but only for two hours, to assist Miss Monkton. For the rest of the day, she would do her sewing at home, either at number Twenty-Six with Mrs Hay, or next door with Lady Agatha and the Miss Makenhams.

"Lady Craston has suggested this arrangement to keep you away from any unsuitable influences, while still fulfilling your obligations," Lady Harriet had said briskly, having summoned Fanny to her room while she supervised the packing. "It is a good point. You are a kindly soul, easily taken in by their stories. Bridget says you buy the girls penny buns on Saturdays, is that so?"

"If I can," Fanny answered. "Sometimes Mr Harper has unsold buns that he sells very cheaply — four or six to the penny, or perhaps stale buns from earlier in the week. The women do not mind if they are stale, and they do not eat very well at Westbury House."

"You see, this is exactly what I am talking about. They eat perfectly well on their own eggs and chickens and pork, and whatever they can grow. They have decent meat once or twice a week, and for most of them, that is lavish indeed. Just because *you* enjoy two full courses every night does not mean they starve to death on boiled chicken and kale. You are too soft-hearted altogether. Do you think I should send them barrels of wine, or a couple of turbot?"

"Oh no, Lady Harriet! I beg your pardon, it was foolish of me. It will not happen again."

"Well, I do not mind the buns, so long as it is an occasional treat and they do not come to expect it. They will be all the better for learning to provide for themselves, and not come to depend upon your charity. Still, it is better if you do not spend so much time with them, especially if Mr Makenham—" She looked sideways at Fanny.

"Mr Makenham?" she said, puzzled. What had he to do with the Westbury House women?

"Fanny, do you like Mr Makenham? You get on well enough with him, for all his finicking London ways?"

"Oh yes, I like him very much," Fanny said, not quite liking to say that she very much approved of his finicking London ways.

"Then, in that case, it is better if you spend more time with Lady Agatha and the Miss Makenhams, and less with common people."

"But I am a common person myself," Fanny said. "I am not a gentlewoman any longer."

"Now, that is not true," Lady Harriet said gently, sitting down on the bed and gesturing to Fanny to sit beside her. "You are a gentleman's daughter, and your appearance, your manners, everything about you is commensurate with that. No one, meeting you in a drawing room would think you anything but a lady. I know you are very self-effacing, but you must not lower yourself beyond reason. Alloway tells me that you use the back stairs. Is that so?"

"Indeed I do when I am going to the shop, or returning from there, but I do not mind."

"I daresay you do not, but I do," Lady Harriet said, although a smile softened her words. "I do not employ you to creep about like a servant, Fanny. My purpose in inviting you here was to have someone who is indubitably a lady of style and taste displaying the clothes from the shop, which you do to admirable effect, but only when you are visible to the population of Sagborough. If you wish to please me, you will pay and receive morning calls, accept invitations to dinner, attend the assemblies and act in every way as the lady you are, and if you intend to be a countess one day, you—"

Fanny squeaked. "A countess? No!"

Lady Harriet rolled her eyes. "Heavens, child, you cannot possibly be so innocent! Can you? It is hard to credit, when the poor man was struck dumb by his very first sight of you. *Of course* he wants to marry you, so bear that in mind if ever Mr Hawes plucks up the courage to speak. Personally, I think Hawes would be a far better match for you than a future earl. Not everyone is suited to the nobility."

"Oh, indeed, I do not think— I cannot believe that he— No, no, you must be mistaken, my lady. Mr Makenham has never shown me the slightest attention that would suggest such a thing."

"Not every man becomes a dribbling fool around a woman when he is thinking of matrimony, Fanny. I think the better of the boy for showing some delicacy about the business, but he is serious enough. His mother said so."

"Oh dear. I do so hope she is wrong about that. It is so *disheartening* to disappoint a gentleman."

Lady Harriet raised one delicate eyebrow. "Disappoint? Well... that is not what I had expected, although it shows surprising sense. But perhaps you will change your mind."

"Oh, no, indeed I shall not, not at all. I can never marry without feeling the strongest affection for a man."

"Hmm." Lady Harriet eyed Fanny thoughtfully. "Fanny, let me say this just once, and then we shall never speak of it again. When a woman contemplates the idea of matrimony, there are a great many considerations to be taken into account. Affection is only one of them. One must also be pragmatic, and weigh the benefits of the match against the decided disadvantages of remaining single. When a man makes an offer, one can never be sure that there will be another offer in the future, or, if there is another offer, that it will be superior to that already before one. It is a great risk to reject a man out of hand, especially one so eligible as Ferdy Makenham, so do consider very carefully. One need not be wildly in love with one's husband to enjoy a very satisfactory marriage. And that is all that I shall say to you on the subject."

Fanny could not quite say why, but she found this conversation very lowering to her spirits. The prospect of receiving an offer from Mr Makenham and being the means of blighting his hopes and reducing him to dejection, even for a short time, made her very unhappy. And then Lady Harriet's talk of a loveless marriage being *'satisfactory'* was depressing beyond words. Not for one second could she contemplate a marriage that was merely *'satisfactory'*. It was inconceivable. She had sooner live her life in perpetual poverty than surrender herself to a man she did not love passionately, and who loved her just as passionately in return. Long after Lady Harriet and Miss Hay had gone off to London, Fanny was quite subdued.

For a day or two, she felt uncomfortable with Mr Makenham, but he was so unfailingly courteous, and gave not the slightest hint of lover-like behaviour, that she was quite reassured. If he had brought her posies of flowers, or written poems in her honour, or pressed impassioned kisses on her hands, she would have suspected him, but he did no such things. He liked to sit beside her, it was true, but he was interested in the most mundane subjects, like sleeves or the quality of various silks, or else talked in the most comfortable way of his family and all that they were doing in London, or asked her about her sisters and what they were doing.

So it was that she came by indefinable degrees to regard him as a friend. She found herself telling him whenever she had a letter from one of her sisters, and sometimes she even talked about Mama and Papa and about poor Jeremy, who had gone away to sea and been drowned. She could tell Mr Makenham everything, and he never minded and always listened carefully and spoke good sense on every subject, just as a brother might.

When Lucy's long letter came, with everything that her Mr Audley had discovered about Jeremy from Mr and Mrs Moreton in Liverpool, she told Mr Makenham all about it, even as she cried tears of joy to hear such wonderful news of her long-dead brother.

"So kind of him to go to so much trouble!" she said over and over. "So very kind. He must be quite in love with Lucy to do such a *romantic* thing for her. How reassuring to know that Jeremy was happy in his last days, and had made a friend — this Johnny Moreton. He was the same age as Jeremy, it is hardly surprising. Jeremy was so amiable, he made friends wherever he went. He was staying with the Moreton family in Liverpool while he waited for his ship, so they knew him during his last weeks on earth."

"Did Mr Audley speak to Johnny Moreton himself?" Mr Makenham said.

"No, for he was not there. He is gone to an uncle in the north of Lancashire to learn to be a mill owner. I wonder if he would remember Jeremy after all this time? Perhaps not, for it was a long time ago — five years now."

"If his parents have such vivid memories of Jeremy, I imagine that this Johnny Moreton would remember him even more clearly. He seems to have spent a great deal of time with your brother."

"Oh yes! So often they say *'Jeremy and Johnny did this'* or *'Jeremy and Johnny went to that'*. They do sound like such good friends. Is that usual with boys, Mr Makenham? To make friends so easily, I mean?"

"Some boys do, if they have a great many common interests, or if they have the happy knack of making themselves agreeable wherever they go. Did you say that Johnny Moreton went to Lancashire? What part?"

She shuffled through the many pages of Lucy's letter. "Ah, here it is — Branton. I have never heard of it."

"Nor I. I shall ask Diana — my sister. She lives in Lancashire now."

But Diana had never heard of Branton either, and there was nothing more to be learnt of Johnny Moreton.

Somehow, Fanny could not quite say how, not a day went by when she did not see Mr Makenham. On the two days of the week when she was with Mrs Hay, he would just happen to call. On the two days of the week when she sat in the morning room of number Twenty-Five with Lady Agatha and the Miss Makenhams, he would be there. And on the two days of the week when the Makenham ladies took their carriage and went visiting, taking Fanny with them, somehow Mr Makenham would always be visiting at the same time. On Sundays, he was in church, his smile reaching across the aisle and bringing her the warmth of friendship.

It was no surprise, then, that he was there with her when Dr Hay came back unexpectedly early from the hospital with two constables and told her that he was very sorry to be the bearer of bad tidings, but a body had been fished out of the canal and it might be Martha's.

19: Turkish Carpets

Martha's body had been found some five miles from Sagborough, in a deep pool off to one side of the canal. It was a popular spot for barges to rest overnight in the summer, but little used in winter, and so the body had probably floated undisturbed for some time, hidden under willow trees.

"What was she doing there?" Fanny whispered.

"I daresay she went into the water somewhere in or around Sagborough," Dr Hay said. "The movement of the water from the barges passing by would have carried her onwards until her clothes seemingly snagged on tree roots on the bank."

"But how did she happen to fall into the water?"

"One can only speculate," Dr Hay said. "Most likely she had taken a drink or two after the ball before setting out to walk along the canal to Westbury House. In the dark, I daresay she missed her footing and fell in and could not get out again. The water would have been so cold that she could not have survived long. I am sorry, Fanny, but these tragedies do occur. However, I have asked the coroner if I may also examine the body, to ensure that nothing worse than an accident occurred."

When Dr Hay and the constables had gone, Fanny said, "What do you think, Mr Makenham? Is it likely that she would simply fall into the water, in your opinion?"

"It is possible," he said thoughtfully. "Although... the moon was up, for I walked home by its light myself. The canal towpath would have been clear enough to walk by. I wonder, though, whether she was truly on her way back to Westbury House. If she fell in there, her body must have been washed through both the Sagborough locks unnoticed, and that seems unlikely. But the Carrbridge Arms is situated on the far side of the locks, and the canal is free of obstruction from there almost to York. So my own guess would be that she went down to the canal there, for some reason, and fell in at that point."

"Why would she do that?" Fanny said.

"Who knows? But there was a great deal of wildness after the ball, so it may be that something happened to cause her to go that way. A disturbance or a fight, perhaps, so she wanted to get away quickly and not walk through the town, as she normally would."

"Yes, I can see that," Fanny said. "Poor Martha! And now her little boy is an orphan. Well, not exactly an orphan, for he still has a father, somewhere. Perhaps he will step forward and take responsibility for the child now."

"Only if he can be found, and can be persuaded to act," Mr Makenham said quietly. "That does not seem likely now."

"Poor little boy!" Fanny said sorrowfully. "I shall write to Lady Harriet and ask if he may be allowed to stay on at Westbury House, at least until he is old enough to be apprenticed. I can spare a few pennies now and then to buy him new clothes. I should hate him to go to an orphanage."

"I shall have a word with Miss Kelly about him," Mr Makenham. "He will not go to the orphanage, I give you my word, Miss Winterton."

"Oh, thank you, Mr Makenham! How kind you are! How very, very kind."

~~~~~

'My dear sister, I was so sorry to hear about the housemaid who fell into the canal, especially as you had made something of a friend of her. What an unfortunate end for the poor girl, after all Mr Makenham's efforts to find her, and just as she had begun to rebuild her life a little. You do not say what tragedy had befallen her, but it must have been grave indeed to leave her destitute and dependent on charity. So kind of Lady Harriet to help such people. I am glad to hear that you are beginning to go out into society a little. The Makenham sisters sound lively company, and Lady Agatha's society will certainly be good for you, Fanny dear. I did not quite like to hear about you working all day, and then long evenings with only Mrs Hay for company. Do make the most of these opportunities to enjoy yourself. You have been too serious lately, and deserve a little frivolity. You have not mentioned Mr Hawes in your last few letters. Has he gone away again? Your loving sister, Annabelle.'

~~~~~

Martha's death was the talk of the town, but not everyone was surprised that she had met an untimely end. When Draper came to arrange Fanny's hair that evening, she pursed her lips and said, "That's what happens to them as isn't particular in their habits, if you ask me. Once a woman discards her principles, she falls in with the worst type of scoundrel and this is what comes of it."

Fanny could not quite follow her reasoning, but one did not argue morality with a lady's maid, so she said nothing. She soon found, however, that the higher ranks of Sagborough's population were of a similar mind. Lady Agatha and the Miss Makenhams had taken Fanny with them on a morning call to Lady Gilbert Marford, and there they encountered Mrs Malpas and Mrs Trivers.

"Very tragic, no doubt," Mrs Trivers said, with a disdainful sniff, "but what can one expect of girls like that? Lady Harriet means well, I am sure, but it does no good to encourage these people to think themselves respectable and mingle with honest, God-fearing people. Why, it quite leads them to suppose that they are the equal of anybody, and then they get into trouble and see where it all ends?"

Fanny did not quite understand why thinking oneself the equal of anybody might lead to a fall into the canal, but she could not argue the point. She tended to seat herself in a corner somewhere on these visits, with a small piece of sewing to occupy her hands. The Makenhams were all very kind to her, and treated her quite as one of the family, but, despite Lady Harriet's reassurance that Fanny was still a lady, she was acutely aware that she was not as much of a lady as the Miss Makenhams.

"I don't think it is Lady Harriet's fault," Lady Gilbert said, rather pink about the cheeks. "I don't think it's anybody's fault, just happenstance and a bit too much ale or punch after the ball. Everything got very wild, so it seems. Gil and Humphrey got into a fight with some of the farmers — well, Gil got into a fight, anyway, for he came home covered in blood and with a dreadful black eye. Humphrey had more sense. He was betting on the outcome, and won twenty pounds, apparently. This poor girl probably fell in with the wrong crowd and got mixed up in something she'd better have avoided."

"You are very generous, Lady Gilbert," Mrs Trivers said. "Still, she would never have been in Sagborough at all had not Lady Harriet brought her here and given her a home and employment, for all the world as if she were a decent, respectable person."

"I'm sure you're right, but she seemed like a nice enough girl to me," Mrs Malpas said hesitantly. "Aren't we all supposed to offer Christian charity to those less fortunate than ourselves?"

"Not by taking them into our own homes, Ruby," Mrs Trivers said quellingly.

"No, of course not, Mrs Trivers. I am sure you are quite right, but I daresay Lady Hay meant it for the best."

Lady Gilbert summoned the footman to pass around the room with the macaroons again and the conversation turned, to Fanny's intense relief. Any criticism of Lady Harriet, her benefactress, made her very uncomfortable.

Under cover of the conversation, Mrs Trivers leaned closer to Mrs Malpas to whisper, "Lady *Harriet*, Ruby. If you call her Lady Hay you promote the good doctor to the peerage, you know, or at least a knighthood." She tittered. "I am sure you will not mind me giving you just a little hint."

"Oh no, not at all," Mrs Malpas said, flushing beetroot red. "Much obliged, I'm sure. I am very ignorant."

Seeing her discomfort, Fanny rushed to introduce a less distressing topic. "I am sorry Miss Malpas is not with you today, Mrs Malpas. I hope she is well?"

"Oh, how kind of you to ask, Miss Fanny. Yes, Emmy's very well, but her father's taken her to visit the warehouse today. There is a shipment of Turkish carpets just arrived, and Jacob likes her to have her pick, you know. That, and it does the workers good to see the master's daughter in all her finery, just like a lady. She's no oil painting, my Emmy, but she's all we have and she's a good girl and a credit to us, for all some people—" She threw Mrs Trivers a quick glance, then said in a lowered voice. "Well, I don't mind for myself, but I'd like Emmy to make us proud and find herself a good husband. Proper quality, if you understand me."

"Of course," Fanny said in ready sympathy, "but surely you also want her to marry for love? To be happy?"

Mrs Malpas laughed, a deep rumble that made her whole body shake. "Ah, you're such a romantic, Miss Fanny. Love's not the only way to be happy. There's money, too, or at least the comforts it brings. And there's having a place in the world, being *somebody*. Emmy has the money, and if her husband gives her a position in society, then they'll have all the time in the world to fall in love later, if they choose. She knows what's expected of her, but we won't blame her if it don't happen. Oh look, here's Mrs Drabble and Miss Celia. I expect Mrs Trivers will want to be off at any moment. She don't like Mrs Drabble above half, for all she was Miss Harbottle once, and she very much don't like Celia outshining Miss Marianne."

And so it was, Mrs Trivers rising smartly and making her farewells in very short order. Marianne waved to Fanny sadly as she followed her aunt from the room. She would have loved to sit beside Fanny and chatter away, as they had done on the journey north, but Mrs Trivers would not allow her niece to be friends with a seamstress, and Fanny could not blame her. Not all the patronage of Lady Harriet and Lady Agatha could protect her from being sneered at by the Mrs Trivers of the world.

Neither Celia Drabble nor her mother had any such qualms, however, for Celia bounced across the room and plopped herself down beside Fanny. The Miss Makenhams followed her, and immediately Fanny was absorbed into a little gaggle of young ladies talking, not about drowned housemaids, but of gowns and bonnets and balls and young men.

Within moments the door opened once more, to disclose Mr Makenham.

Mrs Malpas rumbled with laughter again. "Well now, won't Mrs Trivers be wishing she'd stayed a bit longer. They must have met on the doorstep, too. Aye, but such a pity Emmy isn't here. Not but what he's never looked at her, beyond politeness, but Jacob does like to hear that she's been in company with him, even if nothing comes of it. Which it won't, of course." She looked sideways at Fanny. "Anyone can see that. Anyone except my husband, of course. Ah, Mr Makenham! Delighted to see you. Thank you, yes, I am perfectly well, but you need not waste your smiles on me, when there are pretty young ladies to enjoy them."

Mr Makenham, however, had perfect manners. He pulled up a chair and talked with every appearance of the greatest interest about Miss Malpas and Turkish carpets and the relative merits of carpets from Axminster or Wilton.

"You're very knowledgeable," she said suspiciously.

Mr Makenham smiled his sweetest smile. "When you dined at my house, I had the very great pleasure of sitting beside Mr Malpas after the ladies had withdrawn."

"And he bent your ear with carpet talk, did he? Aye, that's just like him."

"I was very happy to talk about carpets, I assure you, Mrs Malpas. Dr Hay was discussing a very complicated medical issue, something to do with the lungs, and Sir William was talking about political matters, and I had nothing to contribute to either conversation. Carpets are a much more reassuring subject. Everyone may have an opinion on carpets, for we all walk about on them every day, and your husband explained a great deal on the subject that I had not fully appreciated before. A fascinating area of study, carpets. I had no idea."

She laughed merrily, and again told him to go and talk to the young ladies, and this time he did as he was bid, moving a chair to sit between Fanny and Celia, turning first to Celia with a civil question.

Fanny watched him covertly. Ever since Lady Harriet had told her that Mr Makenham had marriage in mind, Fanny had watched him. At first, she had seen not the least sign of any particular attention towards herself, but gradually she had become aware of... she could hardly say what. His eyes upon her, perhaps, more often than they should be. When he had been seemingly engrossed by Mrs Malpas just now, two or three times he had glanced up at her and his eyes had softened. Twice as he talked to Celia he had moved his head a little to catch Fanny's eye. And when he turned his attention fully on her, his voice changed in some indefinable way. Why had she never noticed it before?

Then there were the extraordinary attentions bestowed on her by his family. Lady Craston had talked to Lady Harriet, and after that Fanny had spent much of her time with the Makenham ladies, almost as if she were one of the family. Almost as if they were expecting her to become so one day, and fostering Mr Makenham's suit accordingly. They were making it easy for him to meet Fanny, while also gradually absorbing her into their midst. How many times had they talked of Abbeymount, the earl's seat, or Lennister Hall, where the viscount and viscountess lived, and said, "You would like it there, I am sure, Fanny"? And, without realising what they were about, she had agreed wholeheartedly that she would, for who would not enjoy being part of such a large and affectionate family?

Even now she could hardly believe that Mr Makenham had any serious intentions towards her. Never had she experienced so subtle a suit! Her previous admirers had pressed flowers upon her, or even kisses, once or twice. They had written poetry to her, and serenaded her, and whispered ardently into her ears. One had stolen a lock of her hair, and another had loitered outside the gates every day to catch her as soon as she set off for the village. They had given her books and ribbons and sheet music and even a pocket watch, when her own had broken, although Papa had insisted on her giving that back. But never had she had a suitor who treated her exactly like every other lady of his acquaintance. If indeed he truly was a suitor.

After a while, Mr Makenham rose to take his leave.

"Yes, we must go too," Lady Agatha said. "Goodness, look at the time! We have quite overstayed our welcome."

"Oh, must you go?" Lady Gilbert said. "I do so enjoy your visits, Lady Agatha. You could never outstay your welcome."

"You are kind to say so, but we must indeed go. Ferdy, is it tolerably warm outside? Warm enough to walk home? I feel the need for some exercise, and the carriage is so stuffy."

"It is delightfully mild, and the clouds have all blown away," he said. "Perfect walking weather, and that will give me the pleasure of accompanying you. What is more, Miss Crisp has two new bonnets in her window, just in from London, unless I mistake the matter. One of them would suit Cordelia admirably."

The ladies needed no further persuasion to walk home, for a milliner with new wares was not on any account to be missed. Fanny was glad of it, for she was used to walking and far preferred it to the carriage, especially in a town like Sagborough, where the pavements were wide and clean. As they emerged from the house, she breathed deeply of the air, the wind from the moors making it clearer and less heavy with smoke today. At home, the hedgerows would be crowded with star-like flowers, and in the woods— No, she would not think of that. Sagborough was home now. She set off resolutely after the others. The Miss Makenhams skipped on ahead, arms entwined, and Lady Agatha strode briskly after them. Mr Makenham waited for her.

"Would you like to take my arm, Miss Winterton?" he said with a little bow. Always so polite, so correct!

She accepted at once, for there was nothing so comfortable as a gentleman's arm as one walked about. Any of her sisters would have declined the offer, but Fanny would always rather have a supporting arm than not, and would rather have Mr Makenham's arm than any other. Her reasons for this were quite unworthy, she knew, but she could not help a thrill of delight in walking beside a man so perfectly attired as he always was. From his highly polished boots to his beaver hat set at precisely the right jaunty angle to his delicately coloured gloves and matching cane, he always looked magnificent.

They walked at an easy pace, stopping at interesting shop windows to examine the contents within, and Mr Makenham asked Fanny her opinion a flattering number of times. When they paused at the jeweller's shop, he said, "Which stones do you like best, Miss Winterton?"

"Oh, diamonds," she said, without thinking. "They go with everything. But if I were exceedingly rich, I should have a different set for every gown."

"How very sensible," he said. "Then you would always have the perfect accompaniment for every occasion. I hope one day you achieve your ambition."

It struck her then that he might take her words to imply that she would like to have a rich husband to buy her so many jewels, and went hot and cold at the thought. It would never do to be seen to be encroaching in that way.

She said quickly, "Oh no, I shall never be rich, nor do I wish to be." And that sounded too much like an outright rejection, which was exceedingly improper when he had not yet made the offer, and may never do so. To cover her embarrassment, she rushed on, "I should have had Mama's jewels, or some of them, at least. She had a very famous set of sapphires, and several other good pieces, supposedly, which were to have been our dowries, but they could not be found."

He raised his eyebrows. "Could not be found? Had they been stolen?"

"No one knows. Papa looked for them when Rosamund was betrothed, but they were nowhere to be found and he was obliged to mortgage the house to pay the dowry he had promised to Lord Westerlea. Oh dear, look how far ahead of us the others are. If we make haste we may catch them before Miss Crisp's shop."

They walked on at a brisker pace, but the three Makenham ladies were out of sight, hidden by the throngs of shoppers enjoying the afternoon sunshine. Out of the crowd, however, emerged a familiar figure. Fanny gave a squeak of surprise, and stopped dead, causing Mr Makenham to stop abruptly too.

It was Mr Hawes.

20: Miss Crisp's Elegant Millinery

Ferdy almost groaned with annoyance. Hawes, of all people. He had not been near Fanny for weeks, as far as he could tell, but she was such a gentle creature that she would accept whatever excuse he offered and bask in his insincere smiles.

At first Mr Hawes did not see them, and came on relentlessly, head lowered against the wind, one hand holding onto his beaver hat. Then he saw Fanny, started, smiled and made his way towards her where she stood beside Ferdy.

"Miss Winterton! What a delightful surprise! I had no idea you were to be found out and about, or I should have sought you out sooner." He bowed with a flourish, sweeping his hat from his head.

"Mr Hawes," she said, dipping a slight curtsy. "You are well, I trust?"

"Oh indeed, perfectly well, and if I had not been so, the sight of your pretty features would have driven away every ill upon the instant, and rendered me in the best of health forever more. I do not insult you by enquiring as to *your* health, Miss Winterton, for it is patently clear even to the most unobservant eye, which I flatter myself mine is not, that you are in the rosiest of good health. Never have I seen you blooming so delightfully."

Ferdy tried not to roll his eyes at this hyperbole. He stood very still, frozen in place, unacknowledged and perhaps forgotten, as the other two exchanged greetings. He was too polite to interrupt the conversation, but he felt Mr Hawes' rudeness exceedingly. He had not even offered the courtesy of a greeting, even though he had dined at Ferdy's house.

Fanny noticed, too, for she said, in a slightly puzzled tone, "You remember Mr Makenham, of course?"

That brought forth a slight exchange of bows, and Hawes' vacuous smile slipped a little. Fanny looked uncertainly from one to the other, as if unsure what to make of their behaviour. Perhaps she was aware of the animosity between them, for her hand tightened instinctively on Ferdy's arm. To reassure her, he gently covered her hand with his own. She trembled a little under his touch, like a timid mouse, trusting but still a little afraid.

Mr Hawes licked his lips and looked from one to the other. Then the smile returned. "Are you making your way home, Miss Winterton? I should be delighted to relieve Makenham of the duty of escorting you, if so, and apprise you of all the news from Brinshire as we walk."

How would she respond to that? Naturally she would want to talk to Mr Hawes and hear the news from Brinshire, but she already had a perfectly good escort, and there was also Aunt Agatha and his sisters to be thought of. To Ferdy's delight, she raised questioning eyes to him, as if asking how she should answer.

"There may be too much news to impart for one short walk," Ferdy said smoothly. "Perhaps you might call on Miss Winterton when she is at home, Mr Hawes, when you would have the leisure to relate everything that has happened since you last met."

"Oh yes, for it is such a long time since I have seen you, Mr Hawes," Fanny said disingenuously. "You have not even been in church lately."

Hawes had the decency to look ashamed of himself. "I... I have been attending services at St Etheldreda's. It is very convenient for my lodgings."

"Oh, St Etheldreda's! Oh yes, I know of it," she said. "Celia says the sermons are agreeably short. She and her mother attend there. Oh, but you would know that, of course. You will have seen them there. I do not like a short sermon myself. One feels let off too easily if the clergyman does not take his time over the business, do you not think?"

Hawes agreed to it rather abstractedly, while Ferdy held his breath. Would she realise that Hawes had transferred his attentions elsewhere? But she mentioned the days when she was at home, and expressed her hope that she might receive Mr Hawes there soon, and they parted company, with great affability on Miss Winterton's part, and rather studied courtesy from the two men. Ferdy was glad to have escaped so easily, but he wondered very much what she was thinking, and whether she was much affected by the encounter, for all her seeming composure.

They came to the milliner's, but there was no sign of the Makenham ladies, and Ferdy quickly realised why. "The new hats are no longer in the window," he said with a sigh. "Shall we enter? We may perhaps be in time to forestall them from buying every bonnet in the shop."

Fanny giggled, raising her hand to cover her mouth in that way he adored. She was so enchanting!

They went in, pausing on the threshold, for the shop was dark after the sunlit brightness of the street outside.

"Ferdy! There you are!" boomed Aunt Agatha from the gloom. "Do come and decide between these bonnets for Cordelia."

He blinked once or twice as his eyes adjusted to the poor light, then, identifying his aunt and sisters at the far side of the shop, he led Fanny across.

"There!" said Cordelia. "Is it not charming? Shall I not look quite the thing in it?" She wore an elegant little bonnet, and gave a quick twirl to display all its finer points. "It is the very latest thing in London, so Miss Crisp assures me. Is that true?"

"It was certainly true about three years ago," Ferdy said. "Miss Winterton, what is your opinion? Does Cordelia look quite the thing?"

Fanny looked up at him uncertainly. "It is a very pretty bonnet," she said hesitantly.

"But does it look well on Cordelia?"

"Oh no!" She flushed scarlet. "I beg your pardon, Miss Cordelia, but it is not the best shape to flatter your face. It suits a more rounded face, like Miss Makenham's."

"Or yours," Ferdy said.

"Oh yes, but I am not thinking of buying it," Fanny said at once.

"But you should," Emilia said. "I do not want it, for I have bonnets enough for my needs, but it would suit you admirably. You need not regard the cost, for Ferdy will pay. Cordelia will very likely buy two or three, so one more will be neither here nor there, and the bill will go to Ferdy, you know."

"Oh no, I could not!" Fanny said at once. "It would be most improper for Mr Makenham to buy me a bonnet."

"But he would buy it for me, and then I should give it to you," Cordelia said. "There is nothing improper in that."

"Now, Cordelia, do not tease Fanny," Aunt Agatha said. "She must be the best judge of what would be proper for her. Miss Crisp, may we look at that velvet one with the feather, if you please? There now, Ferdy, what about this one?"

"No, that is too dowdy for you, and too fancy for Cordelia. The straw with the pink muslin is better."

"Pink muslin, Ferdy?" Cordelia said faintly. "Please do not make me wear pink muslin."

"Certainly not," he said. "You and pink muslin should never be in the same room together. It is the shape that is important, Cordelia. Miss Crisp can trim it with something more suitable — blue, I think, quite bright, like your velvet pelisse, and no feathers, just simple bows here, here and here, a little like that one over there, only smaller, and then wide ribbons to tie. But if you want something even more fetching, that one over there, with all the artificial flowers taken off and just strings of tiny ribbon rosettes all around the edge and the crown. Lady Carrbridge wore one very like it only last year."

"How comfortable it is to have a brother who is so knowledgeable about fashions," Cordelia sighed.

"Especially when he pays the bills for them," Emilia added.

Miss Crisp smiled and fetched even more bonnets for inspection, and the ladies settled down for a lengthy discussion of the relative merits of each. Ferdy felt it was safe to creep away and find Fanny. She had retreated to a chair on the opposite side of the shop, although she was gazing around her with interest at the various headpieces and decorations on display. Ferdy sat beside her, his arms folded. For a while, neither of them spoke, but as the silence lengthened, he said,

"I am sorry you did not buy the bonnet, but I daresay you could make one just like it at home."

"Oh yes, I could," Fanny cried. "I believe I will do so, although I shall change the way the material is pleated, and I shall use the same material as my pelisse, so that it will be a perfect match. I like the way the brim curls up at the sides. That is a new style to me. I shall experiment a little to get the same effect."

"You enjoy such work, I think, Miss Winterton."

She blushed a little under his gaze. "Oh yes, very much. There is something greatly pleasing about wearing a garment one has made with one's own hands.

"I hope you *will* make such a bonnet, Miss Winterton, for it would suit you admirably," Ferdy said, smiling down at her.

To his delight, she smiled back at him. "Oh, you are not offended! I am so glad!"

"Why should I be offended?"

"Because I would not accept a bonnet that you had paid for. But I do think it would be improper."

"You would have been uncomfortable with the arrangement, so that is enough to render it ineligible," he said.

"Thank you! You are always so correct yourself, Mr Makenham, so if you agree with me, I know I was right to refuse it."

He was reduced to speechlessness by this ingenuous compliment. She was so open and natural, and could no more dissemble than a child. He thought of all the society women he knew, with their false smiles and empty compliments, caring only about rank and wealth and obtaining invitations to all the most glittering occasions. Fanny was worth a thousand of such women!

When he said nothing, she went on quietly, "I am so glad to have seen Mr Hawes. It quite puzzled me to know what had become of him."

He had no idea how to respond to that, and before he had got his words in order, she glanced up at him and said, "He has done this before, you know. When I first knew him, he was so attentive and gallant. He wrote a play for us all to perform — my sisters and me, the Claremont boys, the Whites, some of the Sheridans, Mr Hill and Mr Keeling. At least, we rehearsed parts of it a few times, but Papa said it was not suitable and I do not think Mr Hawes ever finished it. He and I were to play the leading roles, and there were some speeches—"

She paused, blushing, and then went on, "I quite see why Papa disliked it so, but it was such a romantic thing to do, and poor Mr Hawes seemed so... so *impassioned*, that I decided I would accept him if ever he should be so obliging as to offer for me, for I could not bear him to be disappointed." She gave a little laugh. "Rosamund said that was a silly reason to marry a gentleman, and that I should consider every offer on the basis of suitability and prudence, as well as affection. Rosamund talks a great deal about prudence. She is very lowering to the spirits sometimes. But anyway, not long after that, Miss Turner came to stay in Brinchester with her aunt, and… and Mr Hawes came to see me less often. When Miss Turner went back to Hampshire, Mr Hawes went to visit a friend, also in Hampshire. After a few months, he came back and started making up to me again, but then when Papa died he was nowhere to be seen. Now here he is again. But I am not surprised that he is drawn to Celia Drabble, for she is so beautiful, and that is so *romantic*, is it not? Every gentleman must be drawn to such beauty." She sighed.

Ferdy was powerfully affected by this recitation. He was thrilled that she trusted him enough to tell him the story, but also pleased that she seemed unaffected by Hawes' duplicity.

"You do not mind?" he said cautiously.

"Oh no, not a great deal. Well… apart from the blow to my self-esteem. It raises one's consequence so to have an *eligible* suitor, does not it? Most of mine have been dreadfully *in*eligible, like Thomas Claremont and Mr Waterford, who was *not* an agreeable man at all. He frequented places that innocent young ladies should not know about, so Rosamund said. She is married, so she is permitted to know about such things. Mr Waterford kissed me once and it was exceedingly unpleasant. Quite horrid, and he did not even ask if he may, for if he had, I should have said no, of course. I should never kiss a man unless I were betrothed to him, and I should not agree to become betrothed unless I were violently in love, and never mind about prudence."

"What was wrong with Thomas Claremont?" Ferdy said, smiling at the image of Fanny violently in love. "Did he kiss you, too?"

"Oh *no!* Thomas is sweet, but he is a third son with no prospects. He is to be an attorney and he says if he studies hard, he may be able to afford a wife when he is forty, so I suppose *he* is being prudent, and perhaps that is a good quality in a gentleman. Or at least in a prospective husband. Oh dear, I am getting as bad as Lucy for chattering away. I do beg your pardon, Mr Makenham. You are very kind to listen to my nonsense."

"I—"

"Ferdy! Ferdy! Which of these shall I have? Or both?" Cordelia called optimistically from the far side of the shop, waving two bonnets in a flurry of ribbons and feathers.

He sighed. "Pray excuse me, Miss Winterton. I had better intervene before they purchase the rest of Miss Crisp's wares."

She laughed, and smiled up at him with such an impish expression that for an instant every thought flew out of his head, and he wanted to kiss her so badly that he could barely restrain himself.

"Ferdy!" Cordelia's impatient screech penetrated the lovelorn haze that surrounded Ferdy and, forgetting even to bow, he turned and stumbled across the shop.

"This one is hideous, do not you agree?" Emilia said. "Tell her, Ferdy."

"Nonsense! It will look very well with a little more trimming. You agree, I am sure, Ferdy," Cordelia said.

"Great Heavens, girls, stop arguing," Aunt Agatha boomed. "Ferdy, they cannot agree, so you must say which one will be more becoming."

"I do not care," he said, with a casual wave of one hand. "Buy both."

Miss Crisp whisked the bonnets away to be boxed up before he changed his mind, but the three women stared at him.

"You do not *care?*" Cordelia said in astonished tones. "How can you not care? You care more about bonnets than I do. Are you ill?"

"Leave the boy alone," Aunt Agatha said, laughing. "I am sure he has more interesting things on his mind than bonnets just now. Emilia, do you want to look at gloves while Ferdy is in such a benevolent mood?"

But Emilia, smiling knowingly at Ferdy, shook her head, and as soon as it had been agreed where the hat boxes and the bill for them were to be sent, they left the shop, and made their way without haste to Harlington Terrace.

There they heard news that drove all thoughts of bonnets out of their heads. Dr Hay's examination of Martha's body showed a narrow but deep wound in her stomach, such as might be produced by a long, thin knife. Such an injury, combined with a fall into bitterly cold water, would have quickly put the sufferer beyond all aid.

Martha's death had not, it seemed, been an accident at all.

21: Investigations

Fanny was distressed beyond measure. She went about her usual daily round, doing everything that was expected of her without complaint, but tears would keep welling up in her eyes. All evening she sat in the drawing room, sniffing from time to time, and dripping tears onto the stitchery she was engaged in. She could hardly see to place her needle.

"Really, Fanny, you must stop being so lachrymose," Dr Hay said, setting down the book he was reading. "It is rather trying. You have had a shock, certainly, but you must not allow it to overset you."

"I will do my best, sir," Fanny said meekly. "I am very sorry." She pulled out a damp handkerchief, blew her nose fiercely and tried hard to stop being so lachrymose. Crying never helped anything, after all, or so Rosamund always said.

Dr Hay grunted. "It will be for the best if you do not go to the shop tomorrow. I shall send William round with a note. You may spend the day next door."

"It is not my day to be at number Twenty-Five," Fanny said. "I should be with Mrs Hay tomorrow."

"Mama will not mind, and I think it better for your spirits that you should be in uplifting company, rather than dwelling on tragedy. Be ready to leave straight after breakfast, and I shall take you there myself and explain the circumstances. Lady Agatha will be perfectly agreeable, I am sure."

So it was that Fanny found herself shown in to the breakfast parlour of number Twenty-Five while the Makenham were still at table, and was able to observe Mr Makenham's face light up when he saw her, before he carefully schooled his features to a more restrained degree of pleasure.

"Of course she may stay with us today," Lady Agatha said with a wide smile, almost before Dr Hay had finished his explanation. "Nothing could give us greater pleasure. Fanny, do take off your bonnet and pelisse. Will you join us for breakfast? We have seed cakes — Ferdy's favourites, you see. Good girl. Yes, do sit there beside Ferdy. Well, is this not cosy? But what of Mrs Hay? Shall we call upon her later this morning?"

"My mother enjoys quiet and solitude," Dr Hay said. "She had a disturbed night, so she will sleep for much of the day, I expect. Forgive me, but I have a very busy day ahead of me, and—"

"Of course, of course. Do not let us detain you from your important work. Thank you so much for bringing Fanny to us. Poole, do show Dr Hay out. Peters, some chocolate for Miss Winterton, or should you prefer coffee, my dear?"

"Oh, chocolate, if you please. Thank you, Peters."

"Well, this is a dreadful business and I am not at all surprised that you are upset," Lady Agatha said. "That poor girl, murdered right under our noses!"

"There is no need to assume intent, Auntie," Mr Makenham said in his calm way. "There was a great deal of disruption after the ball, quite an affray by all accounts, and the most likely explanation is that Miss Smith inadvertently became embroiled in one of the many fights and found herself in the path of a knife."

"And then conveniently fell into the canal, I suppose?" Miss Makenham said tartly. "Of course there was intent, Ferdy, and we may guess why. After all, this was not just another housemaid on her night off, this was a woman who had already threatened violence in this very house, with a knife of her own. Undoubtedly she got into a dispute with someone, the knives came out and she came off worst. Then the fellow rolled her into the canal. But no one will ever confess to it. A great deal goes on under cover of darkness that no one ever finds out about."

"You may be right, Emilia," Mr Makenham said equably. "Whatever may be discovered, however, the constables will discover it. Miss Winterton, will you try one of these seed cakes? They are quite delicious. Eduarde has such a light hand with cake."

His calm voice and composed manner were infinitely reassuring to Fanny. There was nothing to distress her, for the constables would find out what had happened to Martha, and in the meantime, Mr Makenham and his family were there to surround her with comforting affection, and there were seed cakes to be enjoyed.

~~~~~

The constables asked questions and discovered that Martha had not been seen since the end of the ball. Nobody had seen anything, heard anything, knew anything. Dr Hay became very cross and stormed off to see Lord Gilbert, letters flew between Sagborough and London, Lord Carrbridge's secretary arrived in great haste and Dr Hay, Lord Gilbert and the secretary went to York together. A day later, four serious gentlemen came from York and began the investigation all over again.

"This time, it will be done properly," Dr Hay said, with a tight smile. "Martha was under my care and I shall see justice done on her behalf if it is humanly possible. No stone will be left unturned."

Fanny wondered that he had not displayed such zealousness when Martha was merely missing, although it was true, as Mr Makenham pointed out, that no search, however diligent, could have found her any sooner. She had almost certainly died on the night of the ball, and was well beyond earthly help before she was even missed. Still, Dr Hay had been lamentably unconcerned before, and should have made more effort to find Martha, in Fanny's opinion, instead of leaving it all to poor Mr Makenham.

The York constables were very thorough. They interviewed all the women from Westbury House, they interviewed everyone they could find who had attended the ball, and they interviewed everyone who resided at number Twenty-Six Harlington Terrace. Naturally, this included Fanny. She was a little nervous, but both Dr Hay and Lady Agatha sat with her while she answered the gentlemen's questions, their silent presence a great reassurance, and she knew she need not be afraid, for Mr Makenham had told her so.

"Everyone is being talked to, Miss Winterton," he had said. "There is nothing to fear, for this is perfectly normal. All you have to do is to tell the constables everything you can remember about Martha. You do not need to concern yourself with whether a detail is important or not, for they will be the judges of that. It is all for Martha's sake, after all."

"Nothing I say can be of use to Martha now, except prayers," Fanny said sorrowfully.

"That is true," Mr Makenham said gravely, "but if we can help to find out how she died and perhaps bring a murderer before a judge, then we may save another person from dying as Martha did."

"I should like to do that," she said.

In fact, the process was not frightening at all. The constables were very matter-of-fact, and joked about the clerk's trouble with his pens, and how they would never be able to read his notes for the ink blots all over the paper, and then the clerk had offered to ask the questions while they wrote the notes, and they had all laughed and everything was very easy. Nor were the questions at all difficult to answer — they wanted to know when she had first met Martha, how they had gone together to the Malpas house, which they knew all about, and then the time when Martha had gone storming next door to see Mr Brant. They were very interested in all that Martha had told Fanny of herself when they had sat in the tap room with coffee to warm them, for that was something they had not heard before.

" '*His face is burned into my mind...*' Those were her words?" one of the constables said, as the clerk's pen scratched away.

Fanny nodded. "She said she had thought about him every waking minute and one day she would find him."

"And she came all the way from Grantham to find him? Goodness me!"

It was striking, now that Fanny thought about all her dealings with Martha, how bent on vengeance she had been. No, not necessarily vengeance. If she had found the man responsible and he had made reparation for her difficulties, she would have been content, perhaps, keeping her knife sheathed. But if he would not help her... *then* she would have taken her revenge, and if the body in the canal had been that of a man, perhaps that would have been the reason for it. Instead, it was Martha who had ended up in the canal with a fatal stab wound.

The constable went on smoothly, "Tell me about the night of the ball, Miss Winterton. You saw Miss Smith there, I believe?"

"Yes, she was serving drinks to the ladies and gentlemen. I spoke to her once, because I was surprised to see her there, but she explained that it meant extra money and an extra day off for her."

"Did you see her drop the tray of drinks?"

"Oh yes! Poor Martha! That was very close to where I was sitting. She just seemed to miss her footing and down she went. I wanted to help her but Mr Makenham told me not to. I wonder if she got into trouble for that, and that was why—?"

"She was chastised for her clumsiness, naturally, but Lord Carrbridge always pays for breakages without any questions asked. There were no repercussions from the incident for Martha. Who else was on the platform near you at that point, Miss Winterton?"

"Oh... let me see... Mr Brant was there, and Lord Carrbridge and some of his brothers. Lady Harbottle and Mrs Drabble. Mrs Plumstead. One of the footmen, who came to Martha's assistance, but I do not know his name. I cannot think of anyone else who was nearby."

"And did you see Miss Smith again after that?"

"Only in the distance, helping to replenish the food tables. I suppose they would not trust her with trays of drinks after that."

"You did not see her after the ball closed?"

"Oh no! Lady Harriet wished to leave quite early, so I did not stay to the end. Poor Martha! Shall you be able to find out what happened to her, do you think?"

The constables exchanged smug glances. "Oh, I believe we might, Miss Winterton. I believe we might."

~~~~~

Ferdy was rather harassed. The constables had wanted to know all about the occasion when Martha Smith had come to number Twenty-Five, brandishing a knife. Then they had asked a great many questions about Edgar, and had he ever been to Grantham? Had Ferdy ever been to Grantham? Did he know of anyone who lived in Grantham?

"No, I do not," he said testily. "I know nothing at all about Grantham, and never wish to."

Then the constables had asked for Edgar's direction in London. "And why did he go to London just at that time, sir?"

"He always goes to London after Easter. It is the height of the season, and everyone who is anyone is in London."

"But not you, sir," the constable said affably. "Here you are still in Sagborough."

"Yes, I... I have personal business that keeps me in the north," Ferdy said.

"Personal business. I see, sir."

"It is a family matter, if you must know."

"Of course, sir. Not our concern, I'm sure. Are there any other gentlemen by the name of Edgar Brant?"

Was it his imagination, or were they eyeing him with deep suspicion? They sounded pleasant enough, and very polite, but why did they want to know about Edgar, and why did every question make him feel guilty? He had done nothing wrong, and he strongly disliked being made to feel as if he had.

"I have no idea why you are so obsessed with Edgar," Ferdy said. "There are a great many Brants in the world, and Edgar is a traditional family name. However, none of them live in Grantham."

A glimmer of a smile flickered across the questioner's face before being extinguished. "That would have been too much to hope for," he said.

The constables were tight-lipped about their progress, but they were reporting daily to Lord Carrbridge in London, by way of his brother, Lord Gilbert Marford, and Lord Carrbridge's agent, a man called Merton. Ferdy had the happy idea of inviting these two gentlemen to dinner, in hopes of finding out something of events. Then, because it seemed courteous to neighbours, he invited Fanny and Dr Hay as well. And even if he learnt nothing of the constables, he would at least enjoy a pleasant evening.

There was one additional guest, Cordelia's suitor, Julius Whittleton, who had, so far, been little seen in Sagborough. In his role as manager of Lord Humphrey Marford's gaming house in York, he was obliged to be at work every evening except Sunday, and his days were spent in the eternal chore of managers everywhere, paperwork. There were endless letters to be written, bills to be paid and records to be kept. While Lord Humphrey had been in London, Whittleton had been unable to do more than ride hastily to Sagborough for a snatched hour with his beloved once or twice a week. But now Lord Humphrey was returned, and he was at liberty to take an occasional night off.

Ferdy had taken the earliest opportunity to draw Whittleton aside and play the stern older brother, well aware of his history as an accredited fortune hunter, but he need not have worried. As soon as they were alone, all Whittleton's hopes and fears poured out.

"I know I have not always behaved as I ought," Whittleton said. "It is the very devil being poor, Makenham. I spend weeks at a time at Drummoor with Carrbridge, with the table groaning at every meal and the cellar full to the rafters with the best wines and Carrbridge with a dozen different coats a day, if he wishes, while I had to pay pennies to a sewing woman to remake mine over and over. So whenever an heiress was dangled in front of me, naturally I was tempted. Who would not be? But when I met Cordelia — Miss Makenham, I should say — I was so thankful I had never succeeded with any of those heiresses. When one is in love, everything changes, does it not?"

Ferdy could not disagree with him on that point. Nor did he dislike the fellow. He was handsome and personable, with excellent manners, he had a fine singing voice, and his fair good looks were a perfect foil for Cordelia's dark prettiness. No one could say, as they performed duets together, that they were not well matched. He had already made his intentions known to Lord and Lady Craston, and laid out details of his financial position, and apart from the unstable nature of his employment, he was well able to support a wife. His suit seemed well-founded and Cordelia, always slightly mercurial, seemed almost a different person when Julius was around. Ferdy could only hope that his own suit would proceed as amicably.

Dinner was a relaxed affair, the company pleasant and the food a credit to Ferdy's expensive French chef. Aunt Agatha bore the brunt of Dr Hay's medical conversation, while Ferdy had the gentle Lady Gilbert to one side of him and his lovely Fanny to the other. He could hardly imagine a pleasanter way to pass an hour or two. By the time the ladies withdrew, he was in a very mellow frame of mind, and hardly remembered his original intent for the evening.

It was Julius Whittleton who raised the subject. "So, Gil, how are these constables of yours getting on? Might we expect an arrest soon?"

"They tell us very little of substance," Gil said. "Who they have talked to, who they plan to talk to next and so forth. Nothing of their thinking at all."

"But we may glean certain elements of it," Merton said. He was a narrow-faced man, not prepossessing, but Ferdy felt that Lord Carrbridge's secretary must be a person of some aptitude, to manage the marquess's many estates and holdings. He dressed unobtrusively, too, as a gentleman but plainly and soberly, as befitted his station.

Gil laughed. "You could glean elements from the clouds, Daniel, if you set your mind to it. Come on, man, enlighten us."

Merton made a small bow to acknowledge the compliment. "Given the circumstances," he said, "there are only limited possibilities to account for Miss Smith's injury — self-immolation, accident or murder."

"She did not injure herself," Dr Hay said. "The angle of the knife wound was such that she could not have accomplished the injury unassisted."

"Ah," Merton said. "So... accident or murder, and some other person caused the fatal injury and, presumably, tipped the unfortunate woman into the canal. So the constables will be considering the reasons why such an event may have occurred, and out of sight of the great crowd congregated around the yard of the Carrbridge Arms. Was this other person someone she knew before? Was it a casual acquaintance, or a stranger? If the latter, there is not much to be done except to attempt to discover whether Miss Smith was seen with another person during the evening. But if it were *not* a stranger, then one would expect the constables to enquire into Miss Smith's history and all her acquaintances."

"It is surely obvious what happened," Dr Hay said. "This woman has already lost her respectability. Is it not likely that she took the opportunity to entice some unsavoury fellow aside for immoral purposes, they fell out over payment and she ended up in the canal? Can there be any other explanation?"

Ferdy shifted restlessly. "She did not strike me as a person who would behave in such a way," he said. "She was very angry at the loss of her virtue, which was taken forcibly from her by a gentleman who gave her the name of my cousin, Edgar Brant. In point of fact, she came to Yorkshire from Grantham for the sole purpose of finding him and insisting that he do what was right by her. But it was *not* my cousin's doing, as she admitted when she saw him, so I cannot at all understand why the constables keep asking about Edgar."

"Because of the connection," Merton said at once.

"What connection, Daniel?" Gil said.

"The man who abused Miss Smith was a gentleman, who told her his name was Edgar Brant from Yorkshire. There is indeed an Edgar Brant from Yorkshire, so the gentleman did not simply invent a name out of whole cloth — he used a real name. Therefore he was someone who knew Edgar Brant."

"Everybody knows Edgar," Ferdy protested. "He spends every season in London, he is invited everywhere, he is known to hundreds of people."

"Undoubtedly," Merton said. "But only some of those people were in Sagborough the night of the Easter ball."

Ferdy frowned. "I still do not quite see—" Light dawned. "Oh, you mean that whoever it was who mistreated her was here that night? And she recognised him, perhaps?"

"Recognised him and challenged him, yes, it is possible. Threatened him with exposure. Perhaps he is a respectably married man, or a clergyman, or someone with ambition to marry well — such a story could well damage his reputation severely."

"So he murdered her?" Ferdy said. "That seems — an extreme response. Why not pay her off? That is all she wanted, I daresay, some money to free her from dependence on charity."

"Perhaps he has none to spare," Merton said. "Or perhaps he is a gambler, a risk-taker. There they were, beside the canal, let us suppose, and quite alone. He could give her money, but she might want more, or she might still talk and get him into trouble. Or he could pull out his knife and get rid of her once and for all."

"Good God, that is appalling!" Ferdy said.

"But it is a possibility," Merton said. "And the worst of it is, that the constables are looking at those few gentlemen who were at the ball and stayed on afterwards — principally Lord Gilbert, Lord Humphrey, Lord Monty, Lord Reggie and Lord Carrbridge."

"That is ridiculous!" Ferdy said, appalled.

"Of course," Merton said. "But if any of them have ever been to Grantham—"

"Well, it was not me," Gil said sharply. "I have never been to Grantham in my life, and while I freely admit that I have not always been the pattern-card of rectitude that I ought to have been, I have never bedded a housemaid, not even in Grantham. Where is Grantham, anyway? Is it in Essex? I went to Essex once, and a devilish dull place it was too. I am sure I have never been to Grantham… tolerably sure, anyway. I would remember if I had, I think. Hmm… now I begin to wonder." He frowned.

"Even if you have no memory of the place, you would certainly remember the housemaid," Merton said.

"Naturally I would, if I had ever…" Gil said, but the frown deepened.

22: To And From London (June)

Edgar Brant returned from London in a post-chaise and four, his face creased with anxiety.

"Whatever brings you haring back in such haste?" Ferdy said, watching Edgar's mountain of luggage being disgorged from the carriage.

"Had a letter about this girl who went into the canal from some Bertram fellow. A constable, all terribly official-sounding. Wanting to know what I did on the night of the ball, but Ferdy, I did nothing except drink some punch, watch the dancing and then walk home with you. Did you not tell them that?"

"I did, but presumably they want confirmation. You are not accused of anything, Edgar."

"No? Well, it sounded very accusatory to me. So I thought it best to get back here and tell them to their faces that they are far out if they are looking at me."

Ralph accompanied Edgar, but when Ferdy asked what had brought *him* back to Sagborough, he only laughed and said, "Unfinished business."

"A lady," Edgar said sorrowfully. "He is as bad as you, Ferdy. You will both be caught by parson's mousetrap before you are much older. But he will not tell me who it is."

"Miss Trivers, I would guess," Ferdy said, laughing. "Or it could be Miss Malpas, I suppose, but those are the only two fortunes to be had in Sagborough at the moment."

"You are getting cynical, cousin," Ralph said, with his ready smile, but there was a coldness in his eye that made Ferdy suspect he was not too pleased to have his intentions known.

Ferdy took Edgar at once to see the constables, before he expired altogether in a puddle of terror. Once Edgar had been reassured that he was not suspected of any crime and they only wanted to know if he had ever been to Grantham or knew of any of his friends or relations who might have been, Edgar relaxed somewhat and was able to answer their questions with tolerable composure. They asked him about the ball, but apart from agreeing that he had seen Martha drop the tray of drinks and had gone home with Ferdy even before the dancing had finished, he had nothing to contribute.

"There, now," Ferdy said affably as he and Edgar walked home again. "That is all over with, you have done your duty and may forget about the business. Should you like to call on the Trivers?"

"The Trivers? Is there a reason why I should?"

"I am sure they would be delighted to see you," Ferdy said with a beaming smile. "And it is just possible that they may have some other callers just at this time."

"Ah. Miss Winterton, I take it. Lord, Ferdy, just offer for the girl and be done with it."

"In the fullness of time, cousin. There is no rush. Besides, I should like to see how the wind blows regarding another person." Edgar blinked at him. "Another possible suitor."

"Oh, you mean Hawes? Is he still sniffing about, then?"

"Hush, hush!" Ferdy said, for they were on the York Road by this time, the pavements thronged with passers-by. "Yes, him. I should like to know what he is about and that he is not an obstacle before I put my future to the test."

"She will not have him when she could have you," Edgar said, surprised. "Stands to reason. Any girl would take a future earl over a plain mister."

"I cannot be sure," Ferdy said, as they turned onto the street where the Trivers lived. "Fanny is very romantic, and if she has already formed an attachment to Hawes..."

"Nonsense," Edgar said. "Hawes is nothing to you. Fellow can barely tie his neckcloth in a simple knot."

Ferdy laughed and shook his head. If winning Fanny were merely a matter of neckcloths he would have some confidence, it was true, but he could not forget her animated face and shining eyes when she had met Hawes again. There was some attachment there, beyond doubt, and while it might diminish if Hawes continued to neglect Fanny, there was no point in Ferdy risking an outright rejection of his own suit by offering before she was ready to receive it favourably.

The Trivers' morning room was rather crowded. Apart from Mrs Trivers and Marianne, Celia Drabble was also there, working quietly at some stitchery at the worktable, as well as Fanny and the Makenham ladies. Sitting beside Marianne, both of them laughing, their heads close together as if they were just sharing a joke, was Ralph.

Ferdy and Edgar made their greetings around the room, and looked about them for seats. There was no chair available beside Fanny, and Edgar had spotted the empty seat beside Mrs Trivers, so Ferdy, from politeness, made his way to Celia Drabble's worktable. She smiled shyly at him, and he was immediately engrossed in a conversation about the correct shade of blue thread for the peacock she was embroidering. Then the door opened again.

"Mr Roland Hawes," said the footman.

The room fell into silence.

"Mr Hawes," Mrs Trivers said, with a little trill that might have been a laugh. "How delightful to see you again. I thought you had quite gone away."

"Indeed, I have been much occupied of late, madam. Much to do... visits to York... and so on. I do hope you will forgive my laxness, but it was through no wish of my own, you may be sure. Nothing could have kept me from your charming company, had I any say in the matter. You will observe that I make no enquiries as to your health, madam, for I may see for myself that you are positively blooming. Why, I do believe if you are not careful, you and your niece may be taken for sisters."

He bowed over her hand with a great flourish and she coloured up like a girl.

"Oh, Mr Hawes, what nonsense you do talk! You know everyone, I think. Do pray sit down. Yes, bring a chair forward. We would not have you excluded from the conversation."

Hawes found a chair set against the wall, then looked about the room. His eye fell first on Marianne, with Ralph close by. Then he looked across to Celia, observing Ferdy in attendance. Then, to Ferdy's dismay, Hawes placed his chair within inches of Fanny's and sat down beside her.

At first Ferdy was caught up in covertly watching Fanny's face, and observing with just a little triumph that her response to Hawes was distinctly cool. This kept him too occupied to notice anything else, but when he happened to look round, he saw Celia's face aflame, tears welling up in her eyes. Ferdy's gentlemanly instincts immediately rose to the surface, and he gallantly began a long monologue about peacocks, and then other garden fowl, then pigeons, and eventually, in desperation, the weather, until Celia had composed herself. This she did discreetly, wiping her eyes surreptitiously with a handkerchief, and eventually, in trembling tones, agreeing that it was indeed quite cool for May, and there was a good chance of rain later. After that, she bent her head to her sewing again and seemed more her normal self. She was too sensible a girl to repine for long. Still, Ferdy was disinclined to abandon her and kept to her side with a stream of inane nothings for the remainder of the visit.

The morning did not improve, for when the Makenham ladies and Fanny rose to leave, Ferdy's hopes of another pleasant walk home with Fanny on his arm were dashed at once.

"I think we must keep to the carriage today," Aunt Agatha said. "The risk of rain is too great to walk."

"Rain?" said Edgar in alarm. "My chest…"

"We can squeeze you into the carriage, I daresay," Aunt Agatha said.

Ralph seemed reluctant to leave Marianne Trivers, so Ferdy prepared to walk home alone, but just as he was setting off he heard himself hailed. He turned to find Hawes puffing after him.

"Shall we… walk together?" Hawes said, stopping to catch his breath. "I must go… to the post office… to collect my mail. We are bound the same way, so… you will not object to my company, I am sure."

There was nothing Ferdy wanted less, for his anger still burned brightly. Not because of Fanny, for he could not blame any man for wanting to enjoy her company, but because of Celia Drabble. It was cruel to pay attention to any lady and then veer away leaving her broken-hearted, and especially so with one who had so few enticements to draw a suitor, beyond her own person. She was a lovely girl, both in looks and in manner, with a great deal of sense, and Ferdy heartily wished her a good husband, and not one so erratic as Roland Hawes.

But politeness was impossible to set aside, so Ferdy assented to Hawes' company, and they walked on down the street in what must have looked to outsiders as companionable discourse. Hawes expounded at some length on Fanny's virtues, sentiments to which Ferdy readily agreed, while wanting very much to punch Hawes on the nose. For perhaps the first time in his life, Ferdy had some inkling as to why gentlemen sometimes got into fisticuffs with each other.

"It is so *difficult* to know what to do," Hawes sighed. "How hard it is to know if a lady is perfectly suited to one, or whether there may be another elsewhere even better suited."

That was when Ferdy had his clever idea. He was not, as a general rule, much given to clever ideas, and if he ever did, they usually ended by getting him into some sort of bother, but this time he surpassed himself. "Have you never thought of placing yourself on, shall we say, a wider stage, Hawes? One where all your good qualities may be fully appreciated, and you may have a much larger selection of potential Mrs Hawes to choose from? Why, you might even find one who encompasses all your preferences — the beauty of Miss Drabble, the fortune of Miss Trivers and the good-nature and demureness of Miss Winterton."

"I have been in York lately—"

"No, no. York is far too small a backdrop for Mr Hawes of Kellingborough. What about London?"

"Oh!" Ferdy could see Hawes thinking about it. "I do not think... I know no one..."

"But I know *everyone*," Ferdy said genially. "Everyone who matters, that is. I can write you letters of introduction — my grandfather, for instance, the Earl of Belwarren, or how about the Duke of Camberley? Did you meet the Marquess of Carrbridge at the ball? No? Oh, but you will, if you go to London. I can get you in to a couple of my clubs, just until you find your feet, you see, and my sister and brother-in-law would be thrilled to show you around. He is Viscount Lawston, you know."

Hawes' eyes were round, and his lips mouthed, "Earl... Duke... Marquess... Viscount..." in awe. Ferdy would not normally bandy about the names of his noble acquaintances in quite such a shameless fashion, but there were times when he was glad of his heritage and this was one of them.

He parted from Hawes on the most amicable terms possible, as Hawes rushed away to his inn to pack and pay his shot, while Ferdy wrote a stack of letters to friends, relations and useful acquaintances in London.

By the end of the day, Hawes was already on the road south, his pockets stuffed with letters of introduction, and Ferdy was at last free of his rival for Fanny's hand.

~~~~~

JUNE

Fanny found herself quite settled in her new life. She had congenial work, she had a comfortable home and she had friends whose company she greatly enjoyed. Now that she could go into society again, she could meet her particular friends, like Marianne, Celia and Emmy. Lady Agatha and the Miss Makenhams made her welcome at number Twenty-Five Harlington Terrace, and occasionally took her out into the countryside for a drive in the carriage, which thrilled Fanny. Apart from one outing with Lady Harriet and Miss Hay, which had turned out to be a visit to Lord Montague's church, she had not yet seen anything of the Yorkshire countryside. Now, with summer coming in and everything a-bloom, she could appreciate just how beautiful it was, in a wild and rugged way.

Lady Harriet and Miss Hay were still away, although almost every letter came from a different place as they moved about from one friend to another, but Fanny felt rather guiltily that they were not greatly missed. Dr Hay and his mother were undemanding company. He spent almost all his time at the hospital, and his evenings studying medical treatises and books. Mrs Hay was happiest when left to doze away the hours, waking properly only at mealtimes.

Fanny was not sure what to think about Mr Hawes. After travelling from Brinshire presumably for the sole purpose of finding her, he had been drawn away by Celia Drabble's greater beauty, which Fanny could not in the least blame him for, and had then gone off to London. He was a very unsettled sort of man, and, on the whole, she felt she was better off without him.

Her opinion of Mr Makenham was rather more positive. He was a pleasure to look upon, for he was always immaculately dressed — when not tramping through the mud to find missing housemaids, of course. His manners were so delightful, too, and Fanny never felt the least awkwardness with him, even though she was fairly sure that he would one day offer for her. Such an agreeable man! No matter what happened, he always set her mind at rest and made her feel less distressed.

Only one thing happened at this time to distress her, or rather, two things, but two occurrences of the same thing. Two more young women were found dead in the canal, stabbed and then pushed into the water. Dr Hay described them brusquely as *'bad women who have done bad things, and no doubt fell in with bad men and got what they deserved',* but Mr Makenham had put it rather more gently.

"They were unfortunate women who had no Lady Harriet to rescue them and give them a chance to recover from their mistakes. They were obliged to scrabble for money however they could, and in such cases one may meet with unscrupulous types who will stop at nothing, who might even kill for the slightest of reasons, or for no reason at all."

Fanny felt confident that she could say anything to Mr Makenham, but even so, she was hesitant when she said, "Dr Hay said they got what they deserved."

To her great pleasure, Mr Makenham's answer was robustly expressed. "No one deserves such an end. Stabbed and then tossed into the water like yesterday's dinner? It is despicable. But there is one good thing about it, for the constables now know why Miss Smith was killed, for it must have been the same sort of... encounter."

"Martha was not a bad woman," Fanny said sadly.

"No, but perhaps she made a mistake, just that once, and it cost her everything," Mr Makenham said gently. "It means that her death had nothing to do with her previous life in Grantham, and my cousin need not worry about his name being dragged into the business."

"Oh yes, poor Mr Brant!" Fanny cried. "How dreadful that was, to have the constables asking about him in that way. How he must have suffered!"

"Yes, indeed. But the constables are looking elsewhere for reasons for Miss Smith's death, and so my cousin may be easy."

Now that she was moving in society, Fanny had begun to attend the assemblies. Since Dr Hay had no interest in such occasions, Fanny went in the Makenham carriage. Their numbers meant that the carriage was obliged to make two journeys, and as often as not Fanny found herself travelling with Mr Makenham and his two sisters, while Lady Agatha came later with Mr Brant and Mr Ralph Makenham.

The upper room at the King's Head was much smaller than the barn at the Carrbridge Arms, but then it had no need to accommodate every farm labourer and scullery maid in Sagborough. The assemblies were subscription only, so only the gentry and the highest levels of professional families attended. There was no dais here for the gentry, and the seats ringing the walls were mere inches from the dancers, so that one was in constant fear of an energetic leaper landing in one's lap, but Fanny was enchanted. It was not as sophisticated as the assemblies at Brinchester, but it was the most tremendous fun. She leaned forward, tapping her feet to the music, counting in her head the number of weeks before she could be comfortable dancing herself. She still wore black gloves and black ribbons in her hair, but those were the very last vestiges of her mourning for poor Papa.

Lady Agatha was officially chaperon to Fanny, Emilia and Cordelia, but since she stood up for every dance, Fanny was glad to place herself near Mrs Trivers and Mrs Drabble, who stayed decorously on the chaperon's seats. Not that Fanny was without other company, for there was always one or other of her friends sitting out a dance or just glad of a rest, for while the people of Sagborough were not elegant dancers, they made up for any lack of gracefulness in an abundance of energy.

After one particularly vigorous country dance, Marianne flopped down beside Fanny, gasping for breath. "Goodness! So lively! I shall be… quite exhausted… by the end… of the evening."

"You could have asked Mr Ralph to partner you for the cotillion instead," Fanny said. "I am sure he would have been happy to oblige you."

Marianne pulled a face, then, with a quick glance at her aunt to ensure she was busy talking and not attending, she said, "I daresay he would. He has asked for the supper dance, too, but… I have put him off."

"You dislike him?" Fanny said, surprised. "He is so handsome, and he dresses very fine. Such broad shoulders!"

"Oh yes, and he is very amusing, but sometimes when he looks at me…" She shivered. "I feel… undressed, somehow. He makes me uncomfortable. Not like *your* admirer." She tilted her head towards the set just forming, where Mr Makenham was leading Miss Malpas to the head.

Fanny blushed slightly, but she did not pretend to misunderstand. "Oh yes! Such a gentleman."

"He will not keep you waiting much longer, I feel sure. See how he glances in your direction even now — he is very discreet, but he loves to look at you. Oh, here is my partner to claim me. I shall see you at supper, I expect."

Fanny loved to look at Mr Makenham, too. His perfect evening dress always made her sigh with pleasure, and he was quite the most graceful dancer in the room. At one time she had not thought him especially handsome, but his features were so familiar to her and his expression so full of the good humour that characterised him, that she had long thought him a fine looking man. She next turned her gaze on Mr Ralph, and realised at once what Marianne had meant. He was excessively handsome, he smiled a great deal and there was no dispute at all about the manliness of his form, but there was something in his eyes that was unsettling. As he danced, he caught her eye and his smile slipped a little. Annoyed with herself for staring at him, she dropped her gaze and then, when she thought it safe, turned back to the more pleasing subject of Mr Ferdinand Makenham.

Mr Makenham very kindly sat out the supper dance with her, and then led her into supper. That was a relief, for otherwise she would have had to go in on her own, which someone like Miss Hay, perhaps, would not care about, but Fanny cared very much. How mortifying to have no partner for supper! And then Mr Makenham was so good at bringing her everything she wanted to eat and drink, with not the least thought of himself.

When the carriage returned them to Harlington Terrace, he escorted her to her own door and raised her gloved hand to his lips with a bow. In the flicker of the lamp above the door, his eyes gleamed softly.

"Miss Winterton, I wonder if I might be permitted the favour of an interview with you tomorrow — in private?"

Fanny's heart lurched in sudden fear. She lowered her eyes. "Of course, sir. Would two o'clock be acceptable to you?"

"Perfectly, thank you. Good night, Miss Winterton. Until tomorrow, then."

With another neat bow, he turned and walked back to his own steps, but then he stood and watched her until William opened the door and she went inside.

Tomorrow. Tomorrow everything would change.

23: An Offer Of Marriage

He was nervous, and that was a surprise. All her previous suitors had been nervous when it came to the point and the solemnity of the moment overcame them, but Ferdy was so supremely assured in every situation that she had not expected him to be discomposed in the slightest. Yet there it was, that slight hesitation in the smile, the hint of anxiety in the eyes. It was rather endearing.

"Mr Makenham."

"Miss Winterton."

His bow was as finely executed as ever. Somehow, she always felt more dignified in his presence, her curtsy more graceful. She felt more like a lady.

She gestured towards a chair. "Will you sit down?" She sat herself, and realised at once that she had forgotten to arrange the furniture. Rosamund, always so practical, had once said that it was important to choose one's seat carefully for a proposal. If it is welcome, then sit on a sofa so that the impassioned lover may steal a kiss afterwards, but if one intends to refuse, it is better to sit in a chair so that one need not be importuned. But Fanny had not thought of that when she had told William last night that Mr Makenham was to be shown into the drawing room, and it was too late now. She could only take the nearest seat.

William bowed himself out, a little smile on his face. All the servants would know, of course. The significance of a private interview could not be misunderstood. The door clicked shut behind the footman, and she was alone with Ferdy. It was clear that he was not going to sit down, so she rested her hands on her lap and waited.

He cleared his throat. "Thank you for permitting me to see you," he began. "I... am sure you know what I am about to say. I myself have known that this moment would come for a long time now, in fact, from the very instant I first saw you on that gloomy day in January, when we had both of us just descended from our carriages. Two strangers, newly arrived in the town — it seemed like fate at the time. It still does. You looked—"

His face lit up eagerly as he sat down abruptly opposite her. "Miss Winterton, I had never seen any woman so charming, so... so entrancing. When you looked round at me, peeping out from your leghorn bonnet with the velvet rose on one side, you looked as beautiful as a flower turning its face to the sun, and I was struck dumb at the sight. I daresay you remember how mesmerised I was! How foolish I must have looked at the time. But every day since then has only served to increase my admiration for your beauty, your kindness, your gentle nature and your delightful conversation which so captivates me."

Here he jumped up again and began to pace about the room. "Miss Winterton, I could expound on your many virtues all day, but let me not try your patience. Let me get to the point. You know something of my family, so you are aware that one day, a great many years in the future, one must hope, I will be the Earl of Belwarren, and my wife a countess and mistress of Abbeymount. I know that such considerations will not weigh with you, but it pleases me to offer you a position and a setting worthy of your many perfections. It might seem a little sordid to talk about money to a lady, and I will be happy to discuss the matter in more detail with your brother-in-law or solicitor, but be assured that you would want for nothing, and my grandfather has agreed to settle a large sum on you... if you should... if I were so fortunate as to... so... so you would have plenty of pin money. And the house is mine... number Twenty-Five, that is. It is a fine house, I think, and I should be very happy... if you were to... I mean..."

Finally his composure slipped altogether, and he knelt at her feet, taking one of her hands in his, anxious eyes fixed on hers. "Oh Fanny, my sweet Fanny! I want to marry you more than I have ever wanted anything in my life. I... have not the words to express how much I love you. Please say you will marry me, because my life would be utterly empty without you in it. Could you...? Do you think...? Would you do me the honour of becoming my wife? Please?"

Fanny's heart was pounding. This was the moment she dreaded, the moment when everything changed.

She licked her lips. "Mr Makenham..." She could have stopped there, almost, for she could see at once that he knew. The formal language was not the happy acceptance he had hoped for. "I thank you from the bottom of my heart for the very great honour you do me. I am so very obliged to you, but... oh, I am so extremely sorry, but I cannot!"

"Cannot?" His voice was a mere thread.

"I am afraid not. You see... oh, I would not cause you pain for the world, but it must be so! You see, I do not love you, Mr Makenham."

"Oh." A long pause. "Not at all?"

"I *like* you very well, and if I could marry a man I only liked, then you would certainly be the man I should choose. But marriage must be based on love, do you not agree? A great passion, an overwhelming, all-encompassing love that is impossible to deny. *'There is no form in which the fire Of love its traces has impressed not.'* Do you see? *'What subtle pain is kindled now, Which from my heart doth overflow Into my senses?'* I need my heart to overflow, Mr Makenham."

Another long pause. "You do not feel that... perhaps... in the fullness of time, you might grow to love me?"

"Oh no, because I have known you for a long time now and I have not yet experienced the fire of love. I am sure it would have happened by now, if it were meant to be, for surely it would be quick and overwhelming, like being struck by a thunderbolt."

"A thunderbolt. Oh. As... as with me?"

"Exactly so, and that cannot happen after one knows a person, can it? One cannot have a pleasant little friendship, and *then* be hit by a thunderbolt, can one? You do see why it would be impossible, Mr Makenham?"

He smiled a little wanly. Releasing her hand, he rose smoothly to his feet. "Not... not entirely, but I see that it is an obstacle for you, Miss Winterton."

She jumped to her feet too. "I am so very sorry!"

Another slight smile. "There is not the slightest need for any apology from you, Miss Winterton. It is for me to apologise for misunderstanding you so completely. I beg your pardon for importuning you. May I... may I wish you a future which brings you all the love and happiness you desire, and a man who is worthy of you. Good day to you."

In three steps he had reached the door, opened it and passed through. Fanny waited, listening for the rumble of male voices as the footman showed him down the stairs, and then the front door opening and closing again. He was gone. Fanny picked up her skirts and fled to her room in tears. Whether she wept most for Ferdy's disappointment or her own lost friendship, she could not say.

~~~~~

Ferdy pulled on his gloves mechanically, and accepted his hat and cane from William. He might even have spoken to the man, he could not say. Probably he did, for it would be expected of him. William opened the door for him, and Ferdy walked slowly out of number

Twenty-Six, down the steps, along the street and up the steps to number Twenty-Five. Poole opened the door, Ferdy handed his hat and cane to Hill, peeled off his gloves and entered the book room. There he sat in his favourite chair beside the hearth and stared at nothing.

For a long time he sat motionless, too numb to know what he was feeling. Grief, perhaps. Despair, just a little. Fear of the long, empty future before him, a future that had no Fanny in it. And besides that, a sweep of formless regrets and melancholies that were beyond his ability to describe.

In all the long months he had courted Fanny, he had never thought much about the possibility of rejection. He had not thought much about an acceptance, either. He had not, in point of fact, dared to look beyond the proposal itself. Every step on the road to this moment he had weighed and considered and contrived. The offer itself he had rehearsed in his mind a thousand times. He had even written it out a few times, to ensure that the phrasing was the most felicitous he could manage, although in the event it had come out rather differently from his imaginings. But he had never dared to anticipate Fanny's answer, and so he was wholly unprepared for the ocean of anguish in which he now found himself drowning.

Had he erred in some unknown manner? Was there any way he could have made his case that would have brought a happier outcome? He could not see it. There had never been the slightest hope for him, if he had but known it. If he had considered the matter at all, he would have supposed that the only real obstacle to his suit was a prior attachment on Fanny's part. Hawes, perhaps. But Hawes had gone, and Fanny seemed unaffected, and that was not the obstacle at all. She did not love him, and, what was worse, could never love him. There was no getting past that.

Dimly he was aware of a carriage on the cobbles outside, then the front door opening and girlish chatter in the hall. Footsteps on the stairs, and then silence fell again. After a while, the book room door opened, and Aunt Agatha's head appeared.

"Ferdy? Oh Ferdy, my poor boy! I am so sorry."

"So am I, Auntie."

She came in and sat on the matching chair across the hearth. "What did she say?"

"That she does not love me, she can never love me and there is an end to it."

"But you seemed to get on so well. I cannot understand it. Is it Hawes, do you think?"

Ferdy sighed. "She did not say so."

"No, she did not seem distressed when he went away, and she is a sensitive soul. If she were suffering, we should have observed the signs. So not Hawes, then. Did she give you *any* hope?"

He shook his head, picking unseeingly at a worn patch on the leather arm of the chair.

"Oh dear. What will you do? Shall you feel obliged to go away?"

For a moment Ferdy could not even grasp the idea. He had been fixed in Sagborough, his thoughts only on Fanny, for so long that all alternatives had long since vanished. Even now, he could not contemplate leaving his beloved Fanny behind. "I shall stay, I think. In a day or two, I shall be able to meet her again with equanimity."

"But what if *she* cannot meet *you*? After all, Sagborough society is very confined. You will encounter each other everywhere."

"If that is the case, I shall leave, of course. I would not for the world cause her any discomfort. But for myself, it would please me to see her sometimes, and perhaps, in time, she may change her mind."

"Yes, dear. Of course she may."

~~~~~

Fanny wept for fully half an hour. Then she resolutely dried her eyes, aided by the powerful image of Rosamund's bracing practicality. *'Do pull yourself together, Fanny,'* she would say sternly. *'So many tears!*

Where do they all come from? Crying never helps anything. Besides, your eyes and nose will go red, and then you will look a complete fright.' So Fanny obediently pulled herself together, and washed her face and tried not to think about Ferdy's hopeful expression gradually turning to bewilderment and then disappointment. But it was always so, with her suitors. They always looked so disappointed.

She could not explain it to Mrs Hay, for such intimate disclosures did not lend themselves to being bellowed at a pitch loud enough to be heard by the scullery maid two floors below. However, she told Dr Hay about it when he came into the drawing room before dinner.

"Hmph. So you are not minded to be a countess, eh?"

"Mr Makenham's title is of no interest to me," she replied stiffly.

"Even without that, he is rich, presentable, well-mannered and behaves himself. He will never give you the least trouble, so what was so objectionable about him that you would turn him down?"

"I… I do not love him, sir."

"Love! Pah! What does a child like you know of love? Still, it is your life wasted with a needle in your hand, when you could walk amongst the nobility."

And that was all he offered on the subject, for his friend Dr Wellbeloved arrived just then for dinner, and Dr Hay set aside the gruff manner he reserved for Fanny, and became the genial host.

Through the long evening, as Mrs Hay's gentle snores and the click of the dice on the physicians' backgammon table were the only competition for the ticking clock on the mantel, Fanny pondered the question. Was her life wasted? Should she, perhaps, have set aside her own feelings on the subject and agreed to marry Ferdy anyway? It was not as if there were anything repellent about his person, after all. On the contrary, he was a delight to look upon and to be with, always so immaculately dressed and his manners perfection. A lady felt like *somebody* on Ferdy Makenham's arm.

But how dreadful to marry without love, purely for one's own comfort, and then be hit by a thunderbolt later. How easily that might happen, if one's heart were not entirely given to one's husband already. Here again, Rosamund's words were like a ewer of cold water. *'Thunderbolt? And what happens if the thunderbolt arrives and the object of your sudden passion is a married man, or a wastrel, or a gambler? What if he is a ditch-digger or a pirate? Love grows, Fanny, and no thunderbolts are needed.'* In vain Fanny had protested that she had never met a pirate, and could not think it likely that she would. *'Well, a Romany, then,'* Rosamund had said impatiently. *'Would you throw away your life to follow him, ragged and barefoot? It is not sensible, Fanny. Marriage cannot be sustained by love alone, for who will see that the meals are ordered and the bills paid? All that is needed is enough money to live upon without scrimping, and two people who rub along tolerably well. One must be prudent.'*

Enough money to live upon without scrimping. Ferdy had all that and a great deal more, and marriage to a future earl would be prudent enough even for Rosamund to approve. All her sisters would rejoice in such a match, would they not? Ferdy's wealth could support any number of unmarried sisters in tolerable comfort. A little cottage somewhere, with a bit of garden in front and an orchard behind it, and the expense would be nothing to him. Annabelle would not need to be a lowly governess. Lucy would not be driven to distraction by her two young charges. Poor Margaret need not be companion to two old ladies. Deep inside Fanny, a little flame of guilt was lit, and refused to be extinguished.

~~~~~

After a sleepless night, Fanny woke to a long, dreary day ahead. She ought to be going to number Twenty-Five today, but that was out of the question now. She could never go there again, she supposed. How angry they would be that she had refused the heir to the earldom! After all the kind attentions they had paid her, she had rebuffed the family in the strongest manner possible. The loss of

Lady Agatha's company, and of Emilia and Cordelia too, was almost as painful to Fanny as the loss of Ferdy. Her spirits were so low that she could not help crying again, just a little, as she dressed, so she sent William to the shop with a note to say that she felt unwell — which was true enough — and would not be in attendance that day.

She tried her very best not to cry or sniffle at breakfast in front of Dr Hay and Dr Wellbeloved, who had stayed the night, for she knew that gentlemen had little tolerance of female sensibilities. Or at least, Dr Hay had little tolerance of Fanny's sensibilities. Once the two physicians had gone to the hospital for the day, and she had settled down with her needle and thread, the tears blurred her vision again. In the end, she gave up even trying to sew, and sat miserably in her corner, wondering how long her distress would last this time. Three days was the usual length of time before she began to recover her spirits, but she was unaccountably lower than expected this time.

The doorbell rang, and she hastily blew her nose and tried to wipe her face with her sleeve. It was not Mrs Hay's day to receive callers, but some people came anyway, without regard to the proper days.

"The Lady Agatha Makenham, madam," William intoned.

Fanny jumped to her feet, a spasm of pure terror spearing through her. Lady Agatha! To berate her for refusing Ferdy, no doubt.

Mrs Hay looked up, startled, and dropped her tatting. Lady Agatha stooped to pick it up. "THERE YOU ARE, DEAR. YOU CARRY ON. JUST HERE TO TALK TO FANNY."

"Oh. Of course," Mrs Hay said, looking at her tatting in bewilderment as if she had never seen it before.

Fanny bowed her head in terror as Lady Agatha swept across the room, a blue satin ship in full sail. Fanny was not sure she could face a scolding without collapsing altogether. But Lady Agatha did not scold. Instead she looked searchingly at Fanny, said, "You poor child! How you must be suffering!" and scooped Fanny into her arms for a fierce hug.

When, eventually, she let Fanny go, she gently steered her to a different seat. "There now, let us sit here so the old lady cannot see your tears. My poor, dear Fanny! Have you been crying all night?"

She shook her head. "I am trying to be sensible."

"Of course you are, for you are a good girl, but it distresses you to cause pain to anyone, I know."

"Oh yes! It is so upsetting to be the means of... of *disappointing* a gentleman."

"Indeed it is, but one cannot marry a man on that account, can one? That would be absurd."

Fanny nodded. "If I could have hinted him away... but it is so awkward. One cannot tell a gentleman not to offer for one."

"No, indeed," Lady Agatha said. "One can say nothing until he makes the offer. It would be the height of bad manners to presume that an offer is to be made, after all. You did just as you ought, my dear."

Tentatively, Fanny said, "You are not cross with me? You are not going to tell me that I have made a dreadful mistake?"

"Cross with you? Good gracious, child, who could possibly be cross with you? As to whether it is a mistake — well, that is between you and Ferdy, and if you do not wish to marry him, there is an end to the matter. I am sorry, naturally, because I should have loved to welcome you into the family, but the decision is entirely yours. Now, my dear, let me get to the reason for my rather irregular visit, which is to invite you to come next door today just as usual. Yes, yes, I know you feel you should not, but Ferdy has gone to York for the day, so you will not encounter him at all, and Julius is to take the girls to Drummoor in the barouche, so they will be gone soon and I shall be all on my own. It would please me greatly if you would bear me company for the day, and if you wish to talk about anything at all, why, there I shall be, a sympathetic ear. And if you do not, then there is no need at all to say a word. We shall have a cold collation and a little Madeira, perhaps, and I have a new box of bon-bons from that delicious little shop in Mill Road, so we will have a very comfortable time together. What do you say?"

Fanny was quite unable to refuse such a kindly invitation, and so, against all her expectations, less than a day after she had refused Ferdy, she went back to Twenty-Five Harlington Terrace.

24: In York (July-August)

Ferdy had no great desire to go to York on that or any other day, but Aunt Agatha in autocratic mood was not to be denied.

"Trust me, Ferdy," she had said. "If we can but persuade Fanny back into the house on the same easy footing as before, then we can gradually get her used to your presence again. Then you may see what comes of it. So long as she is not betrothed to anyone else, there is always a possibility that she will come to appreciate you as she should."

He had seen the sense in it, and was grateful to Aunt Agatha for making the attempt, although he himself could see no cause for optimism. Still, if he could but meet Fanny in company without discomfort on either side, he would be content with that.

So it was that he found himself driving his curricle along the York road well before breakfast. At first he was fully occupied with his pair, for they had not been out for a few days and were rather frisky. Ferdy was a perfectly competent driver, but he had never been as accomplished or as stylish as Ralph, and the first few miles stretched his capabilities rather. Beside him, his groom sat with arms rigidly folded, no doubt wishing he had the reins himself. Once they left Sagborough behind, and were bowling along the wind-blown lanes, he got on rather better and was rattling through Micklegate Bar in no time. He left the curricle and groom at the Black Swan, while he himself went to Eridge's Hotel for a late breakfast.

He had not planned a trip to York, but now that it was forced upon him, he would make good use of the opportunity. Accordingly, he made his way to the offices of Bertram, Smith and Bertram, solicitors. The younger Mr Bertram graciously agreed to see him without an appointment, and Ferdy was ushered into an office so well-appointed that any lady would be happy to entertain there. Apart from a desk strewn with papers and a few larger than usual leather-bound volumes on the shelves, there was nothing to indicate that this was a place of business.

Mr Bertram greeted him courteously, poured Canary for them both and sat Ferdy in a comfortable wingchair beside the hearth, where a small fire burned despite the warmth of the day.

"Now, Mr Makenham, how may I be of service to you?" Bertram said.

"It is about the business of the young ladies found in the canal at Sagborough, in which you acted as constable."

"Ah, yes. My uncle is the appointed constable at present, but he is not a well man these days, so I act as his deputy when required. Is there some new information? Not another murder, I trust?" he added, in alarm. "I had hoped we were finished with the business."

"Nothing new, but it is the question of being finished with the business which I hope to discuss with you," Ferdy said. "Three women are dead by infamous means, and yet it seems no one is to hang for it, and you appear to have given up the case altogether."

"Not given up, so much as reached an impasse," Bertram said thoughtfully. "We have three dead women, and not the slightest hint as to a possible culprit."

"None at all?" Ferdy said, in a small voice. "That is... disappointing."

"Such a situation is almost inevitable, given the... ah, *career* of these women."

"Whatever the latter two may have been, Miss Smith was not a lightskirt," Ferdy said sharply. "She was a housemaid."

"Indeed, indeed," Bertram said, pushing his spectacles more firmly onto his nose. "She had a respectable profession, but she also had a fatherless child. It may be that, given the rather rowdy nature of the evening of the ball, and the quantity of punch consumed, matters may have turned... *amorous*, shall we say, and she took the opportunity to make a few extra coins."

"That is a most insulting—" Ferdy began hotly, but Bertram cut in quickly.

"You do not, I feel sure, frequent such places as the... ah, *establishment* beside the canal a short distance from the Carrbridge Arms, Mr Makenham. There are two brothers who look after the women who reside therein, and they feel very strongly that such women should not... ah, *ply their trade* outside the accommodation provided, and that under no circumstances should they be undertaking business on their own account. Nor should any other women be providing similar services within the domain the brothers regard as theirs. Now the other two women found dead in the canal, Sally Turner and Jenny Melton, were both... ah, *employed* by these brothers, and Sally at least was known to have had private arrangements with favoured clients, so you see..." He raised his hands, palm outwards, with a little shrug.

"So that is it?" Ferdy said, in rising indignation. "They were lightskirts, so nothing can be done about it? Have these brothers been interviewed?"

"Of course, but naturally they proclaim their innocence, and no one will speak against them. I would love to see the blackguard who murdered those women swing for his crimes, but it cannot be done without some evidence, Mr Makenham."

Ferdy pondered the point, but he could not see a way around it. "I appreciate the difficulty, Mr Bertram. As to the other two women, I did not know them, so I cannot say anything about their characters, but I have met Miss Smith, and she did not strike me as a person who was likely to succumb to an amorous encounter, whether coins were involved or not. When she accosted my cousin, Mr Brant, she was outraged by her treatment at the hands of an unknown gentleman, and she was very glad of her place as a housemaid."

Somehow his glass had emptied. The solicitor rose from his chair and silently refilled both glasses.

"When we first began our enquiries," he said, resuming his seat, "we had only Martha Smith to consider, and so it seemed possible that her death was connected to her seducer in some way. Perhaps she had seen him at the ball, and drew him aside to remonstrate with him? He, perhaps, had seen a way to prevent her from making damaging revelations. But... I have to tell you, Mr Makenham, that our enquiries led us in a most unexpected direction. We looked for a gentleman who had been at Grantham at the time Martha Smith was there, and who was *also* in Sagborough when she was killed. Most likely, it would be a gentleman who was at the ball itself and stayed on afterwards. Also, he would be a gentleman who liked to seduce innocents. There are very few names who fit all requirements."

"I cannot think of any," Ferdy said. "No one seems to have been anywhere near Grantham."

"No one admits to it, certainly, but there is one person who fulfils the other criteria."

"I cannot think—" Ferdy began, then hesitated. "You cannot be suggesting—"

"Lord Gilbert Marford."

"No!" Ferdy whispered. "Good heavens, I have known Gil for years, and he would never—" He stopped, recalling Gil's reputation as a rake, his trail of mistresses, his wild reputation. And now he had a wife he loved, a respectable life, and he might not want his past returning to haunt him. But murder? Surely not.

"All the Marford brothers were present after the ball, but Lord Gilbert seems the only one likely to seduce a housemaid. We did wonder about *you* at one point, Mr Makenham, but Martha knew your face and would surely have recognised you at your house if you had been her seducer. We settled on Lord Gilbert when we heard that he came home that night covered in blood."

"He had been in a fight! His nose bled, I expect, or his opponent's nose."

"Indeed so. But that might have made him more reckless. He might have thought that he could get away with knifing the poor girl because he was already bloodied. It all fitted horribly well. So you see why we were relieved when a second body appeared, and then a third, and it looked likely to be a squabble amongst lowlifes."

"So you stopped looking for a gentleman. Yes, I see," Ferdy said thoughtfully. "But I cannot believe it of Gil Marford. He has always been wild, it is true, at least until he married, but his mistresses were from his own class, married women bored with their husbands, that sort of thing. Not housemaids. And I cannot believe he would kill merely to keep the story quiet. The whole world knows him for a rake, so it is hardly a revelation. No, it was not Gil, I would stake my life on it."

Bertram removed his spectacles and began to polish them with a handkerchief. "Would you stake money on it, Mr Makenham?"

"A wager? That seems... inappropriate."

The solicitor laughed. "No, no. I am not a gambling man, I assure you, but I am a man of the law and it would please me to bring a man to justice for these crimes. These women have no family to seek justice on their behalf, and although we constables do what we can, we are constrained somewhat. When Lord Carrbridge asked for constables from York to intervene, he agreed to pay our expenses, but we could not call upon his purse indefinitely, so once our investigations trickled away to nothing, we returned here. There is still much that could be done, however, if a benefactor could be found to foot the bill. There is Grantham, for instance, where all my letters have not even discovered the house where Martha worked. I should dearly love to go there in person to make enquiries."

"A benefactor..." Ferdy said slowly. "I can certainly pay, if you are willing to undertake the work."

"I am willing, but are you prepared for the possible outcome, Mr Makenham? Are you prepared to put a hangman's noose around the neck of Lord Carrbridge's brother?"

"If he has done this wicked deed, then yes, I would see him swing for it. And if he has not, I would have that known also."

"So be it," Bertram said. "I shall depart for Grantham tomorrow."

~~~~~

'Dear Fanny Aunt Letty has died Margaret'

~~~~~

Seven days. That was how long it took Fanny to feel comfortable again. On the first day, she did not see Ferdy at all. On the second day, he put his head round the door of the morning room, smiled and said hello and how was she, before disappearing again. The third day was Sunday, and they exchanged a few words after church. Then he was at the Trivers' house when she called, but on the far side of the room, so she did not speak to him at all. The next day, they were both dining at Lord and Lady Gilbert's house, so they spoke briefly before dinner, were at opposite ends of the table during the meal and were part of a large, noisy vingt-et-un game afterwards. The day after that, he sat with the ladies in the morning room at number Twenty-Five for a few minutes while he waited for Mr Brant to be ready to go out. And on the seventh day, they met in Mrs Malpas's crowded drawing room, and he took one look at Fanny and came straight towards her, his face wreathed in anxiety.

"Miss Winterton, whatever has happened? You are in full mourning again."

"It is my aunt who has died, Mr Makenham. She has been ill for a long time. That is why my sister Margaret went there, to be of help to her in her infirmity."

"Oh, your *aunt*. Thank goodness!" He sat down on the seat beside her. "Such a relief! Well, not your aunt's demise, of course, but I was afraid it might be one of your sisters, for I could not immediately recollect any other relatives. Now that I think upon it, there were two aunts and an uncle, I believe. And she was ill beforehand? So it was not unexpected. But your poor sister, how she must feel it! Shropshire, I think you said? Near Ludlow, was it not?"

No reserve could withstand such genuine concern. Certainly Fanny's could not, and all reticence between them was at an end. They talked of Margaret and Aunt Letty and Aunt Pru, and Fanny could have wept at Ferdy's kindness and sincere interest in her relations. He said all that was proper, expressing his concern in such heartfelt terms that she was quite overwhelmed and talked to him in the most open manner, just as she always had. They were sitting at the table, for Fanny always took a little piece of sewing when she paid a call, so that she could sit quietly occupied and not put herself forward, but her work lay forgotten in the excitement of talking to Ferdy again, talking properly, as friends.

"Oh, I am so glad you did not go away, Mr Makenham," she burst out. "I was so afraid that you would, and that Lady Agatha and your sisters would not wish to talk to me again, and it makes me very happy to find that it is not so."

There was just the tiniest pause before he said, "I am relieved to hear you say so, Miss Winterton. I would not for the world distress you, and if ever my presence should do so—"

"Oh no! Not in the least! I should have been very sorry indeed if you had gone away on my account."

He smiled a little, but she thought it was not a comfortable smile. For a moment he was silent, looking down at the table, as the chatter in the room swirled around them. With one finger, he idly traced an imaginary pattern on the cloth. Then abruptly he raised his head, and Fanny was shocked at the pain in his eyes. It was as if she looked straight through to his heart.

"Miss Winterton, I am… very pleased that we can remain friends, for I value your friendship above all others. I shall not speak again of the matter that lies between us, for I honour your wishes in all things, but… but if ever you should reconsider, be assured that a single word to me would be sufficient. And now, I have kept you from other company long enough. I bid you good day, Miss Winterton."

He rose, bowed and moved away, leaving Fanny shaken, but also exultant. He would not leave! And he valued her friendship above all others. They could still be friends, and somehow, despite her sorrow that she had disappointed him, she was insensibly cheered by his continuing presence.

~~~~~

'Dearest Fanny, What dreadful weather you seem to be having in Yorkshire! Does it always rain so much or is this unusual, would you say? At least you are keeping well, and I am relieved to hear that there has been no recurrence of the grippe which so afflicted the town in the spring. I hope the weather improves so that you may get out of the town occasionally. There is nothing like country air to set one up, so do take every opportunity to escape. Is Lady H returned yet? She has been away for a long time. Mr H must miss her dreadfully, but it is only natural that she should want to see all her old friends and I daresay they would not care to visit Sagborough. How soon do you feel it would be proper to leave off the black gloves, for I confess that I am very tired of being in mourning and it is not as if we had ever met Aunt Letty. But one would not wish to be lax in the proper observances. I am sure Rosamund will know what is appropriate. Perhaps we will hear more from Margaret now that she is freed from her duties attending Aunt Letty. You have not mentioned the lovestruck Mr M in your most recent letters. Has he gone away, like Mr H? Do let me know what has happened to him. Your loving sister, Annabelle.'

~~~~~

JULY - AUGUST

The rain of June gave way to the marginally warmer rain of July. Outings were arranged; outings were cancelled. Entertainments were planned to be held in gardens, and then hastily squeezed into drawing rooms far too small for them. In one week alone, three picnics, two outdoor Venetian breakfasts and an afternoon of battledore and shuttlecock were ruined. In the end, in desperation for some activity that might be conducted indoors, it was suggested that they might get up some readings from Shakespeare. With choosing the extracts to be performed, preparing properties and designing suitable costumes and hangings, even wet days might be filled with activity.

But this interesting scheme immediately ran aground as the putative acting troop fell into dispute. Some were for Romeo and Juliet, as being most suited to the ages and temperaments of the participants, and having besides some stirring sword fights. Others, however, felt that a play where both hero and heroine died was too morbid for words, and would it not be better to choose one of the comedies? Ferdy, however, insisted that it had to be The Tempest.

"That is *my* play, you see," he said proudly. "Prince Ferdinand, the son of the King of Naples. I like The Tempest."

"It is pretty silly, though, Ferdy," Mr Ralph said. "All that magic, and everything comes right in the end, and even the shipwreck was not true."

"That is the best kind of story, where everything comes right in the end," Ferdy said.

"Oh, yes! I completely agree, Mr Makenham," Fanny said. "It is so much better when everyone is happy and safe eventually. I am always in an agony of suspense watching a play in case someone dies, which is too horrible. And I am sure you would make an excellent Prince." Ferdy turned and smiled at her with such warmth that she blushed hotly.

But the actors could not agree and so nothing ever came of it.

Fanny and the Makenhams were gathered in the morning room of number Twenty-Five one day, about to depart for the Trivers' house for a morning of sketching, when Poole sidled in. Fanny knew him well enough now to interpret his countenance, which varied from the embarrassment of a domestic crisis to the triumph of announcing a particularly grand visitor, but now his behaviour was decidedly odd — a strange mixture of excitement and dread, as if the message he was about to impart was both gratifying and at the same time terrifying.

"Beg pardon, milady, but I have a message for Miss Winterton from the footman at number Twenty-Six."

"For me?" Fanny said. "Oh, is it Mrs Hay? Oh dear!" She leapt to her feet, and would have bolted for the door at once, but Poole coughed discreetly.

"It is *not* Mrs Hay. There is a gentleman who wishes to see you, madam. In private." He proffered a card on a silver salver.

The room was utterly silent, and Fanny went cold. Was it Mr Hawes? It could be no other. She was aware of every eye turned on her, but she dared not look at any of them for fear of what she might see there. Especially she could not look at Ferdy. What must he be thinking and feeling now? If it were indeed Mr Hawes, then—

Lady Agatha's voice was reassuringly normal. "Read the card, dear. You will not know who it is until you do."

"Oh yes." With trembling fingers, she picked up the card and read it. "Oh." Then, "Oh! *Thomas!* Good heavens. Thomas Claremont. What can he—? I mean, he could not— Oh, my goodness."

25: Another Offer Of Marriage

For a moment, Fanny could not think straight. Thomas Claremont here in Sagborough? And asking to speak to her in private? Surely that could not mean...

"Well, you had better go and see him," Lady Agatha said gently. "Should you like me to come with you, my dear?"

"Oh... oh no, thank you. You are very kind, but it is not necessary. I have known Thomas all my life. He is a very old friend, but I never thought— His family live very close to mine... to where we used to live, I mean. I daresay... it is just news from home. Yes, I must go to him. Pray forgive me, my lady, but I shall not be able to go with you to the Trivers. Please make my apologies."

"Of course, dear. Off you go."

Fanny went, almost in a dream. She collected her bonnet and gloves from Hill, carefully tied the ribbons and pulled on her gloves. Poole opened the door, and she made her way slowly down the steps, but all the time her thoughts revolved and revolved. What could it mean? What could it possibly mean?

Thomas was in the drawing room, standing head down, lost in thought, near the cold hearth. His face lit up when she entered the room.

"Fanny! How... how are you?"

She curtsied demurely, although it always seemed odd to treat her childhood playmate so formally. He bowed in return, but she thought it rather a perfunctory bow, not as elegant or precise as Ferdy's. Now there was a gentleman who always knew the correct degree of familiarity to impart through his bows.

Thomas looked the same as ever, although his coat was new, she thought. But then she had not seen him since Christmas. Plenty of time for a man to buy a new coat.

"I am very well, Thomas. And you? Your parents? Your brothers?"

"Oh yes, yes, everybody is well. Fanny, you will hardly believe it — indeed, I can scarce credit it myself — but I have had the most extraordinary good fortune. Do you remember — well you will not, of course, for you never met him, but you will have heard me speak of him — my Uncle Jasper? He died a few months ago, and just imagine it, he has left everything he had to me! Not that it is a vast fortune or anything of the sort, only eight hundred a year at present although the attorney thinks more could be done with it and it might reach twelve hundred with care. And when Mama dies I will have another two or three hundred, too, so a comfortable income, very comfortable. Quite an independence. And the prettiest little house, just perfect, and in very good order and just right for—" He blushed scarlet then and hung his head. "Just right for... for a *wife*. And so I thought to come and rescue you from being a seamstress. Oh Fanny, I should think myself the most fortunate creature alive if you would... if you could... do you think...?"

He trailed off, perhaps seeing from her face that his suit was not going to prosper.

"Oh Thomas, I am so flattered that you came all this way on my account."

"No, no, I am not come from Brinshire. I have been at Helsford — my estate, you know," he said with simple pride. "It is in the East Riding, not so far from here. It is beautifully situated, Fanny, you would love it, and not isolated at all, for there is Helsford village beside it, and it borders Abbeymount. Do you know who lives there? Lord Belwarren, so you would be rubbing shoulders with an *earl*, you see. What do you say, Fanny? We should deal so well together, you and I."

"Abbeymount," Fanny said faintly, with a vision of a lifetime of morning calls and dinners and balls with the Makenhams, when she would have to make conversation with Ferdy as the wife of another man. Faintly she said, "No, Thomas, I cannot."

"Oh," he said. "Are you sure, Fanny? You can think about it, if you like. I am fixed here for a week — paid in advance at the King's Head, you see. It is cheaper that way. Why not take a few days to consider?"

"Oh no, I do not need to. Thomas, I am very sensible of the honour you do me, but I cannot marry you."

"Is there... anything you dislike about me? Because I always thought we got on very well, actually."

"Oh yes, indeed we do, but that is not enough."

"But the house, Fanny! You would love the house if you were to see it. We should be so cosy. Are you sure you would not like to think it over?"

"Quite sure, Thomas. I am very sorry."

"Oh. Did I... did I do it wrong? Because I have never offered for anyone before. Tell me what I did wrong."

"You did it very well, Thomas, but... it was not terribly romantic. I think the next time you make an offer of marriage, you should talk more about love and less about the house. You should tell a lady that she looks like a flower turning to face the sun, and that your life would be empty without her — that sort of thing."

He pulled a face. "I am no good at flummery, Fanny. I am a very ordinary sort of fellow, but I should have dearly liked to make you my wife. Just because I am not good with words does not mean I have no regard for you. I... I do love you, Fanny. I have loved you for years and years, and never thought I would have a shot at winning your hand, and it is hurtful to be rejected just because I am not *romantic*. I am very sorry. Good bye, Fanny."

~~~~~

Ferdy was in an agony of suspense. Thomas Claremont! The childhood friend. What had she said about him? *'Thomas is sweet'* Sweet! She would accept him, he was sure, and then all hope would be over and how would he go on without any possibility that she would be his? How could he even meet her in tolerable composure, and see her happy with another man? No, that was ungenerous. If she had an attachment to this Claremont, then he would wish her joy and he would mean it, even if it broke his heart. Of course he wanted to see her happy! As if—

"*Ferdy!*"

"Oh! Your pardon, Aunt Agatha, I was not attending."

"Of course you were not. You are far too distracted, and you will not wish to go to the Trivers today, I am sure. I will take Emilia and Cordelia, for they are expected, but then I will come straight back and bear you company."

"Thank you. You are very good, Auntie. I cannot imagine what I would do without you."

"There now... hold up your chin, Ferdy. It may be nothing at all, or she may refuse him, you know. Do not give way to despair."

But he did, of course. As soon as the ladies had left, even before the rattle of the carriage wheels on the cobbles had died away, Ferdy had raced down to his book room and settled on the window seat, half hidden by the curtain. From there, he would see Claremont the instant he left the house. He took out his pocket watch, but then decided that he could deduce nothing from the length of time the fellow stayed. If he was in there for an hour or more, it might only mean that they were reminiscing over old times. And if he—

There he was! No more than ten minutes, and he had a face like thunder. Ferdy's heart leapt in joy — she had turned him down! It was all right! He need not yet face the terrible prospect of smiling and offering good wishes as another man walked away with Fanny on his arm. Thank God!

His heart had not yet returned to its normal pace, his hands shaking as he poured himself a celebratory glass of Madeira, when the knocker clattered at the front door. Moments later, he heard her oh-so-familiar voice in the hall. He was there instantly, and her tear-stained face tore him apart.

"Miss Winterton?" She wore neither bonnet nor gloves, her agitation too great to delay even for the proprieties.

"Oh, Ferdy, is Lady Agatha here?" she sobbed.

His name! She called him by name! Breathe, he told himself. It means nothing. Keep breathing. "She... she has gone to Mrs Trivers, but she will be... back soon. Come into the book room and let me pour you a brandy." He gently shepherded her through the door.

"Oh, no, thank you. No brandy, but... oh, Ferdy, he said I was *hurtful* and I did not mean to be, not at all. I would not hurt *anyone*, not for the world, you know I would not, but I could not help it and he was *so* disappointed."

Ferdy quietly shut the door to exclude the servants. It was terribly improper to be alone with Fanny, but it was preferable to having every word related to the servants' hall, and very likely to next door's as well. He proffered his handkerchief.

"Thank you! Oh, thank you!" She held it to her eyes, weeping, too distraught to say another word.

Ferdy could not bear to see her in such distress. His rational mind knew that it was a temporary affliction, brought on by the suddenness of Claremont's declaration and a quarrel with a childhood friend. She would soon recover her usual composure, he was sure. But in that moment, she sought comfort, she needed it, and he could not forbear to offer her what succour was his to supply.

By insensible degrees he drew nearer, and then, quite unable to help himself, he wrapped his arms around her and drew her to his chest.

She made no resistance. To his infinite joy, she leaned her cheek against his coat, and wept piteously into his neckcloth. "Hush now," he murmured. "Hush, hush." And she only wept all the more.

Her unbonneted head was just below his chin, and one or two stray hairs tickled him. Hardly daring to breathe, by infinitesimal degrees he turned his head and lowered it so that his cheek rested upon her hair. So soft, so exquisitely soft... Her scent drifted around him, and he breathed it in, eyes closed, feeling the touch of her hair upon his skin, holding her tight in his arms, wishing this moment might never end.

Impossible hope. From the street came the unmistakable sounds of the carriage returning, Aunt Agatha descending, Poole's voice no doubt explaining. Ferdy had time to release Fanny from his arms before the door opened and Aunt Agatha bustled in. She glanced at Ferdy, seeing at once, no doubt, all that had happened, but she spoke only to Fanny.

"My poor, dear girl! Whatever has happened to distress you so? Come upstairs with me now while I get rid of this wretched hat, and we can sit in my room until you feel more the thing. Come now, dear."

Still sniffling and clutching his handkerchief, Fanny allowed herself to be led away, without looking back at Ferdy. He was left alone, shaking from head to foot, his breath rasping in his throat. Closing his eyes again, he let himself sink into the glorious memory of holding her tight, remembering the feel of her in his arms, her scent, the butterfly-wing softness of her hair tickling his cheek, her perfume...and the shuddering sobs that gradually diminished as he held her, safe, in his embrace.

If only he could always do so.

~~~~~

A summons to Aunt Agatha's dressing room before dinner was unusual, but Ferdy had an idea of what it was all about. He kissed his aunt's powdery cheek as she sat at her dressing table having her hair done, and pulled up a chair as the maid silently withdrew.

"Now, Auntie, you need not say a word, for I know it was wrong of me, but I did not want the servants to hear anything they should not."

"What? Oh, the door being closed. No, you did quite right, dear, although you did not take full advantage of the opportunity. You should have kissed her, you know."

"Take advantage of a lady in distress?" Ferdy said, scandalised. "Certainly not!"

"You can be *too* correct sometimes, Ferdy."

"One can *never* be too correct," he said stiffly.

"There are times... and it would have been ideal. Well, it is a pity, but remember for next time."

Ferdy jumped to his feet. "Fanny's friends must all hope there is no next time. No one would wish her to be so distraught ever again."

Aunt Agatha smiled. "No dear, of course not, but if it *should* happen... Ferdy, I know she told you that she does not love you, but I do not believe her. It seems to me that she loves you very well, without having the slightest idea of it. If you were to make love to her just a little, then—"

"Auntie, no," he said quietly. "It would make me uncomfortable, and if she still rejects me, it would make *her* uncomfortable too."

"Well, no one expects you to force yourself upon her, or rush her off to Scotland, or anything excessive of that nature. Just... unbend a little. Woo her. Reach out and pluck her."

"She is not a piece of fruit," Ferdy said tersely. "She must come to me of her own accord, Auntie, and not just because I... because I *plucked* her."

Aunt Agatha sighed. "Oh, Ferdy. She is such a sweet little thing and would suit you admirably, and you are going to let her slip through your fingers. Well, it is your own affair, I daresay. Go along with you, and tell Pritt to come back in, will you, otherwise I shall be horribly late for dinner."

~~~~~

Ferdy had set out early with Edgar for the assembly at the King's Head, leaving the ladies to follow in the carriage whenever they had finished titivating themselves to a satisfactory degree. Ralph was dining with the Trivers family again, as so often lately. That was an interesting development, and the whole town was buzzing with rumour and speculation. Ralph had said nothing about his hopes in that direction, but Ferdy had a shrewd idea that there was no particular affection on his side, except towards the lady's dowry. As for Miss Trivers herself, she was so composed that it was impossible to tell whether her affections were engaged or not.

The moment Ferdy walked into the assembly rooms, he saw Claremont loitering uncertainly near the entrance, his eyes scanning the room. For an instant, Ferdy burned inside, but then he remembered that Fanny had rejected Claremont too, and his sympathies were aroused. He knew exactly how abject the poor man must be feeling. Accordingly, he left Edgar to his own devices and made his way without haste to the spot where Claremont stood all alone, a little island of solitude in a sea of people in friendly groups.

"Good evening, sir," Ferdy said, then wondered what he was to say to a man he was not supposed to know anything about, and to whom he had not been introduced. Improvising rather, he said, "How delightful to see a new face here. Have you just moved to Sagborough?"

Claremont looked relieved at the approach. "No, just... just staying for a few days. Here at the inn, as it happens. The innkeeper suggested I come tonight. Do you live here yourself, sir?"

"Yes, on Harlington Terrace." Claremont started on hearing the name. "Ferdinand Makenham at your service, sir. May I be one of the first to welcome you to Sagborough, but not the last, I hope."

"Oh... how very kind. Thomas Claremont of... of Helsford. Did you... did you say Harlington Terrace? Then you must know—?" Then he laughed at himself. "No, of course not. You need not know her just because... no, forgive me, I am being foolish. The one acquaintance I have in Sagborough also lives in Harlington Terrace, but the likelihood that you know her—"

"I know everyone," Ferdy said with simple pride, and it was true. Everyone who went into society in Sagborough was his acquaintance. He had danced with every unmarried lady, drunk tea with every matron and played cards with every gentleman. And dreamed of a certain young lady from Harlington Terrace. Oh yes, he knew her.

"Fanny Winterton?" Claremont hazarded.

"My next-door neighbour," Ferdy said. "She is not arrived yet, but she will be here directly with my aunt and sisters."

"Oh... your aunt? And sisters? Forgive me but did you say your name was—?"

His voiced tailed off into nothing, as he stared into space, mouth hanging open and eyes bulging. Ferdy's first alarmed thought was that he had suffered some kind of seizure, and might fall to the floor at any moment. But then he realised that Claremont was gazing transfixed at the entrance, at someone arriving. Ferdy turned to look. Sir William Harbottle? No, surely not. But behind him, drifting into view, an ethereal vision in silvered tulle over the palest icicle-blue slip, with tiny spangles in her hair and about her corsage, was Celia Drabble. She looked like an angel descended to earth to tempt mortal men, and if that had been her aim, she succeeded admirably.

The room fell silent as she entered, every eye drawn to such a vision of beauty.

Claremont's eye was drawn, certainly. He stood spellbound, unable to speak or move or, quite possibly, breathe.

"Oh, a *thunderbolt*," Ferdy murmured. "Well, well, well."

26: Confidences

Ferdy wasted no time in introducing Claremont, not to Celia herself, who was already surrounded by admirers, but to Mrs Drabble, who understood immediately the significance of *'the nephew of the late Jasper Dagsby, of Helsford'*. Plenty of young men were smitten with Celia, but few of them could afford to marry her, penniless as she was. She would have preferred a man of more substance, able to be of help to the rest of the Drabble family, but she would settle for a gentleman of property and a modest competence, if Celia should take to him.

Celia did take to him. Claremont had pleasant features and easy manners, was neither high in the instep nor a flirt, and was soon discovered to be an energetic dancer who showed his partner off to perfection. Ferdy occupied himself during the first dance by strolling round the room, enlightening the good people of Sagborough as to the identity of the stranger. Then, duty done by Mr Claremont, he stood up with Emmy Malpas for the country dances, putting a beaming smile on her father's face.

Fanny had arrived by this time. Finally, she was out of black gloves and able to dance again, but Ferdy was too late to secure her hand for the next two. Instead, he found himself eagerly sought out by Claremont, wanting information on Celia Drabble. Ferdy told him the facts as baldly as possible, but he was not put off by the troop of indigent relations or her lack of fortune.

"Thank goodness! I was afraid she might be quite above my touch, a veritable high-flier. That gown is not any work of a provincial seamstress."

"Unless I am very much mistaken, it is the work of Miss Winterton," Ferdy said with pride.

"Oh! Fanny, eh? She always was deft with a needle." Then he paused, chewing his lip, before taking a deep breath and plunging on. "Mr Makenham, I have a confession to make. I came to Sagborough with the sole intent of making Fanny my wife. I... I have always admired her... admired her greatly, and so... when I came into my inheritance I thought... but she turned me down. She told me I was not romantic. Well, of course I am not! It is all nonsense, to expect a man to stuff his head with high-flown balderdash. Likening her to a flower turning its face to the sun, indeed. How ridiculous! I was angry with her, just at first. And now... now I am glad of it. Is that wicked of me?"

A flower turning its face to the sun... she had quoted Ferdy's own words to Claremont, and had told him he was not romantic. Did she think, then, that Ferdy was? He was dizzy with hope, suddenly. He had to take a long, slow breath before he could constrain his distracted mind to answer Claremont.

Honesty would compel Ferdy to absolve Claremont of wickedness, but his behaviour was unforgivably fickle. Suppose Fanny had thought better of her answer, and decided he was, after all, an appealing prospect for a husband? It was a grievous insult for her suitor to instantly fall in love with another, and she would be bitterly hurt by his defection. Ferdy could not pardon any action which distressed Fanny in the slightest. But, rather selfishly, he had no wish to remind Claremont of his obligations towards her.

"Certainly not!" Ferdy said robustly. "You need feel no guilt in what has happened. You offered, she refused, so you are as free as the air, Mr Claremont."

"She does not seem to mind me being free," Claremont said. "Look how happy she is as she dances. Who is that she is with?"

"Lord Gilbert Marford."

"Ah, yes, of course," Claremont said absent-mindedly. "I think... I think I might just wander down the room a little way, and watch the dancing from a different vantage point."

He took off at once, leaving Ferdy's head spinning. Was it possible that Fanny thought him romantic? Could there, perhaps, be some hope for him after all? Only the sight of her shining face smiling up at Gil Marford reminded Ferdy just in time that she treated everyone in the same open and confiding way. He was not special to her, not in the slightest. His spirits plummeted.

Thus brought back from the brink, he was able to calm his racing pulse and begin to act normally again.

Fanny danced every dance... except one. The supper dance saw her sitting alone, her feet tapping, but with no partner. Before Ferdy could make his way to her, one of the Harbottles solicited her, but she shook her head and he drifted away.

"Miss Winterton." Ferdy made his bow. "Might I have the honour of this dance... if you are not otherwise engaged?"

"Oh yes! Or rather, no, I am not otherwise engaged, for I have saved these two for you, Mr Makenham. You have always been so kind as to sit with me before supper, and I hoped you would do so again for I should like your advice upon a matter."

Saved the supper dance... wanted his advice... His volatile spirits soared again. He cleared his throat. "Of course... always at your service, Miss Winterton."

"Oh, how kind you are! Thank you! But you see..." She leaned her head towards him so that he had to bend down to hear her, and whispered, "It is a confidential matter. And I do not quite know..."

"Ah. Then let us walk down the corridor outside the card rooms," he said. "If we stand at the far end of it, we will always be observed, so there is no impropriety, yet we will be able to talk privately."

"Oh, yes! That is the very thing. You always know the correct way to do things, Mr Makenham."

He offered her his arm, and they perambulated slowly around the room and then down the long corridor past the card rooms, echoing to male voices and bursts of laughter, a hint of cigar smoke in the air. Beyond the last door was a little-used space with a small table and two chairs, and here they sat, catching glimpses of the dancers whirling past in the distance, almost as if they were looking through a telescope.

"It is about your cousin, Mr Ralph Makenham," Fanny began.

"Ralph? He is not here tonight."

"No, the poor gentleman. I expect he is too upset to think of dancing. He offered for Marianne, you see, and she would not have him."

"She refused him? No, he would not be happy about that," Ferdy said thoughtfully. "But I do not quite see what I can do about it. If a lady refuses a gentleman's offer—" For a moment, grief welled up inside and rendered him mute. He took a deep breath, then another, and in a ragged voice went on, "—there is not a great deal anyone can do, except... except to be sorry about it."

Perhaps detecting his churning emotions, for he could not entirely conceal them, she raised anxious eyes to his face. To cover his own agitation, he went on hastily, "Is there any particular reason for her refusal? Most young ladies would regard him as a good catch. He is handsome enough, I should have said, and his manners are polished."

"Oh yes, it is not his person. She says he is very agreeable to look at, and most affable and attentive and so forth, but it is his eyes, you see. She said that when he smiles at her, his eyes are cold, not like when—"

She broke off in confusion, blushing violently. *Not like when you smile at me.* That was what she had almost said, he was sure of it, and his breath caught in his throat. Heavens, but he was out of his depth! It was madness to talk so intimately to her, alone in their far corner of the corridor. He knew it, and yet he could not deny himself the pleasure of her confidences.

Her glance veered away from him, and she went on in a rush, "Marianne is quite determined that she will not marry him, but you see, her aunt and uncle are very angry, for they think it an excellent match for her very first offer and they have told her that she will *have* to marry him and she has led him on and will be called a jilt and... and they said a great many other things. They will not let her go out into society or meet her friends until she agrees to it. She is to stay in her room and eat nothing but bread and water and beef tea and she does *not* like beef tea at all. It is abominable, she says, although I quite like it myself, especially when I am not feeling quite the thing. It perks me up tremendously. But she greatly dislikes it. She wrote me a very long letter which her maid smuggled out and she begged me to help her, but I could not think what to do. But I knew that *you* would know, Mr Makenham. You always know what to do."

Ferdy's chest swelled with pride at this encomium, even though he could not think what advice he might offer. "One cannot interfere between a young lady and her guardian," he said slowly. "I daresay Mr and Mrs Trivers do not intend to treat their niece harshly, but in their disappointment..." That word again! "...in their disappointment, people sometimes speak rashly. Do you know, Miss Winterton, I cannot imagine why anyone would be upset if a lady refuses her first serious offer. Miss Trivers is barely out, and here in Yorkshire no one expects a girl to succumb to matrimony in her first season. The Trivers should take her to London if that is their aim, or perhaps Bath."

Fanny shook her head. "They do not want to go all that way and put themselves to a great deal of expense when they are not a great family or noble or anything of the sort. And Marianne does not want it either, for imagine how dreadful it would be if her uncle spent a vast amount of money trying to fire her off in London and she did not take. She would feel obliged to accept any offer she could get, and it might not be someone comfortable, and one has to be comfortable with one's husband, is it not so?"

Ferdy nodded, not quite trusting his voice. Comfortable... he and Fanny were so comfortable together, but she would not settle for that. She wanted something more, and he could not blame her. A woman need not accept a man just because they were comfortable together.

He chided himself for such thinking, for really he ought to stop puzzling over every word she spoke, looking for encouraging signs. Such foolishness! Why would she ever change her mind? She knew him well enough to decide, she had known his offer was coming so she had had plenty of time to consider her response. Waiting and hoping and *seeing her* on a daily basis was driving him to the brink of madness. He should have left, and yet... how could he? How unbearable life would be if he could not enjoy even these small moments with her. And sometimes larger moments, too, as when he had held her in his arms and she had dampened his neckcloth with her tears.

"Mr Makenham?" She looked at him expectantly, and he tried to gather his disordered wits. Marianne... what to do about Marianne? He cleared his throat.

"The law is clear that no one may be forced to marry, and the clergyman must be very sure of the bride's willingness before he proceeds. That does not mean that pressure cannot be brought to bear, and there are clergymen open to bribery, as in any profession, but a knowledge of the legal position may strengthen Miss Trivers' resolve. If you are able to convey that information to her—"

"Oh yes!" Fanny said. "Yes, I can do that. Is there anything else I might do?"

"Perhaps there is something that *I* might do," Ferdy said thoughtfully. "Miss Trivers is not present this evening, and it would be remiss of her friends not to enquire after her wellbeing. I shall call upon Mrs Trivers tomorrow, and perhaps a title would help... not Gil, he has his duties to attend to, but perhaps Lady Gil will accompany me... Yes, it will not hurt to remind Mrs Trivers that her niece has friends amongst the nobility. Her life is not blighted because she refused her first serious suitor."

"You are so very good, Mr Makenham. I cannot thank you enough for your kindness," Fanny said, and her shining eyes and pleased smile sent his spirits aloft again.

But as he led her back down the corridor and thence to the supper room, he wished with all his heart that he had the strength of mind to leave Sagborough, for both their sakes.

When he and Edgar returned to Harlington Terrace, Ralph was ensconced in the book room, draped over an armchair with a brandy glass in his hand, neckcloth askew.

"There you are," he called out loudly, as they peered round the door. "Been out enjoying yourselves, have you? Had a wonderful time, no doubt, being fawned over by all the hoity-toity females of this God-forsaken town who look down their noses at *me*. *I* am not the heir to a title and a vast estate."

"Heavens, Ralph, have you been drinking all evening?" Ferdy said mildly, picking up the brandy decanter, which was almost empty. "You had much better have gone to the assembly and danced your megrims away, instead of moping about here on your own. She was not even there, so there was no need to hide away."

"Oh, are you giving me cousinly advice now? Very kind of you. Much obliged, I'm sure."

"Really, Ralph, stop feeling sorry for yourself," Ferdy said in sudden irritation. "You have no complaint worthy of these blue devils. So she turned you down. It is not as if you were even in love with her."

Ralph uncoiled himself from the armchair and thrust himself at Ferdy, his face inches away. "Do *not* patronise me, cousin." He jabbed Ferdy in the chest with one finger. "Just because you will be *somebody* one day…" Another jab. "…does not give you the right to talk to me…" Jab, jab. "…in that supercilious tone." Jab, jab, jab.

"I say, Ralph!" Edgar said. "No need for that attitude. Calm down, old fellow."

Ferdy refused to yield even an inch of ground, although he was uncomfortably aware that Ralph was half a head taller than he was and considerably broader about the shoulders. It was all muscle, too. Ralph boxed and fenced and hunted and drove his curricle to an inch, the epitome of the well-honed sportsman. He had only to raise his fist and Ferdy would be flat on his back and bleeding copiously. But he would not give his cousin the satisfaction of showing the least fear, so he merely raised a questioning eyebrow.

For several heartbeats they stood motionless, Ralph's pugnacious face looming over him, while Ferdy's stomach churned in dread. Then Ralph whirled away.

"Deceitful little hussy," he muttered. "Leading me on all these weeks, wasting my time. Pah! Women! They're nothing but schemers and cheats, the lot of them."

And he hurled the brandy glass against the wall, where it shattered into a thousand tiny shards, sparkling in the candlelight as they arced to the floor.

It took an hour of sympathetic listening, gentle encouragement and another decanter of brandy before Ralph had descended sufficiently from his high dudgeon to recover his usual insouciance and even laugh at himself a little. Ferdy was relieved to escape to his bedroom intact. He found Wrackham waiting for him instead of Wright, and he knew exactly why. The whole house must have heard raised voices and breaking glass, and a quarrel between cousins was not a circumstance that could be left in the hands of a junior valet.

"A good evening, sir?" Wrackham said with studied casualness.

Ferdy allowed his valet to ease him out of his coat before answering. "Eventful."

"Indeed, sir. I trust these events were not unpleasant ones, sir?"

That made Ferdy laugh. "A valiant attempt, Wrackham, but daresay you will be able to piece it all together and answer that question for yourself when you compare notes with the other servants."

"I do not *gossip*, sir," the valet said, in disdainful tones.

"Naturally you do not," Ferdy said. "Nevertheless, I am sure you will know the whole story by morning. Do you know, Wrackham, I believe a little brandy may have been spilt on these breeches. I do hope they are not ruined."

"I have a method of my own invention for dealing with that, sir, not to worry."

"Excellent." After that, they proceeded in silence, Wrackham no doubt burning with curiosity and Ferdy wondering whether the fellow would feel obliged stay up all night applying his secret method to the brandy stain.

It was a relief when Ferdy was alone at last, the curtains drawn around his bed, but if he was free of other people, his own thoughts crowded uncomfortably in his brain. What a turbulent day he had had! First Claremont's arrival and the terrible fear that Fanny would accept him. Then the relief of her rejection, followed almost at once by those tender moments when she had rested in his arms, sobbing as if her heart would break. He closed his eyes for a moment, remembering. Then, in the evening had come her very flattering confidences, and his own violent emotions — up one minute and down the next. And to round the evening off, Ralph's ill-humour, when he had feared blood would be spilt. This was his life now, lurching from one state to another. He could barely remember a time when he had sailed through his days untroubled by either joy or misery or terror.

For his own peace of mind he ought to leave, he knew it. He should go to Abbeymount and let the country air soothe him and learn to live without Fanny. He no longer had any hope of winning her, now that he knew her better. How had he ever imagined he might do so? He was too ordinary, too down-to-earth ever to attach her. She wanted a knight in armour to ride up on his white charger and sweep her off her feet — a hero, strong, manly and romantic. Ferdy was no hero, and nothing could turn him into one. He should give up the hopeless quest for Fanny's love. And yet he could not. Until the dreadful day when she became betrothed to another man, he could not abandon the dream. His sweet, beloved Fanny, who was his whole life now. If only he were hers.

27: Rosebuds

'My dear Fanny, I have some very exciting news! Lord Brackenwood has asked me to marry him, and I have accepted. I know what question will be uppermost in your mind, Fanny dear, and yes, I am very much in love with him and he with me, and we have settled it between us that we are to be the happiest people in the whole of England. Are you pleased for me? I hope you are, and that you will one day find someone just as wonderful as my Allan to cherish you as you deserve. I am too dizzy with joy to write more. All the details of my wedding clothes to follow. Your most fortunate sister, Annabelle.'

~~~~~

It would be overstating the case to say that Fanny was put out of frame by Annabelle's betrothal, for what could possibly give her greater pleasure than the happiness of a very dear sister? And had she not secretly harboured hopes of just such an outcome? Annabelle had talked so favourably of the earl, and she herself was so clever and good-natured that every man must love her. It was so wonderfully romantic that his grief for his late wife and Annabelle's unhappy circumstances should find solace in each other's love.

Still, Fanny was not quite as contented as she felt she ought to be. It was in her nature always to find the best in her situation, and so each morning and evening when she recited her prayers she thanked God for the food and shelter she enjoyed, and her work which put coins in her purse each quarter day. She was grateful for her friends, too, but here she always hesitated. Who were her friends now? Lady Harriet and her family, for all their generosity, were too distant to be called friends. The women at the shop were forbidden her, and although she understood the reasons, she was sorry for it. Even Miss Monkton and her mother treated her like a lady condescending to undertake a little charitable work, rather than just another seamstress. On the other hand, for all she paid them morning calls and knew them well, the ladies of Sagborough were out of her reach now, separated from her by the needle constantly in her hand. They embroidered fire screens and trimmed bonnets, while Fanny stitched gowns for paying customers. It was a gulf too wide to be bridged. Even so, when she named the Makenham ladies for their share of her prayers, her gratitude was deep and genuine. They had treated her almost as a member of the family.

And that brought her to Ferdy, and always at this point she could not find the words, and was obliged to shed a few tears, hastily wiped away. Dear, kind Ferdy, who was such a good friend to her! And she had turned him down and made him miserable. He never said so, of course, and his manner was just as it had always been, but there were times... oh dear, there had been *several* times when his composure had slipped and she had seen something in his eyes. It was elation, sometimes, when she paid him some trivial compliment, but at other times it was something like despair, and it almost broke her heart. She could not bear to be the means of making such a good, honourable man unhappy.

Yet she could hardly marry a man just because he wanted it badly enough to be miserable when she refused. She had perfectly sound reasons to reject his offer, after all, such as... such as... It was curious how her certainty at the time had gradually melted away. Sometimes now she lay awake in bed wondering what it would be like to be Mrs Ferdinand Makenham and be mistress of the house next door, and pay regular visits to his parents at Lennister Hall and his grandparents at Abbeymount. It would make her very proud to walk beside Ferdy in such places, and it would not matter if everything was strange and she felt a bit lost, because he would be there to explain everything. Ferdy always knew what to do, and she would be entirely comfortable with him.

Sometimes, in the silence of the night, when her thoughts crowded round her in the most agitating way, she had thought that Dr Hay had the right of it. There was no reason not to marry Ferdy, no reason at all. He was everything that any sensible woman could want, so kind and courteous as he was. So gentlemanly. She liked him far better than any of her other suitors, and unlike Thomas Claremont and Mr Hawes, Ferdy had never wavered in his devotion. From the first moment he had seen her, he had been her admirer. He made her feel so comfortable, always. So she had wavered, and thought of her sisters and how delightful it would be to marry a man rich enough to rescue them all from their menial employment. She ought to do it, and a part of her wanted to, and she did like Ferdy so much...

But liking was not love. She could not marry without that overwhelming love, a love so strong and instant it would hit her like a thunderbolt and change her life utterly, and especially now that Annabelle had found her own true love. She sounded so happy! That was what Fanny longed for, that all-encompassing mutual love, strong enough to sustain two people through all the trials of life. She would never condemn those who married prudently, but for her, romantic love was everything and she could not give up the chance of finding it, not even for a man as appealing as Ferdy, who would suit her so well in every other way. She tried very hard not to think such dismal thoughts, but she could not quite escape them.

The summer brought back to Sagborough many of those who had enjoyed the delights of London's season. Lady Harriet returned in an ill-humour, on account of some mix-up with the lawyers, which would not be resolved before the autumn.

"These legal people always have something more important to do," she said with a sigh. "It is very trying. My business is not, perhaps, a matter of life and death, but I should like to get it settled, all the same, and set Westbury House on a proper footing. And do not ask me about the fashions this year, Fanny, for I cannot describe how hideous they are. I never saw so many frights in my life. I have brought you some journals to look at, however, so your clever fingers can copy the least appalling styles."

Miss Hay was the same as ever. "Still here, Fanny? I felt certain some dragon-slayer would have rescued you from your high tower by now."

"I have not been in any towers, Miss Hay," Fanny replied, puzzled, but Miss Hay only laughed.

Lord and Lady Carrbridge returned to Drummoor, their seat a few miles from Sagborough, and Lord and Lady Gilbert closed up their house to go there too.

And the house next door was filled with Makenhams. The servants had the full list of arrivals within a day, and through Draper, Fanny soon had it too. Lord and Lady Belwarren were the principals, the earl and countess who were Ferdy's grandparents. Then his parents, Lord and Lady Craston and his young brother Gregory, on his way home from Harrow. Mr Brant's parents were there, too, and another Brant uncle, and Fanny wondered how on earth so many guests had been squeezed into the house without some of them sleeping above the stables or in the attics with the servants. Most were staying only a few days, but they were a sociable family and they wanted to see Ferdy in his new home before they moved to Abbeymount for the summer months.

Naturally, this necessitated a dinner for guests. All the Hays and Fanny were invited, and even old Mrs Hay deemed the presence of an earl and a viscount of sufficient importance to require her presence. She would wear the court dress she had worn when her husband had been presented, she decided, and a diamond tiara, and hoped their lordships would forgive an old lady if she left immediately after dinner, for she would be ready for her bed by then.

Fanny trembled when she realised that she would be in the same room as Ferdy and all the important members of his family. Would they know that she had turned down the heir to the earldom? Of course they would, for Lady Agatha knew. Whatever would they think of Fanny? For the first time in her life, she dreaded an evening engagement.

Like Mrs Hay, however, she had a special gown to put on, one of her ball gowns from last year which she had made for her birthday in February but never worn because Papa had died and put them all into black. Well, she would wear black no more, not even a ribbon for Aunt Letty. It was time to put her mourning behind her. The slip was pure white figured silk, with some stitchery around the bodice, which Margaret had helped with, and tiny silk rosebuds around the neck and sleeves. She had planned to wear a heavier satin over-tunic for the winter, but for summer wear she had a gauze over-skirt trimmed with more rosebuds. In her hair, she would wear yet more rosebuds, since it was the right time of year for flowers.

Thus fortified, she walked the few steps to the front door of number Twenty-Five without too many palpitations, and only one fleeting thought that, had she chosen differently, she might even now be inside the house and receiving the Hays, not walking behind them as a guest herself. Ruthlessly, she suppressed the notion, but it straightened her spine a little to consider it. And had Ferdy not told her she might still choose that way? His offer remained open, and she knew he was still willing and bore her no resentment, generous man that he was. She need not fear the Makenhams, for they might yet be her own family if she wished it so.

Even so, her nerves rose with every step up the stairs to the drawing room until she could hardly breathe. Peters and Hill threw open the doors and Poole intoned, "Dr Hay and the Lady Harriet Hay, Mrs Andrew Hay, Miss Hay, Miss Winterton."

The drawing room was crowded, and at first Fanny could see no familiar faces amongst those she could glimpse from her place behind the others. But then she heard Lady Agatha's booming voice above the murmur of conversations — greeting them, and then, with Dr Hay's assistance, gently guiding Mrs Hay in her strange hooped skirt to a seat specially prepared for her near a low fire, so that she might suffer no chill from her two minute exposure to the night air. Lady Harriet waved cheerfully to several of the strangers, obviously well known to her, and then wandered off to talk to one of her acquaintance, with Miss Hay in tow. Fanny stood uncertainly in the doorway.

As if magically summoned, Ferdy was there. "Miss Winterton." Oh, that perfect bow again! Such a graceful man. And his eyes — Fanny blushed at the look in his eyes, which there was no mistaking. "You look quite lovely tonight," he said, his voice even softer than usual. "Rosebuds — how appropriate! Cordelia and Emilia have been denuding the garden of roses all day." He gestured to a console, where three large Chinese bowls were filled with blooms. "Come, let me introduce you to a few people you have not met before. This young man with the lop-sided neckcloth is my brother Greg, the brains of the family."

Greg was about twelve years old, and reminded Fanny with a pang of grief of her own brother, Jeremy, who had been just that age when he died.

"It is not lop-sided!" Greg protested. "Not everyone is a perfectionist like you, Ferdy."

"Make your bow to Miss Winterton, brother."

He made a passable attempt, and she curtsied to him with a smile. "How do you do, Mr Gregory," she said gravely.

"My Uncle James Brant. Uncle Edward Brant, who is Edgar's papa. Aunt Maria Brant, his mama. You know Lady Craston, of course, and this is Lord Craston. This is Miss Winterton, Papa. And here we have Lord Belwarren and Lady Belwarren, my grandparents. My neighbour, Miss Winterton."

Fanny bobbed up and down as each was introduced, the gentlemen standing to bow, the ladies smiling at her.

"Miss Winterton, do come and sit beside me," Lady Belwarren said. "We have heard so much about you..." For an instant, Fanny's insides roiled in fear. What had they heard? But then the countess went on smoothly, "...and how your poor papa left you in such difficulties. How dreadful for you and your sisters to be broken apart in that way, and sent to quite opposite ends of the country. My heart goes out to all of you, coping so bravely. But there is good news, too, for I saw the announcement in the newspaper. Lord Brackenwood and Miss Annabelle Winterton. She is older than you, I take it?"

"Yes, my lady, the second oldest of us. She went as governess to his lordship's three daughters."

"It sounds a sensible arrangement, as much practical as romantic. It would be natural in a widower to look for a new wife to mother his girls, and she might see it as a matter of duty, to marry well and provide for her sisters, and who could blame her?"

"Oh no!" Fanny said, shocked. "They are quite in love, and it has been coming on these many months. I could tell from the way she wrote about him, although Rosamund would say that I see romance everywhere and allow my fancy to run away with me sometimes, but I was right about Annabelle and I still think I may be right about Lucy, too, although she denies it."

Lady Craston nodded at these confidences. "Rosamund... that must be Robin Dalton's wife, I think."

"Oh yes. The eldest of us."

"Such a very pretty girl. I was talking to her only a week ago at Marford House, and when she heard that I might see you, she asked me to tell you that she is very well, her husband and children too. They are all well. Louisa had a long chat with her, too."

"Louisa?"

The countess smiled, making dimples appear in her powdered, wrinkled cheeks so that she looked ten years younger. "Lady Craston. Louisa Brant, as she was, of course. And I, in case Ferdy has not mentioned it, was Alicia Marford."

"Oh, Marford! Then you are related to Lady Harriet."

"Well… somehow, I am sure, but I could not tell you how. Cousins, I expect. Twice removed, most probably. Gregory! Come here, my boy, and help out your ageing grandmama. How am I related to Lady Harriet Hay? We are both Marfords by birth so we must be related. I am the daughter of the sixth marquess, and Harriet is sister to the ninth, so—"

"Great-niece," Greg said.

"What? Impossible! Are you sure we are not cousins of some sort?"

He shook his head. "Seventh marquess was your brother, so eighth was your nephew, ninth is your great-nephew. His sister is your great-niece."

"Well, upon my soul! Such brains! It is very worrying, my dear," she said in a lower voice to Fanny. "Nothing good ever came of having brains. But perhaps he will grow out of it. It would be very upsetting if we had to send him to India." Then, seeing Fanny's puzzled face, she added, "I do beg your pardon, Miss Winterton. Makenham history. We had a clever fellow in the family once, but he went to India and promptly died. We always say that anyone too clever to be a Makenham must be sent to India. Do you see? Just a little family joke, but you are so easy to talk to that one quite forgets that you are not one of the family."

~~~~~

Ferdy watched her surreptitiously all evening. Heavens above, but she looked wonderful tonight. Such a gown — simple, and yet exquisitely beautiful, draping itself so elegantly. How much he longed to touch it — to touch *her*. To put his arm around her waist, and feel the cool silk under his fingers and the warmth of her body beneath that. To run one finger down her soft cheek. To take all the rosebuds out of her hair, one by one, and watch her dark locks fall, smooth and shining, down her back. A man could drive himself mad with such thoughts. He made no effort to suppress them, however, savouring each thought as it rose inside him like a bubble, only to burst when he had to turn his attention elsewhere. And in all his watching, sometimes he had the shivering delight of catching her looking at him, too, and then blushing in that enchanting way she had, lowering her eyes demurely. Such looks gave him, for the first time in weeks, a tiny sliver of hope.

There was such joy in seeing her here, amidst all his family. Talking composedly to Grandmama before dinner. Laughing at Uncle James's feeble jokes at dinner. Playing Commerce very badly with Greg, Cordelia and Emilia, and not minding when she lost. Then, much later, playing cribbage cheerfully with Grandpapa for a full hour without the slightest complaint, although Ferdy knew that she disliked the game. Ah, Fanny! So eager to please, so generous, so enchanting. *'A taking little thing,'* Aunt Maria said after the guests had left. *'Charming, quite charming,'* Uncle Edward whispered, with a paternal smile. Even Greg approved. *'She called me Mr Gregory,'* he said with simple pride.

"Miss Winterton is always very correct," Ferdy said, equally proud.

When the ladies had all gone to bed, and the men of the family settled down for a final brandy, Lord Belwarren said, "Well, Ferdy, I like her very much. She would be an asset to the family."

"Not clever," Uncle Edward said. "I cannot abide clever women. In a man it might be tolerated, but it is unseemly in a female. Ladies should be decorative and demure, in my view."

Ferdy smiled, knowing that Aunt Maria was neither decorative nor demure, nor was she clever, but she kept Uncle Edward on a short rein all the same.

"It is a pity she won't have you," his grandfather said. "Still, she may come round to it, now that you have seen off that Hawes fellow. That was devious of you, m'boy, and I cannot blame you for foisting him onto us, but upon my soul, the fellow was tedious."

"Kellingborough this, Kellingborough that... we all got sick of hearing about it," Uncle James said. "It was amusing for the first ten minutes, but then I felt under an obligation to point out — purely for comparative purposes, you understand — that the stables at Abbeymount were rather larger than his entire house."

"He was quieter after that," Uncle Edward said, laughing.

Ferdy shook his head. "You were supposed to dazzle him with London spectacle and introduce him to eligible young ladies who might like to be mistress of the place, not try to puncture his vanity."

"No danger of that," Lord Craston said. "The fellow is as pompous a windbag as I ever saw, quite impervious to slights, and your Fanny is much better off without him."

"What have you done with him for the summer?" Ferdy said. "I do not want him wandering back up here."

"Bianca and Rufus have taken him down to Brighton with them," Uncle James said, grinning. "The poor chap was positively drooling at the prospect of bumping into Prinny, since we never could get him an invitation to Carlton House. Even the Prince of Wales has *some* standards, it seems. After that, we can send him to Cousin Delia in Bath. But Ferdy, why is Ralph not here tonight?"

"He has gone haring off to Abbeymount," Lord Craston said. "Who is he avoiding, Ferdy?"

"Miss Marianne Trivers," Ferdy said. "He offered for her, and she refused him. Her uncle and aunt are not at all pleased with her."

"Which was the Trivers girl?" Uncle Edward said. "The spectacular beauty in pale blue?"

"No, that is Celia Drabble," Ferdy said. "Marianne Trivers was the one with the gold-trimmed chemise robe with the cream satin slip and—"

"Thank you, m'boy, we get the idea," his grandfather said genially. "Pretty girl, and well-mannered. Well-dowered, too, one might guess?"

"Very," Ferdy said. "I have heard the sum of fifty thousand mentioned. Adam Trivers is a very warm man, and his niece is his sole heiress, now that her sisters are married."

"But she would not have Ralph. Any idea why?"

Ferdy hesitated, for he could hardly relate Fanny's confidences on the subject. In the end, he said, "It is my understanding that she was not entirely comfortable with him."

"He is not nursing a broken heart, I take it?"

"If he is, he keeps it well hidden," Ferdy said, smiling at the thought. Ralph with a broken heart? He would be astonished if that day ever came.

"Hmpf. And who was the young sprig drooling over the beauty, then?"

Ferdy laughed. "That was Thomas Claremont, who recently inherited Helsford. You remember Jasper Dagsby? Left the place to Claremont. Quite unexpectedly, by all accounts. He came here in a great lather, intent on marrying his childhood sweetheart, Fanny, but she turned him down. Before anyone could catch their breath over that, he saw Celia Drabble and was instantly smitten. She has not two farthings to her name and she seems just as smitten, so I suspect they will make a match of it."

"Good heavens, what a great deal goes on in a small town like Sagborough," Lord Craston said. "It was a sleepy sort of place when I lived here, I assure you. But you have had murders and who knows what going on here."

"Yes, that made the London newspapers," Lord Belwarren said. "Did they catch the fellow?"

Ferdy sighed. "They stopped looking, because the last two were lightskirts. But the first was a housemaid at number Twenty-Six, and for all she had a child out of wedlock, I never thought it likely she turned to the oldest trade. There was more to it, I was sure. I even paid the constable to continue his enquiries, but he found nothing helpful. I had a letter from him just a couple of days ago, presenting his bill and reluctant to waste any more of my money on futile avenues of investigation. So it seems all is at a standstill, and whoever the culprit is, he has got clean away with it."

"That is very unsatisfactory," Lord Belwarren said. "One does not like to hear of any man getting away with murder. Never heard of a man reluctant to spend another man's money before, either, especially a lawyer. Generally they go on running up bills forever. Makes me wonder whether he found out something best left in the dark. But you never know, m'boy, something may yet turn up to enable the law to be brought to bear, as it should."

~~~~~

Fanny crept out of bed as soon as Draper had left the room. Winding a thin wrap around her, she sat on the window seat and gently pushed up the window. She was two floors higher than Ferdy's drawing room next door, but their windows were open, too, and in the still night air, bursts of male laughter drifted up to her, wreathing around her like perfume. Gently she inhaled, fancying she could detect a thread of cigar smoke, or the delicate pomade Ferdy used, or a hint of brandy.

Closing her eyes, she sighed, thinking back over the evening. Thomas had been there, so attentive towards Celia. He had looked sheepishly at Fanny, but she had not minded. Celia would make him an excellent wife, and it was so romantic! Their very first glimpses of each other had sent them both tumbling into love. Fanny sighed with pleasure. As for Marianne, she had not had a chance to talk to her, for her aunt had hovered about rather. Marianne had looked pale, but at least she was out in company and not locked in her room, subsisting on bread and water and beef tea.

And then there were the Makenhams and Brants. Parents and grandparents and uncles and aunts, all of them amiable, friendly people, not stiff or superior or disapproving of an impoverished seamstress. They had family jokes that had to be explained to outsiders. They gently teased each other, but with real affection. There were fathers who were not morose and did not hide away in their book room every night getting drunk. There were aunts and uncles and cousins who got together as one jolly family every summer and were real, known people, not just names on once-a-year letters. She had a sudden vision of Abbeymount, its many halls filled with laughing Makenhams and Brants and Marfords, and she wanted to be a part of that so badly that the aching need was a physical pain. If only she could!

But it would be dishonest to marry Ferdy solely to be gathered up into the embrace of his wonderful family. It was Ferdy's embrace she should be longing for, and without that, she could not possibly marry him.

Fanny laid her head on her arms and sighed. If only her heart were more malleable. Why could she not have been struck by the same thunderbolt as Ferdy? How convenient it would be to fall violently in love with so eligible a man. But life was very disobliging, sometimes.

28: The End Of Summer (September)

Ferdy was required to leave Sagborough for a few days to act as escort to his sister. Emilia was bound to Lancashire to visit their sister Diana and manage the household as she awaited her first confinement. Such a role would normally fall to Aunt Agatha, but she was still fixed in Sagborough.

"I shall not leave here until you are safely wed, nephew," she told Ferdy firmly. "Besides, I have no intention of abandoning your Fanny to the mercy of the Hays, what with Lady Harriet and Marina Hay forever gadding about here, there and everywhere, Dr Hay always at that hospital of his, and Mrs Hay asleep in her chair most of the time. Fanny will be good company for me once the girls have gone elsewhere. Besides, if Emilia wants to take over my position as the family's pillar of support in a crisis, then she may begin with Diana. And she could do worse than to take Marianne Trivers with her."

"Miss Trivers? Are they especially friendly?"

"Ferdy, you are not usually so dense. Marianne is a flower who needs to bloom in a larger garden than Sagborough. Diana's husband has a fine shooting estate, and three younger brothers with many friends. The house is full of eligible bachelors just now."

"Ah. I see."

So it was that Ferdy found himself travelling in a convoy of three vehicles, to accommodate himself, Emilia, Mr and Mrs Trivers, Marianne and the number of servants and boxes deemed essential for the journey. They were two days on the road, but they encountered no difficulties and were greeted with joy by Diana, with affable but slightly distant pleasure by her husband and with enthusiasm by the multitude of guests ensconced there, delighted to have the novelty of fresh faces in their midst.

The Trivers were to stay a week or so to see Marianne settled, but Ferdy could not bear to be away from Fanny for so long. He needed to see her sweet face at frequent intervals, not to mention the letters from Brighton that assured him that Hawes was still far away. Accordingly, after two nights he left Diana and her overflowing house and began the journey back to Sagborough.

He had a small diversion in mind, however, for he had not forgotten the friend of Fanny's brother, who had gone off to a Lancashire town. Johnny Moreton, that was the fellow's name. Jeremy had been staying at Moreton's family's house while waiting to board his ship, and the two boys, being of similar age, had fallen into friendship. Jeremy had joined his ship, which had tragically been lost at sea, but Johnny Moreton had ended up in Lancashire, learning to be a mill owner like his uncle.

After reaching the main road through this part of the county, Ferdy turned not north but south until he came to the sprawling and unprepossessing town of Branton. Everywhere he looked he saw mills and warehouses, and the road was clogged with wagons piled high with bales of the many textiles which the region produced. Yet amongst so much industry, there were also fine churches and, towards the centre of the town, rows of well-proportioned houses, not stylish but solid and prosperous, like their owners.

Ferdy found the inn recommended by Diana's husband, and made enquiries regarding Jeremy Winterton's friend, Johnny

Moreton. Here was the point where his scheme might have foundered, for the only name he knew of was Moreton, yet he had no idea whether Jeremy's friend still used the name. If his uncle were on the maternal side, and the boy had adopted his benefactor's name, Ferdy's plan would be sunk at once. But he was in luck. The innkeeper knew of Mr Giles Moreton, and even had a direction for his mill.

"'e lives 'ard by t'mill, so just ask there, sir."

So Ferdy did, and in no time found himself before a cheerful red door, opened by a prim housekeeper. Ferdy handed over his card and the note he had prepared earlier to explain his quest, and waited patiently in the hall, watched over by a curious footboy. The clock struck the quarter and then the half hour before the housekeeper came back.

"Mr Moreton can spare you a few minutes, sir. This way, if you please."

Ferdy was shown into a large study, clearly a place of business. Piles of papers were heaped up in an orderly fashion, and the shelves held ledgers rather than books for reading pleasure. A secretary scuttled away through a back door as Ferdy entered.

"Mr Makenham, you are welcome. Giles Moreton, sir." He was a rangy man, quite elderly although the exact age was hard to determine, his hair lightly powdered and worn long in the old-fashioned style, or perhaps it was a wig. He was dressed for practicality rather than fashion, a man who was more used to walking amongst burghers and businessmen than the sons of the nobility, with a shawl around his shoulders for warmth, despite the heat of the day. He stared rather vaguely at Ferdy, with an old man's bewilderment at an event so out of the ordinary.

"Ferdinand Makenham." Ferdy executed his best bow. "Forgive my wholly unexpected arrival. I will not detain you for long from the many important calls upon your time, I give you my word. However, I have been staying with my sister, Lady Masters, at Wrayforth and I could not resist the opportunity to call when I realised how close my route would bring me to Branton. You have read my letter of explanation?"

"I have but, forgive me, sir, I do not quite understand what it is you want of me. Your letter mentioned my nephew?"

"Yes. His name is Johnny Moreton, I understand, and he was from Liverpool originally?" The old man nodded. "I have the good fortune to be acquainted with a lady by the name of Winterton, whose brother Jeremy was known to your nephew. In fact, your nephew was one of the last people to see him alive, for Jeremy was drowned at sea on his first voyage shortly after staying with the Moreton family in Liverpool. It may be that, being of the same age as Jeremy, he will have memories of his last days which would comfort his family."

"I hardly think so," Moreton said with a dismissive wave of one hand. "Johnny left Liverpool years ago. Never mentioned this Winterton fellow, not once. Quite forgotten him, I daresay."

"You will not object if I speak to him myself?" Ferdy said politely. "It may be that—"

"Not possible."

"Oh. That is... disappointing, when I have come here specially to see him. Perhaps if I come back tomorrow?"

"Not possible because he is not here. Not in the country. Gone to America to look at the plantations there, learn about the business from the other end, so to speak. Daresay he will be there for years. May never come back."

Ferdy was not clever, but he had moved in society for long enough to know when he was being lied to. Those who were skilled at the art of deception could look him straight in the eye and tell him that a particular black gelding was a sure thing for Newmarket, he had it direct from the stable lad, or that a certain establishment would never use loaded dice, on his word of honour, and Ferdy would *almost* believe them, so convincing were they. Why, even

Greg could deny all knowledge of missing jam tarts with an impressively plausible look of wounded innocence. But Mr Giles Moreton had not that skill. His eyes slithered away from Ferdy's in a clear admission of guilt.

But there was no point in pressing a man who wished to keep his own counsel. Ferdy thanked him for his time, bade him farewell with unimpaired civility, and returned to the inn and his waiting carriage not angry, but very, very puzzled.

"Why lie about it?" he said to Aunt Agatha when he returned. "What possible difference can it make to them?"

"People lie for all sorts of reasons, Ferdy," she said sadly. "Every family has secrets they do not wish to expose to the world."

"Still, it is strange that the Moretons in Liverpool were so helpful and friendly, and wrote down everything they remembered of Jeremy, and yet this branch of the family is downright obstructive. It is a pity, for now there is nothing to tell Fanny."

"But you will tell her of the attempt, surely?" Aunt Agatha said. "She will be very grateful for it, and that can only be helpful to your cause."

"I did not do it to be thanked," Ferdy said tersely. "My only intention was to bring her some happy news, if I could, but since I cannot, she need know nothing of the obstreperous Mr Moreton."

"As you think best, dear," Aunt Agatha said with a sigh.

~~~~~

'My dear Fanny, I have news of Margaret! I fretted so about her that Leo set off for Ludlow determined to find out what has become of her, for I will not hide from you that I had begun to fear the worst. But she is alive and well and happy, so Leo says, although he will tell me nothing more, except that a great deal has happened and Margaret was not able to write to us at all for a long time. But now she can and so she wishes to write herself to each of us and explain everything. Oh yes, and she has a gentleman friend, a curate, but Leo

will not tell me another thing, irritating man, so we must just contain ourselves in patience until Margaret takes up her pen. Your affectionate sister, Lucy.'

~~~~~

SEPTEMBER

The summer wore away, day by day. Almost everyone of importance in the town disappeared to their country estates, or, if they had none of their own, visited friends who had. Mrs Drabble and Celia went south to Brinshire to visit the Claremonts, with an engagement announcement expected any day. Lady Harriet and Miss Hay went off to Drummoor, and most of the Makenhams went to Abbeymount or Lennister Hall, which adjoined it, and Cressington Manor nearby, where the Brants lived. Fanny listened wistfully as Cordelia talked of all the comings and goings between the three houses, the outings and long walks and lawn games and archery. It all sounded delightful. Eventually, even Cordelia left for Abbeymount, where Julius was to be invited to stay periodically, when his duties permitted. From further south, news arrived that Mr Hawes had left Brighton and was settled in Bath, where he was reported to be very popular, single gentleman of means being in short supply there.

Now only Ferdy and Lady Agatha and Mr Brant remained at number Twenty-Five Harlington Terrace, and they became almost Fanny's only society, apart from the indefatigable Malpas family, who still had faint hopes of Ferdy for Emmy.

It was at a dinner engagement at the Malpas house that Fanny found herself sitting next to Ferdy. For much of the first course he devoted his attention to Emmy on his other side, but when the second course was laid out and the footmen had drawn back, he turned to Fanny with a smile.

"And how are your sisters, Miss Winterton? Has Miss Annabelle set a date for her wedding yet?"

"Oh yes, it is to be in November, and they will not have a wedding tour at that time of year, but may consider it for the spring.

But I have had news from Rosamund — her father-in-law, Lord Westerlea, wishes to invite me and all of my sisters to Westerlea Park for Christmas. Is that not wonderful? He will send his own carriage for me, and Robin Dalton — Rosamund's husband, you know — will collect Margaret and Lucy. Annabelle will have her own carriage by then, naturally. Is it not the most delightful scheme? We will all be together again at last."

"That... that is very generous of Lord Westerlea."

"Oh yes! Rosamund says that his lordship felt some regret that we were forced to separate — scattered to the four winds, he said, is that not poetic? He felt he should have done more to help us, so now he wants us to be together again, for a little while. He is not terribly well, I think, so perhaps it will cheer him a little to have the house full of friends. Oh, and there are some papers relating to the house for us to sign. Mr Makenham? Are you quite well? You look a trifle pale."

"Perfectly well, I thank you. I... I am just a little surprised by this news. No..." He frowned. "Not surprised, exactly, because clearly there would be a change in your circumstances, but—"

"Change in my circumstances?"

He laid down his knife and fork, and turned slightly to look her full in the face. "Had you not realised? Your sister will be marrying the Earl of Brackenwood, a man of great wealth and influence. He will be more than capable of supporting two or three unmarried sisters of his bride. You will not need to be a seamstress, Miss Winterton, but may live out your days as a lady, as you deserve. When you go south for Christmas, I doubt you will return to Sagborough."

Fanny could barely breathe. Leave Sagborough for good? It was unthinkable. "No," she whispered. "This is my home now. My friends are here, my work... *everything* is here."

"You will not need to work," he said gently, "and you will make new friends. Your amiability and good nature must win you friends wherever you go, Miss Winterton." But his voice was almost as low as hers, and there was a bleakness in his eyes that made her want to cry.

That night, Fanny sat in the window seat in her bedroom pondering her future. Would she be obliged to go and live with Annabelle? Or perhaps, if Lucy were to marry her Leo, they would find a home for her. There would be no shop, no customers and no endless work on other ladies' gowns. She could sew for her own pleasure and for her sisters, as she had always done. She would make new friends in Cheshire or in Shropshire or in Bath. There might even be a season in London, who could say? She would meet new gentlemen, and perhaps she would meet the one who would make her heart leap out of her breast the moment she saw him, and she would be hit by the thunderbolt of love. Perhaps there would be a glorious future ahead of her. So why did she feel so miserable at the thought?

~~~~~

Late in September, Lady Harriet returned from Drummoor, and two days later her lawyer arrived.

"Not before time," she said, as they were shown into the morning room. "I have been awaiting you since the spring. I could have had any number of lesser beings, but Sir Rathbone assured me you were the best for disentangling these messy situations."

The lawyer bowed. "We were distracted by a murder or two," he said, smiling genially at her. He was an unlikely lawyer, in Fanny's view, for he was not much above thirty, and ostentatiously attired in a style similar to that of Mr Brant. "However, we are here now, Lady Harriet. I am Pettigrew Willerton-Forbes, and—" Fanny squeaked, recognising the name, then covered her mouth with her hands, as if to hide her embarrassment. Mr Willerton-Forbes smiled at her, but continued smoothly, "May I present my colleague, Captain Michael Edgerton, formerly of the East India Company Army?"

Edgerton was a very small man, flamboyantly dressed in the garish blue and yellow striped waistcoat of the Four-Horse Club. He bowed in a florid manner, but his eyes twinkled roguishly at Fanny.

Lady Harriet harrumphed. "I am not sure why you need the assistance of an army captain, Mr Willerton-Forbes. However, you must do as you see fit. This is my mother-in-law, Mrs Hay, and my sister-in-law, Miss Hay. My husband is at his hospital just now, but you will meet him at dinner, I daresay. You will stay for dinner? You will forgive me if I do not offer you accommodation here. We are a small household, ill-suited to guests."

"The King's Head will suit us very well," Mr Willerton-Forbes said. "And this must be Miss Winterton."

"You know Fanny?" Lady Harriet said, her voice sharp with suspicion.

"We have never met before, but I know two of her sisters," Mr Willerton-Forbes said. "We were called in to investigate a possible murder at the Earl of Brackenwood's house, where Miss Annabelle Winterton lives, and then we moved to Shropshire, to look into another possible murder at the house where Miss Lucy Winterton lives. And here we find yet another Miss Winterton, but no murder this time."

"Oh, but there is," Fanny cried impulsively. "The housemaid here was murdered just after Easter, and then two more ladies, and no one has been able to find out why, or who has done such a wicked thing."

Mr Willerton-Forbes' eyes gleamed. "How fascinating. Do tell me more, Miss Winterton."

"Oh no," Lady Harriet said sharply. "No, no, no, no, no. I shall not allow you to be distracted by any more murders. Sort out the mess regarding Westbury House, and then you may worry about murdered housemaids, but not before, I beg you."

Mr Willerton-Forbes bowed, but he grinned conspiratorially at Fanny. At dinner, he contrived to sit next to her, but there could be no private talk, for they were a small company and Lady Harriet monopolised the conversation at first.

"You understand the position with Westbury House?" she said.

"Not entirely," Mr Willerton-Forbes said. "There is a question regarding the current ownership, that is all I know at present."

Lady Harriet sighed, and rolled her eyes. "Really, Sir Rathbone should have explained it to you. I made it very clear in my letter. Westbury House used to be part of Lord Carrbridge's estate, but it was gifted to me when I came of age, including the income from the surrounding tenant farms, to provide me with a home and an independence should I choose not to marry. It would revert back to the estate on my marriage or death. But then there was a crisis when it looked as if everything would be lost, so Carrbridge made it over fully to me at that time. I established it as a home for women in unfortunate circumstances, and now I should like to set up a legal trust of some sort so that it may continue to be used in that way even after my death. However, I am now married and there is some confusion over who currently owns the property. It may even be that Carrbridge still owns it, or it may be me or perhaps Dr Hay. And then there are the tenant farms, which are subject to some medieval constraints. So you see, your job is to disentangle the mess and set up this trust for me."

"I can certainly try to disentangle the mess," Mr Willerton-Forbes said gently. "Once that is done, however, it will depend on the exact terms of the property's title as to what may be done with it, and who may make that decision. It may not even be possible to do what you wish."

"That is what I am paying you for, to make it possible."

"I will do my best, Lady Harriet, but a lawyer must work within the law, sadly. It is a great hindrance at times."

She glared at him, and although she fell silent and allowed the conversation to become more general, there was no opportunity to talk about Martha's murder.

It was not until the two gentlemen were leaving that Mr Willerton-Forbes was able to whisper, "You must tell me about this murder another time, Miss Winterton."

She whispered back, "Ask Mr Makenham in number Twenty-Five. He knows all about it."

Mr Willerton-Forbes' eyes glittered with excitement.

Fanny felt no remorse in distracting him from Lady Harriet's problem, which was merely a dry legal argument over a house that had stood for a hundred years and would stand for a hundred more, no matter who owned it. Surely a woman's life was more important? And perhaps Mr Willerton-Forbes, who had been so successful at solving murders already, could do the same for poor Martha.

29: *The Lawyer*

"A lawyer?" Ferdy said, reading the card Poole had proffered. "Willerton-Forbes? I do not know him."

"He says that Miss Winterton sent him to you," Poole said.

"Oh, then show him in at once, and his friend... Captain Edgerton," Ferdy said.

In just five minutes of civil conversation, Ferdy established that Willerton-Forbes was the son of a recently elevated earl and that they had several mutual acquaintances. Social niceties satisfied, Ferdy enquired politely what they wanted of him.

"We should like to hear about this murder. Miss Winterton said you would know all about it."

It took two hours to relate all the details of Martha's disappearance, the search for her, the dreadful discovery in the canal, the investigations and the two subsequent murders. By the time Ferdy had reached the point of his own visit to Bertram in York, the morning was all but gone, and Willerton-Forbes had begun to make polite noises about leaving.

"But I have many more questions," he said. "May I call again to continue this discussion?"

"I suppose you will not be free for dinner?" Ferdy said hopefully, for he very much wished to hear Willerton-Forbes' opinion of the situation. "You will not like to abandon your hosts so soon, I daresay."

"We are not staying next door," the lawyer said ruefully. "It is too small a household for guests, seemingly, but the King's Head is perfectly comfortable."

"Oh, that will never do," Ferdy said. "You must stay with me. I have a staff of fourteen kicking their heels here, not counting the valets, with only myself, my aunt and my cousin to benefit by my grandfather's generosity. Eduarde, my French chef, is always grumbling that his talents are underused."

Before the lawyer could demur, Captain Edgerton jumped in to say, "We would be delighted. It would be a kindness to allow your chef to demonstrate his talents, for think how dreadful it would be should he feel so underemployed as to give notice. We must unselfishly aid you in keeping him contented. Should you like us to assist you in depleting your cellar, too? We are always happy to oblige a gentleman in so worthy an endeavour."

Ferdy laughed in delight. "How excessively thoughtful you are. I will send my troop of footmen to the King's Head to retrieve your things. We dine at seven, and I should perhaps warn you that my Aunt Agatha is a fearsome whist player and she likes to play high."

"Better and better," Captain Edgerton said, grinning.

~~~~~

Willerton-Forbes and Edgerton set about their self-appointed tasks with energy. During the day, they strode about Sagborough together looking at the scenes of tragedy and talking to anyone they could find about their memories of the murdered women, and each evening they did their level best to drink Ferdy's cellar dry and impoverish Aunt Agatha. They went to York one day and recruited Mr Bertram to their cause, and thereby took hold of all the notes taken by the constables' indefatigable clerk. Ferdy supposed that they also devoted some time to Lady Harriet's legal problem, but they never mentioned it.

After dinner, when Aunt Agatha had withdrawn in state to await them in the drawing room, the two men described for Ferdy and Edgar all their discoveries.

"A fascinating case," Willerton-Forbes said one evening. "I am increasingly convinced that the later murders were not connected to that of Martha Smith. You have said all along that she was not a lightskirt, Mr Makenham, and I agree. None of her friends see her that way at all. She was very bitter about her ruin and therefore hardly likely to multiply the offence, and the servants next door say that she was glad of her place there, and was a hard worker. She was not desperate for money, and she loved her little boy. She could only see him on Sundays, but she never missed a visit. It seems to me that something happened at the Easter ball that set the tragic events in motion, and led to her murder."

"Is it because of the child?" Ferdy said. "Might she have encountered her abuser at the ball? He supposedly came from Yorkshire."

"That is possible, perhaps, but the reference to Yorkshire may have been just as false as the giving of Mr Brant's name," Willerton-Forbes said thoughtfully. "In any case, the Grantham trail was useless. Bertram found the house where she had been employed and examined the guest records, and can you guess what he found?"

"Not my name," Edgar said, running a finger nervously around his neckcloth. "I was never anywhere near Grantham."

"No, in fact the name was *Makenham*," Willerton-Forbes said. "Another false name, you see, but Bertram was embarrassed in case it might be thought that *you* were the person in question, so he dropped that line of enquiry instantly."

"Why do you assume the name is false?" Ferdy said with interest. "It is exceedingly difficult to get oneself invited to a place as a guest without being known personally to at least one of the family."

Willerton-Forbes' face changed. "You mean—? But it was not you, Makenham? It cannot have been you, or Mr Brant either, because Martha saw your faces clearly and did not recognise you."

"No, no! I have never been to that part of the country, nor Edgar. But there are almost as many Makenhams in existence as there are Brants."

"But how many of them were at the Easter ball?" Edgerton said, leaning forward. "There was only you, sir."

"There was my cousin," Ferdy said. "No, not Edgar. I have a great many cousins, but Ralph is my only first cousin to bear the Makenham name."

"*Ralph* Makenham?" Willerton-Forbes said. "But no such person was ever interviewed or mentioned."

"Nevertheless, he was here at the Easter ball," Ferdy said. "He was never interviewed, I expect, because he left for London very shortly thereafter. But he is no more a murderer than I am."

"No doubt," Willerton-Forbes said. "Still, *somebody* murdered those poor women, and I find it interesting that there were three murders and then no more."

"Whatever does that mean?" Ferdy said.

"I have no idea," Willerton-Forbes said. "It is just... interesting."

The very next day, Ralph himself arrived, ambling unannounced into the house with his valet and boxes as if he owned it. Ferdy was pleased to see him, of course, but his mind was too full of murder and the approaching desolation of a life without Fanny to be as welcoming as usual.

"I wonder you did not let us know of your plans, Ralph," he said testily, stepping around the heaped array of boxes in the hall to greet his cousin. "It puts everyone out to have you turn up out of nowhere like this, and we have dinner guests tonight, as well, and Eduarde has something special in mind."

"Good Lord, Ferdy, you pay your staff to cope with such contingencies," Ralph said. "What is the matter with you? Is it your courting that is amiss?" He laughed and to Ferdy's strained nerves the sound was harsh. "You are a slow-top, sometimes, cousin. Shall I woo her for you?"

"Devil take it, Ralph, you can be such a rattle," Ferdy muttered.

The dinner guests were only the Hays and Fanny, and the half hour before dinner was entirely taken up with Lady Harriet catechising Willerton-Forbes on his progress into the legal position regarding Westbury House. Ferdy was amused by the lawyer's deftness in deflecting her enquiries without her realising that he had, in fact, done very little work on the business.

Ferdy thought Fanny seemed pale and subdued. She answered questions with her usual willingness, but the sparkle was missing. His heart ached for her, although he had no idea what had happened to put her out of frame. Her sisters were all well, she told him, so it was not that. Perhaps Lady Harriet had been berating her for some perceived misdemeanour, for the woman could be snappish sometimes, and her brisk manner was at odds with Fanny's gentle ways. Poor Fanny! It was so dispiriting to see her so cast down.

But then, that was much how he felt himself, as if he had been hit over the head with a very large stick and all the life beaten out of him, and in his case he knew the reason very well. In a few months — no, weeks! — Lord Westerlea's carriage would be outside the door, and Fanny would enter it and disappear from Ferdy's life. And even if he were to follow her, for he would follow her to the far side of the ocean, if need be, she would still not look at him as a possible husband. He had nothing but loneliness and dejection ahead of him. How could he possibly go on as if nothing had happened? And yet he must. Good manners demanded it.

With such depressing thoughts hovering in his brain, the murders and Willerton-Forbes' eager investigations were almost a relief. When the ladies had withdrawn after dinner and the gentlemen were enjoying the port, Dr Hay enquired on their progress.

"Oh, we proceed slowly," Willerton-Forbes said, in his calm, lawyerly way. "Very slowly. There is much to be considered, and much still to be discovered, I fear. For instance, we learnt only today of the existence of Mr Ralph Makenham, who was at the Easter ball, seemingly, yet no mention was made of his presence in any of the interviews."

"Oh, you have read the notes of all the interviews, have you?" Ralph said, with his easy smile. "You gentlemen are reassuringly thorough. I feel sure you will solve the puzzle before too long. Yes, I was at the Easter ball, and did my share of dancing with the yokels, but it seems unlikely that I could tell you anything you are not already aware of."

"Did you stay on after the dancing finished?" Willerton-Forbes said.

"A little while. I was in the crowd watching Gil Marford get a bloody nose, but after that things got rather rough and I left the locals to their own little fights. I got back here not long after Ferdy and Edgar, for they were still not abed."

"It was more than an hour!" Edgar said indignantly. "I was worried sick about you, Ralph, so I was watching the clock compulsively. As if we could have slept while you were mingling with drunken mobs. I felt sure you would be caught up in a riot and killed. As it was, you were—"

"Good God, Edgar, what a worrier you are! I can look after myself, you know. Ferdy, are you holding on to the port for any particular reason? Saving it for Christmas, perhaps?"

"What is there to save it for?" Ferdy muttered, refilling his own glass before passing the decanter. By Christmas, Fanny would be far away and he would be back at Abbeymount for his birthday having failed utterly to secure the woman he loved. What was there in his future to look forward to?

But Christmas was a long way off still, and Fanny was in his house tonight. His spirits lifted as he went upstairs to the drawing room once more. She looked up as he entered, and gave him a tremulous smile. How could he resist? He crossed the room and sat down beside her. Again she smiled, before bending her head to her sewing again. Dear Fanny! She was always sewing, even at an evening engagement, as if her hands could not bear to be still.

"I like your new gown," he said. "I am so glad you are no longer in mourning, for white suits you much better, and the way you weave colours around the bodice and sleeve is very clever."

"Thank you! I copied the style from something I saw Lady Carrbridge wearing when she was here in the spring. The fullness of the skirt, and the way the bodice is arranged... she is such an elegant lady. Of course, being married, she wears far more colourful gowns than I can, but I liked her way of mixing two or three colours in striking combinations, and I can do that in the trimmings of mine, even if the gown itself is white."

"It works very well," he said. "You use the same colours in your hair, too. This fuller sleeve is very pretty. Did you copy that from Lady Carrbridge, too?"

"Oh no, I just invented that. Do you know, Mr Makenham, it is such a pleasure to talk to you, for you understand all about clothes, and you do not tell me you are sick of hearing about silk and lace like Lady Harriet does."

"I never get sick of hearing about silk and lace," he said at once, which was the plain truth of the matter. Fanny smiled up at him with such warmth that it was all he could do to restrain himself from kissing her on the spot. He was so absorbed in the conversation that he failed to notice Ralph's approach.

"Miss Winterton, I never see you without a needle in your hand," Ralph said in his lazy drawl, sitting down a little closer to Fanny than Ferdy thought necessary. "What are you making today?"

"A reticule to match a gown I made for Miss Malpas," she said. "It is small enough work to bring with me for the evening, and I enjoy sewing, Mr Makenham. I feel a little lost without a needle in my hand."

"Well, it is a relief to leave our male concerns behind for a while and focus our attention on female pursuits, such as needlework," he said lightly. "See how we are all drawn to your side, Miss Winterton, by your feminine charms."

Edgerton drew up a chair beside them, with a roguish grin to Fanny that made Ferdy fume. Edgar was helping Aunt Agatha set up the card tables and Lady Harriet was haranguing Willerton-Forbes about her house again, but with both Ralph and Edgerton clustered around Fanny, Ferdy felt himself rather crowded out.

"Indeed we cannot help it," Edgerton said. "Every man is inevitably drawn to the prettiest young lady in the room, as a moth is drawn to the flame."

Ralph sighed and rolled his eyes. "Such flummery, Captain. Take no notice of him, Miss Winterton, although I suppose it is better than all this talk of murder. Do you really expect to find out anything after all this time, Edgerton?"

Edgerton's flirtatious manner dropped away, and he answered seriously, "Oh, we may, sir. We may. Mr Willerton-Forbes is very thorough, although it is proving tricky to obtain a coherent view of events. There are some serious discrepancies in the reports."

Ralph laughed. "Of course there are! Have you any idea how much punch and ale was consumed that night? We were all too drunk to know what we were doing even at the time, never mind six months later."

"Miss Winterton was not drunk," Ferdy said, offended on her behalf. "I expect you remember a great deal, do you not, Miss Winterton?"

"Oh yes! It was my first ball in an age, you see, although I could not dance, being still in mourning. But it was so pleasant to sit and watch everyone else dancing. I enjoyed it very much and I only had a few sips of the punch, for it was rather strong, so I was not in the least drunk. I remember everything very well."

"Captain Edgerton!" Aunt Agatha called. "Are you playing? Ferdy? Ralph? Or Fanny, dear — would you like to play whist tonight?"

"Oh, no, Lady Agatha, you know I am not a good player," Fanny said. "Pray hold me excused."

"You will have enough for two tables without me," Ralph said. "I will bear Miss Winterton company while she sews in her quiet corner."

So Ferdy had to sit for more than an hour with the galling sight before him of Fanny blushing and giggling and smiling as the focus of Ralph's considerable charms. Ferdy had never played whist so badly.

As soon as the visitors had left, Aunt Agatha rounded on Ralph. "What on *earth* are you about, to be making up to Fanny right under Ferdy's nose? Really, Ralph, have you no sense of honour to be stealing her away like that? It is the outside of enough! You should be helping him win her, not getting between them like that."

"Good heavens, Aunt, am I not to do the pretty to any young lady now in case Ferdy wants her? I was just being civil to a guest, that is all."

"If that was just being civil to a guest then I am the Queen of Sheba," she said tartly. "Leave Ferdy's young lady alone."

"She is not *my* anything," Ferdy said tiredly. "She has a mind of her own, Auntie, and since she does not want me, if Ralph can make her happy—"

"What poppycock! Really, Ferdy, can you not stand up for yourself, just this once? Stop being such a gentleman and *fight* for her, like a man!"

"No fighting, Auntie," Ferdy said firmly. "Especially no fighting within the family."

"Well, I wash my hands of you, and when Ralph has whisked her off to the altar and you are sunk in gloom, you will get no sympathy from me, you may be sure."

And so saying she flounced out of the room in a swirl of green satin, and up the stairs. There was silence for a few minutes, as Willerton-Forbes and Edgerton studiedly ignored the altercation and pretended to be folding away card tables and replacing cards in boxes.

Edgar exhaled noisily. "Heavens! Is there any brandy about?"

Ferdy poured and saw them all settled, before quietly stealing away to his room and Wrackham's sympathetic silence. Then he sat in his dressing robe on the window seat, his forehead resting against the cool glass, drowning in his own unending misery. If only he were braver or more articulate or just had the confidence to sweep Fanny off her feet and *make* her love him by the power of his own dominance. As Ralph could do. As Ralph *would* do. And Ferdy was helpless to do more than watch and pray that Ralph would be kind to her and make her happy, as she deserved to be. Dear, sweet Fanny, the love of his life, who was lost to him for ever.

30: *Westbury House*

Fanny was very unsettled. In fact the whole household at number Twenty-Six was unsettled, for Lady Harriet was out of sorts and that put everything out of alignment, even the servants. Fires died down for lack of attention, washing water failed to appear and meals were late, the latter putting Dr Hay quite out of frame. Fanny tried to help by offering to fetch this or that, or run down to the kitchen when no one responded to the bell, but that did not answer, either. *'Why should you run about here and there, Fanny? You are a guest in this house, not a servant. The Good Lord knows that I employ enough of them, but they are never where they are wanted. The simple management of one small household is beyond them, it seems. What is the matter with everyone at the moment?'* and much more in the same vein. So Fanny kept to her sewing corner, head down, and hoped the storm would blow over.

The lawyer was at the root of the problem, for he had been engaged to resolve the question of the ownership of Westbury House, and instead he was *'gallivanting about investigating these murders, and pretending to be a constable, and all at my expense'.* So Lady Harriet said, and a great deal more besides. It was fortunate that Miss Hay was there, for she was the only one who had the power to cajole Lady Harriet out of her megrims.

Then there was Mr Ralph Makenham. Fanny had known him for several months, and he had never taken much interest in her before.

He had always been polite, but in a careless, teasing sort of way, as if she were a younger sister, and sometimes she wondered if he were merely laughing at her.

Now he had turned his full attention onto her, and she was not sure that she liked it. He was very handsome, of course, and she supposed there were women for whom his well-shaped legs and broad chest were great attractions. For Fanny, they were more like distractions. When he sat beside her, and especially when he leaned close to talk more intimately to her, she was dreadfully conscious of his nearness, and was apt to become flustered, blushing and tripping over her words in a way she had not since she was first out. There was something mesmerising about him, especially his eyes — a vivid blue, ringed with dark lashes, piercing eyes which seemed to drill into her very soul. She remembered what Marianne had said, that *'His eyes are cold when he smiles, not like the way Mr Ferdy looks at you.'*

He was not put off by her reticence, however. Somehow or other, he contrived to meet her every day, and when that happened, whether it was at Lady Harriet's house or Ferdy's or at some other place where Fanny was visiting with Lady Agatha, Mr Ralph would sit himself down beside her with a meaningful grin, and no consideration of the polite protocol for morning visits prevailed. He would not be shifted from her side. Sometimes he even loitered in the circulating library to catch her as she emerged from the shop, and would insist on escorting her home. Nothing she said seemed to deter him.

If Fanny had been in love with him, such devotion would have thrilled her, and she would be dreaming happily of the day when he would declare himself. Instead, he made her feel uneasy. She could not understand what he might mean by paying her such attentions. He was in love with Marianne, was he not? At least, he had proposed to her, and when she refused him, he had taken himself away to repair his broken heart, or so she supposed. Now that Marianne was gone away with Miss Makenham, he felt safe to come back to

Sagborough. But still, he could not be in love with Fanny, not so soon after courting Marianne, yet he did not seem to be merely flirting with her, either. His manner was too intent for that. She could not make him out in the least, but there was nothing to be done except to wait until he either made her an offer or lost interest.

Lady Harriet's grumbling to the lawyer had an effect, for he decided that he must visit Westbury House to see if any relevant papers were to be found there.

"Apparently there is a desk full of old documents in the study there, so that must be my next endeavour," he said to Fanny as she sewed in Lady Agatha's morning room. "Miss Winterton, may I prevail upon you to accompany me? Westbury House is an entirely female household, and its occupants moreover not kindly disposed towards the male sex. It would be helpful to have a female amongst the party, and one who is known to the residents, for we do not wish to cause them undue alarm by our presence."

"That is very thoughtful, Mr Willerton-Forbes," Fanny said. "I shall have to ask Lady Harriet if I may go, for she does not like me to mingle with her unfortunate women any more."

But when she approached Lady Harriet with the proposal, she said, "Good gracious, Fanny, you need not ask my permission for every little thing, you know."

"I beg your pardon," Fanny said, flushing. "I should not wish to do anything you dislike, and you said I should not mingle with them, so—"

"One would not wish you to become too friendly with them, it is true, but it was mainly Lady Craston's wish because of— But nothing came of that. Why *did* you turn Ferdy down, Fanny? It seemed like such an eligible match for you, and Mr Hawes had gone off to be dazzled by London society by then."

"I do not love him," Fanny said sadly. "I know I should be prudent and so forth, but marriage would be unbearable to me without the deepest love, on both sides. It must be wonderful to be transported by love."

"Transported... yes, it is very like that, and it *is* wonderful, Fanny," Lady Harriet said, a little smile playing about her lips. "Perhaps you are right to wait and hope and keep searching for the one person who fulfils every need in you, and makes you joyously happy every day." She sighed and fell silent, her face softened by some pleasant memory, while Fanny tried to reconcile these romantic sentiments with the rather stuffy Dr Hay. Eventually Lady Harriet returned to her usual brisk manner. "By all means go to Westbury House with Willerton-Forbes, if it brings me closer to a resolution of my problem, Fanny, for I have to say that the man has been very dilatory so far. At least he has not put me to the expense of accommodating him at an inn — not to mention his army friend, his valet, his grooms and his horses. *So* expensive to feed, horses, but at least they drink water, not claret and port."

So it was arranged. With Miss Kelly to accompany her, Fanny set out with Mr Willerton-Forbes and Captain Edgerton in Lady Harriet's carriage for Westbury House. It was not a long journey, with nothing of much interest visible from the windows beyond glimpses of browning trees and grey skies until they drew up outside their destination and the groom jumped down to open the door.

Westbury House was a plain building of grey stone with little adornment, but it looked well-kept, with freshly painted window frames, and honeysuckle and roses growing over the porch. The crisp autumn air was heavy with their scent, together with a wisp of woodsmoke. The gravel drive was free of weeds, and shrubs bordered the short drive. To one side of the house were neat vegetable beds, and further away an orchard heavy with fruit, where a woman on a ladder could be seen harvesting the crop. A cluster of children, with two young women in attendance, appeared from nowhere to admire the horses.

Miss Kelly showed the gentlemen into the study, and Fanny was claimed by the women and led, unprotesting, to the kitchen for ale and cakes. Fanny had not come empty-handed, bringing sweets for the children and a quarter pound of tea for the women, all she could afford, for she knew they had not the means to purchase their own. For a while, all was laughter and friendly gossip. The women bore no grudge for her previous avoidance of them, knowing perfectly well the reason for it. When Bridget Kelly joined them, there was not the slightest constraint amongst them.

Fanny looked around at the children gathered in the warm kitchen, some sitting on their mothers' knees, others in groups on the floor, playing games with pebbles and wooden cups.

"Which one is Martha's?"

"This is Eddy," Susan said, picking up a sturdy boy of two or so.

"You will not send him to the orphanage?" Fanny said. "I can spare a few more coins if—"

"Lord, no. He's the same age as my ragamuffin — like twins, they are — so I'm happy to look after him, and Lady Harriet don't mind. Besides, the fancy gentleman's been paying for him as well as you. He has brand-new nankeens, and there was enough left over for a couple of spare pairs, too. You want to hold him?"

"Oh, may I?" She had no difficulty in identifying *'the fancy gentleman'*. How kind Mr Makenham was!

She held out her arms to take the boy. Susan lifted the child, and he raised his head and looked straight at Fanny. His eyes locked on hers and she saw... someone else.

"Oh!" Her arms wavered, then, recollecting herself, she scooped Eddy onto her lap and smoothed his dark curls away from his brow.

The women all fell silent, staring at Fanny. The fire in the range crackled away, pots bubbled and the children clacked their stones against the flagged floor, but amongst the women there was a tension as thick as soup.

"You *know*," Susan said accusingly. "You recognise his father — it's someone you know."

"I… I do not *know,*" Fanny said miserably. "No one can be sure, and anyone may have eyes just that shade of blue. It need not mean anything."

"But—" Susan began.

"Now, Susan, don't tease Fanny," Bridget said. "Even if she gave you a name, it doesn't mean he was the one who killed poor Martha, does it?"

"But he could've done right by her," Susan said.

"He could still do right by the boy," one of the others said.

"And perhaps he will, given the opportunity," Bridget said. "Who knows what may happen? The future is ours to make, my friends, but until then, there's sewing to be done. Shoo, back to your needles. Edith, have you gathered enough apples for the pie? Doreen, have you finished upstairs yet?"

One by one, they drifted away, while Bridget watched them go in silence. All the while Fanny sat, cuddling Eddy, rocking him gently as he sucked his thumb and rested his curly head trustingly against her. It was a relief when Mr Willerton-Forbes declared his work to be done, and they could return to Sagborough.

"Was your search successful, Mr Willerton-Forbes?" Fanny said, as they swayed about in the carriage.

"Indeed it was," the lawyer said. "We discovered many interesting documents, and one in particular that points in a most unexpected direction. There are still some records in York to be examined, but I can leave that to Mr Bertram, and with a favourable wind we might yet resolve the matter of ownership."

"Lady Harriet will be pleased," Fanny said.

The lawyer laughed. "Oh, I very much doubt that, Miss Winterton. But how about you — was your visit enjoyable?"

"Very, thank you."

"Fanny has also been making discoveries," Bridget said. "She has discovered that Martha's baby was fathered by a man with blue eyes."

"Oh no... I could not... one cannot be sure... besides, a great many men have blue eyes," she finished, hot with embarrassment.

"So they do," Mr Willerton-Forbes said genially. "So they do. One must not jump to conclusions, Miss Kelly. When one is investigating such cases as Martha's, one must weigh *all* the available evidence. Goodness, that was a severe jolt! This road is badly rutted, I fear. Are you injured, Miss Winterton? Miss Kelly? Dear me, and now I fear that it is beginning to rain. How fortunate that Lady Harriet's carriage is so snug. I was once in a carriage that jolted so badly that the coachman was quite thrown from his perch and ended up in the footwell, and so unsighted that the horses took a wrong turn at the next crossroads onto a narrow lane and it was twenty miles before there was anywhere to turn about. And then..."

He kept up this gentle burbling all the way back to Sagborough, but Fanny was acutely uncomfortable for the whole journey.

~~~~~

Ferdy found himself alone at breakfast one morning. Aunt Agatha had already eaten, and then bustled away with her long list of tasks for the day, and none of the other guests had yet descended the stairs. His solitude was disrupted first by the sound of raised voices from the hall outside, followed almost immediately by the door bursting open. Ferdy rose as Lady Harriet Hay strode into the room ahead of the harassed Poole. Ferdy dismissed the butler with a slight tilt of the head.

"What is this!" Lady Harriet hissed, waving a letter under Ferdy's nose. "What ridiculous and offensive nonsense is this? I have never been more angry in my life, and to think that I brought him here and paid his expenses, after waiting on his convenience for months first, mind you, and how does he repay me? He is a viper, I tell you, and I will have him sent straight back to London and

Carrbridge will have him thrown out of his chambers and he will never work again, I swear it. Ungrateful toad!"

Picking his way carefully through this tirade, Ferdy deduced that it had something to do with the lawyer. "What has Mr Willerton-Forbes done that offends you so?" he said politely.

"Offends me! I should say it does. As if my brother has anything to do with the matter! Gil has not always behaved as he ought, but this is ridiculous. Here — read it."

She thrust the letter under his nose. Taking it, Ferdy read, *'Hatty, Do not be alarmed, but I do not wish you to hear this from any other source. W-F informs me that I am suspected of murdering those women and he wishes to speak to me on the matter. He advises me to take legal counsel. I have sent word to Merton to attend me, for I would rather have him on my side than a hundred lawyers. I am to meet W-F at noon. Since I am entirely innocent, there is no cause for concern but I thought you should know. Gil.'*

"Good God! Oh, I do beg your pardon, Lady Harriet, I should not speak so in your presence."

"I do not care how you speak. Where is that *worm* of a lawyer?"

As if summoned, the door opened again and in walked Willerton-Forbes, Edgerton, Ralph and Edgar, all laughing as if sharing a joke. They stopped as they saw Lady Harriet there, her face a picture of fury, the laughter dying on their lips.

"What is the meaning of this?" she said in her most imperious manner, waving the letter again. "Gil is perfectly innocent, as any imbecile could see."

Willerton-Forbes looked her straight in the eye. "Nevertheless, I should like to talk to Lord Gilbert. I am sure there is some perfectly reasonable explanation."

"There is — that you are a fool and a hare-brained nincompoop. Carrbridge will not stand for this, you know."

"The marquess is an honourable man and would wish justice to be done, I am sure, Lady Harriet," Willerton-Forbes said equably.

This outraged the lady so greatly that she went purple in the face, quite unable to think of epithets insulting enough. Then, with an exasperated "Huh!", she whisked out of the room.

"Well!" Edgar said, eyes wide. "It is *far* too early in the day for hysteria, if you ask me."

"It is almost half past ten, Edgar," Ferdy said mildly. "A lady of spirit may engage in hysteria at any time from eight o'clock onwards, as Bianca daily reminded us before Rufus took her off our hands. Willerton-Forbes, you handled Lady Harriet masterfully. My congratulations."

The lawyer smiled, with a small bow of acknowledgement. "It was nothing. I have survived the wrath of the Duke of Dunmorton, so no lesser being can fluster me."

"You do not really suspect Gil of murder, though?"

The smile slipped a little. "There is evidence, unfortunately. The possibility must be considered. We are to meet Lord Gilbert at noon. Should you like to accompany us? Having his friends around him to offer support and provide their own view of events may be helpful."

"I am perfectly willing," Ferdy said.

"Let us all go," Ralph said. "We should bear Gil company in his hour of need."

"The more the merrier," Willerton-Forbes said easily.

Ferdy, Ralph and Edgar all went, to find Gil surrounded by his family — Lord Carrbridge, Lord Reginald, Lord Humphrey and Lord Montague, as well as Mr Merton, the marquess's highly competent secretary. Mr Willerton-Forbes was accompanied as ever by Captain Edgerton, and also his valet, Neate, who was to act as secretary and take notes. The book room was too small to accommodate so many people, so they were forced to commandeer Lady Gilbert's drawing room. Willerton-Forbes placed a table in the middle of the room, with Gil on one side of it and himself, Edgerton and Neate on the other. The rest of the company brought chairs to sit where they would. Ferdy had never been in a courtroom, but to his uneasy mind this room had the feel of one.

Gil was quite at ease, however, making no complaint but sending the servants for whatever was needful and joking with his brothers. Eventually, Willerton-Forbes was ready.

"Tell me about the Easter ball, Lord Gilbert," he began. "What you did and when, that sort of thing."

"We were there quite early," he said. "I went on ahead with Monty and Carrbridge, who were staying with me, so that the ladies could have the carriage a bit later. The dancing was just getting lively when we arrived. I danced most sets with a variety of locals — that is expected of us. I drank some punch, but not enough to call myself bosky. I ate some of the food from politeness, but it was not very good. Afterwards, we mingled with the locals in the yard and someone — probably Humphrey — put up a wager that I could beat some likely local fellow in a bare-knuckle fight. The devil was in it, though, for he was a blacksmith and a more solid lump of flesh I've never seen. Damned near killed me. After that we walked home together."

"You were never alone?"

"Not for a moment." Gil stretched out his legs and folded his arms. Ferdy thought him a little too insouciant, but if confidence would acquit him, he had enough and to spare.

"Did you see Martha Smith that evening?"

"I never knew the girl, so I could not say."

"Did you see the maid drop the tray of glasses? That was her."

"Oh, yes, I remember that. Clumsy girl. She must have tripped on the steps."

"Where were you at the time?"

"On the platform with my brothers. It was between sets, so we were allowing our toes to recover from the indignity of being stamped on by dairymaids."

"Really, Gil!" Carrbridge muttered. "Do you take nothing seriously?"

"Sorry," Gil said cheerfully. "I shall try to be less flippant, brother."

"Apart from your brothers, who else was on the platform at the time?" Willerton-Forbes said, taking no notice of the interruption.

Gil chewed his lip. "Do you know, I have not the least idea. I was not paying much attention. Brant here, I think. A woman in puce with a dreadful turban — that must have been Lady Harbottle. Miss Winterton, who was not dancing. Other than that, I cannot remember."

Neate's pen scratched away.

"Did you know Sally Turner? She worked at Mr Keele's establishment near the canal."

For the first time, there was a hesitation in Gil's answer. "Well... I did know her, after a fashion. Not that I had... dealings with her, but I visited the place once, with a friend, and—"

"The friend's name?"

"Must I say?"

"It is all right, Gil," Ralph said quietly. "Best to tell everything. Not that there is much to tell, frankly. The place was rather tame. There is a tap room on the ground floor, and I had heard there was often some action there — bare-knuckle fights with some wagers on the side, that sort of thing. I persuaded Gil to go with me, since two are better than one in such places. There were no fights, however, just the girls plying for trade. We had a couple of drinks and then left."

"Thank you," Gil said, and there was relief in his voice. "We met Sally Turner there, and she clung to me rather. I had to be brusque to persuade her that I was not interested. Why would I? I have a wife I adore at home."

"That is not always the deterrent one might expect," Willerton-Forbes said mildly.

"Well, it is for me," Gil said with a spurt of anger. "Besides, I have never had to pay for my pleasure, and I saw nothing to tempt me in a woman like that. But she seemed to have borne me some grudge, for I had a letter from her, and frankly, I was astonished she could write. Then there was another, and finally, she asked me to meet her at night on the canal towpath."

"You have these letters?" Willerton-Forbes said with sudden interest.

"I burned them."

"But you went to meet her?"

The room became quiet suddenly, as if all the occupants were holding their breath. Ferdy was astonished — Gil had met the woman who was murdered! Had received letters from her! Had had an assignation... the walls of the room pressed in on him, and he wished he had tied his neckcloth a little less tightly.

"Yes, I went to meet her," Gil said, head defiantly raised, and eyes flashing. "I went to meet her at midnight beside the canal, but I am no fool, Willerton-Forbes. I had no wish to end the day with my head bashed in and my pockets empty, so I took Davy with me, who is my valet, and Jack, my under-groom, who is built on the same scale as Humphrey here and a useful man in a mill. If Sally Turner had brought friends with her, we could have given them a nasty surprise."

"And did she have friends with her?"

"No friends. No Sally Turner either. She never came, and the next day she was found floating face down in the canal. But it was none of my doing, I assure you."

"And Jenny Melton, the third woman to be killed?"

"To my knowledge, I have never met her."

"Thank you, my lord. I have no more questions. Did you get all that, Neate?"

"Yes, sir," the valet answered, scattering pounce everywhere as he sanded his writing.

"Well?" Lord Carrbridge said acidly. "Are you going to arrest Gil, or do you accept that he is innocent?"

Willerton-Forbes hesitated. "I am not planning to arrest Lord Gilbert, no."

"So you accept his innocence?" Lord Carrbridge persisted.

Another hesitation. "It is my belief that he had nothing to do with any of these murders."

He gathered up the papers, the three men bowed and composedly withdrew.

Gil exhaled noisily. "Brandy, I think," he muttered. "A large one."

"Is that it?" Lord Carrbridge said, in a puzzled voice.

"That does seem to be the end of the matter," Merton said.

"A lot of fuss about nothing," Ralph said, with a little laugh. "Thank goodness it is all over, and you have been exonerated, Gil."

"Well, I'll be—!" exploded Lord Humphrey. "What the *Devil* was that all about?"

Mr Merton laughed. "I think, gentlemen, we have just witnessed a masterly piece of misdirection."

"But what does it *mean?*" Lord Carrbridge said plaintively.

"I have not the least idea," Merton said, eyes gleaming. "But it was interesting, all the same. Very, very interesting."

31: Fireworks

Fanny was very glad to have an evening engagement to look forward to that day, for the prospect of an entire evening in the same room as Lady Harriet was too awful to be borne. The whole household knew that Lord Gilbert stood accused of murder, and was to be questioned by Mr Willerton-Forbes, and Lady Harriet was too incensed to contain her rage. Fanny had never seen her so unstoppably angry before. She could sometimes be gruff when irritated, but her ill-humours rarely lasted long. Even Miss Hay, who was usually able to soothe her ladyship, could do nothing with her.

Late in the morning Mr Willerton-Forbes himself came to explain that he had concluded his questioning and was now satisfied that Lord Gilbert had had nothing to do with any of the murders. This brought another tirade, which he bore with his customary placidity, but after he had left Lady Harriet was a great deal calmer, apologising to everyone for her ill-temper.

"What a bear I have been! But I brought him here," she said more than once. "It is my fault, for I brought the man here." Then she turned to Fanny with a smile. "Poor Fanny! Did I terrify you? But he is my baby brother, you see, and I cannot allow anyone to abuse him so shamefully. I shall go and see him, I think."

She left in her carriage to call upon her brother, and the house returned to somnolence with no little relief.

Fanny dressed with care that evening, for she was to attend a ball at the Malpas's house. The ballroom was a new addition to the property, and this was the very first ball to be held there. A great many people had been invited from York and even some from Newcastle, so it was to be a grand occasion, on a scale comparable with the spectacular events of London. The Hays had declined the invitation, but Fanny was to go with the Makenhams, and so she was asked to dine there first.

As soon as she walked into the drawing room, Mr Ralph was there, smiling at her, with those blue eyes mesmerising her.

"Miss Winterton, how delightful to see you in all your glory, ready for the dance. Am I presumptuous in hoping to secure your hand for the two first? Please allow me to be the first to partner you this evening."

She curtsied politely. "Thank you, Mr Makenham, I should be honoured."

"There is a seat over here near the fire. I would not have you chilled, Miss Winterton."

"You are all consideration, sir, but I must make my curtsy to Lady Agatha. Good evening, my lady. Mr Makenham. Mr Brant."

"How lovely you look, my dear," Lady Agatha said, with her ready smile. "Do come and sit between Ferdy and me, and tell me how things go next door. Is Lady Harriet any calmer now?"

Gratefully, Fanny sat beside her, but there was no avoiding Mr Ralph during dinner, where he monopolised her attention so greatly that she was forced to neglect Mr Willerton-Forbes, who sat on her other side.

There was one pleasant moment as they gathered in the hall to await the carriage. For once Mr Ralph's attention was distracted, and she found Ferdy standing beside her.

"Miss Winterton, may I take the liberty of soliciting your hand for the second two dances? If you are not engaged."

"Oh no, I am not, and I should like that very much!" she cried. "You dance so well, Mr Makenham, so when I am your partner, I always feel that *I* am dancing well, too."

She had the pleasure of seeing his face light up at the compliment, but it drew Mr Ralph to her side again, and Ferdy bowed slightly and moved away.

The carriage only accommodated four, and there was a brief discussion as to which of the gentlemen should accompany the ladies.

"Edgar dislikes the walk, so he at least must ride," Ferdy said.

"And you should take the remaining seat, Ferdy," Lady Agatha said. "It is your carriage, after all, and it is no distance for the others to walk."

"I think I should ride with Miss Winterton since she is engaged to me for the first two," Mr Ralph said. "I should not like her to miss a moment of the dancing waiting for me to arrive."

"There is still time for me to order my own carriage as well," Lady Agatha said. "Then we can all ride."

"No need," Ferdy said, with a tight smile. "I am quite content to walk. It is a fine, clear night, perfect for a stroll, and it is no distance to York Road. Ralph may take my place if he likes."

So it was arranged, and in the event there was such a press of carriages arriving at the Malpas's house that the walkers were there before the carriage. The first sight to meet Fanny's eyes as the carriage door was thrown open was Ferdy's smiling face.

"Oh, you are a fast walker, Mr Makenham," she said, unable to repress a smile of her own. It was odd how she felt so comfortable with Ferdy, and yet with Mr Ralph she was quite unsettled. Nor was it the gentle flutterings she had felt with Mr Hawes in the early days, before she had seen his true nature. It was almost as if she were afraid of Mr Ralph. Yet how could that be? Goodness, her nerves must be overset, to make her so fanciful.

The Malpas's house was one of the large, new buildings on the road to York, home to the wealthy merchants and mill owners and shopkeepers, and not far from the warehouses and manufactories that brought them their wealth. The whole of the rear of the house had been extended to create the huge ballroom, larger even than the assembly room at Brinchester. The room dazzled with crystal and gold and a multitude of chandeliers, with larger-than-life replicas of famous Roman statues arranged to create small seating alcoves. Along the outside wall, four rounded ante-chambers protruded into the garden, partially screened from the ballroom by elaborate draperies.

As their party was announced the musicians were just warming up, an orchestra brought all the way from London for the occasion. Mr Malpas had spared no expense, for there was even to be a display of fireworks later in the evening, the first such event ever to be held in Sagborough.

Mr Ralph was an excellent dancer, and Fanny would have greatly enjoyed her half hour with him, had he not spent much of the time cajoling her to save the supper dance for him. She had hoped to keep that for Ferdy, as was her habit, but Mr Ralph would not take no for an answer and in the end she had to give way.

After that there was the pleasure of two dances with Ferdy. Mr Ralph was accomplished in the art, but there was a gracefulness about Ferdy that could not be matched. Fanny liked to watch him dance at least as much as she liked having him as a partner. Then she danced with Lord Gilbert, another graceful dancer and so handsome. His bright blue eyes fringed by such long lashes were arresting. He was surprisingly good company for a man only that day accused of murder. No one would have guessed it from his joking good humour.

Then she danced with Captain Edgerton and then Mr Brant, who was not terribly good and sometimes sent Fanny wrong, too. She did not mind, for his attire was so garish that no one looked at Fanny at all. After that, Mr Ralph claimed her for the supper dance.

When the dance ended, it was time for the display of fireworks, which were to be exploded in the Malpas's extensive gardens. All the guests streamed to the windows to watch from behind the safety of the glass. Mr Ralph tucked Fanny's hand onto his arm and drew her into one of the round ante-chambers, elbowing his way to the front of the crowd.

"Here we are," he said, depositing her in front of one of the deep windows. "You will have an excellent view of proceedings from here."

Fanny had never seen anything like it. She had heard of fireworks, of course, and read descriptions in books and newspapers, and once or twice had seen an illustration of a display, but all of them were a faded imitation of the reality. So much brilliant light, so many wondrous shapes, so much noise, even through the glass! The whole sky was lit up, and the smoke cast a thick haze over the garden. She watched, mesmerised, barely aware of Mr Ralph still holding her arm. Once or twice she glanced at him, to see his deep blue eyes fixed on her.

"Why are you not watching the fireworks, sir? You are missing a spectacular display."

But he only smiled.

The performance finished all too soon, and the crowd began to disperse to the dining room for supper. Fanny turned to follow them, but Mr Ralph held her back.

"Let us see how soon the smoke clears," he said. "I have a mind to see the stars with you by my side, dear Fanny."

Such an intimate use of her name made her uncomfortable. She tried to remove her hand from his arm, but he had placed his other hand over hers and she found she could not disengage herself. Fanny was not one to make a fuss, but she could not allow him to detain her alone in the ante-chamber, half-hidden from the ballroom by wide draperies across the entrance. Such a thing was most improper, unless they were betrothed and that they most certainly were not. Nor did she ever intend to be. It was absolutely necessary to protest.

"Sir, pray release me. Everyone is leaving and we should follow them. This place is too secluded."

"No, it is perfect," he said. "*You* are perfect, Fanny."

"I beg you not to talk such nonsense. I am leaving now."

She pulled away, determined this time to free herself, but to her astonishment, he caught her around the waist and pulled her towards him.

"No, sir, no! Let me go!"

"Ah, Fanny, relax, sweetheart. I mean you no harm."

With a violent jerk, she detached herself from him and made at once to leave the ante-chamber, which was now quite empty. She had taken no more than two steps before he caught her again, and pulled her into his arms with a roughness that made her catch her breath. Before she could say a single word, he had bent his head and clamped his lips onto hers.

Fanny had been kissed before, and unwillingly, but there was something brutal about this kiss that terrified her. She struggled and pushed and even kicked out, although what her slippered feet could do against a man of Ralph Makenham's strength she knew not. But eventually she must have hit something that hurt, for he made an 'Oof' sound, and slackened his grip. At once she spun out of his grasp, and then, her anger too great to be contained, she slapped him as hard as her gloved hand could manage.

"Miss Winterton? Do you need assistance?"

Ferdy was there! Of all the miracles, that was the one she might have hoped for.

"Oh, Mr Makenham!" She tore across the ante-chamber, hurled herself into his arms and burst into tears. One arm, sturdy and reassuring, came round her shoulders. The other rummaged in a pocket for a handkerchief.

His voice was very calm. "Everything is perfectly all right now, Miss Winterton. Edgar, go and find Aunt Agatha, and order the carriage. I believe Miss Winterton would like to go home."

~~~~~

The business of getting Fanny out of the house and safely home without attracting comment occupied Ferdy's thoughts at first. The practical matter of stemming the tears, and encouraging her to appear her usual untroubled self, and then getting cloaks and waiting for the carriage to be brought round took some time, and then there was the journey home — Fanny, Aunt Agatha, Edgar and Ferdy himself. He watched Fanny go into number Twenty-Six first, then he saw Aunt Agatha away up the stairs to bed. Then he gave his orders and settled down in the book room with Edgar to await Ralph's return.

They were in jovial mood, the three of them. Ralph, Willerton-Forbes and Edgerton, all slightly the worse for drink but still at the convivial stage, not morose or belligerent. The footman opened the door to them, they came, laughing, into the hall, then silence fell. Ferdy had left the book room door open, and Ralph's face appeared, bewildered but not yet angry. The other two peered over his shoulders.

"What the Devil is going on, Ferdy? Why are my boxes in the hall?"

"Come in, Ralph," Ferdy said evenly. "Mr Willerton-Forbes, Captain Edgerton, you will forgive me if I do not include you in this invitation, but we have family business to discuss. Kindly shut the door behind you, gentlemen."

They nodded, bowed, made their farewells and withdrew. The door closed behind them with a soft click.

"Ferdy, what the deuce are you about? You are not going to get all Gothic, are you? Just because I kissed her."

Ferdy was out of his chair in a moment, anger welling up inside him like a spring. Ruthlessly he suppressed it, and attempted to speak calmly. "Your boxes are in the hall because you are leaving this house at once."

Ralph laughed. "Good God, Ferdy, where am I supposed to go at three in the morning?"

"I do not care. You will leave this house tonight, and you will meet me at a time and place of your choosing."

Ralph groaned and rolled his eyes. "Positively medieval, cousin!"

"Edgar will act for me," Ferdy went on. "Have your second contact him, and I tell you now, I will only agree to pistols. I have never been a swordsman, but I am tolerably comfortable with pistols. At least I have practised a little at Manton's."

"This is ridiculous, Ferdy," Ralph said, and there was still an unconcerned air about him, as if he refused to take Ferdy's challenge seriously. "She is not yours, you know. You have no right to—"

Ferdy stepped nearer to his cousin, and perhaps Ralph began to recognise his implacability, for he took a step backwards.

"She has no father or brother, no male relatives at all," Ferdy said, his quiet tone belying the rage inside him. "It therefore falls to her friends to defend her honour when *blackguards* try to take advantage of her."

"Oh, blackguard, is it? Really, Ferdy, you had better be careful with your language or I might just take you up on this foolishness."

"I am perfectly serious, Ralph. Accept my challenge or be branded a coward."

"Nonsense! You will be glad tomorrow that I refused to be drawn in."

Another step forward. "You *will* meet me, Ralph."

"Calm down, man. I am your cousin, remember."

"Are you going to meet me or not?"

"I am not."

Ferdy took another quick step nearer and lashed out as hard as he could, hitting Ralph's cheek with the back of his hand so hard that his head snapped to one side.

"Meet me!"

"Damn you, I will! Gil Marford will act for me, I daresay. Good God, Ferdy, that girl has turned you into a drooling imbecile. All right, all right! I am going. I will send for my things in the morning, and the next time we meet — you die, cousin."

"Not if Ferdy kills you first," Edgar said, holding the door open for him.

Without another word, head high, Ralph strolled out.

Ferdy collapsed into a chair, shaking from head to foot. "God help me, whatever have I done?"

32: Rumour And Truth

The next day seemed so normal. Ferdy rose at his usual time, dressed with his usual care, wrote three letters and ordered flowers to be sent to Mrs and Miss Malpas, all before breakfast. Then he ate with Edgar, Willerton-Forbes and Edgerton, just as usual. They talked about the ball the previous night, the weather and the news from France. No one commented on Ralph's absence or the boxes still sitting in the hall, or the wagon from the King's Head which arrived to remove them while they were eating.

Not long afterwards, Gil Marford arrived, and he and Edgar were closeted in the book room for an hour. Then they asked to speak to Ferdy.

"Are you quite sure about this, Ferdy?" Gil said. "As Ralph's second, I feel obliged to point out that he is a crack shot, and it is rumoured that he has already survived a couple of duels. He will have a very steady hand."

"I am determined on this," Ferdy said quietly. "I know your role is to persuade me to back down but I will not. Has he offered to apologise or anything of the sort?"

Gil shook his head. "Do you have an understanding with the lady? Because that would make a difference if—"

"No understanding. In fact, when I offered for her she turned me down, but that does not mean I can stand aside and see her good name dragged through mud."

Gil looked at him thoughtfully. "It was just a kiss. It seems... an excessive response for a kiss, even if the lady was reluctant."

"*Reluctant?* She was fighting to get free of him, Gil, and when she finally got out of his grasp she slapped him. He deliberately held her there until everyone had left and then took advantage of her. It is insupportable to treat a gently-born lady in such a manner."

"Hmm. True, but... Ferdy, I must be completely honest with you, and I speak now as your friend, not Ralph's second. You are the heir to the earldom and it is true that you have a younger brother, but after that the next heir is Ralph. He is... an opportunist, and also very calculating. There is a hard edge to him that makes me fear for you if you proceed with this duel."

"That is a chance I must take," Ferdy said gently. "I cannot allow him to dishonour Miss Winterton. She does not wish to marry me, but I would not see her forced to marry Ralph simply because he tarnished her reputation. Last night I was watching over her, but I cannot always be there and she is too diffident to deal robustly with encroaching suitors."

"And that is what I cannot understand about this whole business," Edgar said. "Why should Ralph take an interest in Fanny Winterton, who has not a penny piece to her name? He was dangling after Marianne Trivers, and she was much more in his style, but now he will not leave Miss Winterton alone. What can he mean by it?"

"Is he jealous of you, Ferdy?" Gil said.

"Jealous of me? Why ever should he be? He is the one with all the good looks and the charm and a way with the ladies."

"But you have the title and the fortune coming to you," Gil said. "So have a care, Ferdy. However, if you are set on this course, then be at Maggot's Field at six o'clock tomorrow morning. If at any time you change your mind, send Edgar to me with a note. There is no shame in withdrawing."

"You know that to be untrue," Ferdy said. "I have made the challenge and I cannot honourably withdraw unless Ralph apologises."

"That he will not do," Gil said ruefully.

"Then I will meet him tomorrow, and may God have mercy on us both."

~~~~~

Ferdy's mood varied from gloom to despair and back again. Of his own death, he had no fear. His faith was strong, and he had done his best to live a virtuous life, so he felt he could meet his Maker with equanimity whenever he should be called upon to do so. Nor was he concerned that he might kill Ralph and be forced to flee for the continent, for he intended to delope. His object was not to kill his cousin, but to bring him to account for dishonouring his beloved Fanny.

He was, however, terrified of being injured, and then dying slowly and painfully from some putrid infection. He was also terrified of disgracing himself by losing his courage at the crucial moment. Both these concerns preyed upon his mind so greatly that he was forced to remember Fanny's distressed face and tears to bolster his resolution. Not that he wavered in his determination to face his cousin, but he wished with all his heart for greater bravery in the enterprise.

His nerves kept him awake for most of the night with a queer, sick feeling in his stomach. He was already up when Wrackham and Wright arrived at four in the morning to dress him, making no comment on the unusual hour as they lit candles and laid out his clothes in preparation.

"Wet morning, sir," was all Wrackham said. "Steady rain."

"It might ease off," Ferdy said.

"Looks very settled to me," Wrackham said.

Rain. That was all he needed.

By half past five, he was ready. Edgar, wide-eyed and solemn-faced, awaited him in the hall, carrying the box containing Ferdy's expensive pair of duelling pistols, wrapped in waxed cloth. Duelling pistols. Ferdy had bought them for their elegant beauty, never expecting to use them, and he had no wish to use them now. If only he could back out! But of course he could not. Honour forbade it, and he had been right to call Ralph out, of that he had no doubt. Honour was both the greatest attribute of a gentleman, and also its greatest curse. How pleasant it must be to be a footman or a carpenter or some such, and not be bound by it, although he supposed even footmen and carpenters must have some sense of fair play to bind them just as much. No man could behave just as he wished, or society would crumble into anarchy. But just at that moment, Ferdy wished his own sense of honour were not quite so acute.

He and Edgar made their way to the coach house at the back of the house so as not to disturb the sleeping residents of Harlington Terrace by rattling a carriage over the cobbles in the street. The horses were put to, they got into the carriage and, after collecting a surgeon recommended by Gil, they began the short drive to Maggot's Field. It was apparently a place favoured for secret assignations, being close enough to the town for convenience in reaching it, but not so close that a gun shot would be noticed. The rain fell steadily. In his imaginings of the occasion, Ferdy had never considered the weather, but now it seemed very much of a piece with his low spirits. Perhaps the dampness would inhibit the powder, and the whole escapade would be a waste of time. He spent the whole of the short journey trying to decide whether he would be glad of such an outcome or not.

They stopped the carriage on the nearest road, but Maggot's Field was three fields away.

"Can we stay in the carriage until the others arrive?" Edgar said plaintively, looking at the downpour.

"They may come from the other direction, or even walk here along the canal towpath," Ferdy said. "If we are not in the agreed place, we will be held to have defaulted."

"I know," Edgar said sadly. "It is so *wet* out there."

"Sorry, cousin," Ferdy said with a rueful little smile. "I hope you will not catch a chill."

Edgar took a deep breath. "If I do, then so be it, for it is in the cause of a lady's honour," he said stoutly.

"You are a good friend to me, Edgar," Ferdy said. "I shall not forget it. Well, gentlemen, shall we go?"

They climbed the gate into the first field, trudged across it, climbed again, trudged again, climbed a third time. There they stood, under the shelter provided by a few meagre trees, and waited.

It seemed a long wait.

Edgar examined his pocket watch, leaning over it in an attempt to keep it dry. "It is ten past the hour. They are late."

They waited. Ferdy's nerves, already frayed, began to unravel altogether. "How much longer?" he muttered, pacing up and down. Why was it so cold? Surely it should not be so cold in September.

"It is gone seven," Edgar said at last. "He has defaulted. We can go home now."

Ferdy's spirits soared. It was over!

"Wait," the surgeon said. "Someone is coming."

For an instant Ferdy's stomach lurched and he thought he would be sick. He took a deep breath, and Edgar's worried face and gentle hand on his arm steadied his nerves.

A rider on a black horse was crossing the fields from the canal direction, jumping gates with a recklessness that Ferdy both admired and deplored simultaneously. But it was not Ralph, unless he had borrowed both horse and coat. Ferdy took another breath, this one of relief.

The horse slithered to a halt, and Gil Marford slid from its back.

"He has gone," he cried, his voice high with alarm. "He did not come in last night and has not returned this morning. I have been everywhere I can think of, looking for him, but he is nowhere to be found."

"I cannot believe he would run away," Ferdy said, bewildered. "It is impossible."

"Wherever he has gone, he is not here," Edgar said. "This affair is over, and we can all go home and dry off."

~~~~~

Fanny had spent the day after the ball quietly. She had gone to the shop, as usual, but clearly the ladies of Sagborough were still recovering after their exertions in the ballroom, for there were few customers. Then she had spent the rest of the day at her stitchery, while Mrs Hay slept. Lady Harriet had come in just once.

"Are you all right, Fanny? I heard that there was an incident at the Malpas's ball."

"It was nothing, Lady Harriet. I was... a little upset at the time, but Lady Agatha very kindly brought me home, and I am quite recovered."

Lady Harriet looked at her for a long time, then said, "Hmpf. You would not complain if your hair was on fire, I suppose."

Fanny could only stare at her in bewilderment. "My hair?"

"Oh, never mind," Lady Harriet said, laughing suddenly. "You must not take me so literally." And she had gone away, still laughing, and Fanny could not see the joke at all.

Dinner and an uneventful evening saw her composure almost recovered, but she wondered if she would ever be able to think about Mr Ralph again without feelings of revulsion welling up. He had seemed so pleasant and amiable on the surface, but beneath the charm lay a man who took what he wanted, regardless of her wishes. Had she not made it perfectly plain that she did not want to be alone with him, and certainly not be kissed by him? No gentleman would disregard her wishes in such matters, but he had done just as he pleased. And if Ferdy had not come in at that moment... she could not imagine what might have happened. It did not bear thinking of.

A full night's sleep saw her quite restored. Her composure would be tested when she first met Mr Ralph again, but for now she felt well. It was raining steadily — a good day for writing letters before breakfast, she thought, since she could not go out to do any shopping. She finished a letter to Annabelle, and began one to Lucy, and then went down a little late for breakfast. Lady Harriet and Miss Hay were nowhere to be seen, Mrs Hay never rose before noon, and Dr Hay ate quickly and then left for the hospital, so Fanny was left alone to finish her meal slowly, as she preferred. She was lingering over her second cup of chocolate when she heard voices from the hall, a half whisper but still loud enough to catch many words. She would not normally have listened to the servants' gossip, but the urgency of the tone was unusual. And then she heard Ferdy's name mentioned. She rose from her chair and crept towards the slightly-open door.

"...Mr Ferdinand called him out, and... a duel at Maggot's Field... Mr Ralph... pistols... no, I tell you, it is perfectly serious. To the *death*."

She pulled the door open. "Mr Ferdinand Makenham?" she said, her voice quavering. "And Mr Ralph? A duel?"

Mrs Bell, the housekeeper, sprang to attention, and Patty, the housemaid, dropped into a deep curtsy.

"Now then, Miss, you shouldn't know about—"

"Tell me the truth. At once, if you please. Is he to fight a duel?"

"It's just a rumour, Miss. There may be nothing in it."

Fanny's world crumbled to dust around her. She was dizzy, her ears roaring as if she were about to faint. Ferdy fighting a duel? With pistols? To the death? Ferdy *dead?*

And in that instant, as abruptly as if she had been shot through the heart, she understood herself. Life without Ferdy was no life at all. How could she have been so unutterably stupid as not to realise it? Ferdy was as necessary to her as the air she breathed and the water she drank and the food she ate. Ferdy was *everything* to her, he was her friend, her wise counsellor, her unquestioning supporter, her faithful companion, the love of her life. She had never loved any man before, but now she loved Ferdy with every ounce of her being, and would love him for ever.

Without a word, she turned and fled from the house.

~~~~~

Ferdy had changed out of his rain-sodden clothes, thrown on a clean shirt and dressing robe and was sitting down with Edgar to a late, and most welcome, breakfast when there was a hammering on the front door, then a violent ringing of the bell, followed by more hammering. Voices from the hall suggested that the door had been opened, and then there were impatient steps running towards the breakfast room.

Ferdy put down his coffee cup and rose, expecting Ralph to burst into the room, but when the door was flung open, it was not Ralph but the much more agreeable sight of Miss Winterton, although without bonnet, gloves or coat, her gown spotted with raindrops, her face wreathed in the greatest agitation.

"Tell me it is not true!" she cried. "It cannot be true, I am sure. You would not... Surely... You are not, are you?"

Ferdy could not have been more astonished, but the training of many years took over and he bowed as if they had met in the most commonplace way, then waved the interested footman away.

"Miss Winterton?" His voice sounded high to his ears. What could have distressed her so? And oh, if only he could soothe her by sweeping her into his arms and kissing away all her fears, whatever they may be.

"You are not, are you? Going to fight a duel?"

Oh, that. Ferdy smiled, attempting to convey amused tolerance, but not altogether sure he succeeded. "Now who told you a thing like that?"

"The servants. Is it not true? Oh, I can see from Mr Brant's face that it is, it is! Oh but you must not, truly you must not!" She stretched out one hand towards him imploringly.

"Miss Winterton," Ferdy said, with greater command of his voice. "Even if it were true, and I do not say that it is, mind you, but even if it were so, it is a matter between gentlemen. A lady is not supposed to know about such things, ever."

"But I *do* know, so *pray* do not fob me off and treat me like a child. I understand that it is a question of honour, and if it must be so, then it must, for you cannot honourably withdraw, but please, *please* do not pretend, because you might be injured, or...or even..." She gulped, gazing up at him with tear-filled eyes. "You might be *killed* and I would never see you again and how could I bear it if you were *not there?*"

Edgar edged out of the room and closed the door quietly behind him.

Ferdy's heart burst with joy. *'How could I bear it if you were not there?'*

He took a deep breath. To his surprise his voice was almost steady. "You need not be under the slightest degree of apprehension for my welfare, Miss Winterton. The... er, meeting was to have taken place this morning, but... er, the other party did not make an appearance."

"And will you be obliged to... reschedule?"

"No. That is the end of the matter."

"Oh." She collapsed backwards onto Edgar's abandoned chair, as if her legs had given way, and burst into tears. Between sobs, she murmured repeatedly, "Oh, thank goodness!" and then, "So sorry, so very sorry!" in equal proportions.

Kneeling at her feet, Ferdy gently possessed himself of her hands. So warm, so soft... he stroked them lightly, hardly able to believe that all her agitation was for him. "Not the slightest need to apologise, Miss Winterton. I am deeply gratified that my foolish person can evince such concern." Even as he spoke the words calmly, his heart was singing. *'How could I bear it if you were not there? How could I bear it?'* They were, he thought, the most glorious words he had ever heard. "I beg your pardon, but I have no handkerchief upon me to offer you."

She laughed then, and cried at the same time, but after a while, as her sobs lessened, her face changed, and became serious.

"May I ask... was it about me? Because he kissed me?"

"He took advantage of your innocence, Miss Winterton, and I could not allow that. You have no father or brother to protect you, so—"

"Oh, yes, I quite see how it was."

"It was presumptuous of me, but—"

"Oh no! Not at all." She removed one hand from his clasp to wipe her tear-streaked face on one sleeve, and then, to his inexpressible delight, placed her hand back in his. "I am very much obliged to you, but... but I should not like you to be killed over such a thing. It is not the first time that a man has kissed me against my wishes, it has happened *several* times, for some reason, and so I do not regard it as a matter necessitating such a drastic response. Even so, I am *very* much obliged to you. It was such a chivalrous and... and *romantic* thing to do." She heaved a satisfied sigh at this thought.

"Was it? I confess, I did not consider it in that light. I was very angry that he had abused you so. If you had wanted him to kiss you—"

"Oh but I did not, not in the least, and an unwanted kiss is quite an unpleasant thing. If I had wanted to be kissed... but I do think he should have asked me first. That is the correct procedure, is it not?"

"I believe it is," he answered gravely.

"Sometimes I wonder what a *wanted* kiss would be like."

She fell silent, looking at him thoughtfully, and then, as if a decision had been reached, she took a deep breath. Or perhaps she suddenly realised their extraordinary situation. They were quite alone, neither of them suitably attired for a morning visit, and so close their faces were almost touching.

"Oh, Mr Makenham, I do not think this is quite proper, is it? You are not yet dressed, and I quite forgot to put my gloves on. Whatever shall we do about it?" Her face was such a picture of innocence, he half wondered if she even understood what she was saying, until he realised there was a decided twinkle in her eyes.

"Well," he said, trying to speak prosaically, but his heart was overflowing so much that a smile would keep breaking out, "there are two ways we might deal with the awkwardness which naturally accompanies a situation such as this. We could spring apart, clearing our throats loudly, and pretend this has never happened. Or..."

"Or?" she said, smiling at him with such sweetness that he was almost undone.

He took a deep breath. "Or... or I could kiss you," he said hopefully.

"I see." Her voice was solemn but she was trying not to smile. "What is your opinion on the matter?"

"My personal preference," he said, his voice not quite steady, "would be to kiss you. But... but your wishes are paramount, Miss Winterton."

"I am willing to be guided by you, Mr Makenham."

He gave a little laugh, and said, "Then I think I should kiss you, Miss Winterton."

"I do think that would be for the best," she said.

Somehow, while they talked, the gap between them had narrowed, so that Ferdy had only to move forward the smallest amount. Their lips touched so softly that he would almost not have been aware of it, if not for the thrill that coursed through his veins at the precise moment. Perhaps she felt it, too, for she pulled back momentarily, with an "Oh!" of surprise. Then, closing her eyes, she leaned forward and pressed her lips against his more firmly.

Ferdy had never experienced anything like it. He had thought himself equal to anything, undaunted by any social occasion, but nothing in his twenty-five years of gentlemanly training had prepared him for the sweet kiss of the woman he loved. When, eventually, they drew apart, his heart was pounding so hard it was a wonder the whole town could not hear it.

She gave him her most enchanting smile. "Does that mean we are now betrothed?"

"Oh." His voice sounded strange in his ears. "I... am not sure."

"Not sure, Mr Makenham? But you are always so certain of the proper protocol."

That made him laugh. She was so adorable! How could he focus when his darling Fanny was so close, her hands still resting in his. He took a deep breath, and tried very hard to concentrate. "Such has been my dearest wish since the first moment we met, as you must be aware, Miss Winterton. But, as always, your wishes are paramount."

"Are they? Would you do whatever I wished?"

"Of course," he said. "Although, if you were to ask me to jump off the roof, I might enquire if you were absolutely certain that such was your wish."

She laughed merrily. "I shall not do so, however, for you might be injured or even killed, and that was very much how we started this conversation, was it not?"

He laughed too, raising both her hands to his lips to be kissed, and pressed against his cheek, and then kissed again. "Fanny — dearest Fanny — I think—"

But the thought was destined to remain unexpressed, for the door burst open for the second time that morning, and Lady Harriet strode in, Edgar twisting his hands nervously in her wake.

"Whatever is going on? Ferdy, good gracious, you are not even dressed!"

Ferdy and Fanny jumped to their feet and sprang apart.

Fanny said quickly, "I believe… I am not quite sure, but I think we are betrothed, Lady Harriet."

"Well, I should hope so… what do you mean, you *think* you are betrothed?"

"The matter is not quite settled," Ferdy said. "We were just debating the issue when you arrived."

"Well, you will not debate it any further, not in such a state of undress."

"Of course, Lady Harriet. Perhaps I might be permitted to call upon Miss Winterton later today? Fully dressed, naturally."

"Really, Ferdy!" she said, but there was a twinkle in her eye. "Three o'clock, then. Come along, Fanny."

"Yes, Lady Harriet. Goodbye, Mr Makenham." She had just reached the door, when she turned with her most innocent expression. "Oh dear! I forgot to clear my throat when we sprang apart."

And then, with a low chuckle, she was gone, leaving Ferdy smiling. His lips still tingled from her kiss, and softly he raised his hands to touch them, as if to reassure himself that he was not dreaming, that his Fanny really was *his* Fanny at long last.

33: *Abbeymount*

Fanny changed into her newest, never before worn, morning dress and waited demurely for three o'clock. At ten minutes to the hour, Lady Harriet appeared in the morning room.

"I would like to talk to Ferdy for a few moments when he arrives," she said. "There is an odd rumour flying about."

"You mean about the duel?" Fanny said.

"Good heavens, do you know about that? Oh but of course, that was why— Nevertheless, I should like to hear it from Ferdy. Then he may have his interview with you, but I shall be in the drawing room next door if you should wish to discuss any matter with me. Although," she chuckled and added in a lower tone, half to herself, "it seems that you have everything in hand."

Precisely on the hour, the doorbell rang and Lady Harriet disappeared. Fanny moved from one sofa to another, and then, thinking better of it, moved back again so that she would have the earliest possible view of Ferdy as he entered the room. *Her* Ferdy, she thought, with delight. Or was he? This brought a frisson of alarm. Perhaps he had thought better of it? She had taken him unawares, bursting in on him before he was even dressed, so perhaps, in his punctilious way, he now felt obliged to offer for her because she had compromised herself. She was not quite sure what compromising a lady entailed, but she was fairly certain that kissing a gentleman wearing only a dressing robe would be regarded as such.

Low voices on the stairs, then the door of the drawing room shut with a snap and silence fell. The minutes ticked by. Whatever was taking so long? Discussing the duel could not absorb them for such an age, surely. Was Lady Harriet telling Ferdy about all Fanny's faults? Would he change his mind and go away again? She could not bear to lose him now!

She jumped up, and paced anxiously about the room. Then, because she could suffer the uncertainty no longer, she turned away from the door and pressed one ear to the wall between the rooms. Thus it happened that she did not, after all, have the earliest possible view of Ferdy when he entered the room.

Spinning round excitedly, she beheld him in all his glory, his hessians polished to a high sheen, his pantaloons clinging to his thighs, his neckcloth immaculate and was that a new coat?

"Oh Ferdy, you look splendid!" she cried impulsively, holding out her hands to him.

"Not as splendid as you, Fanny," he said, and the smile on his face drove away all her tenuous fears. He came straight to her and somehow, without any conscious thought, she was in his arms, his lips on hers and everything in the world was wonderful.

When at length they moved a little apart, she said shyly, "So *now* we must be betrothed?"

"Well, I have been considering the question carefully," he said, still holding her tightly, "and it is my opinion that the thing ought to be done decently, with me making my little speech, you know. Make you an offer in form. Perhaps I ought to kneel at your feet — that would be the correct thing to do, would it not?"

"But Ferdy, you have already made me an offer in form, and as I recall, you said everything that was proper, and all very eloquently expressed."

"Oh. Did you like it? I must say, I had practised quite a bit beforehand."

"It was charmingly done," she said. "You said everything that needed to be said, I believe. You paid me some very pretty compliments — you said I looked as beautiful as a flower turning its face to the sun, and I am sure I never had anything half so delightful said about me before. Then you told me all about how you will be an earl one day, which neither of us much cares about but it is the sort of thing which ought to be said on such occasions. And how you have a great deal of money to live upon, and a house of your own, which is a great comfort, naturally. And then, you know, you told me that your life would be empty without me in it, which is a perfectly poetic thing to say, and so romantic, and really, Ferdy, I do not think your previous offer could possibly be improved upon. It was quite perfect."

"Not *quite* perfect," he said, kissing her forehead and then her cheeks and then her lips again, so that for a while not another word was spoken. But then he sighed. "However charming a speech it was, it could not have been perfect, for you turned me down."

"Oh. So I did. How foolish I was. So it was my part in the conversation which was deficient. May I try again?"

"Please do, Miss Winterton."

"Now you have gone back to calling me Miss Winterton again."

"One feels one ought to be formal on such occasions."

"Oh. You are quite right, Mr Makenham. I stand corrected. But I believe the first part of my original response may stand — about thanking you for the very great honour and so forth, may it not?"

"I believe it may," he said gravely. "It was very felicitously expressed."

"Thank you. Then all that remains is for me to tell you that it would give me very great pleasure to accept your most obliging offer, and I should be very happy — very, *very* happy — to be your wife."

"Oh, Fanny!" he whispered, pulling her tightly against him.

"*Now* we are betrothed, are not we?"

He laughed, and she was so pressed against his chest that she felt him shaking. "Indeed we are, dearest Fanny."

"So what should we do next?"

He paused, and then said in surprised tones, "Do you know, I have not the least idea. I have never been betrothed before. What is your opinion?"

"I believe we should kiss again," she said demurely.

"That sounds like a sensible plan."

So they did, and, having nothing further to say to each other, they continued for quite some time.

This idyllic scene was disrupted by the door knocker below, and then raised voices, getting louder, as if someone were coming up the stairs. Reluctantly they separated, although Ferdy kept hold of her hand. The door opened, and Mr Willerton-Forbes rushed in, followed by Lady Harriet.

"Thank goodness!" Mr Willerton-Forbes cried, which seemed so odd that Fanny could make nothing of it. "Miss Winterton, I am very relieved to see you safe and well."

"As you see, I am perfectly well," Fanny said, puzzled. "Why should I not be?"

"I have reason to believe that your life is in grave danger, and until Ralph Makenham is found, I shall not be easy."

"Ralph knows something of this?" Ferdy said sharply.

"Is he in danger too?" Fanny said.

"Makenham, have you somewhere safe you can take Miss Winterton, where she will be surrounded by people day and night?"

"I can take her to Abbeymount, which is full to the rafters with my relations at the moment."

"Perfect! And — forgive me if I am presumptuous but am I to wish you joy?"

"You may do so," Ferdy said, with a small bow. "Miss Winterton has done me the very great honour of—"

"Excellent, because no one will think it odd if you whisk your betrothed off to meet your family. But you must go at once. There is no time to be lost."

"At once?" Ferdy said. "Today?"

"As soon as the horses can be put to. Any delay could be fatal. I cannot explain it to you now, but believe me, I am very serious about this. I will come and tell you all as soon as I may."

Fanny looked at Ferdy. She could see the indecision on his face, wondering that a relative stranger should make such an outlandish claim and drive them from their homes at a moment's notice. But then he looked down at her and smiled.

"I would have taken you to Abbeymount soon anyway. It might as well be today. Let us go next door and talk to Aunt Agatha. She will know how it may best be contrived."

"Yes, do take Lady Agatha," Mr Willerton-Forbes said, "and someone should stay with Miss Winterton at all times. She must not be left alone."

"You are frightening me, Mr Willerton-Forbes," Fanny said. "Who would want to kill me? I am nobody!"

"I will explain it all to you when I can. Besides, I may be wrong. God knows, I hope I am, but go now, quickly! Get out of Sagborough as soon as you may."

They were in Ferdy's carriage and on the road within the hour, Fanny, Ferdy, Mr Brant and Lady Agatha huddled in silence inside, with Captain Edgerton, his pockets full of pistols, sitting beside the coachman. Their boxes, valets and maid were to follow in Lady Agatha's coach. And none of them were easy until they turned in past the western lodge at Abbeymount.

~~~~~

Abbeymount was exactly as Fanny had imagined it. The house was vast, with odd wings everywhere, and if she had not had Ferdy or Lady Agatha or one of the footmen to guide her about, she would have been hopelessly lost. Ferdy's uncounted relations accepted her into the family with cries of joy, the aunts weeping over her and clasping her to their ample bosoms, and the uncles squeezing her hand between both of theirs, telling her she was a pretty little puss and assuring Ferdy that he was a very lucky fellow. Lords Belwarren and Craston and their ladies beamed delightedly, and told Ferdy that they knew just how it would be as soon as he moved to Sagborough. And there was Ferdy himself, a smile permanently on his face, and his eyes shining as he looked at her.

Yet everywhere she went, Captain Edgerton was not far away, his face grim. Two footmen sat outside her door all night and her room had bars across the windows. No one talked about Mr Ralph, and if one of the aunts wondered aloud where he might be, one of the others would shush her. Sometimes Fanny came across several of the gentlemen huddled together, talking in low, serious voices, and she heard Ralph's name mentioned, but they broke apart when they saw her and became jovial again. She knew they were worried about Ralph, wondering what had happened to him, just as she was. And she wondered, too, why anyone would want to harm her, and whether Ralph was in danger too, and whether he had fled because of the duel or there was some other matter altogether that had caused him to disappear. It was very disturbing.

But then Mr Willerton-Forbes arrived and was whisked away to talk to the earl, the viscount and Ferdy in private. A little while later, Ferdy came to find her.

"Fanny, Mr Willerton-Forbes would like to talk to us of his fears for you. He wishes us to understand what has happened — or rather, what he thinks has happened, and he would like you to be there, if you can bear it. It concerns Ralph."

"Oh, has he been found? Is he all right?"

Ferdy shook his head. "No one knows where he is, or what his intentions are, but I believe we need to be prepared for any eventuality. Will you come and hear what Willerton-Forbes has to say? It may upset you."

"Oh yes, I should like to know everything, even if it is distressing to hear. I can be brave if you are with me, Ferdy."

He smiled at her, and her heart somersaulted alarmingly. Sometimes it frightened her to realise how much she loved him — how much she *needed* him. She had always liked to have her sisters around her, but she could manage without them if she had to, as she had proved at Sagborough. But Ferdy — she felt as if she would fall to pieces if ever he were lost to her. Her beloved Ferdy.

She followed him to some previously unsuspected corner of Abbeymount. There was so much of it! Would she ever get used to its maze of corridors and vast number of rooms? This was a dark-panelled room with a faint hint of cigar smoke — a very masculine room. Apart from Mr Willerton-Forbes and Captain Edgerton, Fanny and Ferdy, Edgar was there too, and Lords Belwarren and Craston. Lord Craston fussed about finding Fanny a chair and bringing it forward, and then providing brandy for her to drink if she felt at all faint.

"You are all consideration, Lord Craston, but I should think my smelling salts would do the trick a little better," she said, pulling the bottle from her reticule and placing it beside the brandy glass.

"No harm in having both to hand," Lord Craston said. "Now then, Willerton-Forbes, enlighten us."

"Thank you, my lord." He looked around at his assembled audience, as if assessing them. His eye fell on Fanny, and a small smile lightened his serious expression. "Let me first say how relieved I am to see you safe and well, Miss Winterton. Even though you have had Captain Edgerton guarding you, and Lord Belwarren has had his own people watching over you, I could not be sure... even now I am not sure that you are entirely safe. But the time for secrecy is over, I believe, so let me tell you at once where my greatest fear lies. It is Ralph Makenham who would harm you, I believe."

"Mr Ralph?" Fanny said, bewildered. "He has not always behaved towards me as he should, but he would not *hurt* me, would he?"

Ferdy tucked her hand around his arm and stroked it gently. "I think we must accept, Fanny dear, that Ralph was very wicked, for all his gentlemanly appearance."

"I am afraid that is all too true," Mr Willerton-Forbes said. "But let me begin at the beginning — with Martha Smith. She came to Yorkshire looking for her abuser, but it was *not* Mr Edgar Brant, and it was also not Mr Ferdinand Makenham. However, it seemed likely that it was someone who was at the Easter ball, someone whom she saw there and recognised, who startled her so much that she dropped her tray of drinks. Someone, then, who was on the platform at that time, and we have Miss Winterton to thank for a very complete list — Mr Brant, Mr Makenham, Lord Carrbridge and his brothers. Those were the names you gave to the constables, were they not, Miss Winterton?"

"Yes, although..." She glanced at Ferdy.

"Exactly," Mr Willerton-Forbes said. "You said *'Mr Makenham'*, and the constables knew of no other apart from Mr Ferdinand. Ralph Makenham had already left for London before Martha Smith's body was found, so he was never interviewed or considered. The most likely person at the time was Lord Gilbert Marford, a man who already had a certain reputation as a... as a ladies' man, shall we say. When Sally Turner and Jenny Melton were killed, he became even more likely, since he lived locally and, unlike his brothers, had been in Sagborough at the time of each murder. But there was no real evidence, and no one liked to accuse the brother of a marquess without very clear proof, so nothing came of it."

"Rank should have nothing to do with it," Lord Belwarren said tersely.

"No indeed, but it does make one think more carefully about hurling accusations around," Mr Willerton-Forbes said. "But then Captain Edgerton and I came along and were immediately intrigued. What could be more fascinating than an unresolved murder? Apart from *three* unresolved murders, of course. We were fortunate enough to uncover two facts that changed everything. The first of these was that there was a second Mr Makenham, Mr *Ralph* Makenham, who was himself a known ladies' man, who was in Sagborough for all three murders and who was also on the platform when Martha dropped her tray. Is that not so, Miss Winterton?"

"Yes, for it was Mr Ralph not Ferdy who sat beside me at the time. He grabbed my arm to stop me helping Martha. He was... quite rough."

"He was afraid, no doubt, that she would say something to you to reveal his secret, that he was the father of her illegitimate child. He was, in fact, the man she had sworn revenge upon, the man who bequeathed his blue eyes to his son. You recognised his eyes in the child, did you not, Miss Winterton?"

She nodded helplessly. Ferdy squeezed her hand in silent sympathy, and she threw him a grateful glance.

"But that does not make him a murderer," Lord Belwarren said. "A rake and a scoundrel he may have been, but murder is another matter."

"Very true," Mr Willerton-Forbes said. "But it was enough to make me suspect him, and one may imagine how events transpired. He stayed on at the Carrbridge Arms after the ball, and perhaps Martha approached him and drew him aside to talk privately. We know she had a knife, so perhaps she brandished it, he grabbed hold of it and, in the heat of the moment, used it to silence her. Then he had only to carry her to the canal—"

"No," Ferdy said slowly. "He was wet... he must have fallen in himself. Edgar, you must remember that Ralph came home wet that night."

"So he did! He said he had had an argument with some locals who had tipped him into a water trough," Mr Brant said. "It never seemed likely, to me. He was a bruising fighter. Could have tackled any number of locals. He asked us to keep quiet about it."

"Ah. Interesting." Mr Willerton-Forbes tapped his chin thoughtfully. "So they went to the canal, fell into an argument, she pulled out the knife, there was a tussle and they both went into the water. He swam to the ladder and escaped, she had a deep wound and perhaps could not swim, so she drowned."

"So just an accident, then?" Ferdy said hopefully.

"Perhaps, yes, but—"

"Mr Willerton-Forbes," Lord Belwarren said, "everything you have said so far is as insubstantial as gossamer — a few lightweight facts held together with a web of conjecture. I have known Ralph since he was a babe, and I can no more believe any of this than believe it of myself."

"But I can," Ferdy said quietly. "There was a ruthless side to Ralph that perhaps you never saw, sir. He took what he wanted, and let nothing stand in his way. I would not have suspected him of murder, but I have seen very recently how callous he can be when something he wants is beyond his grasp. I should like to hear *all* that Mr Willerton-Forbes has to say."

There was a long, tense silence as the two men stared at each other, grandfather and grandson. Fanny clung to Ferdy's arm, bowing her head in distress. Let them not argue! She hated discord, and it was one of the most lovable characteristics of her betrothed, that he was generally the most mild-mannered and easy-going of men.

But this was a new, determined Ferdy — not loud or forceful or belligerent, but making his point with steady determination.

In the end it was Lord Belwarren who gave way.

"Very well," he said. "It peeves me to be such a poor judge of character, but I accept your view of the matter, Ferdinand. Willerton-Forbes, you may continue."

Fanny breathed again.

34: Happington

Ferdy raised his eyebrows in surprise. His grandfather deferring to his opinion? That had never happened before. But he had no time to savour the pleasure, for Willerton-Forbes continued his recitation immediately.

"Thank you, my lord. But now we get to the truly wicked part. Ralph Makenham returned from London with Mr Brant in part, I suspect, because the investigation was focused on Martha's child. Sooner or later his rôle in that would be discovered, so he set out to create a distraction. Two distractions, in fact. He murdered two more women, purely to make it seem that the cause of Martha's death was..." He glanced at Fanny. "...let us describe it as the unsavoury interactions between men and women. Nothing to do with Martha's young son. And that worked. The constables shifted their focus and the investigation petered out."

"This is still speculation of the wildest kind," Lord Belwarren said, although with less confidence than before. "You have no proof of any of this."

"Indeed not. Nevertheless, I am confident of my deductions, my lord. I have seen nothing yet to make me doubt them. But I must return now to the *second* fact which changed everything. There was an evening at your house, Mr Ferdinand — a dinner which Miss Winterton attended. Mr Ralph had just arrived that day — he had been sulking at Abbeymount after Marianne Trivers refused him, but he returned rather abruptly."

"Ha! You see something underhand in that too, do you?" Lord Belwarren said, with a glimmer of a smile. "A man may not come and go as he pleases with you, except it must mean some evil is afoot."

Mr Willerton-Forbes smiled too. "Ah, now if I were a vain man, my lord, I might suppose that Mr Ralph had heard of my digging around in the events surrounding the murders and came to see what I had discovered. But let it be no more than whim, if you wish. In any event, the Easter ball was mentioned and Mr Ralph asserted that there was no possibility of settling what had happened, since everyone there had been drinking freely of the punch. At which point, Miss Winterton brought fear to his wicked heart — she reminded him that she had drunk no punch, and had sat on the platform all evening watching everything that happened. In short, she had the power to hang him."

Lord Belwarren grunted, but he frowned too, as if considering the matter carefully.

"From that moment on, Ralph became inseparable from Miss Winterton, paying her the most determined court."

"That is true!" Ferdy said indignantly. "It *did* start then! But I do not see why—"

"Because a wife cannot give evidence against her husband," Mr Willerton-Forbes said gently. "If he married her, he would be safe. But it was a dangerous game, for he stood to be discovered at any moment, and his behaviour aroused concern in more minds than mine. Lord Gilbert's, in particular. He came to me and revealed his part in affairs — that after the first murder, Mr Ralph had become very friendly with him all of a sudden, drawing him out to establishments of male interest, such as the rather unsavoury place by the canal where Sally Turner and Jenny Melton worked. Mr Ralph had introduced Lord Gilbert to Sally Turner, and when he received notes from her, and then an invitation to meet her, and she turned up dead the next day, he suspected that he had been led into a trap. Nothing came of that, but when Mr Ralph began to pursue Miss Winterton, Lord Gilbert was alarmed and told me the whole. From then on, we watched Mr Ralph constantly, and when Mr Ferdy threw him out of his house and—"

"What?" Lord Belwarren said. "What happened there?"

"Long story," Ferdy said sheepishly. "Not relevant to the matter in hand." He had no wish to have the duel known about here. He hoped the whole episode could now be forgotten.

"We began to watch Miss Winterton," Mr Willerton-Forbes put in quickly, with an apologetic glance at Ferdy. "We were concerned about the possibility of an enforced elopement but there were darker possibilities also, so I or Captain Edgerton or Neate, my valet, was nearby at all times. But then when Ralph failed to appear at… er, an engagement, had disappeared, in fact, I felt it best to send Miss Winterton away to safety until we could be sure of his whereabouts, just in case he resorted to violence. A man who has already murdered three times would not hesitate to do so again, if the opportunity arose, and by this time it is my belief that Mr Ralph would have been very glad to see Miss Winterton dead and unable to speak against him. Your lordship has been most helpful in ensuring a constant watch against that possibility, even if you did not know and perhaps do not believe the reasons for that."

Lord Belwarren grunted but said nothing.

"Even if I am wrong in all my conclusions, I hope you will agree that there were sufficient grounds to be alarmed for Miss Winterton's safety. One would not wish to take the least risk."

"That I will concede," Lord Belwarren said.

Ferdy frowned. "But if you suspected Ralph all along, what was that business at Lord Gilbert's house?"

"There were two reasons for that. One was to extract from Mr Ralph a public admission that he had taken Lord Gilbert to meet Sally Turner, which, to my surprise, was very readily achieved. Perhaps he truly believed that Lord Gilbert was on the point of being arrested, so he admitted his role freely to appear like an honest friend. The other objective was to see the two men together, to determine to my own satisfaction that Ralph had fathered Martha's child. I went back to Westbury House to look at the child, and indeed, those blue eyes are very distinctive, as Miss Winterton had observed, but as she also pointed out, many men have blue eyes. Lord Gilbert, in particular, also has very distinctive blue eyes, and I wanted to compare his and Ralph's side by side, in daylight. But Lord Carrbridge forced me to admit that Lord Gilbert was not suspected, so Ralph must have known that he was next to fall under suspicion. That was why we watched him so carefully, and, when he left Mr Ferdinand's house, we watched Miss Winterton. When he disappeared altogether, we became greatly concerned, and advised Miss Winterton to leave Sagborough. But now..."

"Yes?" Belwarren said. "But now...?"

Willerton-Forbes had the grace to look embarrassed. "We made enquiries, naturally. Ralph was widely known in Sagborough, so we enquired for him there, and along all the routes out of the town, and he has not been seen. His horse was still in the stable at the inn. We neglected to enquire — and I blame myself entirely for this error — for his valet. When we belatedly did so, we discovered that he had disappeared at the same time as his master, and that he had hired a gig and horse from a farm on the far side of the canal."

"From a farm!" Ferdy said. "That is peculiar."

"The gig is even more peculiar," Craston said. "Ralph would never be seen in a gig."

"Unless he were desperate," Belwarren said.

"When did Pike hire the gig?" Ferdy said, his brows creased as he tried to make sense of it.

"A little before noon, two days after Mrs Malpas's ball," Willerton-Forbes said carefully.

Ferdy worked it out. That was the day he should have met Ralph at Maggot's field. "Something must have happened to him," he said slowly. "He must have been injured, probably the night before. Yes, that would explain it. Pike would have gone looking for him in the morning, found him under a hedge somewhere and went off to find transportation."

"That is my conclusion also," Willerton-Forbes said. "We have only traced one sighting of the gig since then, and I regret to inform you that it was seen heading in this direction."

"Here? Would he come here, knowing he was looked for?" Craston said.

"He knows the estate as well as his own hand," Willerton-Forbes said. "If he *is* injured, he could easily find some secluded spot to wait it out until he recovers."

"Or his own house," Ferdy said. "Happington, about five miles from here. It is a tiny little place, and has been closed up for years, but he could easily hide there and no one any the wiser."

"It will need to be checked," Willerton-Forbes said. "All the outbuildings and empty cottages, too. Miss Winterton, I am sure I do not need to tell you not to venture outside the house until we have established Ralph's whereabouts. And you must never be alone, not for a moment."

"I understand," she said, white-faced.

With the revelations over, everyone began to drift towards the door, and Ferdy offered his arm to Fanny.

"Ferdinand." Lord Belwarren's voice was commanding enough that Ferdy stopped at once.

"Sir?"

"Craston will see Miss Winterton safely restored to the ladies," his grandfather said. "Stay a moment, m'boy."

Ferdy could not remember a time when he had talked to his grandfather alone, without his father present. It was always the three of them, the earl and the next two generations who would each be an earl when their time came, God willing. Lord Belwarren unhurriedly poured brandy while everyone trooped out, but as soon as the door clicked shut and they were alone, he offered Ferdy a glass and drank deeply himself.

"Now then, m'boy, you can tell me why you fell out with Ralph so badly that you threw him out of the house."

Ferdy toyed with the idea of prevaricating, but his grandfather's piercing eyes gave him pause. He sighed. "He dealt dishonourably with Fanny," he said eventually. "He kissed her — forced her into it, in fact — and I could not allow it. So I called him out."

Lord Belwarren's eyebrows shot up. "Did you, by Jove? And he agreed to it? Pistols, I take it?"

"He did, and it was indeed to be pistols. I can at least shoot a little. We set a time and place, but he failed to appear. I believe now that he must have come by some accident and been injured, for he would never otherwise have defaulted, but I had no knowledge of that. If something has happened to him, it was none of my doing, I give you my word. Had he appeared at the agreed hour, I had intended to delope."

"Were you afraid?"

Ferdy laughed. "Terrified! But I could not let it pass, sir. Fanny has no father or brother to defend her honour — I had to do it."

Lord Belwarren grunted, and then, to Ferdy's astonishment, held out his hand to Ferdy. "Well done, m'boy. You have proved you have backbone. That was a brave thing to do, taking on a crack shot like Ralph."

Ferdy smiled in surprise, offering his hand to be vigorously shaken. "Thank you, sir."

"We will make something of you yet, m'boy, but then I thought there was something different about you when you arrived here the other day. You have changed, no doubt about it, and not just because you have won your heart's desire. Calling Ralph out — that shows rare courage. When you are safely wed and have got your feet back on the ground, I shall take you down to London and let you into the secret of what I get up to down there."

"What *do* you get up to?" Ferdy said, smiling.

"Ha!" His grandfather laid one finger on his nose. "Not yet, m'boy, not yet. Government business, that's all you need to know for now, but Their Royal Highnesses are very appreciative, you may be sure. Other families are openly political, and some like to be flamboyant and engage in all manner of exciting derring-do, but that is not the Makenham way. Quietly and unobtrusively, that is how we work, and we are such an uninteresting family, no one would ever suspect us of involvement in matters of high state. You're a good lad, Ferdinand, a good lad. You will be a credit to this family, and your Fanny will make you an excellent wife. You chose well, m'boy, very well."

~~~~~

It took Willerton-Forbes three days to discover that someone other than the caretaker was living at Happington.

"There are three chimneys smoking, and the valet was observed going off in the gig to purchase supplies, including laudanum and a mixture for poultices from the apothecary."

"So he *is* injured," Ferdy said. "That was why he defaulted over meeting me."

"What do you wish me to do, my lord?" Willerton-Forbes said to Lord Belwarren.

The earl gazed at him through bushy eyebrows. "What would you do if you believed a wheelwright had murdered three people?"

"I would arrest him, and haul him off to the constables to have the case examined in law."

"Then you have your answer," he said.

Willerton-Forbes smiled. "As a lawyer, I must approve of your viewpoint, but are you not afraid of the resulting scandal, my lord? You are a peer of the realm, so—"

"Precisely," Lord Belwarren said. "You are a lawyer, Willerton-Forbes, so you implement and interpret the law. I am a peer, so I and my noble friends *make* the law. We are equally bound to follow it, in all cases. By all means arrest Ralph, but have a care. A man who has already killed will not scruple to do so again. Take the constables with you, and loaded pistols."

"I should like to go with them, sir, if you permit," Ferdy said.

"Old scores to settle, Ferdinand?"

"Not at all. The quarrel between us has been addressed, and honour is satisfied. I should like to talk to him, however, to see if I cannot persuade him to give himself up."

"Surrender himself to be hanged? That would be courageous."

"Ralph has never lacked courage, and facing up to what he has done must be better for him than running off to the continent, and living some nightmare of a twilight life, always looking over his shoulder. It is worth a try, is it not?"

Lord Belwarren made a "Hmpf" sound, which Ferdy took as assent.

So it was that he found himself riding across the Abbeymount estate two days later accompanied by Willerton-Forbes, Edgerton, Neate, several grooms and six constables. To his surprise, Edgar had also chosen to come.

"Not much of a one for confrontation, Ferdy," he had said, "but — well, Ralph, you know. The three of us have done everything together for years. Have to be in at the end."

"Let us hope it is not quite that final," Ferdy said, with a slight smile, although at the back of his mind was the burning fear that he would not survive an encounter with Ralph. He had that queer, sick feeling in the pit of his stomach again. He cursed himself for a fool.

He could have left the whole business to those who enjoyed the excitement, and not risked his new-found happiness on Ralph's uncertain temper.

Fanny had looked up at him, her face white. "Must you go?" was all she said.

"I must. Sometimes a gentleman has obligations of honour."

And she had nodded and said nothing more, but he knew she would not enjoy one moment free of anxiety until she saw him again. If he emerged unscathed, he swore he would never do anything so perilous again.

Happington slumbered in the late September sunshine. It was a small house, not much more than a cottage, which Ralph had occasionally used as a summer lodge to escape the hordes filling Abbeymount. In recent years it had been closed up, mouldering into slow decay while Ralph lived on the lucrative rents of the surrounding farmland. It looked now much the same as ever, the shutters all closed, and the grounds a mass of weeds and overgrown shrubs.

"It does not look as if anyone is here," Edgar said.

But the smoking chimneys told the true story, and when they made their way to the stables, they found a horse inside.

"So the valet is still here, and possibly the caretaker too," Willerton-Forbes said.

"We're not attempting to approach quietly," one of the constables said. "Might the fellow make a run for it when he hears us?"

"We have people positioned in those woods over there," Ferdy said. "I also took the precaution of warning the neighbouring farmers, who will be on the watch. If he runs, he will not get far."

Leaving the horses with the grooms, the rest of the party made their way to the front door. The knocker had been removed but Ferdy rang the bell several times. The house was small enough that they could hear it clanging each time, but no one answered. With a sigh, Ferdy produced a key but before he could use it, Willerton-Forbes tried the doorknob. It turned and the door opened at his touch.

"Not locked," he said with a shrug.

"Or bolted, luckily," Ferdy said. "I have no key for the kitchen door, so we would have had to break in."

The hall was in darkness, but Neate had brought lamps which they quickly lit.

"Ralph?" Ferdy called out. "Are you here? It is Ferdy, Ralph, and Edgar is here too. We mean you no harm."

There was no answer.

They made their way through the house. It did not take long. The stairs had rotted away, so there were only three rooms to examine. They were all empty, although two had fires burning low, and one had clearly been used as a bedroom. There was only one door left, leading to the kitchen.

"I hope he is not in the cellar," Edgar said unhappily. "I do not like cellars. Too many spiders."

"The kitchen is more likely," Willerton-Forbes said. "Remember, all of you — possibly three people, very likely armed. No heroics, if you please, and do not stand in front of Captain Edgerton, in case he has to fire his pistols."

At a signal, Neate threw open the kitchen door, and stood aside. The room seemed as black as pitch, but as Ferdy's eyes adjusted he saw a shaft of light from a broken shutter, and a red glow from the fire.

"Ralph?" he said, his voice wavering slightly. "Are you there?"

No answer.

Captain Edgerton stepped slowly over the threshold, a pistol in each hand. Ferdy followed him through the door. Behind him, more soft footsteps as the others entered. Two of the constables held their lamps high, and the centre of the room could be dimly seen — some chairs, disarranged as if their occupants had left hastily, and the large kitchen table, with bowls and pots and a heap of beans being chopped.

At the far end of the table was a seated figure.

"There you are, Ralph," Ferdy said in relief. Then he noticed the pistol in his hand. "Oh, are you going to shoot me?"

"Give me one reason why I should not," Ralph growled.

He lifted the pistol so that it pointed directly at Ferdy's heart.

35: Lennister Hall (October)

Every person in the room was frozen. No one moved an inch. Perhaps everyone had stopped breathing, and for a moment, so did Ferdy. But he knew better than to show any fear.

"I can give you *two* reasons why you should not shoot me," Ferdy said, attempting to sound insouciant. "You would not wish any harm to come to these." From the pockets of his greatcoat he produced two dusty bottles, and set them on the table. "The finest from Grandpapa's cellar, since your own is probably not well stocked just now. It would be tragic if a stray bullet were to shatter them, do you not agree? Have you any glasses in this dismal place? Where is your man? He can find us something to drink from."

With a grunt that might have been amusement, Ralph set the gun carefully down on the table. "The trouble with you, Ferdy, is that it is quite impossible to dislike you. Are you never out of humour? It is very annoying."

"I beg your pardon," Ferdy said. "Shall I introduce everyone to you?"

Ralph winced. "Spare your breath. I know Edgerton and Willerton-Forbes. No desire to know the rest. Edgar? What are you doing with this rabble? Come and sit down, cousin. I promise not to shoot you."

Edgar inched forward from his position behind the constables, but did not sit down. "I say, Ralph, you look terrible. Whatever happened to you?"

Ferdy had thought it was merely the poor light which made Ralph look like a ghost, but now he noticed the grey pallor of his skin, and eyes that had lost their habitual shimmer of amusement. Was he holding one arm oddly, too? It was in a sling, tucked inside his coat, and Ralph was hunched over, as if in pain. That was it... pain... his eyes were full of it.

"Set upon," Ralph said, shifting in his chair and wincing. "Some *blackguards* jumped me... brought me to this pass..." He stopped, and took several shallow breaths, eyes closed, as if the effort was too much for him, then swore violently. But after a moment, he seemed to recover a little. "Are you going to open those bottles or not, Ferdy? Sit, and drink with me, for friendship's sake. You too, Edgar. Glasses in that cupboard behind you. You will have to serve yourself, for my man is hiding in the cellar and the caretaker ran off two days ago. Willerton-Forbes, send your little army away and you can drink with us. I exclude Edgerton from the invitation, for I am sure he wishes to..." He winced again suddenly, and caught his breath for a moment until the pain receded. "...keep his hands steady with those pistols. Got to be ready to shoot me, eh, Edgerton? God knows, I wish you would."

"You must not talk like that, Ralph," Edgar said, rushing forward to the table and sitting down beside him. "We shall get the physician out and he will have you right as a trivet in no time."

Ralph shook his head. "I am... done for, Edgar. Only a matter of time. Some damage inside... getting worse."

"Have you tried laudanum?"

"Not much help. Wears off. Dear God, I wish the pain would stop!" He bent his head over the table, eyes closed.

Ferdy covered his distress by busying himself fetching glasses and opening the two bottles, while Willerton-Forbes dismissed the constables with a flick of his head. He opened a couple of shutters to let the summer sunshine into the room, so that it was dazzlingly bright for a moment. When Ferdy could see again, he gazed around at the empty, dusty shelves, with a few cobwebby pots hanging from ceiling hooks. He pulled out a chair, sat down and poured wine for them.

That hour was as strange as any Ferdy had experienced. They sat, Ralph, Edgar and Ferdy himself, praising the wine and reminiscing about their boyhood misadventures, for all the world as if nothing was amiss. All the while, Willerton-Forbes watched them in silence, and Captain Edgerton stood motionless to one side of the table, both pistols aimed at Ralph. And Ralph himself... he smiled sometimes, and once he even laughed, but mostly he sat rigidly, unable to move without setting off a wave of debilitating pain. The sight of it distressed Ferdy beyond enduring.

"I cannot bear to see you like this!" he burst out, his voice cracked with grief. "Will you not come to Abbeymount? Or Lennister, if you prefer. Let Mama look after you, get the best physicians out to set you straight, get well in comfort."

"To what purpose? So you can send me off to be hanged in the best of health? Better to...uuuh!" For a moment the pain overwhelmed him and he paused for a long while before continuing, "Better to die here, do you not think? My pistol has been loaded for days now, and not for you, Ferdy, you may be sure. I shall choose my own end."

"What kind of end is that for a man, to die in the dark, like a rat in a hole?" Ferdy cried.

From across the room, Captain Edgerton growled, "It is all he deserves."

"No one deserves to die like this, untimely and in grievous pain," Ferdy said with some heat. "Whatever Ralph may have done, it is for the law and God to pass judgement, not some gang of thugs."

Who were they, those thugs, who had chosen Ralph of all people to set upon? It was hardly likely to be a chance event. More likely that the assailants were friends of the women Ralph had killed, driven to vengeance by the slow and plodding processes of the law.

He thought of the women at Westbury House, looking after the child with Ralph's blue eyes, knowing that he had killed the boy's mother... a group of them would be able to overpower even a man as strong as Ralph. Yes, it could very well have been so. But it hardly mattered now.

"Come with us, Ralph," Ferdy said again. "I would not have you take the coward's way out like this. If death is truly at your shoulder, then now is the time to face up to the wrongs you have done. Confess all, and make your peace with God and the world."

Ralph gave a small smile. "That would take a better man than I am, cousin. Leave me the wine, but go away now. I am tired of you all."

"I am disappointed in you, cousin," Ferdy said. "As a boy, you were my hero, my big, strong, *brave* cousin. I always wanted to be like you, you see, to have just one tenth of your charm, your looks, your courage. You ride like the Devil himself, you box, you hunt, you drive to an inch, and women adore you. When I realised I could never attain such heights, I was forced to hide myself away behind a well-formed neckcloth. My only achievement is to tie a perfect Mathematical — sometimes. Do not shatter my illusions of my heroic cousin, Ralph. Come home with me and face whatever God intends for you with honour."

And finally his words had some effect. Ralph nodded slowly. "Very well. Let it be as you wish, and I shall die in my bed at... at Abbeymount, confessed and shriven. But tell me, cousin... ah, God, this pain!" There was a long silence before he was able to continue. "If I had met you, would you have deloped?"

"Of course."

"Whereas I would have shot you through the heart, God help me. But I am glad now that I did not. And Fanny?"

Ferdy smiled. "We are betrothed."

"Good. Very good. No hard feelings?" He reached out his hand to Ferdy.

Without hesitation, Ferdy shook it. "None at all."

~~~~~

OCTOBER

Ralph had been conveyed back to Abbeymount, where his childhood nurse and an array of aunts had cocooned him with their tender care. The best physicians from York had conferred over him, the finest treatments had been applied but to no avail. No remedy could be found.

Eight days after Ferdy had brought him home, Ralph died tranquilly in his own bed, with his family at his bedside. He had confessed all to Willerton-Forbes and again to the chaplain, and was as prepared to meet his Maker as any man could be.

While all the Makenhams were deeply grieved by his ending, there was relief also that the family had been spared the scandal of a trial.

Lord Belwarren spoke to Ferdy one day. "Well, we got off quite lightly, I feel. One does not quite like to have a convicted murderer in the family. Still, we shall miss the fellow. Place won't be the same without him." He paused, taking several deep breaths. "Well now, well now, what about your Fanny, eh? Abbeymount will be a bit gloomy for a while. We should be holding a celebratory ball for her, but now everyone will be in black, and there will be long speeches at dinner each night, remembering Ralph as he was. Such a promising young man." He paused again, sorrow written across his features. "Ah well. A house of mourning is no place for a young lady soon to be a bride. Take her to Lennister, and Louisa can mother her, eh? That is what the girl needs, a bit of mothering."

Seeing Fanny in his own family home was the greatest delight to Ferdy. He could not quite believe she was his own dear Fanny now, and there was still a niggle of worry in his mind. Accordingly, as they walked about Lennister Hall one day, Ferdy explaining the family history, and Fanny exclaiming over the views from every window, which looked clear to the moors here, he judged the time was right to approach the subject.

They were in the State Bedroom, so-called since a long-dead prince had once spent a night there. It was a grandiose and imposing room, quite out of keeping with the rest of the house, which Ferdy always felt was exactly what a family house should be — cosy, comfortable and just a little untidy. There were samplers on the walls from every Miss Makenham who had ever lived there, and a small army of badly carved wooden soldiers and horses, the workmanship of their brothers.

"Do you like it here?" Ferdy said, as Fanny gazed up at the ornate plasterwork on the ceiling and the elaborate bed hangings. "Lennister, I mean. I grew up here, so I love the place, but it would please me to think that you like it too."

"I do," she said. "Well, not so much this room, which is a trifle overpowering, but the rest of the house is so homely. It reminds me of Woodside, except more regular in arrangement. It feels like a real home, whereas Abbeymount is a bit... overwhelming, just at first. Do you know, it is very pleasant to have you to myself for once. Shall we sit down for a while? It is a little chilly in here, but if we sit very close together, we will keep each other warm."

She smiled up at him with such innocence in her eyes that he melted inside. Sometimes he suspected she was not quite as artless as she appeared, but he was perfectly happy to be led in whatever direction she chose.

So they sat in the cushioned embrasure of one of the windows, and that led to a certain amount of kissing, which Ferdy had no wish to bring to an end. But when she sighed and rested her head on his shoulder, he said, "Dearest, there is a question I must ask you."

"You have already asked me the only question that matters," she said. "I said yes, if you remember." She tilted her head to look up at him with a mischievous smile, but he had no answering smile of his own.

"It is about that."

She shot upright, her eyes huge with fear. "Are you going to cry off, Ferdy?"

"*No!* No, no, no, no, no! Not in the least. That is the *last* thing I would ever do." He swallowed hard, but it had to be said so he rushed on, "It is *your* wishes I am thinking of, for you were very much against the idea until you thought I might be killed in that foolish duel, so you might have felt *bounced* into it, and then obliged to stick to it on account of not wanting me to be disappointed, even though you are not in love with me and—"

"Oh, but I am."

His heart lurched. "You are?" he whispered.

"Oh yes! I think I have been for ages, but I did not realise it. I thought you were just a friend, you see. A very good friend, a *comfortable* friend, someone to be depended upon always, but no more than that. But then when I heard you were to be in a duel, and you might be killed, I *knew*. It was very sudden, for one moment everything was normal and the very next moment I felt as if the earth had tilted and tipped me over a precipice."

"Oh." Then, hesitantly, "Very sudden? Like a thunderbolt?"

"Yes! Oh yes, it was exactly like that! Out of nowhere. So you see, I *do* love you, Ferdy, truly, so please, please do not cry off because I want to marry you more than anything in the world and… and my life would be empty without you in it."

Oh, the joy of hearing his own words spoken back to him! He laughed a little then, rather shakily. "Dearest… I love you so much."

"And I love you, Ferdy. So when shall we be married?"

"You will not be of age until February, so let us wait until then and not have to worry about permission and so forth. It will be a decent interval after Ralph— And… and there will be plenty of time to get your wedding clothes. You are not going to make them all yourself, are you?" he said in sudden alarm, with a vision of her sewing frantically every day for months.

She giggled. "No! I thought, since there is not a great deal of work going on in the shop, that I might use some of Lady Harriet's unfortunate women, especially since they might have to leave Westbury House."

"Leave it — but why?"

"Because it does not belong to Lady Harriet, seemingly, or anyone in her family. She is excessively cross about it, as you may imagine. Mr Willerton-Forbes found out that there was a mistake made... oh, a hundred years ago, almost, and it belongs to some other family altogether. Which is a lovely surprise for them, but very sad for Lady Harriet's unfortunate women and their children. Oh Ferdy, I am so anxious about poor little Eddy, Martha's son. He has no one in the world to care for him now, except Martha's friends, and it is not like *family*, is it?"

"We will do something for him, you may be sure. After all, he is Ralph's son, and therefore a part of the Makenham family, even if informally. We could even adopt him, if you wish it, my love."

"Oh! Oh, could we? And if the unfortunate women have nowhere to live, we could—"

"No," Ferdy said firmly. "Eddy, certainly, but we are not having all those women and their children to live with us. The Sagborough house could not accommodate them all, even if we wished to. I will try to find them some alternative provision if they have to move, and it is an excellent idea to set them to work on your wedding clothes. After all, I should not like you to be so busy sewing that we will have no time to talk or... whatever else we might want to do," he said, pulling her nearer again.

She closed her eyes and lifted her face for his kiss.

~~~~~

Ferdy went back to Abbeymount for Ralph's funeral, but there was a surprise awaiting him when the will was read, for Ralph had left Happington to him.

His grandfather said, "Were you aware that he had done that?"

"Not at all. I wonder why he did so. Better to have left it to Edgar, I should have thought."

"Ralph never had much time for Edgar, for all the lad followed him everywhere. Edgar worshipped Ralph, but Ralph worshipped *you*."

Ferdy raised his eyebrows, but could find no sensible response to this preposterous assertion. Instead he said, "Not sure what I am supposed to do with Happington. I already have a house in Sagborough."

"Aye, and several more to come to you in the future. Well, sell it or keep it, as you please. The house is quite small, not large enough for a growing family and not grand enough to lease out, but there are some valuable tenancies and coverts on the estate. Ralph lived well on the proceeds."

Once the funeral was over, a stream of neighbours called to offer condolences, and also to offer their congratulations to Ferdy and his future bride. Thomas Claremont was among the first to call. Ferdy was still bemused by his abrupt defection from Fanny's suitor to Celia Drabble's, but since Fanny had not been hurt by it he bore the man no ill-will, and they would be neighbours, after all.

"Fanny, I am so happy for you," Claremont said, his face wreathed in smiles. "I guessed at once how it must be, when you— Well, no matter. All has worked out for the best, and I need not worry that you might have been offended when I became attached to Celia."

"Oh no! It was the most romantic thing in the world," Fanny said. "She is so beautiful that I was sure she would find a husband worthy of her before long."

"Thank you, Fanny. You are very generous. We have some small improvements to make at Helsford and then the banns will be called. Celia's uncle, Sir William Harbottle, is to provide her wedding clothes and a small settlement, and I have ordered my carriage already," he said with pride. "Whoever would have thought I should have an estate of my own and a carriage and be married before John and Rupert? I have some improvements in mind for the farm which will, I think, greatly enhance the pasturage and enable me to enlarge the dairy. I plan to put sheep on the upper fields..."

Fanny smiled and nodded, seeming pleased at his excitement, but Ferdy could not become excited by fields of sheep and wished he would go away.

But then Claremont gave a smug grin, and said, "I have had another piece of good fortune come my way. It seems I am also the owner of a property in Sagborough. There had been some mistake in the past, but now that it has been rectified the property is mine. A fine house, by the sound of it. There are some indigent women living there at the moment but—"

Fanny squeaked. "You mean Westbury House? *You* own it?"

"You know it? Oh, Sagborough... of course you do. Yes, it is mine," he said proudly. "Is it not wonderful? Not that I need another house, for Helsford suits me perfectly, but once I have got rid of these women I can—"

Fanny squeaked again. "Thomas, those women are my *friends*. You cannot turn them out! They have nowhere else to go."

"They can hardly be your friends, Fanny," he said with a reproving frown. "They are... not at all the sort of women you should know." He threw a glance at Ferdy, as if wondering why he allowed his betrothed to associate with such people.

"They are unfortunate women who have been given an opportunity to undertake honest employment by the charity of Lady Harriet Hay," Ferdy said. "The alternatives would be far worse. Would you turn them onto the streets?"

Claremont reddened. "No, not if I could avoid it, but I cannot afford to support such a project myself. A tenant in the house would bring me a useful additional income. Or I could sell the house, perhaps. Would Lady Harriet buy it from me, do you think?"

"I could not say," Ferdy said. Then he had one of his unexpected ideas. "But what do you say to an exchange? I have recently come into the property of Happington, which adjoins Helsford. We could come to some arrangement, perhaps."

"Happington? That would… be of interest. What would it be worth, do you suppose?"

"Close to a thousand a year," Ferdy said. "The house itself is small and of no use to you, since you have Helsford, but my cousin Edgar would perhaps like to have a little place of his own. He recently performed a service for me and I should like to repay him. But the estate — I should be happy to let you have that and the income from the tenancies, if you will let me have Westbury House in exchange. I am sure we can come to some equitable arrangement."

Claremont's eyes gleamed. He left soon after, armed with Ferdy's card and the name of his lawyer in York.

"How avaricious Thomas has become," Fanny said sadly. "I am sure he is getting much the best of the deal, too. You are too generous, Ferdy, but thank you! I am so glad that Lady Harriet's women will not have to leave their home. Oh, another carriage is arriving. Who can this be?"

"Grandmama," Ferdy said with a grin. "I would recognise that old bone-shaker of a coach anywhere."

It was indeed Lady Belwarren, and three of the aunts, come to fuss over Fanny, and to bring her several letters which had arrived for her at Abbeymount. "I am so glad no one had to pay for this one," she said, waving a huge package. "There must be twelve pages at least. It was franked by a Lord Delacrost, so it must be from one of your sisters, I think?"

"Margaret," Fanny breathed. "Margaret has written at last. Oh, goodness, how heavy it is! Do you mind if I—?"

"We do not stand on ceremony, dear, not with *you*. I know how anxiously you have awaited news. Open it at once."

Fanny needed no second bidding. Eagerly she broke the seal and opened out the pages, which were huge, and closely written. "Oh so much writing, and— Oh! She is *married!* Margaret is married! My goodness, I cannot— Oh! *Oh!* OH!"

Ferdy laughed. "Now you are worrying us all."

"She is well, and happy, but— Oh! She owns a house, and— OH! Kidnapped! She was kidnapped!" Rapidly she scanned each page, her eyes enormous, her mouth perpetually agape in astonishment. "Well!" she said, as she reached the final page. "My quiet sister has had some adventures. She is married to Lord Delacrost's heir, although he is a curate, which seems odd. I can hardly take it in. But they are to go to Westerlea Park at Christmas, so I can—" She stopped, turning to Ferdy with pleading eyes. "Oh, Ferdy, you will not stop me going, will you? I must go and see my sisters again."

"Of course you must, and I am going with you."

"Oh, Ferdy, thank you!"

Lady Belwarren raised an eyebrow. "Not spending Christmas at Abbeymount, Ferdinand?"

"Not this year, Grandmama," he said, smiling. "This year you will just have to poke fun at some other hapless Makenham. Next year, I promise you my wife and I will be at Abbeymount, but this year is for the Winterton sisters, and Woodside."

36: Christmas At Westerlea Park (December)

DECEMBER

The carriage rolled slowly up the drive of Westerlea Park. Fanny peered through the windows for the first sight of the house. Everything was drear and dull in the grey light of December, but there was the house at last, unchanged in a year. It was Fanny who had changed. She had left the village as a child, filled with romantic ideals, but she returned to Brinshire a little less romantic, but infinitely happier.

Even before the carriage had stopped moving, the doors of the house were thrown open and four figures emerged, waving and smiling. Her sisters! Finally they would all be together again. There was Rosamund, so stately. Annabelle, tears of joy on her face. Lucy, practically bouncing with excitement. And Margaret, looking so grown-up with her matron's cap. And behind them, four men, smiling too.

Fanny practically fell out of the carriage as soon as the door was opened, and then she was wrapped in the arms of one sister after another, with squeals of glee and kisses and tears — so many tears.

"Inside, quick, before we all freeze to death." That was Rosamund, of course, always so practical.

They poured into the house, five sisters and the five men who had brought them happiness. Especially hers! Fanny turned, and reached out her hand to Ferdy, following in her wake. He smiled at her, that special smile that was for her alone, and, as always, she was warmed right to her heart.

"This is Ferdy," she said, as soon as they were over the threshold. "Ferdy Makenham. My future husband," she added proudly.

Ferdy bowed, the ladies curtsied and the other gentlemen bowed.

Mr Dalton stepped forward. "Welcome to Westerlea Park, Mr Makenham." He turned to the others. "How shall we manage the introductions? It is awkward with so many."

"Fanny must do it," cried Lucy. "She can introduce each of us, but she must guess which gentleman belongs to which lady."

Fanny laughed. "Very well, but let me do the ladies first. Ferdy, this is Rosamund, Mrs Robin Dalton. Annabelle is the Countess of Brackenwood. This is Lucy, Mrs Price for a little while longer, and the shy one hiding behind everyone else is Margaret, Mrs Melville Haymer. Now the gentlemen... oh, but this is easy. This is Mr Robin Dalton, whose father, Lord Westerlea, very kindly invited us all here. The great tall fellow must be Margaret's Mr Melville Haymer. And of the others..." She looked from one to the other. One was a rather ordinary-looking man, attired more for comfort than fashion. The other, a stylish dresser, was a handsome man with very shapely thighs... "Oh, you must be Lucy's Mr Audley, and then this must be Lord Brackenwood."

The gentlemen bowed to each other, and, at Rosamund's urging, they made their way towards the drawing room to meet Lord Westerlea, and his sister, who kept house for him.

"How did you know?" Ferdy whispered in her ear.

She blushed scarlet, not quite up to the task of mentioning shapely thighs. "They described them very well in their letters," she said. He laughed and let it pass.

The first evening was rather awkward, the sisters chattering nineteen to the dozen — even Margaret was talking! — while the gentlemen were silent, watching their ladies with smiles but with little to contribute to the flood of reminiscences.

Breakfast was business-like. It was agreed that they would visit Woodside, to look around their old home and decide what was to be done about it.

"I have a possible buyer for the house and estate," Mr Dalton told them. "There have been others interested, but either they would not pay a sensible price or else I deemed them unsuitable for the neighbourhood, for it has been impressed upon me that certain types of person would not be acceptable to the society here."

"Not acceptable to Lady Elizabeth Drake, you mean," Lucy said, reaching for another slice of toast.

"Well... it is true that Lady Elizabeth has been... er, quite vocal on the subject," Mr Dalton said, with a wry smile. "She is very conscious of her position. But it would be awkward for my father and aunt, too, to have neighbours who were not quite the thing. One could hardly refuse to receive them, when Woodside is barely a mile away. However, the buyer I have in mind is perfectly unexceptionable. A Mr Tyrrell, recently widowed and desirous of moving to the country. His present house, I understand, is the property of his wife's family, and he feels it only right to return it to them. He has four daughters, which seems propitious to me, do you not agree? His mother lives with them, and will raise the girls. He offers a very fair price, too. But perhaps you will not wish to sell at all, now that your circumstances have changed."

Mr Audley turned to the sisters and said, "I should be very happy to buy the house, or settle your father's debts, if you wish to keep Woodside."

"We could all contribute, according to our means," Ferdy said. "There is no reason why any one of us should bear the burden alone."

"You are very generous," Rosamund said. "It is a pity Mama's jewellery was lost or sold off, for then we should never have needed charity."

"But it was the hand of Providence," Fanny said, suddenly tearful. "If the jewellery had not vanished, we should never have left Woodside and I should never have met Ferdy, and Annabelle would not have met her earl, nor Lucy her Mr Audley, nor Margaret her curate. It has all been for the best."

"And how much wickedness did you all have to survive along the way?" Rosamund said briskly. "There has been bad as well as good, for all of you. But now we have the opportunity to look to the future instead of the past. We each have a house elsewhere — in some cases, more than one house," she added with a smile. "We do not *need* Woodside any more. We can let it go, remembering the good times we had there but not held back by the weight of unhappy memories, or Papa's debts. However, let us look around the house before we make any decisions."

They squeezed into two carriages for the short drive to Woodside, for although it was near enough to walk, incessant rain had turned every path to a quagmire. Havelock, the housekeeper, opened the door to them, a huge smile on her face. Fanny threw her arms around the startled woman.

"Oh, Havelock, you are still here! How wonderful! Who else is left?"

"Only me and a couple of girls from the village now," she said. "I'm far too old to find a new place. Well now, we've got all the covers off, so you can wander about as you will. I've laid out refreshments in the dining room. Just ring for tea when you're ready."

They moved slowly from room to room, but it made Fanny very sad. So little remained of them now. The worktable in the morning room was empty of bonnets, feathers and half-made gowns. The books had all been packed up and sent to Annabelle. The paintings from the walls, the silver, crystal and china had been stored at Westerlea Park. The linen cupboard smelled strongly of camphor. Their wardrobes were empty, the beds stripped.

They came at last to their mother's bedroom, with its heavy, over-ornate furniture, which had been made specially for her when she married. Fanny gazed round at it, remembering her mother sitting in the chair before the huge secretary with the clock in the middle of it, writing her letters, or on her stool before the mirror of her dressing table, having her hair powdered. Latterly, she had been a tiny, pale face in the massive bed. She had always had smiles for her daughters, even when the mere act of talking became too much for her.

"This is where Mama's jewellery should have been," Annabelle said softly. "Somewhere in this room. Yet Papa took the room apart and could not find it. Such an upheaval! The floorboards up, the wall panels off, the ceiling probed, and every drawer and shelf emptied. But there was nothing."

"She could not have hidden the jewels anywhere else?" the earl said.

"No, for at the end she never even left her room, yet several of us saw one piece or another. She hid them somewhere here."

"Or Papa found them, and sold them to fund his gaming," Rosamund said sharply.

"Oh no, for he was very upset when he needed them for your dowry and could not find them," Fanny said. "I am quite certain he was truly mystified."

"I agree," Lucy said. "I never saw him in such a rage."

"Well, the jewels are gone now," Rosamund said briskly. "So what are we to do with Woodside, sisters? For myself, I would be glad to see it sold and enjoyed by a family, since I have no need of it myself."

"You are a little squeezed in Holly Lodge," Lucy said. "Woodside would make a charming family home for you and Robin, until he inherits the Park. You would have a bigger garden for the children, too."

"We shall be moving into the Park in the summer," Rosamund said. "Robin's father is feeling his age, and wants us there so that he can have his grandchildren around him. There is a proper schoolroom there, too. Besides, I am not sentimental, you know that. Annabelle, what are your thoughts?"

"I think…" Annabelle said slowly, "keeping it would leave us too strongly connected to what once was. We cannot bring back the happy family that once lived here. We have our memories, but it does not do to dwell too much in the past. We should look to the future, I believe. Lucy?"

"I cannot see how I am to manage even two houses, so a third would be out of the question. I see no purpose to keeping Woodside. Margaret?"

She shuddered, tried to speak, failed. Then, with a convulsive gulp, she reached for her husband's hand, and the words came out in a rush. "Get rid of it. Never want… to see it again."

The others stared at her, astonished at her vehemence. "Margaret, dearest," Fanny said. "Do you have unhappy memories of Woodside? You always seemed so contented here."

"Not contented… had no alternative. Now I have."

Fanny hugged her, the ready tears springing to her eyes again. Poor Margaret! So unhappy, yet no one ever knew! And perhaps she did not quite know herself until she met her Mr Haymer and learnt what true happiness was.

"Well, Fanny," Ferdy said. "I think the decision is yours. Keep it or sell it?"

"I cannot live in it," Fanny said slowly. "My home is in Yorkshire now."

"Then keep it, but lease it out. That way it stays in the family," Ferdy said.

Fanny hesitated. "That would be mere sentimentality. What need do any of us have of it now? Besides, Woodside should have been Jeremy's. If there were any possibility that he were still alive, I should want to keep Woodside, just in case, but... I have had to accept that he cannot be. If he were still alive, he would surely have come back to see us or written to us or let us know, somehow. No, Jeremy is drowned at the bottom of the Irish Sea, and wishing and hoping will not bring him back. I have been too foolishly romantical in the past. I must learn to be practical if I am to be a countess some day."

"You will make a charming countess when the time comes," Ferdy said, smiling at her in that heart-stopping way he had, and tucking her hand around his arm. "But not for a long time yet, I trust."

"Oh no! I like your father and grandfather very much," she said. "I do not want either of them to die."

"No more do I," he said. "So you will have to be content to be mere Mrs Ferdinand Makenham in February."

"So that is agreed," Rosamund said briskly. "You may close the deal with Mr Tyrrell, Robin. Shall we have some tea now?"

~~~~~

Before the carriages had stopped moving outside the entrance to Westerlea Park, Miss Dalton rushed out of the house to greet them, waving a letter in her hand.

"Mr Makenham? Mr Makenham! Oh, there you are! An express came for you from London not an hour ago. Oh, I do hope it is not bad news."

"Oh, Lord," Ferdy said worriedly. "Grandfather went off to London a week or two ago, although he should be back at Abbeymount by now."

"If it were a tragic announcement, it would be sealed in black," Rosamund said.

"Oh yes!" Ferdy said in relieved tones. "So it cannot be... *that.*" He turned it over and over in his hands, and then, with sudden resolution, tore it open. "Oh! It is not bad news at all, it is very good news. My grandfather has been kicked up a notch."

"Kicked up?" Fanny said.

"Read it," he said, laughing. "It is very brief."

Taking the paper, she read aloud, *'Ferdinand, By the time you read this I shall be the Marquess of Dilborough. Congratulations. Your birthday present is early this year. Belwarren.'*

Robin Dalton laughed. "Congratulations indeed! Your grandfather must have performed some great service to the Crown to be so rewarded."

"I believe he has, yes, but why is he congratulating *me?*"

"Do you not see? Your grandfather is now the Marquess of Dilborough, so your father takes as his courtesy title—?"

"Oh! The Earl of Belwarren."

"And as the heir to an earl, you now also take a courtesy title, do you not?"

"Oh!" His eyes widened. "So... I must be Viscount Craston, and Fanny will be a viscountess and *nobody died!* That is perfect!"

"Congratulations, my lord," Miss Dalton said, dipping a respectful curtsy. "Goodness, so many titles in the house at once! It is just like the old days. Robin, champagne, at once, for Lord Craston."

"Lord Craston... that is me!" Ferdy said, bemused. "Upon my soul!"

~~~~~

That evening was far more convivial. The gentlemen were a very long time over their port, and even Margaret had left the pianoforte and joined the others in grumbling about the delay to the tea tray. But eventually they came through, laughing together in the most amiable way imaginable.

"You are all getting very friendly," Lucy said.

"It has been forced upon us by Ferdy's elevation," Mr Audley said. "We have adapted with some difficulty to you ladies changing your names, but there is no bearing it when gentlemen change their names too. So we have decided to dispense with all formality. From now on, we shall all be on Christian-name terms only, for if you are five sisters, then we must be five brothers, you see, so we are all equal."

"All equal?" Lucy said, laughing. "How can that be when you have an earl and a viscount amongst you?"

"Ah, but we have agreed that rank is not the only measure of a man. Allan has the highest title, it is true, but Mel is the tallest of us all, besides being a clergyman, which gives him a different kind of superiority. Ferdy has the most perfectly-tied neckcloth, and it is universally agreed that Robin and his father keep the finest wine cellar in the county."

"A great deal of which you appear to have sampled this evening," Lucy said. "But what of you, my love? What is your claim to greatness?"

"Hmm… we are not so crass as to discuss money, so if I profess to be the richest, they will be too polite to contradict me. And naturally I am also the handsomest and the wittiest and—"

"And the most impudent!" Lucy said. "Although perhaps *I* will not contradict you on those points."

"He has the largest house, too," Ferdy said. "A hundred rooms! That is almost as many as Abbeymount, and when I am a marquess—"

Amidst much laughter, the gentlemen all protested loudly at this premature claim, and it was some minutes before order could be restored. It was again Leo Audley who spoke.

"I am glad we are all friends, for that is only fitting when the ladies are as close as any sisters could be. Which is why I have something very particular to ask Rosamund, Annabelle, Margaret and Fanny. When Lucy honoured me by accepting my proposal of marriage, she told me that she has no male relative who may give a blessing on our union. So I should like to ask you, as her dearest friends, to do so. My only wish is to love and cherish her for the rest of our lives. May I do so?"

Fanny sighed in delight. "Oh, how romantic you are, Mr Audley!"

"Leo, please."

"Leo... You certainly have my blessing."

"And mine," murmured the others.

"Thank you!" he said. He knelt at Lucy's feet and took her hands in his. "And now, my dearest, it only remains for you to name the day when I shall be the happiest man alive, but please, I beg you, make it soon."

"As soon as you can contrive it, my love," she said.

"Then how about now? Right here, with all your sisters by your side to witness it? For it just so happens that I have a special licence—"

Lucy squealed. "So *that* was why you went to London! It was not to see your lawyer at all."

"I said it was legal business, and so it was. And, by happy chance, we have a clergyman on the premises. Will you marry us, Mel?"

"Most willingly. Do you have a ring?"

"Oh!" The chagrin on Leo's face was almost comical. "I knew I would forget something."

"Not to worry," Rosamund said. "I have Mama's ring. Let me fetch it."

So it was that Leonard Henry Audley married Lucy Alice Price in the drawing room of Westerlea Park in the county of Brinshire on the evening before Christmas, in the presence of all the bride's family, with Mel Haymer officiating, and great were the celebrations.

Later, when everyone else had gone to bed, Ferdy and Fanny lingered in the bay window, watching snow drifting gently to earth outside.

"You are the last Miss Winterton," Ferdy said, kissing her fingers one by one. "The last of you to marry. Still, it is not so very long until February and you are of age."

"No, not long. Besides..."

"Besides what?" he said, softly kissing her cheeks, still damp from all the happy tears shed that evening.

"So much has happened this past year. I should like to have time to grow accustomed. And to refurbish the house in Harlington Terrace, of course. I wonder that you did nothing, for that furniture is dreadfully uncomfortable."

"I wanted you to do it," he said simply, his arm slipping around her waist. "Oh, Fanny, you have no idea how happy it makes me to be here with you today."

"Oh, Ferdy! You are a romantic at heart, I always knew it."

"Well, I would be happy to be with you anywhere, but it is glorious not to be at Abbeymount."

She stared at him. "But you love Abbeymount."

"I do, I love it dearly on three hundred and sixty-four days of the year. But Christmas Day is my birthday, and the day when every relative, no matter how distantly connected, recalls every

396

humiliating episode from my childhood for the amusement of the company, and Grandpapa bestows on me some violently hideous present. But this year there will be no humiliation, and the present is a welcome one, for although I care nothing for a title for myself, it will give me unutterable pleasure to share it with you. It is a gift worthy of your beauty, your gentleness and your goodness, dear Fanny. I shall count the days until I may hear you addressed as Lady Craston." He kissed her nose, and then, as gently as a summer breeze, her lips. "I adore you, Fanny Winterton. May we have a great many years of happiness together."

Fanny rested her head on his shoulder, and cried for joy.

THE END

The next and final book in the series is *Woodside*, which moves forward ten years. You can read a sneak preview of chapter 1 after the acknowledgements.

For more information or to buy, go to: http://marykingswood.co.uk

Thanks for reading!

If you have enjoyed reading this book, please consider writing a short review on Amazon. You can find out the latest news and sign up for the mailing list at: http://marykingswood.co.uk..

Book 5, the conclusion to the series, is *Woodside*, wherein you will learn all the remaining secrets of the Winterton family, including what happened to Mama's jewels, why Margaret stopped speaking and the truth about Jeremy. You can read a sneak preview of Chapter 1 after the acknowledgements.

Family trees: Hi-res version is available at the Mary Kingswood website: http://marykingswood.co.uk.. .

A note on historical accuracy: I have endeavoured to stay true to the spirit of Regency times, and have avoided taking too many liberties or imposing modern sensibilities on my characters. The book is not one of historical record, but I've tried to make it reasonably accurate. However, I'm not perfect! If you spot a historical error, I'd very much appreciate knowing about it so that I can correct it and learn from it. Thank you!

About the series: *When Mr Edmund Winterton of Woodside dies, his daughters find themselves penniless and homeless. What can they do? Unless they wish to live on charity, they will have to find genteel employment for themselves. This book is set in England during the Regency period of the early nineteenth century. Book 0 takes place 5 years before books 1-4, and book 5 ten years later.*

Book 0: The Betrothed (Rosamund) (a short novel, free to mailing list subscribers)

Book 1: The Governess (Annabelle)

Book 2: The Chaperon (Lucy)

Book 3: The Companion (Margaret)

Book 4: The Seamstress (Fanny)

Book 5: Woodside

Any questions about the series? You can email me at any time at mary@marykingswood.co.uk. I'd love to hear from you!

About the author

I write traditional Regency romances under the pen name Mary Kingswood, and epic fantasy as Pauline M Ross. I live in the beautiful Highlands of Scotland with my husband. I like chocolate, whisky, my Kindle, massed pipe bands, long leisurely lunches, chocolate, going places in my campervan, eating pizza in Italy, summer nights that never get dark, wood fires in winter, chocolate, the view from the study window looking out over the Moray Firth and the Black Isle to the mountains beyond. And chocolate. I dislike driving on motorways, cooking, shopping, hospitals.

Acknowledgements

Thanks go to:

Jane Austen and Georgette Heyer, who jointly inspired me to try my hand at writing a Regency romance.

Shayne Rutherford of Darkmoon Graphics for the cover design.

My beta readers: Mary Burnett, Barbara Daniels Dena, Amy DeWitt, Megan Jacobson, Melanie Savage, Keti Vezzu

Last, but definitely not least, my first reader: Amy Ross.

Sneak preview of Book 5: Woodside: Chapter 1: A Journey

~~~~~

TEN YEARS HAVE PASSED SINCE THE EVENTS OF *THE SEAMSTRESS*

~~~~~

John Moreton stared unseeingly at the page of the book he held. The only sound in the room was the occasional shifting of the coals on the fire, and his uncle's rustling newspaper. He reached for his port glass, sipped, then replaced it on the small table beside him. Then, with a sigh, he closed the book.

His uncle's newspaper lowered, and he looked over the top of it at John, a wry smile on his face. "It is a big step, is it not? Takes a deal of thinking about. That was partly why I never married myself — never could wind myself up to do it."

John laughed and shook his head in resignation. "You always know what I'm thinking, you old rascal."

"You have the world's most expressive face, Johnny. I can read you like a book — better, at all events, than you are managing with yours. Have you turned a single page since we came through after dinner?"

"Not a one." He grinned ruefully. "It *is* a big step, but it is not the prospect of marriage that makes me thoughtful. I decided long ago on that head, and Ridwell has been tolerably encouraging."

"And the lady?"

"Ellen will follow her father's wishes. She is a dutiful daughter."

"She's a cold fish, that's what she is," his uncle said sharply. "You haven't asked for my advice, but I'll give it anyway. If it were me, I'd look for a cosier wife to bed, and never mind about the mill."

"Never mind the mill?" John said, shaking his head in bemusement. "Cragforth? Ridwell's most profitable? A fine dowry, indeed."

"If it's money you want, I'll increase your share of the profits from Hazlehead — fifty fifty, how does that sound? You do all the work anyway, so it's more than fair, and you'll get the lot when I'm gone. Don't make a wrong choice, Johnny. You're not the type to look for your fun elsewhere, and I'd hate to see you unhappy."

"I'd as soon have a mill of my own than any amount of money. Besides, Ellen's a rare beauty."

"Cold fish," his uncle muttered, but a smile softened the words.

"She will be warmer once we're wed and she's out from under that mother of hers."

"Ha! I wish you joy of *that*. But if it is not the prospect of being leg-shackled that has you ruminating, what is it?"

"Unfinished business," John said thoughtfully. "If I'm to be wed, I must needs settle all the loose threads of my former life. I may need to go on a trip. You will not mind that, I daresay? Hadley and Donwell will take good care of Hazlehead while I'm gone."

"How long?"

"A month, perhaps. Maybe a little more."

His uncle grunted. "To Liverpool?"

"No... Not Liverpool, although some day perhaps I must go back to see the family, I suppose. Not that they take any interest in me. The only time I ever hear from them is when there is a death or a wedding. I never knew I had so many female relations of marriageable age, but ever since I sent twenty guineas to Jenny, they have all come crawling out of the woodwork."

His uncle cackled with laughter. "Aye, when there's money to be had, they're all about. But where, then, if not Liverpool? You never mentioned interests elsewhere."

"Brinshire. Woodside, the home of Jeremy Winterton. Do you recall the tale? He stayed with the family in Liverpool before he went to sea. I have had in mind for some time now to go and see his people, to tell them... well, the truth. They deserve to know what really happened to their son."

His uncle lowered his paper fully, folded it neatly and put it aside. "Winterton, eh? Be careful with the truth, Johnny — it's a very sharp sword."

"I know it, but I believe it must be done before I marry."

"Hmm." His uncle watched him thoughtfully for a moment, then heaved himself to his feet. He was only twenty years older than John, and not yet fifty, but already his joints were showing the reluctance of age. "There is something you should see before you go." He went to his desk, the private one he kept for his personal papers, unlocked a drawer and withdrew a folded paper. "A man came looking for you... oh, it must be ten years ago now. Not a Winterton, but a friend of one of them, wanting to talk to you about this Jeremy Winterton fellow. Walked in here as bold as brass in all his London frippery. I never saw the like! Here... his card, and the letter he sent in with it. You were at the mill that day, but I thought you'd not want to be bothered with it, so I never mentioned it."

John turned the card over in his hands. *'Mr Ferdinand Makenham, 25 Harlington Terrace, Sagborough, West Riding'* "I do not recognise the name."

"Why should you, indeed? Who is he to us? I did not like it above half, I tell you. I gave him my aged imbecile impersonation and told him you were gone to America, and he seemed convinced. Never came back, anyway. But there, if you're going to the Wintertons, it's as well to know."

John read the letter, but it told him nothing that his uncle had not already said. It was high-handed of him, but it was true, he would not have wanted to deal with such a person, not then. Ten years ago, or even less, he would have been discomfited by such a meeting. How fortunate that Uncle Giles had got rid of him, and even more fortunate that Mr Ferdinand Makenham had never thought to return to Branton. John had not been ready to deal with the Wintertons before. But now... now he must. Yes, this was the right time to do it.

~~~~~

It would be an awkward interview, that much was certain. John toyed with the idea of wearing his newest coat, only just delivered from his tailor in Lancaster, but that would impart an unwarranted importance to the occasion. He chose his third best coat instead, and walked briskly out of the house, past the modest mill which brought his uncle's wealth. Almost without conscious thought, he assessed the constant thrum of the engine and the looms, his expert ears listening for the slightest untoward tremor. Lady Hazlehead, he called her, his precious engine, so anxiously tended and cosseted. But today all was well. The engine was alive and well and driving the many looms.

He made his way into town by way of the new bridge, then turned away from the line of mills lining the river and began the gentle climb to the hill. It had an official designation in the parish records, but to everyone in Branton it was merely *the hill* — the place where the wealthiest or grandest of the town's inhabitants lived, far from the bustle and noise and smoke that paid for their fine houses and secluded gardens.

The Ridwells lived in the finest house with the most secluded gardens. A matched pair of bewigged negro footmen in dazzling gold-trimmed livery opened the front door to him before he knocked. He had never had to use the knocker, he reflected, nor the gilt bell-pull. Inside the marble-pillared hall, two negro boys relieved him of hat and gloves, while a butler and two more footmen stood by. Marble pillars and statuary from Italy would have given the hall an air of cool, classical style, were it not decorated with a multitude of silver sconces and crystal chandeliers, gold-framed paintings covering every inch of wall, cherubs flying all across the ceiling, six full sized potted palm trees and a stuffed elephant. The hall was capacious, but it felt very crowded.

The butler bowed low.

"Good morning, Weald, and how are you today?" John said. "Recovered from that chill that laid you low?"

"Good morning, Mr Moreton, sir. How kind of you to enquire about my health. I am happy to assure you that I am quite recovered now. May I convey you to the ladies? They are in the gold saloon today."

"Thank you, Weald, but my business this morning is with Mr Ridwell."

The butler inclined his head. "Then pray follow me, sir."

Henry Ridwell's library was large, an over-sized room filled with over-sized furniture, and shelves of books bought by the yard, although at least there were no cherubs to be seen. Every room at Ridwell Court was large, designed to impress, although it was hard to know who might be impressed by it, for the Ridwells were too important to mingle much with the inhabitants of Branton, and not important enough to be acquainted with anyone of true rank in the county. A man who could see the smoke of his own weaving sheds from his house would never be acceptable company for a gentleman.

Their only daughter, Ellen, had been given two seasons in London in the hope that her beauty would attract a noble, or at least a respectable, husband. But it seemed that London society had no value for a dowry that came in the form of bricks and glass and a very large beam engine, for despite her beauty Ellen had returned unwed and the Ridwells had lowered their sights a trifle. That was when their eye had fallen on John.

"Well now, Moreton," Ridwell said affably, a companionable arm around John's shoulders. "What brings you to me rather than to the ladies, eh? Ellen is looking very lovely today."

"Miss Ridwell looks lovely every day," John said politely. "Regretfully, I am come to bid you farewell, for I have business that takes me away from Lancashire."

"Ah. But it will not keep you from Ellen's side for long, I'll wager."

"I shall be gone for a month or two," John said evenly.

That caused a raised eyebrow. "Serious business, Moreton, to detain you so long."

"It needs to be done. I have delayed it for too long, but can delay no longer. I must... settle my accounts, so to speak."

"Ah — yes, indeed. Clear away all the outstanding matters and start with a clean slate. An excellent notion. Are you away soon?"

"This very day. The chaise is ordered and my valet is packing as we speak, so..."

"Of course, of course, but you will not rush away without seeing the ladies?"

John allowed himself to be led out of the room, across the hall, through the newly refurbished Chinese saloon draped with overpowering red damask, and into the gold saloon, its white walls with narrow green panels cold and unwelcoming to John's eyes. He had preferred the blue that had prevailed last year. Next year, perhaps, it would be pink or ruby red or violet.

The two ladies sat at either end of a chaise longue, Ellen playing with the fringe of her shawl, while her mother waved her embroidery frame as she talked. She broke off at once as the two men entered.

"Mr Moreton! How delightful! What an unexpected pleasure! Look, Ellen, Mr Moreton is here to see us."

She held out her hand to be bowed over, simpering girlishly at him. But then she dressed like a girl, too. The two women wore gowns identically styled, with the same gold sash and shawl, their hair arranged in the same artfully disordered curls. Even their necklaces and bracelets were similar. Only the colours of their gowns — green for the mother, virginal white for the daughter — and the wisp of lace on Mrs Ridwell's head distinguished them.

"Mrs Ridwell, how delightful you look today. And Miss Ridwell, as lovely as ever." He disliked such arrant flattery, but the Ridwells seemed to expect it.

"Thank you, sir. You are most kind," Ellen said with a polite smile, her voice carefully modulated. "How pleasant to see you again."

She was a beauty, there was no doubt, and every man would envy him when she was his wife. From her abundant golden hair and skin as luscious as a ripe peach, to her delicate, slippered feet, she was perfection, a vision to turn heads wherever she went. He could imagine himself entering a drawing room with Ellen on his arm — *'Mr and Mrs John Moreton'*, the butler would say, or perhaps, in time, it would be *'Sir John and Lady Moreton'*. Ellen. His Ellen, in a few weeks. A lovely creature, who moved with grace and smiled a great deal. There was no warmth in her eyes, but he did not ask for warmth in his wife, only compliance.

Perhaps if he had ever fallen in love or felt even the tiniest tremor of affection for a woman he would not view marriage so pragmatically, but in truth, he knew himself to be every bit as cold as Ellen. His heart was as frozen as hers — two creatures trapped in an icy carapace, all warmth leached out of them by circumstances. Or, in Ellen's case, by her mother. But once they were married, they could thaw each other's hearts and be happy. Or at least content.

He did not stay long at the Ridwell's, and in truth he scarcely listened to their expressions of regret at his impending absence. He would be back — he knew it, and they did too. Soon, he would return and then... he would marry Ellen and be master of Cragforth Mill, and he would have taken his first step on the road to being *somebody*.

~~~~~

Brinshire was a shock. Hardly any towns, and the villages poor, with urchins running barefoot in the mud alongside the post-chaise. The villages consisted of a church, a shabby inn and a row or two of dilapidated cottages, that was all. Then farms and scrubby woodlands and scrawny sheep until the next pathetic village. Occasionally he would catch a glimpse of a substantial house tucked away behind high walls or at the bottom of long drives. Once, he saw a shooting party crossing a distant field, dogs at their heels, and he had an unexpected yearning to be part of that way of life, to spend his days in drawing rooms or out on his own land, to dine with lords and dance with ladies. To be not just somebody, but a gentleman. One day, perhaps, he could make that claim.

Frickham was a little larger than most villages, boasting two inns, a well-kept church, a smithy, an apothecary and two properties of substance, Westerlea Park and Woodside. He left his valet to settle in at the Frickham Inn, and walked through the village until he came to a pair of stone gateposts, high and sturdy. 'Woodside', they said, in neatly engraved letters. There was no lodge, and none needed, for there were no gates to be opened or closed. Just the posts, and a short gravel drive, the house glimpsed through the trees lining it.

Taking a deep breath, he passed through the entrance and began the walk up the drive, his boots crunching on the gravel. There before him was the house, a plain frontage with mismatched wings on either side, one of earlier date, and one later. He rapped loudly with the door knocker, then stood back and waited.

After an age, the door opened. A stern-faced young woman stood on the threshold, dressed in neat grey poplin, a small cap on her head, hands clasped in front of her. The housekeeper, to judge by the chatelaine at her waist. "Yes?"

"Good day. Is Mr Winterton at home?"

An odd look crossed her face. "Mr *Winterton?* You will find him in the churchyard. He has been dead these ten years."

The world spun. John felt the blow as surely as if he had been punched in the stomach. *Dead?* How could he be dead? He sagged against the door frame, and would have fallen but for its support. Of all the outcomes he had considered for this journey, that was the one that had never occurred to him. How had he missed the notice in the newspaper? Surely the death of Edmund Winterton of Woodside would have been posted? But — ten years ago! He had not bothered to read the London papers then, so no wonder he had known nothing of it.

"Now, do not collapse like a balloon, for people die all the time," the housekeeper said gruffly. "Here, take my arm. Come inside and sit down for a minute, but whatever you do, do not fall down, for it will take four men to lift you again, a great tall fellow like you."

He breathed, pulled himself off the door frame to stand upright, breathed again. The odd, sick feeling passed and the world stopped spinning. Even so, he felt weak.

"Thank you, I will come in for a moment."

He walked — no, staggered — into the hall unaided, and collapsed into a chair beside the console, the housekeeper hovering nearby.

"Are you about to swoon again like a girl? If so, I have smelling salts to wave under your nose, but if you can manage to stay conscious, brandy might be a more apt remedy for a man as large as you."

"Thank you, yes, a little brandy would be helpful."

She bustled off down the passage to the kitchens, and he heard low voices, then the chink of glass. She came back with the brandy in a wine glass.

"Here, drink this. I never meant to give you such a shock. It never occurred to me, not after ten years. How did you not know? Were you in Australia or some such place?"

That made him splutter into his brandy. "Lancashire," he said indignantly. "There's some that might like to see me transported, I daresay, but it hasn't happened yet."

"Lancashire," she mused. "Yes, I can hear the accent now. For a moment I mistook you for a gentleman. Still, you have come a fair distance to see Mr Winterton, so I am sorry your journey has been wasted."

John pushed down rising exasperation. He had suffered worse insults before, after all, although it was a bit rich coming from the housekeeper. "Who lives here now?" he said.

"My father. Geoffrey Tyrrell."

"Oh... I took you for the housekeeper. My apologies, Mrs... er?"

"Miss. Miss Jane Tyrrell." Her eyes were a cool grey, looking at him with disfavour. Well, at least the insults were evenly balanced now.

"Miss? Then why the cap? You are not so old as to despair of ever finding a husband."

"I thank you for the *compliment*, sir," she said acidly, "but I am five and twenty, and unlikely now to meet a man of sense who is not already wed, or too old to want to be so."

"You astonish me, Miss Tyrrell. Brinshire must indeed be devoid of men of sense if there is not a single one to be found able to lead you to the altar."

"It seems to me that Lancashire is equally devoid of men of sense, if you are typical of the county," she shot back.

He laughed at that. "*Touché*, Miss Tyrrell. I will allow my county to be every bit as wanting in sense as yours. Are you always this waspish, or only to men of Lancashire? It seems to me that we have got off on quite the wrong foot. Allow me to prove myself not entirely devoid of manners. I am John Moreton, manager of Hazlehead Mill in Branton in Lancashire, and, as you so aptly pointed out, not a gentleman." He swallowed the last of the brandy, and set the glass down on the console.

In housewifely fashion, she picked it up, with her handkerchief wiped away the small ring it had left and set it carefully on the cloth beneath the vase of dried stems that stood there.

"Are you *sure* you are not the housekeeper?" he said teasingly, and her lips quirked into the promise of a smile, instantly repressed.

"In a way, I am," she said, her tone softer now. "Havelock gets so muddled now that I cannot even trust her with the keys to the linen cupboard."

Havelock… He remembered that name…

"Thank you for the brandy," he said, rising unsteadily to his feet. "I should go and leave you in peace."

"Not until I am sure you are yourself again," she said firmly. "Let the brandy do its work. Mr Moreton, I do not know what your business was with Mr Winterton, and he left no son behind that you might deal with, nor any male relative that I ever heard, but he had five daughters who may be able to help you. They would know the name of his attorney, if it is a legal matter."

Before he could reply, the knocker sounded.

"And this might be one of them," she said. "I sent word to Rosamund."

END OF SAMPLE CHAPTER of *Woodside*

For more information or to buy, go to: http://marykingswood.co.uk

Made in the USA
Monee, IL
23 July 2022